HELL'S EMPIRE
Tales of the Incursion

**Edited by
John Linwood Grant**

PREFACE

How this book came about and the concept it encompasses are both discussed in the introduction which follows. Rather than a clinically assembled finished piece, this particular anthology has been a work built up with genuine enthusiasm from all sides. Special thanks should go to Sam Gafford of Ulthar Press, a fine writer himself, who became enthused about the idea and agreed to publish it; authors Matt Willis and Charles R. Rutledge, who spared much time to help develop the concept further, and various members of the Imperial Weird Facebook group, who asked questions or offered opinions on a range of topics relevant to the book. Most of all, thanks to the authors for grasping, so quickly and so skilfully, what we were after.

John Linwood Grant

HELL'S EMPIRE
Tales of the Incursion

TABLE OF CONTENTS

DAYS OF DOUBT

     All linking text by John Linwood Grant

INTRODUCTION

Hail horrours, hail
Infernal world, and thou profoundest Hell
Receive thy new Possessor: One who brings
A mind not to be chang'd by Place or Time.
The mind is its own place, and in it self
Can make a Heav'n of Hell, a Hell of Heav'n.

Milton, Paradise Lost Book I

Being someone who rarely ventures into the worlds of steampunk, I was reading one such story a year or so ago, and it did get me wondering. What would happen if the forces of Hell had tried to invade the real, historical Victorian Britain? Not some fantasy or alternate Britain, but the unvarnished realm, warts and all. No armoured airships or astonishingly advanced submarines ready to bolster the defences; no thinking machines; no cape-swirling guilds of sorcerers ready for the fray. Only a lot of sceptical and confused ordinary people, ill-prepared for such an insane occurrence, and a few – a very few – who through courage, learning or natural gift could face the onslaught slightly better than most. The Infernal Throne against the Imperial Throne, in a desperate struggle for Empire...

There was potential here for something rather different. Ideally, I was seeking a series of tales, linked by the broad theme and background, which might combine to tell a much larger story. 'Hell's Empire', if it were feasible, would tell of how at some point in the early to mid-1890s, what appeared to be the Legions of Hell invaded the United Kingdom of Great Britain and Ireland - as it was known then - in an unprecedented event known as the Incursion.

This was a time when the main forces of the British Empire are engaged elsewhere across the globe, and those units still in the United Kingdom itself were quite depleted from sending reinforcements to conflicts overseas for years. A vulnerable time, and an ideal one should the Infernal Prince be looking for an opportunity to expand His realm. To make a Hell not of Heav'n, but of Britain.

So I and Ulthar Press put out a call. Writers were free to get political – perhaps the entire British Empire deserved to be challenged or taken down a peg – but this was a Home Front situation, and so no stories would be set outside the British Isles as they were back then. It was agreed that Matt Willis would provide the anchor tale which started things off – someone had to stick their neck out – and that Charles R Rutledge would take on the equally challenging task of writing the story which closed the anthology. No one else would see these two tales, which ended up as novelettes in their own rights, in advance. We would see what people came up with.

Sometimes when you wish for things, you get them. In this case, we were sent a marvellous range of tales, and as an editor, I don't think I've ever been more pleased by the results of asking for submissions to a project. In the end, I decided to take twelve more stories which were too good to miss – seven by men, five by women (many by British/Irish writers), bringing us up to fourteen contributors. These good folk had, through arcane, telepathic or accidental means, produced pieces which fitted together to allow for the sort of over-arching narrative I'd hoped for.

They also delighted me by selecting such very different protagonists, interpretations of the Infernal forces, and monstrous occurrences. I had tried to offer guidance in the open call, but I'd wondered if we would be sent loads of jingoistic tales of a purely militaristic nature. We weren't – rather the opposite. There was action and excitement, yes, with strong plots, but also much

7

subtlety and pathos – fleeting, personal victories; dreadful losses, and a sense of true horror at a world falling apart.

It was a pleasure to receive so many submissions from women writers, and to be able to include a lot of them in the final book - not through some process of deliberate balance or fair representation (which I have nothing against), but simply because they were so darned good that they had to be in here. Talent rises.

One thing I was asked a number of times was if this was a project which insisted on only Christian symbology and tropes – the classical Hell of the Church. The answer was No. Perhaps the Incursion was not the onslaught of a literal Christian Inferno, but took such an appearance to most people in Victorian Britain because of their own history and upbringing. Another plane of existence, malign, chaotic, and using the most suitable guise for its assault? Entirely acceptable. One of many dark or sad 'afterlives', from Abrahamic or other religions? Fine.

And there remained the possibility that it was Hell itself, most of all, that believed itself to be Hell. Perhaps we shape our nightmares until they take the form we give them? Are demons demons because we tell them that they are?

Writers were therefore free to go down their own paths, with the greatest consensus emerging that Faith and Will, drawn from beliefs of many kinds, might be key to withstanding the Infernal Horde. Given the setting, belief in the God of the Bible, Talmud and Quran was likely to be core, though I was open to other ideas, including deep-rooted folk beliefs. Again, the writers obliged, with some tales being what might be termed Folk Horror – ancient beliefs awoken in remote, embattled communities. You might turn to Shell Bromley's 'Forge', J. A. Ironside's 'Yahn, Tan, Tethera' or Frank Coffman's 'Reinforcements' as examples of folklore and folk memory arising to this new challenge.

As you might imagine, in the early days of the Incursion few people understood what was really happening, and so we have some nice introductory tales, such as Marion Pitman's 'Hell at the Empire', Ian Steadman's 'The Sea Wall', and one with a very different viewpoint, 'The Singing Stones' by Charlotte Bond, to show this aspect.

We do have stories of desperate combat, of course, because the Incursion was a most tangible threat. Thus Matt Willis's 'The Battle of Alma', A. F. Stewart's 'Infernal Patrol', 'The Mighty Mastiff' by Ross Baxter, and Charles R. Rutledge's 'A Swig in Hell' all show the regular and militia forces in direct action against the horrors of the Inferno.

Be warned that this is also a book about darkness within and without, not one where decent and worthy people always win the day. Humanity has its own darkness, as you will see in stories such as J. S. Deel's cunning political tale 'Profaned by Feelings Dark', Martin Gilbert's 'The Ones Left Behind', 'Ad Majorem Satanae Gloriam' by Damascus Mincemeyer and S. L. Edward's worrying 'We have Always Lived in a Colony'.

Finally, although I had no intention of including verse, special mention should be made of Phil Breach, who wrote and volunteered two excellent poetic pieces, knowing that they would probably not be used. In the end, they had to be in.

Between us all, we have managed to chart the Incursion. I hope you enjoy the stories which follow...

John Linwood Grant
Yorkshire, April 2019

PROLOGUE

It began as 'certain curious events'. A mention in a local newspaper; a wry comment in one of the national organs; a letter to the editor of a hobbyist magazine. Shadows and lights, inexplicable scratchings at the door – neither certain nor concrete. And it might have continued as such for months, remarked on by country vicars in their sermons, perhaps investigated with enthusiasm by the type of amateur sleuth who loves a good mystery. Nothing to bother the engines of Empire.

But it did not stay that way. We were not allowed months. From the first mention of a sickly light upon the heath to the first clawed-open corpse was a matter of weeks. Faces which could not be faces were seen in the alleyways, and mediums broke from reporting Great Aunt Mary's comfort in Heaven to stare and scream.

Something was very wrong.

In the corridors of state, certain dust-covered boxes were opened, initially with doubt – 'just in case'. An archbishop was summoned; a senior rabbi was requested to attend at Whitehall. Two or three of the foremost spiritualist leaders in the capital were asked – reluctantly - to have a quiet chat with Ministry officials. The word was of contingency plans - a contingency which no one had ever taken seriously, and plans which made no sense in this new age of thundering steam and the electric light bulb.

As you might expect, in the early days there were many names given to what was happening – and as no one truly understood the unfolding events, those names reflected what people feared. Judgement Day. Invasion. Rebellion.

Her Majesty Victoria, by the Grace of God, of the United Kingdom of Great Britain and Ireland Queen, Defender of the Faith, Empress of India, would have none of that.

"If all that you bring to me is true," she said to her Prime Minister, as she looked up from her daily journal, "Then we shall not be driven by foolish pronouncements. It is... it is merely a passing incursion."

In such a way was the Incursion born and named, to cut a bloody swathe across the land.

Hell would have its Empire...

PART ONE

OPENING SHOTS

One of the defining aspects of the Incursion, which people – and the authorities – were slow to understand, was that the Infernal forces appeared to recognise the nature of an island. Whilst many incidents seemed, and possibly even were, quite random, it became obvious that the United Kingdom was not to be reinforced from elsewhere. Not from its colonies, nor by any notional allies on the other side of the English Channel. The leading news may have been about London, but in fact, ports were the locations hit most heavily in the early days.

We were never sure what teemed in the grey waters around the coast, but trawler fleets returned burned and scarred, half their number missing. The mail and passenger packets between here and Belgium, the Netherlands and France ceased completely after the first weeks – for those who were not pulled into the depths, a cold welcome and quarantine awaited outside foreign harbours. The French alone pressed seven hulks into service as 'relief stations', crowding survivors into them. These people were not allowed to set foot on French soil. "Et si un seul est un démon à l'intérieur?" said the harbour-master at Brest. And if only one of them is a demon within?

Many waited with hope for returning troop-ships, particularly from South Africa, but with the loss of HMS Camforth off the Isle of Wight, that hope was dashed. Witnesses in Ventnor saw the brave vessel torn open as it hove in sight, grasped by tendrils of a monstrous size which carried weeping sores upon their mottled length. Hell was determined that there would be no relief, and the fate of the Camforth, out of Durban and carrying three hundred Army regulars, made that point clear.

Hull resisted; Liverpool was assaulted and fell into anarchy. The great fishing ports held out better than those which relied on passenger and cargo trade; fishermen and their wives understood

14

loss and struggle. The clergy who blessed the fleets had a history of dealing with grief, and a hard faith, tested by the North Sea.

The larger ports of the South Coast faced the heaviest challenges, which may have been no accident. Dover, Portsmouth, Weymouth...

THE BATTLE OF ALMA

Matthew Willis

It was Sunday morning when they came. Alma was at prayer in the chapel. They came anyway.

'At prayer' might be putting it a little strongly. She was standing in a full height stall in this ludicrous 'separate system' prison chapel, wooden screens and doors blocking all contact with anyone apart from the minister, who she could just about see if she raised her head and peeped over the screen in front of her. Not even allowed to acknowledge the presence of her fellow prisoners even if she could see them. She let the words of the sermon drift by, half-listening. At least the hood meant she didn't even have to affect not to look bored.

The first sign was the aether-headache, the one that always came on when the dead were near, plunging into her skull like a splinter of glass through the eye. But never so sudden, never so strong. *I haven't summoned anything*, she thought. A surge of panic. *Haven't so much as drawn a sigil!*

Round and round in her head. *They've found me, all of them, they've found me! The Dead!*

Desperation was overwhelmed in an instant by a barrage of sensations. She sank against the back of the stall as tides of nausea heaved at her and the whistle rose in her ears. The screen gave her a moment's freedom to double over and gag, but the minister, high in his pulpit, would surely notice in a moment. She fought against the sickness assailing her stomach, head, ears... The hood felt as though it had begun to shrink and squeeze her skull. She tugged at the leather. It didn't help.

Something was coming.

Something was here.

16

In the name of heaven and the thirty aethers - what?

Through the lance of pain, a sense. A presence. Not dead. Not lost. Malevolent. She looked behind her, as if there was anything other than white-painted wood there...

The minister, who had been mumbling along in his usual monotone, began to yell. Alma heard something about *Christ protecting us from the fiends of Satan*, and thought for a moment that the man had finally discovered the passion of his vocation. And then the screams started. From the rows behind her at the back of the chapel, yelps muffled by leather hoods. The doors to the stalls rattled, crashed. The sound of something wet, ripping.

Through the pain in her head, something else intruded. A sense of something, even a hint of a name. *Mazzikim*. It was not the spirits of the dead, that was certain. Something from another place. Somewhere forbidden.

Couldn't see a damned thing behind, but still the yells of surprise and fear, banging of wood, and something like meat being inexpertly chopped. Alma looked back to the front, to see the minister, now silent, wide-eyed and holding the huge chapel bible before him at arm's length. The rattling was in the row behind her now. Out. Must get out. She bashed at the door to the adjoining stall. It jammed into the occupant, who toppled and started pushing back.

Alma shoved her head as far through the gap as it would go. The woman stared back from her hood, blank with disbelief and something else. "Go!" Alma shouted, "go through! We need to get out!" They bashed into the next stall, and the next, thudding into another prisoner each time, and finally their combined, panic-fuelled weight broke the bolt on the end door designed to keep the women from escaping. They spilled out into the aisle in a heap, bruised and scraped.

Instantly something was on them, a pack of things, biting and slashing. *Dogs! Wolves! Pigs!* ran nonsensically through Alma's head as she rolled clear of the mass, where the women shrieked and flailed and the whatever-they-were swiped and snapped. Her migraine-fogged eyes saw but could not take in.

17

They were something like men but utterly unlike. Smaller, their outer surface - the word skin didn't occur to Alma in that moment - blueish, wet, rippling as if it wasn't quite there. Long, narrow claws, slightly curved. Something like spines... or wings? Her mind could not make the creature settle into a comprehensible form.

Then, one of lunged at her from the scrum. Unthinking, Alma yelled a phrase in Enochian - *banishment* - the usual last resort to get rid of a persistent spirit. The creature - demon... she now knew they were demons... slumped to the floor as if punched. In a moment it was back on its... feet? hooves?... and about to launch itself at her again. Another word, and a symbol sketched in the air, flung the thing back across the chapel. Thank goodness, it worked! Another word, and the accompanying symbols formed, rough and raw but backed with crackling power, aimed at the knot of demons in the aisle. It threw them back too, and they lay scrabbling on the flagstones. Two, three women picked themselves up, scratched and bloody. Another two lay on the ground, immobile.

Alma was about to make a break for the door when more of the things poured into the aisle from the stalls on either side, and stood, facing her. One of them let out a screech that momentarily drove the migraine-glass back through her eye. No way out! Through the blood-fog she glanced behind her. The minister, up in his pulpit, still holding out the bible, and muttering, eyes like white balloons. The demons hadn't come near him...

"Up onto the gallery, quick," Alma called to the other women, "Get behind the bible." They ran for the stairs onto the little platform behind the pulpit.

"What...what...those...things?" The minister panted.

"Do you have a pencil?" Alma replied. "Something to write with! Anything!" It looked as though the minister was going to question her, but after a second, hitched up his surplice and thrust a hand into his jacket. He brought out a stub of a pencil, which Alma grabbed before he could offer, and began sketching an Enochian sigil on the walls. The Mazzikim crept forward, spreading out along the flagstones below, eyeing her hungrily as she darted from side to side, covering as much of the wall as possible with markings that should - she hoped - keep them safe. Alma noticed they didn't come closer than about six feet.

"Say something!" she hissed at the minister.

"What?"

"I don't know, anything! Something about saving us from demons, maybe? That would be a good start. Anything in there?" she jabbed a finger at the bible. One of the women spoke, but Alma couldn't make out the words through the leather hood. She ripped her own hood off and held a hand up to her ear.

The prisoner removed her hood, revealing a freckled, girlish face, and several missing teeth. "Colossians," she said. "Er, one-thirteen?"

"Oh! Yes!" The minister started riffling through the tissue-thin pages. "Giving... ah, giving thanks unto the Father, which hath made us meet to be partakers of the inheritance of the saints in light! Yes, that's good! Saints in light, who hath delivered us from the power of darkness! And hath translated us into the kingdom of His dear Son in whom we have redemptionthroughhisbloodeventheforgivenessofsins..."

The demons started shuffling backwards. When the priest paused for breath, Alma shouted a phrase of Enochian she had hastily composed, commanding *banishment from this realm into the place of darkness*. The Mazziķim suddenly looked as though they'd been caught in a hurricane, battered and pushed by something unseen.

"...Who is the image of the invisible God, the firstborn of every creature," the minister continued, voice rising an octave. "For by Him were all things created, that are in heaven, and that are in earth, visible and invisible, whether they be thrones, or dominions, or principalities, or powers: all things were created by Him, and for Him, and He is before all things, and by Him all things consist..."

"What, so those things were made by God an' all?" said Freckles.

Alma held a finger to her lips.

"And He is the head of the body, the church, who is the beginning, the firstborn from the dead; that in all things He might have the pre-eminence."

Alma cast her last charm. The Mazziķim toppled like skittles. The air towards the back of the chapel began to flutter as if above a bonfire. A few of the creatures bounded into the wobbling air and disappeared, but most fled beneath it and left by the front door.

The minister collapsed over his bible. Freckles started crying silently. The silence in the chapel was like a roar in Alma's ears. Only then did she hear the screams from outside.

***

For three days it was as though the prison had returned to normal... or what passed for normal when you were forced to wear a hood at all times and forbidden from any communication with your fellow prisoners. It wasn't as though it was exactly quieter - silence was demanded at all times anyway, "speak when you're spoken to," but somehow the silence was emptier. She had no idea how many had been killed by the...things. But it had not been a few.

On the fourth day Alma was brought out of her cell and escorted out of the block. She knew better than to ask where she was being taken. She'd find out soon enough and there was no need to risk a cuff for the sake of an answer she would not be given. It was obvious that whatever it was, only she was being moved.

The answer turned out to be the administration block, and then an incongruously dark wood-panelled vestibule, and then a large, plush office. It must be the governor's. No-one was here. The guard dragged her by the bruised elbow to stand in front of an acre of polished desktop, and left, closing the door. There she waited for what might have been five minutes or half an hour.

The sound of a different door opening somewhere behind her, two male voices in conversation. "...Urge great caution. Is the need really so great?" That one familiar. The governor.

"I'm afraid so," said the other. "The situation is quite dire. We've kept the newspapers from revealing the worst of it so far, but it's clear this is not going to stop, and far from that it's getting worse. Desperate times... well, you know."

It could hardly be more obvious what the desperate times were... So the incident with the Mazziḳim was not isolated? Alma's heart juddered in her ribcage.

"Oh, she's here already." The governor again. "Very well. It seems the authority you bear means I can't stop you, but you must be aware that Separate System requires preventing the prisoners from communicating as far as is humanly possible, and by talking to prisoner Langley, you are interfering with her punishment."

"Nevertheless, I must insist," said the man she did not know.

The governor sat at his desk, facing her. The other stood off to her right. She caught a flash of gold on his dark clothing, but dare not even move her eyes to check.

The governor cleared his throat. "Langley. Commander Wilcox wishes to question you about... the... occurrence on Sunday. You will answer him honestly and briefly."

Alma nodded.

"Thank you, Miss Langley," Wilcox said. "Er, you may look at me." She turned her head stiffly, ignoring the snort of disapproval from the governor. Wilcox was a small man with a narrow face framed with whiskers like thunderclouds, wearing a dark uniform, rather plain apart from the gold stripes round each cuff. "I understand you were of some assistance to the chaplain in fighting off those... er..."

"Mazziḳim," Alma said, voice scratchy. She shoved the annoyance at 'some assistance to the chaplain' aside.

"What's that?"

"I think they're called Mazziḳim. A form of demon," she whispered.

21

Wilcox turned to the governor. "I suppose that hood affair is part of the system?"

"Yes," the governor said, voice thin with irritation.

"You may take it off, Miss Langley."

"But!-"

"Now please. It's quite all right." Wilcox' voice was not unkind. At least any sharpness was directed at the governor. "How did you do it?"

Alma's mind raced. There must be more of these occurrences. Demons breaking through from other realms. And if they were talking to her, did that mean they didn't know how to deal with it? She pulled off the mask, took a breath, and explained, making it as clear as possible without being disrespectful that it was not exactly she who had been of assistance to the chaplain... Explaining the sigils and language from the Book of Enoch, the passage from Colossians, a little of where she thought the intruders came from... nothing at all on why. On that front, she didn't want to speculate. Not yet, anyway. That sense she'd had... unformed, messy. *They hate us. No, not even that. We are almost beneath their notice. Contempt.*

"I'll be jiggered," the officer said. He put his cap on, rubbed his face, whipped his cap back off again. "How did you know to do all that?"

Alma glanced at the governor, took another breath, and suppressed a smile. "It says so on my conviction. I'm a witch."

After the interview, Wilcox, and a couple of bluejackets with rifles, escorted her to the railway station where they boarded a train. Alma did not think it a coincidence that they had a compartment to themselves. After her Parthian shot in the governor's office, the governor had seemed to lose all interest in the completeness of her punishment and gave every appearance of simply being pleased to be rid of her. An hour out of Gloucester, Wilcox cleared his throat. "You haven't asked where we're going, Miss Langley."

She looked up sharply. Well of course not, she didn't want to be struck again... But this was no longer the prison.

22

"Oh. No. I didn't think it would be permitted." She shook herself. "Very well then. Where are we going?"

"Portland. The Channel Fleet anchorage. You're to help us with the defences."

Defences? Alma frowned. "I don't know what you think I can do against the French."

"The... F..." Wilcox mouth fell open and then he began to laugh. One of the bluejackets snickered, the other went pale. "No, no Miss, not the French. Those creature whatnots. Demons. Marzipan?"

"Mazziḳim? There are more of them?"

"Well yes. Not all the same kind though. But you weren't aware?"

"We don't often have the morning papers in Gloucester Prison, I'm afraid, Commander. And we're not supposed to be spoken to. The Queen could die and we wouldn't know about it. She hasn't, has she?"

"What? Oh, no, Miss! We're still subjects of Her Majesty. Bertie's still waiting his turn." He flushed. "His Royal Highness, the Prince of Wales that is." He leaned forwards across the compartment, and whispered "I was a Middie with him on *Bacchante*, you know. That's how we got you, truth be told."

Alma simply stared. She could not make sense of what Wilcox had said. This was more conversation than she'd had in the last year, and her mind was tumbling more than when the demons had broken through. Unanswered questions began to form a heap in her mind, and she'd just begun to think about posing some of them when they arrived at London. The next few hours were a cacophony of conveyances and crowded streets. Even through the sheer psychic noise, she could feel the torn edges of the recent attack. Absences where there should be life, a slight taint of sulphur, spirits of the recently dead who radiated fear and shock, and hid from her.

And then another huge station, all smoke and pillars and cast iron filigree, before they were on another train, this one for Weymouth. Alma, battered by the noise and confusion, drew back

23

into herself and let the countryside spool past through the carriage's window. It had been perhaps an hour when Wilcox addressed her.

"I'm sorry to disturb you, Miss Langley, but there are a few things we ought to discuss before we arrive."

"Am I still a prisoner?" she blurted, the question having bounced around in her head all the way through London.

"Yes, I'm afraid so." Wilcox smiled sheepishly. "I should have said so, shouldn't I? You've been placed under my authority, temporarily, but if you help us, then I'll do my best to secure some reduction in your sentence. Perhaps even a pardon, given that sooner or later your... ah, crimes, might not seem so serious. Or not even a crime."

She looked up. None of that particularly mattered, did it? "Yes, of course. Thank you." So she was not free to leave. Nor to escape. But the feeling she'd had at Gloucester, and again in London - she met Wilcox' gaze. "How bad is it? I can't see why you need me. You must have an army of priests, witches, mediums, sorcerers and so on you can call on."

Wilcox goggled. "An army of... Oh dear. Oh dear, oh dear."

Alma frowned. "Tell me what's happening. And what you're doing about it?"

The Commander wrung his cap, and turned to the ratings. "Fuller, Sharpe, kindly avert your ears."

"Aye, aye sir," the bluejackets nodded and looked out the opposite window.

Wilcox leaned in again. "The truth is, it's rather a muddle. We're getting these things. These... Manticores?"

"Mazziķim."

"They're popping up more and more. To be frank, it took us a little while to know what was going on. Reports of packs of wild dogs attacking villages, roaming bands of frenzied savages..." He chuckled ruefully, "even tales of sailors running amuck, as though Jack Tar on shore leave goes naked and is covered in green spines. And even when the descriptions were a little closer to the mark...well, it took a while before they were believed. We think the attack on Gloucester Prison was the first, but others certainly happened around the same time. And then there was a breakout in London. A sort of hole appeared in the air above Hyde Park and *things* started streaming out. I suspect not quite the same as at Gloucester though, judging by the Reverend's report... smaller. Like monkeys. Vicious little b_____s though. Saw the damage meself. Was over at the Admiralty that day."

Oh, so no-one cared until London suffered? Typical. Alma looked down and discreetly rolled her eyes.

"But as for why you... well, it seems to be that Gloucester Prison was the only time anyone fought the... things."

"Mazziķim."

"Yes, quite. Fought them off. And survived."

"Oh!" *Oh no. Oh, no.*

"Quite. And so although there is now something of a national effort to try and keep a lid on things, I'm not sure the Home Defence Committee is really going about matters in the most effective manner. Which is to say... no army of priests, sorcerers and those other chappies. There are real sorcerers? Extraordinary. Do you know any? Oh, the Committee. They rather think that we can deal with all this with infantry squares and quick-firing artillery."

Alma let her mouth fall open. "But they'll all die!"

Wilcox shifted awkwardly. "Let's hope not, eh? But I read all the reports. I have to say the Hyde Park business rather shook me. And the one case where the... er Mandibles..."

Alma waved the officer to go on.

"...Where anybody had any success to speak of, that we know about with certainty, was your little incident. There may be one or two others but as I'm sure you'll appreciate, they're hard to pin down."

Alma slouched against the seat. This was bad. She girded her loins and for the first time since the demons had broken through, properly probed the edges of the aethers with her mind, gently, like a tongue counting teeth. Silvery fog filled her thoughts. There was nothing identifiably different but something indefinably wrong. Jagged edges. A pricking in the fingers, a dogwhistle needle in the ears. Whatever they were, they weren't coming down the Dead Roads, but there was more than one way into the world. And more than one place to come from. "They don't have anyone who can fight demons? No-one at all? What about the chaplain? Reverend..." Alma realised she didn't even know the priest's name.

Wilcox pursed his lips. "He's with the Royal Family. I had enough authority to see to it that B... the Prince took him on. Which leaves you."

"So... I'm supposed to protect... what was it, the Channel Fleet? From demons?" She bit off what she had been about to follow with. *Isn't it the Channel Fleet's job to protect civilians, not the other way round?*

"Well, that's the idea." Wilcox's shoulders slumped, and he sighed expansively. "Initially we thought sending them to sea would be the answer. But - and this is entirely between you and me - we lost a torpedo boat in the Channel yesterday, not far off Portland Bill. One of those hole things opened up in the sea, beasties swarmed out, slaughtered the entire crew before the other boats of the flotilla could come up in support. They found the vessel listing, half the hull plates popped open, and covered in sulphur. And the men... well, such things are not for the ears of a lady."

Alma's annoyance at being mollycoddled fought with disquiet at what Wilcox had told her. Disquiet won. The frantic struggle in the Chapel. What if that was nowhere near as bad as things could get...?

The Commander gave a sort of shrug with his eyebrows, and looked past her. "I know how it sounds. In view of the unusual nature of the threat, I've been given a somewhat free-wheeling role by the Admiralty to assemble a group of... well, I'm using the term 'specialists'. But the trouble is, no-one's listening to me. I had to start somewhere, and need to buy a little time to convince the Home Defence Committee that we require an... unconventional approach. It was enough for me to secure your temporary release, and pursue a few other avenues, but it's a slow start. I need time, and it's running out, isn't it?"

Alma let her head fell forwards into her hands. She felt sweat begin to prickle at her palms and forehead. It was nowhere near enough! If demons had started coming through the aethers into the physical world in numbers, then something had changed. Surely! They wouldn't just drift away again. It would keep happening. It would get worse. "How bad is it?" Her voice was barely a whisper.

Wilcox shrugged. "Compared with what? I was rather hoping you would tell me."

How was she supposed to know, shut up in that place and starved of communication! She resisted the temptation to snap. But the sense she had from the edge of the between-place... from the chatter of the dead she'd been trying to ignore... from the fact that once these things had started, they would surely not stop until they were stopped...

The Dorset countryside rolled by outside the glass, but beneath that, and above it, things were shifting, tipping. Planes of existence were clicking into new orbits. Something was coming. "I think it's bad," she replied eventually. "And likely to get worse. If there don't happen to be people like me there when an attack comes... a church minister at the very least... There are things priests can do to. If they're prepared, perhaps? There are passages in the Bible, the Apocrypha, that have power. Some work better than others Symbols... inc- er, recitations..." How much dare she say?

Wilcox smiled wanly. "Will you tell me as much as you can about how this business all works? It's all Greek to me, I'm afraid. Anything you can tell me, anything at all..."

For the rest of the journey Alma described as much about the Book of Enoch, the Enochian language, the realms of demons and protectors as she could. The truth was that even she had not realised how much of it was apparently real, rather than lore. Until that day in the chapel she had only used her sensitivity and the skills she had learned to converse with the recently dead.

Well, a young lady of no independent means had to make a living. Wilcox asked her if she could describe the Mazziķim (although he called them the Macaroons), which she did, as far as she could. The memory of them had... not exactly faded, but had become blurred. She had to focus extremely hard, and sometimes come at the demons from the edges, in the way their victims had moved, say, to establish how they had attacked. Her mind seemed to want to slide off, like walking on seaweed covered rocks. Wilcox wrote down the words avidly.

"It's the oddest thing," he said when they'd finished. "I can't retain any sense of what these things are like. Reverend Stack tried to describe them to me, and I'd form an image, but moments afterwards there was just a sort of hole where the image should have been."

Alma remembered the way their shape had flickered and rippled. "They're not from here. They're not supposed to be here. I think our minds are rebelling. That's why you can't remember the name properly."

"Every time I go for the word, it's like trying to grasp a cake of soap. Tell me again, spell it out, and I'll write it down."

Alma gave a rough transliteration from the Hebrew. "It just means 'the harmful', if that helps." They spilled out of the train at Weymouth, and a carriage took them to Nothe Fort.

"Best you don't say anything," Wilcox muttered as they were escorted to the Commanding Officer. "The Colonel isn't exactly the most open-minded fellow."

That turned out to be an understatement. "I'm not having that b_____ witch in my fort!" he thundered when he had stopped cursing enough to form a sentence. "For all I know she brought those b_____ creatures here in the first place. As far as I'm b_____ well concerned the chief enemy I expect to face in this port is the b_____ French and I can't imagine anything these dog-monkey creatures can present that will be worse than a Frenchman!"

Wilcox attempted to explain exactly what he had seen of the capabilities of the 'dog-monkey creatures' and the most effective proven means of combating them, but the Colonel cut him off again.

"I don't need b_____ witchcraft, I have b_____ ten inch RMLs. You can put that witch under b_____ naval orders if you like but not in my b_____ command."

Wilcox argued, dropping the name of the Prince of Wales several times, but to no avail. 'Bertie' apparently held the naval rank of Rear Admiral but no army rank. He was reduced to pleading for Alma to be placed anywhere in the Portland defences.

"As far away from me as b_____ possible," the Colonel blazed.

"Aye aye, sir," Wilcox replied. "Permission to carry out your orders?"

The Colonel agreed, blinking with confusion, and dismissed the Commander. Wilcox hurried Alma, just as confused, out of the fort. As they rushed across the courtyard, she glanced at the massive, black, snub-nosed artillery pieces pointing out over the bay, and found she couldn't blame the Colonel. After all, what on this Earth could stand against such force?

Only something not of this Earth.

"I'm afraid this isn't quite what I had in mind, but if you'll bear with me," Wilcox said as, once again, they hurried from one place that didn't want her to the next. "It's as far away from Nothe Fort as possible within the defences, and under naval command, and I choose to interpret the Colonel's orders in that way. There's a naval detachment on the North East breakwater, you see." He pointed to the edge of the anchorage, past the ships. Alma could see a low grey wall encompassing the harbour. It stretched from the island of Portland back towards the coast at Weymouth, with a break near either end. "The Royal Engineers hadn't finished building the defences there," Wilcox went on, seemingly talking to himself, "and the Royal Artillery is short on men as it is. To be perfectly frank, the whole country is short on men. Most of the regular forces are overseas. Cape Colony and Natal, Sudan, Egypt, Hong Kong. We're stretched perilously thin, and trying to form units out of all sorts." As if remembering her presence, he added "It won't be terribly comfortable on the breakwater, I'm sorry to say."

Alma raised an eyebrow. "Will it be less comfortable than a Separate System prison?"

"Oh. Well. Now you put it like that... I'm afraid I won't be able to stay with you. I have work to do if we're to overcome this menace properly. I just need you to do what you can to help them prepare. And, God forbid, if the place is attacked, help defend it. You might make the difference. I expected an attack would come from the land, but after the torpedo boat incident, it might just as well be from the sea. Just... do your best would you?"

"Aye aye, sir."

Wilcox smiled. "You wouldn't be the first of your sex to fight in a naval battle, if that's any consolation, Miss Langley."

Alma stopped, hands on her hips. "Oh, for heaven's sake call me Alma. I can't stand being called Miss Langley."

Wilcox fluttered and departed. Feeling desolate, alone, and as though the situation was not quite real, Alma was put aboard a puttering steam pinnace which picked its way through massive ironclads, lying low in the water like grotesque armoured crocodiles. She read names on elaborate stern plaques that meant little. *Sans Pareil... St James... Anson...* One of the bluejackets who had accompanied her from Gloucester carried hastily written orders to the Lieutenant in command of Pier Head A.

The thought that she might slip away, run from the ghastly threat she knew was coming, chose that moment to insert itself into her head now it was too late. It was only then that she realised the armed ratings hadn't been there for her protection.

Pier Head A was a circular stone fortification at the end of a section of breakwater, with gun emplacements on the outer face which had, as yet, no guns on them. It was tiny as defences went, and dwarfed by the hulking Breakwater Fort across the shipping entrance two hundred yards to the Southward (which itself was still small compared with Nothe Fort back on the mainland). Everything looked new and disturbingly unfinished, coated in fine grey stone dust. The boat pulled up at a set of weed-slicked steps and she had to step across a sloshing gap, as the petty officer in command refused to tie up. Lieutenant Finch, who was apparently in command, swore more than the Colonel had, and ordered her placed under guard in the powder magazine, on the basis that it was the only room on the breakwater apart from the washroom that had been completed. She spent no more than an hour in the cool, dark confines of the store, before she was ordered out again. She and her guard, the seaman Fuller, had been getting under the feet of the men trooping in and out bringing shells and barrels of powder from the supply boats. The last straw came when two men came in with buckets and brushes to whitewash the bare stone walls. Alma and Fuller were shooed away from the activity. They made their way a short distance down the breakwater and settled themselves out of the way.

Alma watched as three artillery pieces were swung across from a lighter and manoeuvred into place with sheer legs. One by one they settled into recesses along the top of the huge concrete glacis bounding the Pier Head's seaward side. Before today she would have thought of the guns as large, but they were peashooters compared with the artillery at Nothe. She said as much to Fuller, for want of anything better to talk about.

"That one's a twelve pounder breechloader, Miss," Fuller said when the first had been fixed in position. "And those two are three pounders. Fire a much smaller shell than the old RMLs up there but a lot faster. They're quick firing guns, see? Takes a minute to load those big things. These ones can get twelve or more shots off in that time. Fifteen if the crew knows what they're about."

It was little comfort. Earthly weapons might slow down an army of demons a little, but it would take arms of a different kind to drive them off. Alma paid more attention to the breakwater itself. Constructed of great blocks of quarried stone, by the waterline a rough jumble but at the top, almost a paved pathway. It was more or less a very long, thin, artificial island.

"What are those, more gun emplacements?" she asked Fuller, pointing at stubby bunkers, widely spaced, receding along the length of the breakwater. The nearest was a hundred yards away.

"Searchlights," Fuller grumbled. "Steam powered. Bloody bright and noisy. Won't be much sleep tonight if we can't get under cover."

From the scene around them, it was hard to believe they were preparing for something that was not of this reality. The sun glittered on the sea and glowed off the pale cliffs. Vast, squat ships sat on the mercury sheet of the anchorage, their snub guns trained on Earthly enemies. The Earthly industry of men filled the air with metallic sounds and shouts of Earthly labour. And it would all be for nothing. Besides, what made them think they demons would come for their Channel Fleet? Alma's lip curled. What did the Lords of the aether care about ironclads and ruling the waves? What need had they for trade routes? If what she had read was true, many demons disliked iron. It could be that the fleet would protect itself and the people ashore would bear the brunt. There may be attacks taking place even now. Was the attack she had fought off nothing but an advance party?

If only they'd let her do something to help! "Can I not at least prepare some protective sigils?" she snapped at Fuller. "All I need is some chalk, or a little of that whitewash. It would do a power of good. More than any of this," she swept her arm across the martial tableau.

Fuller shrugged. "Sorry Miss. Got my orders from the Lieutenant to keep you out of the way."

"And doesn't he have orders from Commander Wilcox to the contrary?" she fumed.

"Don't know anything about that, Miss, I'm afraid." Fuller said. "There wouldn't be any point arguing the toss with Finch. I'd be wrong even if I was right."

Feeling so stymied she could scream, Alma watched the useless preparations until the sun began to set. She was allowed ten minutes' sole use of the washroom, a bucket behind a screen, and ordered back into the magazine with a thin roll of bedding and a blanket. Despite the sense of powerlessness screwing her into a ball of frustration, the day had been long, tiring and strange, and she fell asleep in moments.

...To wake with a searing, white-hot needle through the side of her skull. Her heart galloped, and for a moment she struggled to haul enough air into her lungs. The salty atmosphere scratched as she gulped at it. Then thought followed sensation.

Alma heaved a shaking breath into her lungs, and another, and hunched as small as possible. The walls seemed to brush her shoulders.

There was something coming. Just like last time. Alma threw the blanket off, stood, and hammered on the door.

The sailor on guard pulled it open a crack. "Yes, Miss?"

"There's..." she started. But they wouldn't listen to her, would they? Maybe if she could get out, then at least she wouldn't be trapped. Then help, or persuade someone, or whatever could be done.

"I need to... ahem."

"Miss?"

"P___! I need to p___!"

The sailor went white, and yanked the door open. "Thank you!" she hissed, and grasping the clean bucket, rushed away up the breakwater before the guard could realise that she ought to have been perfectly capable of relieving herself without leaving the blockhouse, and clambered down towards the water's edge. The tongue of light from the nearest searchlight swung across the black water, blueish-white like concentrated moonlight, until it was almost parallel with the breakwater and Alma felt as though she was pinned in silver glow.

"You shouldn't be out here, Miss!" All her muscles twitched in shock. The shout came from back towards the pier head, and she turned towards it. Caught! But no, the lookout was shouting at someone else. Another woman standing by the water. Alma caught a glimpse of Asiatic eyes and long, wet black hair, before the pain almost knocked her down. The woman launched

33

at the sailor and as she flew, she was both a woman and a bulky, greenish, frog-like horror. Alma gasped in air to shout, but it caught in her throat. The man didn't have time to raise his rifle, and the thing was on him, impossibly long arms ending in curved claws.

Alma wasn't quite sure what happened next. A shriek from the sailor like an express train slaughtering a herd of goats, ending in a gut-churning sound of ripping. Before the searchlight swung away, Alma saw something like the shape of a man lying on the stone, bound in red strips of cloth, purplish lumps stuck to it here and there. Her stomach convulsed, and with a lurch, her breakfast surged in her throat and splattered on the ground. The lookout was inside-out. The frog-creature turned toward her. She shouted the phrase she'd used in the chapel and sketched a symbol in the air as it did it. The demon recoiled slightly, but did not even lose its footing. No use. She froze, muscles locked.

Shouts on the pier head, gunshots. Alma caught a glimpse of grey-green, a horrible rippling in the night, and long arms slicing the air around the pier head. The demon turned and bounded in that direction. Alma bolted for the magazine, and pulled the heavy door to.

Think! The charms that had worked before were barely effective here. Need to find out what works. Someone must know! But to astrally project in the hope of finding someone with the knowledge. Might take hours. By all the aethers, they'd be dead, the lot of them.

The dead! It was worth a shot.

Alma forced herself calm. Shut out the sounds, the percussion in the air. Centre yourself, Alma. A wash of calm despite it all. And almost without thinking she was halfway out of the world, in the fog of the between place, pain lancing behind her eye. She formed a picture of the demon, and sent it as a cry out into the aether. A touch of souls pushed under the fingers of her mind like bones under skin. A couple fled somewhere she couldn't follow. One answered the call. Features formed out of glistening, metallic fog. An oriental woman in a sort of cloth wrapping that left her legs and arms free. Almost exactly as the creature had appeared before its transformation. She bobbed as if the fog were water, and her hair radiated like a halo. Alma thought the description of the demon again.

-*Shiri Koboshi*, the woman said. *Bad*. She showed Alma memories. Even in this non-place, this place of numbness, Alma shuddered. *They came through in the water, and feasted on abalone fishers. They pretend to be like us so we'll let them get close. And then they take those long claws and reach right inside you, and...*

-*How long have they been attacking your people?* Alma asked.

-*For millennia*, the woman answered. *Volcanic eruptions tore open the fabric of worlds many ages ago. The shiri koboshi find their way through. But it is a small tear. Only one or two, and rarely. When I lived, they were just a story. Now I know the truth of it. There are ways to protect against them. But I was foolish.* A grim smile. *I grew lazy. I thought, 'Who needs to protect themselves against a story?'*

The woman described the symbols the abalone divers used to paint on their boats, mark on their skin. The *seiman* - identical to a pentagram - and the *doman* - a grid of five vertical lines and four horizontal, not unlike a table from the Liber Logaeth.

"But why take such a form, here in England?" Alma tried to grasp the logic of it all.

The woman's spirit seemed to shudder. "They steal those shapes they choose from human minds across the world - it... it amuses them."

Alma pulled her consciousness out of the fog. Something to mark the symbols with. She remembered the whitewash, and rushed outside into the night lugging a bucket of the stuff and a brush. The sailors had formed a perimeter, thank the gods, shoving at the advancing demons with bayonets and shooting volleys. With each one, the demons recoiled as if struck, but soon came on again. A *shiri koboshi* rushed a sailor, with the same result, a horrific scream, the wet ripping, the demon oblivious to the blows of axes, cutlasses and bayonets. She had space to work. But precious little time. Hurry, Alma, hurry, but for goodness' sake don't rush.

She set to work painting the biggest pentagram she could manage on the flags of the pier head, ignoring the shouts of the sailors for her to get back inside the magazine, taking care to clog the gaps between the stones with whitewash. There must be no breaks in the line. She finished the symbol and looked for Lieutenant Finch. He was by the twelve pounder, slashing at the shiri koboshi with... what was that, a ceremonial sword? The sailors were maintaining their line, trying to keep the demons at bay with bayonets and cutlasses. "Lieutenant!" she shouted, "get everyone inside the p... the star!"

"Get back in the magazine!" The lieutenant yelled, parrying another slash by the demon. Just then, a blood freezing scream, a wet tearing-canvas sound on the other side of the pier head and two sailors turned inside out. A knot of shiri koboshi rushed through the line, heading straight for Alma. She froze, unable to think of a curse to hurl, but as soon as they hit the whitewashed line, they bounced back, their skin hissing with blueish flame. The demons uttered a scream almost as horrific as the eviscerated men had, and hurled themselves over the edge of the pier head, exploding with a bright flare and a rrpfffft! before they hit the water.

Finch stared, from the pentagram to the demons and back. "Do as she b_____ well says and get inside the lines!" he cried, and as one, the remaining bluejackets fell back inside the pentagram. A few demons pursued, only to suffer the same fate as their brethren when they tried to cross the line. The rest of them swarmed back into the water and retreated a short distance, their frog-like heads poking out above the surface, black unblinking eyes regarding them balefully.

"So much for defending the fleet," Finch spat when they'd taken a roll call and an inventory of weapons and ammunition.

A Petty Officer coughed. "At least they haven't gone for the ships yet, sir. Or the town."

"Nothing to stop them though, Monk, is there?" Finch rubbed his face, leaving white streaks in the soot. Can't exactly draw one of these around the whole anchorage, can we?"

"No, not that," Alma replied. "But there are things we could do... They don't like daylight. A spirit I spoke to said they only attacked at night or in the deep water where it was gloomy. We'll probably be safe when the sun comes up. Safer, anyway. And then we can see to the perimeter."

"Quite the little Admiral, ain't she?" someone muttered

"Stow that talk!" the lieutenant barked. He turned back to Alma. "What did you have in mind?"

"Holy water, perhaps? If it were sprinkled all the way around the breakwater."

Finch's mouth twisted. "You happen to have a few thousand gallons of Holy water about your person, I take it?"

Alma regarded him with narrowed eyes. "I *take it* you have chaplains on those ships? One of them could bless as much water as you liked."

"Oh!" Finch exclaimed, "could we turn the whole anchorage into Holy water?"

Alma shook her head. "It doesn't work like that unfortunately. You can bless a fixed quantity, not an infinite body. But I don't know how to cover the gaps in the breakwater - couldn't use Holy water for that, anyway. Silver would work. Iron, at a pinch. But I dare say we're short of those things."

"Iron?" Finch knitted his brows. "Well, there's the boom defence. It's a big chain between the pier heads. It just lies across the bottom normally, but if we're attacked we're supposed to pull the chain taut and it stops torpedo boats getting into the anchorage."

A tiny spark of hope. "Well that's perfect! I can add charms to the metal, to make it more powerful. They don't much like iron as it is, but it won't actually stop them. With the right magics though, it could be more or less impenetrable. Can we operate the boom from here?"

37

"There's a capstan on the level below. It won't be easy with the men we have, it'll take hours, but we ought to be able to raise it enough."

The steps to the interior of the pier head were within the outline of the pentagram, just. They filed into the darkness, leaving a couple of men to keep a watch. No-one had a lamp. With a lot of bashing and cursing, the men got the capstan bars fitted and began to haul the chain in, link by huge link, while Alma sent what magic she could into the substance of the iron with Enochian words and symbols chalked on the links as they inched it along. Then, when the huge boom had drawn itself, dripping black filth, into the air, she chalked a sigil in full detail on the top of the capstan. One of the men gasped. The chain had begun to glow with purple light, which soaked into the surface of the metal, leaving nothing but a slight sheen. "I think that means it worked," Alma breathed. The men laughed, and Finch clapped her on the back, then apologised profusely.

Without discussing it, they all began to file back outside. Well, it was surely better to be in the open. No sense in being stuck down here if the pentagram began to fail... Even under the gaze of the creatures, who were still out there, watching. She could see them in the sweeping beams of the searchlights, until one by one, the shafts of light stopped moving, each one a stone in Alma's gut. More men suffering that fate.

There wasn't much more they could do before the sun rose. Alma tried to slumber, seated on the flagstones as she was, but it was just too cold. And with those things out there, watching...

Next to her, Fuller cleared his throat. "Named after the Alma, was you Miss?"

"I beg your pardon?"

"The Battle, Miss. In the Crimea? Only I heard you saying your name to Commander Whatsisname with the b_____'s grips and wondered if it was that."

"Oh. No, I don't think so. It's the Spanish for 'soul'."

"Is that right? Well I never." The sailor chuckled.

"Finding something funny, Seaman Fuller?"

"Well we've got our own Battle of the Alma here, ain't we? Your battle, Miss. And the battle for our souls, of course." He laughed heartily at that, delighting in his wordplay. Presently he became very quiet indeed. "There's a pub in Harwich called The Alma," he added, almost at a whisper. "I wish I was there now."

Alma fell into a sort of waking doze, peering out into the gloom. And then, just like that, the black of night had become a grey penumbra, the waves - once discernible only by the twinkling of reflected lights from the ships - suddenly visible in their own heaving mass. Dawn was not far off. She felt Finch seeming to gain energy with every new glimmer. He began jabbering orders at a signal rating, and they fashioned flags from jackets and rifles. As soon as there was enough light, the signal rating began semaphoring towards the fort and the nearest ships. Alma wasn't hopeful. If the attitude of the Colonel over at Nothe and most of the other officers was any yardstick, they'd be ignored at best or at worst...shot?

To her surprise, signal flags began fluttering up masts, and lamps from more distant ships started to flash staccato Morse.

"It looks as though they had a spot of bother in the night too," Finch reported. "Until we raised the boom, that is. Then the beasties mostly withdrew. I think they were impressed with the purple glow."

Really? Alma allowed herself to feel a little real hope for the first time since the demons had appeared... "I've passed on the message about the Holy water, though that was a blasted nuisance to explain in semaphore, I can tell you. If it's true that those beasts don't attack during daylight, *Empress of India* will send their chaplain to us, and *Royal Sovereign*'s padre will see to the Southern breakwater. Unfortunately it doesn't look as though they fared very well on the fort. Only a handful survived. Poor b_____s. Begging your pardon, Miss."

"They're going!" someone shouted. Alma stood, and looked out to see where the cordon of black, glaring eyes and amphibian heads had waited. The creatures were half-swimming, half-running out to sea. For the first time, Alma noticed a fluttering flaw in the air just above the water, perhaps half a mile away. It was like a shredded flag, that had somehow been sewn into the fabric of the sky. She pointed it out to Finch.

"Are they going back, do you suppose? Where they came from?"

"Not sure." She probed the edge of the aethers for information. The sense of wrongness nearby in this plane was just as strong. "I don't think so. My guess is that they don't want to be caught somewhere they can't get back to their portal, if that's what that is, especially not in the daylight." She pondered for a moment more. "If I were to speculate, I'd say raising the charmed boom unsettled them. Even though we couldn't trap them just with that, it raised the possibility that we might be able to with a few other tricks."

"Right, Bailey," Finch barked at the signalman. "Make to *Empress of India*: enemy withdrawing, your support requested soonest." Presently, Alma noticed a launch rowing towards them, picking between the battleships. It pulled up to the steps, a man in officer's uniform and a dog collar hopped across and ascended the steps. He and Finch exchanged salutes at the top.

"Thank you for coming over, sir," the lieutenant said.

"Not at all. I gather I'm to prepare for a rather large baptism?"

Finch smiled. "Something like that, sir. If you don't mind my asking, how did the fleet fare?"

"Better than you chaps out here I gather," the chaplain said. "Lost a few lookouts to those horrific things, but it seems the breakwater was the main target." He turned to Alma. "Is this the young lady who did the trick with the boom chain?"

"It is. Miss Langley, Lieutenant Commander the Reverend Wylie. Lieutenant Commander Wylie, Miss Alma Langley."

The chaplain took off his hat, revealing a shining pate, and nodded to her. "Charmed, Miss."

"Not yet, but I have a spell or two for that," Alma said before she could stop herself. "I mean, thank you, Lieutenant Commander. Likewise, I'm sure."

Wylie bowed. "You must show me how to do the..." He gestured indistinctly. "...glowing chain business." Alma smiled humourlessly, and bit back her immediate reaction. If he had five years to learn and a particular sensitivity to the aetherial, he might one day master it.

"Of course, but it might be advisable to start with something simpler."

"As you like, Miss. Anyway, if you'll show me to your water supply, I'll do my best to bless the stuff."

They found the tank for the drinking water supply and Wylie blessed it. Then someone suggested the water supply for the steam searchlights. The lieutenant pondered briefly, and agreed. Finch detailed Petty Officer Monk with a detachment of seamen to pour the Holy water along the high tide line, and see to the searchlights. "Shut 'em down and attend to any defects, then fire 'em up again at sunset and direct them toward that sort of ripply spot on the sea. Half a mile to the Sou' Sou West. See it? Keep 'em trained and your eyes absolutely peeled for those demon frog creatures, and follow them with the light if they start moving."

After the party had gone, Finch sidled up to Alma. "Might I have a word, Miss? It's just that these symbols and markings and suchlike are all very well. But they strike me as rather defensive in nature."

Alma nodded. "Go on."

"I wondered if there was any way of being a bit more offensive, so to speak? Our weapons were more or less useless. A shot from a Martini Henry could knock one of those things down, but it would just get back up again and charge. Same with the bayonets and cutlasses. We could hold them off a little, with muscle behind the thrust, but not for long. Good God, those creatures were tough. And powerful. Heavy. And as soon as they get their claws into you, well..."

"They're not from the Earth," Alma replied. "They're not even of this universe. As far as I've seen, they still have to obey Newton's laws when they're here - they still weigh whatever they weigh and all that, but they're not made of the same sort of stuff. They're not animated by the same sort of energy. It's like... like..." she racked her brains for an analogy. "Like a fish. Throw as much water as you like at a fish in its element but you'll never drown it. But put it in air and it'll drown in moments, where a man would be fine. We need to find something that works against them on their own terms, and the magics I know a little of do that. Some of it works better, some not so well. I can't be everywhere. But a lot can be done with the right symbols. They have a sort of power, or they can confer a sort of power on the object."

Finch sighed. "I miss the days of scientific design and measurable effects. How does all this work, anyway?"

It was a good question. Alma thought it was probably one that would never be answered, at least not to any of them, in this world. "I wish I could give you a clear and consistent answer, but I don't think one exists. If it did, it would be science. For the record, the general thinking is that the Enochian words and symbols call and direct protective spirits. For want of a better theory, that's what I'm working on."

"Well I never. Spirits, eh? Good Lord. I must say, if it hadn't been for the last day, I never would have believed it. And I'm truly sorry for the way I behaved when you first came here, Miss Alma."

Alma waved the apology away. "I've had worse receptions."

"I'm a Godfearing man, I go to church," Finch went on. "But I don't think I ever expected Heaven and Hell to bother directly with the Earth like this."

"I don't think they're supposed to," Alma said grimly. "But looked at one way, heaven can help us, if we help ourselves. We might be in a bind, but we can help ourselves."

"Hmm. We didn't have a chance to use the artillery, I don't suppose that would be any more effective?"

Magical artillery? Alma pondered. "What do they shoot? Some sort of explosive shell?"

"Yes. Twelve-pound common pointed shell Mark Two, percussion base-fused, gunpowder bursting charge. Steadfast, reliable, and very good at their job."

Alma chuckled. "You sound as though you're introducing a close personal friend."

Finch grinned. "I am, Miss."

But there was something in it. Alma knitted her brows, trying to remember. "Gunpowder? That's carbon powder, nitrate and sulphur?"

"Basically, yes."

"The brimstone on its own might do them a little harm. But I should be able to do something akin to what I managed with the boom - use symbols, sigils and words to amplify the power it has against the demons. Let me think. It'll take some planning, and a lot of work, but we could do it. And come to that, I should be able to do something about the rifles and bayonets. Oh, if only we had more time!"

"Sunset's not until twenty-two-oh-six. And that's just for us. What do you think the rest of the defences and the fleet might do?"

Alma knitted her brows. She didn't have to do it all. In fact, properly directed, anyone might mark a bayonet with the appropriate symbols or even apply a sigil to the breech of an artillery piece if they followed a plan very carefully, and believed in what they were doing. Simple incantations. And the ship's chaplains could be put to use. The more hellfire and damnation their preaching, the better. "Plenty, actually." She sighed, and set out her thoughts. "It will take an awful lot of work."

Finch smiled and patted her arm. "We can do it. You'll get a b_____ medal, I shouldn't wonder."

"Just avoiding having my innards pulled out through my backside would be reward enough."

The lieutenant flushed but laughed. "All right. Tell me what you need. Start with instructions for what others can do. We'll get those to the Admiral for distribution to the fleet. Even a set for that fat martinet in Nothe Fort, if he chooses to listen. We could do with a barrage from a battery of charmed ten-inch guns."

Alma set to preparing instructions for the fleet - remembering to add that any strange women of oriental appearance should be killed on sight - then applying the appropriate charms to their artillery, small arms and other weapons. In her heart, she didn't expect the Navy to carry out much of it. *Well, you're just a witch and a criminal, aren't you?* In the cold light of day, the demonic threat would seem less real, the normal attitudes of the Navy and all those hierarchies of men would snap back down, and they'd do nothing of worth until everyone was slaughtered.

To her surprise, Finch's report, possibly with Wylie's support, did the trick, and the lieutenant told her that the ships in the anchorage had embarked on a feverish programme of making spiritual reinforcements to their weaponry. It seemed that once the Navy had decided something was real, that was that.

At least when the shiri koboshi came back - and it was a dead certainty that they would - they'd find a bit more resistance than the last time. With any luck it would show them this plane would not be the pushover they evidently expected.

"The plan is to sink *Hood* in the Southern opening." Finch told her. "A b____ big iron barrier across the entrance. If you've time, do you think you could apply some spells or whatever it is you call them to her? Thank you. And here, they're going to move the *Thunderchild* up to cover the Southern opening. She's been fitted with ten inch breechloaders, much faster firing than those RML things on the other ironclads."

"*Thunderchild*? I didn't see a ship with that name?"

"That's HMS *Saint James* to me and thee Miss. Don't know why they call her that."

"I suppose because James and John were called the Sons of Thunder. In the Bible?" It sounded auspicious, at any rate.

"Is that right? Could well be, Miss, could well be. Anyway, someone had a bright idea and asked that if you could put charms on the ammunition hoists, would that mean you didn't need to mark up all the shells?"

"If the shells make contact with whatever I'm blessing, yes, I should be able to work it so they take on the charm. It'll be a little more complicated but will save a lot of time overall."

"There's the torpedoes too. If comes to using her ram then we're probably finished anyway."

"Heavens above, Lieutenant, I'm only one woman!"

He spread his hands placatingly. "Sorry Miss. They don't cover this in basic training."

"No, well. I've a mind to write a very strongly worded letter to the First Lord of the Admiralty when all this is over."

"With any luck he'll have his innards ripped through his a___ and we can get on with the b_____ work," Finch muttered sotto voce.

After she had done the more complicated work at the pier head, a boat came and took her across to the *Thunderchild*. The ironclad's hull sat low in the water, almost like a waterlogged ship, with a stem that curved forwards as it descended to the water, like the blade of a plough. Two large gun barrels peeped out from a drum-like turret, set well back on the foredeck. In the centre of the ship, white-painted upperworks towered above the black hull, themselves surmounted by two tall funnels, mounted side-by-side. The battleship had steam up, and thin trails of smoke jetted into the sky, straight up so windless was the day. Alma wondered if the shiri koboshi could see it, and what they made of it. Perhaps pillars of smoke were not unusual in whatever hellish realm they came from. Or perhaps it was a beautiful and pleasant land and she was making unfair assumptions. The demons' purpose here was not, however, open to interpretation. They attacked everyone they met and killed them in a variety of violent means whenever they had the chance.

A lieutenant met her as she came aboard, and took her to the ammunition hoists, deep in the metal rabbit-warren of the battleship's interior. He introduced himself as Crosley. "Is it true

45

you're a witch?" he asked breezily as she carefully painted a sigil on the shell cradle.

"They said as much in the court, didn't they?" Alma replied, not looking up from her work.

"Well yes. But I assumed you weren't really a witch. Just conning gullible folk out of their money by telling convincing lies about their dead relatives."

Alma laughed bitterly. "There are a lot of people who do that, I grant you. Far more than actually have any sensitivity to the dead." And far, far more than have any ability to find the edges of the aether realms. "Or could do any of this." And in any event, Alma didn't care to go into detail as to why she'd really been convicted, and put in the one prison remaining under the Separate System and guaranteed to stop her revealing what she knew... what the dead had told her...

"I suppose," Crosley mused, breaking into her reverie. "What about churchmen? Are they any use against these demon whatnots?"

"Hard to say. Depends how open-minded they are."

Lieutenant Crosley kept peppering Alma with questions until she'd finished. And then, to her utter delight, offered her use of a cot in the First Officer's cabin. "Finch said you'd probably need to catch up on a bit of sleep," the lieutenant said. Alma could have hugged all three of them.

The deadlight had been fixed over the porthole and when the door was closed the cabin fell into total darkness. She collapsed onto the cot, and had no memory of even drifting off when she snapped awake.

The fine hairs on her forearms prickled up. Someone in the cabin with her. *God, no, Saints and Angels!* She scrabbled with her feet and pushed herself to one end of the cot, which started swinging madly. She toppled onto the deck, running from the presence, which was everywhere she tried to go, kicking with her feet, sliding across the deck with covers tangled round her.

Total blackness. Couldn't find the door. *Oh spirits, help!*

Not someone.

46

Something.

Something bitter in the air. No, in her mind. No, in the air. An area of greater shadow. Blacker than black. Before she knew what was happening her consciousness was half out of her body and in the between-place, and the shadow-thing was here too. Heat and sulphur, unbearable. Alma recoiled, as though her soul were physical, a limb she tried to pull it away where it was beginning to singe at the edges. The shadow-thing had no form, no face, and yet it turned to look at her.

-Siren, it said. Was there surprise there?

-NO! She screamed through her soul and wrenched it from the aether, landing back in her body with a snap.

What? Who?

Hands on her shoulders! She raked at them.

"Miss! Miss! You're having a nightmare!"

Alma opened her eyes, only just realising she had had them closed, looking into Crosley's face. She was still in the cot.

"Awfully sorry," the Lieutenant said, "but we have more questions. I did knock..."

She thought about explaining... saying something about the shadow-thing. But what good would it do?

Afterwards, she was introduced briefly to the Captain, who asked if she'd like to stay on board when she'd finished her work. Alma declined, asking to be returned to the breakwater. She ought to see this business out, and Finch had been kind. Seaman Fuller too.

As she stepped up on deck, she noticed a flurry of small boats clustering around a smooth shape like a whale carcass stretching across the gap in the Southern entrance through the breakwater.

"HMS *Hood*," the lieutenant said. "In her new role as a doorstop."

"Oh!" Alma's mind rebelled. A whole ship just to block an entrance. "Isn't that rather wasteful? Couldn't they just have moored it? Her, I mean?"

47

"A floating ship can be rammed out of the way," he said, then laughed. "They intended to sink her level and pump her out when all this was finished, but she had the last laugh and rolled over. Still. More than one way to skin a cat, I s'pose. Surprised it didn't wake you up."

Alma stared but he merely smiled, nodded and escorted her to the entry port where another boat, its bow crowded with paint pots, was waiting. "Thank you, Lieutenant," Alma said, smiling. She was about to step over the side, but something occurred to her and she turned back to Crosley. "Listen. Paint a five-pointed star with a single, unbroken line somewhere on the deck," she explained, telling him to get inside it if there was nothing for it. "In fact," she added, "if I were you, paint as many of the things on the ship as you can."

The boat took her to the pitted and scored bilge of *Hood* where it sat above the waves like a sand bar. The boat's coxwain warned her that the warship was probably b_____ unstable, begging her pardon, and if there was any hint that the hull was about to shift again they'd be pulling out faster than a cruiser commander when Captain Beatty comes home early.

She had them move along the hull as she painted symbols at regular intervals with a thick, gloopy white paint, and as she applied the last element of the charm, she felt it click into place, and a rush of something bright and prickling coursed through her.

"B_____s, will you look at that!" the coxwain shouted. Alma looked up. The whole upturned bottom of HMS *Hood* was sparkling with lilac luminescence, and humming just out of the range of hearing. She grinned as the sailors nearby whooped and cheered, and sat roughly on the stone of the breakwater, heaving in gulps of air. Good heavens, that last ward had taken it out of her!

The boat took her back to Pier Head A. Finch greeted her with a wide grin, and gestured at all the extra men he had been assigned - a good share of Hood's crew. "Good to see you back, Miss. Did you see the *Hood* go over? Stap my vital breath! That'll be a b_____ to shift. Anyway, how are you bearing up? Do you need to rest? Do you want to check our preparations? How about a cup of tea?"

"Yes, oh, God, tea! Thank you!" She sat heavily on a packing crate that had been arranged as an impromptu bench. "I could sleep for a week. Oh, thank you for arranging a bed, Lieutenant, that was kind," she added, shuddering inwardly at the memory of the shadow-thing. Had it just been a dream...?

"Not at all." The bustle of activity stopped for tea and a tot of rum for the men, and suddenly it was a peaceful late afternoon by the sea. The tea was quite awful, and a powerful tonic. All of a sudden, it wasn't long until sunset. That stone of nausea appeared again in her belly. The activity of the day had neatly pushed out any thought of what they were facing, and it all came back with a rush. The ghastly end of anyone falling to the demons. And on top of that, other worries. What if they weren't just facing shiri koboshi this time? What if there were more of them, and they were simply overwhelmed? What if there were other things? Worse things?

Things like a shadow... crackling with more aetheric power than she had ever experienced...

The panic wrapped around her lungs and she fought for air. Breathe, Alma. Slowly. Keep on top of things. And like it or not, you're a weapon. She stood. "Lieutenant Finch, would you object if I spent a short while in the magazine, undisturbed? I need to centre myself, focus my energies." The cool of the magazine was a blessed relief, even with the slightly excessive chill of the early evening. She began to meditate, stripping away Earthly cares one by one, shutting down useless thoughts and emotions, gathering her power and sensitivity. It was almost pleasant. Letting the aether come to her, and meditating on the symbology and words that would be effective against the shiri koboshi, remembering what the diver woman had communicated, what she had seen of them herself. A calm, ordered state. And then a taste of bile.

That prickle between her shoulder blades, and Alma was not alone in the dark.

She could not stop her consciousness being pulled violently out of her body. In moments she was surrounded by choking silver fog, and then the shadow, the darker dark, was there. She thrashed arms that she didn't possess in this place.

-Why do you help them, Siren? the darkness said.

Why did it keep calling her that? She flung curses and wards at it. They bounced off like tennis balls on an ironclad's flank.

-Very well. Yours will be the last soul to burn, the thing said.

That time, when Alma tried to pull back into herself there was no resistance and she snapped into her body with a gasp.

She sagged to her knees. The scent of ozone, and something behind it, filled the magazine. She was alone again. But along with the bitter tang in her mouth she had returned with, there was a name at the edge of her memory.

"Bezaliel," she breathed. So it was him. The thirteenth. The damaged. She rushed outside.

"Are you all right Miss," Fuller yelped as she stormed past him towards the Lieutenant. "You look like you was dragged through a hedge backwards."

"Fine, thank you Seaman," she replied. "You look wonderful yourself."

"What is it?" Finch narrowed his eyes. "Has something happened?"

"Perhaps. They're out there, and they're being commanded. This isn't just a mindless lashing out. I... sensed something."

"All right." Finch started issuing orders to form a perimeter, check the ready-use ammunition for the quick-firers, setting the range. A mere 800 yards, point-blank range for those weapons. Alma saw the *Thunderchild* had been brought up while she was in the magazine, and was now anchored just inside the entrance, guns pointing out to sea. It was all somewhat reassuring. But only somewhat. She had seen what lay behind the incursion through the aether. And He would not be turned aside easily. She knew why they were coming. And what they thought of mere humans. Humans who were in the way.

The sun dipped below the horizon, and shadow blanketed the sea. One at a time, bars of white light began to stab out across the water from the searchlights towards the flaw in the sky.

Finch pulled out a telescope, opened it and scanned it in arcs across the horizon. "Do you think they'll try the trick of appearing as women again?" he asked without stopping his search.

Alma shook her head. "I doubt it. They know we're wise to it."

"There!" Finch hissed, pointing, and passed his telescope to Alma. A quick glance - bands of demons advancing in that half-swim, half-run, like gigantic nightmare toads. "And there. And there. A Gun, cover the port quadrant. B and C guns, the centre. Fire when ready."

The quick firers boomed out, the layers and loaders frantically swinging cranks, opening breeches, shoving shell and cartridge, pulling lanyard. Flares of blue-white flame began to burst around the sea. Thank the angels, the charms were working. *Thunderchild* joined in with her ten-inch guns, which each roared out in a plume of fire in the darkening sky. Alma, looking through Finch's telescope, saw the occasional cluster of demons flung into the air by the shell bursts, but at this point they were still quite a distance away. It looked like the apocalypse out there, the entire sea on fire. She allowed a hope that they could be kept at bay, knowing before it was formed that they could not be so lucky. As she thought it, she noticed the searchlight beams edging forward, keeping tabs on the front rank of the shiri koboshi.

"It's going to be down to us presently," Finch said to the riflemen. "In ranks. Wait 'til you see the whites of their eyes."

"We'll be waiting a while, the b_____s don't have any," Fuller muttered.

Alma chuckled to herself. Finch gritted his teeth. "Keep it to yourself, if you please Seaman Fuller. Miss Alma, if you'd move back behind us." A grim smile. "We might need you if things get sticky."

Despite herself, she tensed. "Lieutenant? Remember the pentagram. Get inside it, if... if there's no alternative?"

"We will. Now go. And Miss Alma? Thank you."

She nodded, and stepped back behind the rear rank.

"In volleys by rank!" the lieutenant boomed. "First rank... fire!" The Martini Henrys spat pink flame. There was an unearthly howl from somewhere beyond the men. Demons, meeting their match. "Second rank... fire!" Bark of rifle fire, bellow of artillery, shriek of wounded demon, yell of angered sailor, clank of spent shell cartridge. For what might have been minutes or hours, the air was filled with noise. Alma tried to see what was going on. She couldn't see much at all, but it seemed the demons were being kept at bay for now. There was gunfire and the flash of wards and spell-enhanced ammunition all around the anchorage now. The men at the artillery pieces had left off firing their guns and were defending them with rifles. The shiri koboshi pushing closer. She concentrated and cobbled together a ward around the men from words and symbols, and with whatever spare energy she had, a blow or two against the demons. *Thank you spirits*, she whispered.

"They're pulling back!" Finch shouted. "Regrouping! Reload, but hold fire. Man the quick-firers."

Unbidden, Alma rushed to the front, re-chalking Enochian terms along the line of the glacis with shaking hands.

"Are you all right Miss?" Finch's face was blackened with burnt powder and streaked white where sweat had run down it. She nodded. "Why are they here?" he yelled, jabbing his arm roughly in the direction of the shiri koboshi and shaking his fist. "What do they want? Don't they know this is our world?"

"They know very well," Alma sighed. "But they like it, they want it, and they think they deserve it more than we do."

Finch goggled at her, shaking his head.

"For us it's Darwin," she went on, "for them it's the cosmic conflict of the physical realms and the demonic, but the end result is the same. If you dominate, it means you are superior. *That in all things We might have the pre-eminence.*"

"Then how on Earth are we supposed to defeat them?"

She shrugged. "I suppose we have to deserve it more."

The shiri koboshi came on again. Somewhere, out in the black, Alma sensed the shadow presence of Bezaliel, but in all the confusion and psychic turmoil it might have been her imagination. This time, they went for the boom defence, and Finch's men were forced to try and maintain a withering enfilading fire with the three-pounders while protecting the guns and their crew. Soon, the space in the middle of the pier head was littered with brass propellant casings, and a ring of spent Martini Henry cartridges were heaped inches high behind the riflemen. Each one meant destroyed shiri koboshi, but for every one felled there were more vomiting over the sea.

This time a few shiri koboshi got in as far as the front line. An anguished cry, a nauseating sound and the riflemen were forcing the dead ruins of men out of the line, closing ranks.

"They're pulling back again," Finch shouted. "Five...six hundred yards. Man the twelve-pounder."

"Sir. We're running out of ammo," a gunner panted. A flash of a sickly green light emanated from out in the bay, and vomited at the breakwater.

"Get down!" Finch shouted, but the energy-pulse was directed at the boom. Alma felt the strike somewhere in her midriff. Counter-magic. The glow from the boom chain started to flicker, then fade.

A hollow opened in Alma's chest. She nudged Finch and pointed to the chain. "I could try and fix it," she panted.

"No, there isn't time." The Lieutenant's eyes flashed, huge and white in the glare of the searchlights. "Protecting the gap is down to *Thunderchild* now. Look, they're massing again. Load!" he called to the men. "And fix bayonets."

A thick, boiling layer started to spill across the darkened sea, like burning oil, closer and closer... and then it resolved into a charging mass of shiri koboshi. Alma mustered the last of her

53

strength. Most of the demons hurtled for the gap, slowed by the now un-charmed boom chain but fighting through as if through treacle. The demons that struggled through the breach converged on the *Thunderchild*. The monitor's guns ripped out again, tearing at the demons but there were so many... Alma watched in horror as they swarmed up the ship's flank, the boom of artillery now punctuated by the crackle of rifle-fire. God help them.

And us. "Here they come," Finch called, strangely calm in the raucous night, and there was a clatter of cartridges reloaded, a mutter of prayer.

And then...a dart of pain shot through Alma's eye. Something else out there! Oh, heavens. There was something in reserve all along... the *power*. A charm died in her throat. It had never even been close. There had never been a chance of seeing the dawn.

From out of the gloom, a sound of thunder, a clanking, thrash. Five flaming columns sprang out across the bay, one disturbingly near the shore. Alma closed her eyes. She could sense nothing, but she was tired, so tired. The dark presence had been toying with them. The end was close.

"Hold your fire," Finch howled. "Hold your fire! I know that sound!" Alma opened her eyes again. A shaft of vermilion light, straight and crisp as an iron bar blasted across the water. Another joined it, and another, criss-crossing the sea. As she realised what was happening, she felt something in the overlying aether move.

"Torpedo boats!" Finch started laughing. "They're ours!"

A pentagram. Cast by searchlights. And backed by a fair bit of powerful magic. Formed around the portal and the shiri koboshi. Alma felt a sob issue from her chest. The boats must have crept in at low power and arranged themselves unseen until it was time to spring the trap. Wilcox! He'd found his specialists after all.

A green glow built at the centre of the pentagram. Alma clenched her fists. Maybe it wouldn't be enough. The green light gathered into a roiling bubble and pulsed outwards - only to dissipate when it hit the line of the searchlights. There was gunfire issuing from the boats now, and they were pressing in, shrinking the pentagram while maintaining its shape, firing at any shiri koboshi who remained.

Finch cleared his throat. "Port arms," he ordered, and the riflemen cautiously lowered their Martini Henrys across their chests. The torpedo boats were almost bow to bow now. There was a final burst of green light, and everything was still. She could feel it. They'd gone.

"B_____ hell, Miss," the Lieutenant said, "Did we win? I think we won."

"Yes!" she said, her voice brittle in the sudden silence. "My God. We won."

Her smile was fixed. Painted on. No, they hadn't won. This was a temporary setback. She'd seen what lay behind it. The shadow thing. The Thirteenth of the fallen. And who was to say there weren't others, too? She'd felt a determination that men could not comprehend. This was not the end. It was the beginning.

For the populace in general, the news in those early weeks was confusing, conflicting, if printed at all. Some editors refused to mention certain strange events, considering them hoaxes or outbursts of hysteria (especially if witnessed primarily by women or the hoi polloi, rather than 'men of quality'). Few people had any idea what was happening. Many did not know that anything so dark could possibly be on its way.

In London, such was the swell of rumour on any normal day that actual examples of demonic appearances could be buried beneath the usual political scandals and shocking assaults committed by all-too-human monsters. A tapestry began to form, though, based on the smallest of incidents...

HELL AT THE EMPIRE

Marion Pitman

The first time I didn't believe it. I'd slept late after a party the night before, and the girl woke me banging on the door, coming in to empty the slops. I sat up, groping for a bed-jacket, and... something, was standing at the foot of the bed. I caught my breath - I must have made a noise, because the girl looked round - but by then the something had gone again. It was... it was very tall. And thin - well, parts of it were thin. I think it was mostly green. And there were teeth...

I thought, Blimey, I must have had a skinful last night.

Dad wouldn't like me swearing, or drinking - he wouldn't like me being on the halls, either, but he's not here. A girl's got to live, and the gin does help you get through the day...

Not if it's going to give me the horrors, though. Anyway, I had to get up and go out; I was supposed to meet Danny and run through a new number he'd written for me, and work out a bit of business. I felt a bit shaky as I got dressed The sight of... whatever it was, although I couldn't really picture it, had made me feel really bad. I was glad to get out in the street.

I went to an eating house and coffee shop round the corner and had eggs and coffee and rolls, and then I went to Danny's rooms (there's no funny stuff with Danny, he's one of those, and he's the best friend I've got).

I was humming the new song - you probably know it, 'By the Garden Gate', it did very well. I use the name Lucy Lilac, and I wear lilac coloured dresses, and have a bit of artificial lilac on my dress, or somewhere on stage. I sing wistful love songs. I wonder if I wouldn't do better if I did the saucy stuff, like Marie Lloyd, but I don't think I could bring it off. She can make the most innocent lyrics sound filthy. Anyway, I do what I do, and I don't do too badly.

Danny offered me a bottle of beer when I arrived, and I was just about to say Yes, and then I thought, and said, "No. I won't have anything to drink today. I had too much last night, and I got the horrors this morning."

Danny stared at me - "You? Give over. You don't drink that much. What - what sort of horrors?"

So I told him about the thing. Like I said, I couldn't remember quite what it looked like, but it wasn't anything normal, and, well, it wasn't really there, was it? Was it …?

While I was telling him, Danny went sort of quiet, then he took a swig of his beer, and said, "Be careful, Luce. There's some funny customers about."

"Well as if I don't know that! What are you on about?"

He just shook his head, and went to the piano, and said, "Let's have a go at this song, love."

***

The second time was at the theatre. I was going down the passage to the dressing room - a rather poky little hole that I shared with a couple of other girls. (I wasn't bottom of the bill - that was the ventriloquist - but I certainly wasn't high enough up to have my own dressing room). As I turned a corner I saw - something - just ahead of me. It vanished almost at once. It wasn't like the other something, well not really, but … maybe it smelled the same. This one was a nasty yellowish pink colour, and it had scales, and tusks...

I couldn't move for a minute, it turned me right up. And I realised there was a smell, a right old pong in fact, a bit like something burning. It was gone in a minute, and I wondered if I was going barmy. I was definitely giving up the drink.

Pauline was in the dressing room, and she looked at me and said, "You all right, Luce? You look like death warmed up."

I shrugged; "Be all right. Hangover."

Then she said, "Here, have you heard about the monsters?"

58

"What?"

"People have been seeing monsters in the street. They say there was one in the Strand that bit a bloke's head off."

"Get away! What are the coppers doing, then?"

She shrugged; "I dunno. That's what I heard. Sounds to me like someone's had too much absinthe." Pauline does novelty dancing, and she gets taken out by one or two well-off Bohemian types.

I still didn't really think I'd seen actual monsters. I did wonder if someone had been slipping something in the gin. Maybe that was what Danny meant... There are always a few rum touches hanging round the theatre, taking the girls to the pub... I shivered. It's not nice to think someone's been doing that, it makes you think about them murders in Whitechapel a few years back, somehow, someone out there... It was worse to think of than monsters, in a way.

Still, the show must go on and all that. I started doing my make-up, and then there was a knock on the door: it was Alf, he's the comic, he's a nice boy, and he's sweet on me, but I'd never take up with another performer. He stuck his long bony face round the door and said, "Luce! Glad you made it here - there's man-eating monsters all over town, they say."

I shook my head at him, and said, joking like, "There's enough man-eating monsters in this business, never mind all over town."

He looked startled, and went away, and I wondered if he thought I meant him. Still, time was getting on, there was no good worrying about it. Pauline helped me into my dress, and I started trying to fix the spray of lilac on the shoulder.

***

There was a new act on the bill, an American, big, busty woman, not much of a voice; she had a weedy little husband who was some kind of doctor, but he spent all his time trying to get her bookings, or get the management to give her better billing. They

59

were standing now in the wings, talking furiously in low voices, and he kept looking round nervously. When they saw me they moved away. I made some arrangements with the orchestra about the new number, then I saw Alf, looking at me rather worried, so I went over to smooth his feathers.

He said, "Luce, I need to talk to you. Can you come back to my room for a minute?"

"Well, I don't know -"

"I promise I'll behave. Do, Luce, it's important."

So we went to his dressing room, and he got out a bottle, and I thought, well, I could have just one drink...

So I took a sip, and I said, "What is it, Alf? What's so important?"

"Luce - I wish you'd let me, well, look after you. Walk you home at least. There's things going on - terrible things - on the way here I saw..."

"Saw what?"

And then he stared past me, went white as a sheet, and fainted - just folded up and fell down. Fortunately there was an old divan behind him, but still he went down with an awful crash. I stared at him for a minute before I thought to look behind me, and I just glimpsed it - blue and scaly, with bat-wings and four arms - before it vanished. Bloody hell, I thought, maybe they *are* real, and I wasn't having the horrors after all. So I took another swallow of gin, and since whatever it was had gone, I concentrated on trying to bring Alf round. When he came round he said, "You see what I mean?"

And I said, "Yes, but I'm not sure I'm the one needs looking after."

He got all huffy at that, and I went out.

***

The next time was when I was standing in the wings, waiting to go on. The act before me was a trio of acrobats and contortionists - amazing what they could do, you wouldn't credit it, they ended up like a Chinese puzzle - and then, somehow, there was - well, it looked more like a snake than anything. It was sort of curled around them, twisted around their bodies; it was huge, and blackish green and red, and spiky... They weren't half bloody troupers, because instead of screaming and falling apart they carried on unwinding themselves; and when they'd finished the thing had gone.

I looked out at the auditorium, afraid that the audience would start to panic, but either they hadn't seen anything, or they assumed it was part of the act, a conjuror's illusion. There was a bit of muttering, but no hysteria. Thank God for that, I thought, we don't need a stampede and people being trampled to death.

The acrobats came off, shaken and wondering what had happened. I didn't say anything; I didn't know what to say, and anyway I had to go on.

I can't say I wasn't nervous, but once you're on stage the act takes over, you go into the routine, and the other things you were thinking about drop to the back of your mind. I got through, and the new number went down well, and as far as I could tell, nothing appeared or disappeared. It wasn't till I came off, and found my whole body shaking so much I had to sit down, that I realised what a strain it had been.

Often I'd stay around a little while after my spot, chatting with people, going on somewhere for supper and a drink, but tonight I just wanted to go home and go to bed, on my own. Alf asked me to wait and he'd walk me home, and I almost said yes, but then I realised he'd probably take it the wrong way, so I said I'd be all right. He was angry again at that and he flounced off. I was just going out when one of the chaps that hang around the stage door came up to me. He wasn't the usual type - he looked about forty, very quietly dressed, in black, with a long, pale face, and no watch fobs or rings or flowers in his buttonhole or anything - and he said, "Miss Lilac, may I have the honour of accompanying you? The streets are dangerous at night."

He had very piercing dark eyes, and he looked at me like he could see right inside me, and somehow I found myself saying, "Yes, thank you".

I took his arm and we started walking. He made polite conversation, nothing out of line, nothing out of the ordinary. Somehow I never found out his name, or what he did for a living, but the way he talked was very soothing, and by the time we reached the house I wasn't nervous at all. He kissed my hand and said goodnight, and waited for me to get inside the front door before walking away. The perfect gentleman. I found myself wondering if he had money. I know it's wrong, but you have to think of these things. Some of the girls I know have a protector, and it does make life easier.

I made myself a cup of tea and took it to bed. The landlady doesn't like you to do that but I felt I needed it. It would be all right if I remembered to wash up the cup before she had a chance to complain. I wanted to think about all the things that had happened, but my brain was like the parrot house at the zoo, everything shouting and drowning out everything else. I still half thought I was seeing things, but if other people saw them - what could they be? If they were real, why did they disappear? And what *could* they be...? In the end I gave up, took a sleeping powder, and woke up in the morning in the same state of confusion.

I went to the usual place and had a bloater for my breakfast. It put the lid on the idea that it was just me - people were talking about the things, the monsters, whatever they were; everyone had a different idea. None of the ideas made much sense. Everyone seemed to have heard about the man who had his head bitten off, but no-one had seen it. I looked at the papers: there were some lurid headlines, but nothing I hadn't heard. There was a lot about Gladstone, and the Sudan, and what have you, and the monsters were only described as rumours. The Times thought it was all advertising for a new play. If I hadn't seen anything myself, I'd have agreed with them.

I decided to go to confession, and ask Father Murphy what he made of it all. Another thing Dad wouldn't have liked - when I became a singer I 'went over to Rome'. A lot of people in the theatre are Catholics, and so would you be if you heard what some of them Methodist preachers say about the stage. (Mind you, poor old Will's still a Presbywhatsisname - he's a Scotchman, he does historical monologues, he says they're educational and not frivolous. His church is all hellfire and brimstone, and hating your neighbour as much as yourself, and he drinks a lot of whisky, which makes him even more miserable).

There was quite a crowd for confession at St Aloysius', I had to wait a while. Some people were saying the end of the world was coming, others that it was some kind of attack, by unspecified Foreigners. Anyway, I waited till the end, and after we'd done the confession and absolution thing, I asked the Father what he thought about the "monsters", and whether he'd seen anything. I told him I'd seen a couple of them. He thought for a bit, then asked me to describe the things I'd seen as well as I could. I told him what I could remember, but somehow the things were hard to picture. Still I did my best, and he got up slowly and went out through the door to the sacristy; he was gone for some time, and I was wondering whether to follow him when he came back with a book - quite a large book, bound in dark brown leather. He opened it and laid it on a pew, and said, "What do you think of those?"

Well, blow me down if there wasn't a picture of the very thing I'd seen the morning before - or near as damnit. And several others, similar, with horns and tusks and bat wings.

"Yes," I said, "that's very like them."

"These," he said, "represent our mediaeval predecessors' notions of what demons look like."

"Demons." I wasn't sure what he was getting at. "You're not saying London's full of demons wandering the streets and in and out of ladies' bedrooms? *Is* it the end of the world?"

"As to the end of the world, it may or may not be; if it is, we shall soon know. As to whether the things people are seeing are demons, it seems, from the evidence, the obvious conclusion to be drawn. I don't know whether these pictures are taken from life or from imagination, but I would suppose that the denizens of Hell can take whatever form suits their infernal purpose, and sometimes they choose to appear as we expect or imagine them."

"So you don't think it's something in the water, or the gin, or a massive outbreak of DTs?"

"Also possible, but to be honest no more probable."

"You don't think … it's some disease, like the cholera, only that makes people see things?"

"If that were the case, surely two people would not see them at the same time? You say that you and Alf saw something in the same place at the same time."

"Well, he seemed to see something, and I turned round, but I was expecting to see something then, wasn't I?"

"You are admirably scientific about it, Charlotte." (Charlotte's my real name). "Well, we shall see."

"But if they're biting people's heads off -"

"A hallucination is unlikely to bite anyone's head off. Do you have evidence of this incident?"

"No. Only what people are saying."

"I will pray and study. Come and talk to me again whenever you want."

I saw that the queue was building up again, so I went out. Demons. Well, strike me pink. Demons. How about that? I went to a tea shop to have a cup of tea and a bun, and think. My stomach told me it was dinner time, so I had a ham sandwich as well. The tea was very hot, and I started to eat the sandwich, and the steam coming from the tea seemed to swirl around into a shape, and it got bigger, until it was definitely something rising out of the tea - it was mostly like a tiger, but with the face of a woman with huge tusks - she rose out of the tea, and I started back, but she drifted away and disappeared through the wall of the shop. I looked around; several people were watching her, but at the same time trying to pretend they couldn't see her in case she wasn't there. And a chap in the corner with a cup of coffee was more concerned with the black leopard that was climbing out of his cup ... it seemed about to spring, but then it turned back into steam and blew away...

We were all still pretending there was nothing there, and of course there was, now. I ate my sandwich and looked a bit sideways at my tea, but when I tasted it it seemed all right, and nothing happened, so I finished that and the bun, and since we had a matinee, I went home to change. I didn't see anything strange on the way back, except a lot more people than usual in the street proclaiming the end of the world and calling on everyone to repent, but most of the passers-by were ignoring them; I mean, that's London, isn't it?

***

The first thing I saw when I came into the theatre was three people - Belle, the American woman, her husband, and the gentleman who'd walked me home the night before. They were talking, and seemed to be getting on very well. I was a bit miffed - how did he know them? What were they talking about? How did he get in? Were they talking about me? I suppose it was jealousy - I'd thought he fancied me, and here he was with - let's face it - a woman less attractive than me and with a worse voice, chatting away like a house afire. It was silly, but for a minute that was how I felt.

But then my gentleman saw me, and turned and smiled and said, "Good afternoon Miss Lilac. You are looking beautiful. I came here to look for you, and I find some old friends." He smiled again, and I felt ... sort of triumphant. Which was rather strange, really.

Well, Belle had to go and change - she's on before me - and her old man drifted away as well, and the gentleman took my hand, and kissed it, and said, "May I buy you flowers? And - may I call you Lucy?"

Well, I was a bit flummoxed, because gents don't often ask either of those questions - they just call me Lucy and don't

65

buy flowers, without any asking. So I sort of stammered, and said, "Well - uh - yes, I mean, yes, I suppose so. But -" a sudden fear popped up - "Please don't buy me lilacs. I get fed up with it."

He laughed gently, kissed my hand again, and moved away - not towards my dressing room, but not towards the stage door either. It looked like he was going towards the stage; but it wasn't my business. Outside my dressing room Alf was waiting for me, looking like thunder. Oh Gawd, I thought, not now. He said,

"Who is he? Where did you meet him? What's he up to? Up to no good, I'll bet. How can you let him kiss your hand like that? It's disgusting. He's too old for you anyway -"

I waited till he ran out of breath, then I said, "I hardly know him. He's an old friend of Belle's. I quite like having my hand kissed. And it isn't any of your concern." And I went in and shut the door before he could get started up again.

The whole afternoon felt prickly and electric, like a storm coming on. There was a bit of a gap between shows, and I went round to the presbytery to see Father Murphy again.

"Come in, Charlotte. Has something further happened?"

I told him about the tiger and the leopard at the tea shop.

He frowned. "Interesting. These were not like what you saw before?"

"No, not really. Nor like your pictures."

"You say they seemed to rise out of the tea and the coffee? It may be that they are foreign demons - Indian, African ... You say they faded away, just as the others did?"

"They faded more slowly - the others were there one minute and gone the next. They didn't turn me up like the others, I was startled and frightened but I didn't feel sick. But, in the theatre ... everything feels bad. Everyone's in a bad temper, and there's been a, well, an atmosphere. I'm... frightened. Is that silly?"

"I should say not. I have an idea that these phenomena are only a prelude, that they are building up to something. I suspect you do well to be afraid. Is there something I can do for you now?"

"I don't know, really. I'm just frightened, and I can't tell anyone else. Everyone's carrying on as if they're not real, I don't even know if everyone can see them. Father, if they're demons - could you exorcise them, or something?"

"I understand people hoping they are not real. As for exorcism … that generally applies to a person, or perhaps a house, possessed of an evil spirit … there may be something, though. Now, I will give you a blessing. Remember that no-one can harm your soul - that is in God's keeping."

He gave me the blessing, and I went back. Everyone was still there, which was weird, no-one had gone out to have their tea or anything. My gentleman was still there; he and Belle's husband were talking again. The little doctor looked rather strange, worried and fascinated. When he saw me, my gentleman - I realised I still didn't know his name - excused himself and came over to me. He seemed excited, but in a good way, not the dreadful anxiety I was feeling.

"Oh Lucy," he said, "you are such a lovely sight. Almost… edible. My dear, great things are happening. Soon they will all come together."

I frowned. "What sort of things? What do you mean?"

"The greatest empire the world has seen. Is that not something to admire? You should appreciate that, my dear. The empire, and the Empire." He laughed, and it wasn't a pleasant laugh, and he pulled me towards the stage. The conjuror, Chin-Ho (his real name's Rajiv, but people expect conjurors to be Chinese...) was fiddling with one of his devices - making sure he didn't really saw a lady in half, or something, I supposed - and everyone on the bill seemed to be standing around watching, as well as all the stage hands, and even the manager.

I said, "What's going on?"

Pauline turned and saw me, and said, "When Raj was going through a new bit of his act, with a guinea pig, the guinea pig exploded. He's trying to find out what went wrong. Didn't you hear the bang?"

"It must have been while I was out," I said. "What on earth could make a guinea pig explode?"

I realised the gentleman beside me was laughing, and then we were all distracted by a grinding noise in the middle of the stage. There was a star trap there, you know, the thing the demon king in the panto pops up through - he's shot up through a star-shaped opening that falls shut immediately so you can't see where he came from. Raj had been using it in his act, but it shouldn't have been operating now. Suddenly it flew open, and - demon kings weren't a patch on what flew out. They poured across the stage, big ones, little ones, blue, green, red, yellow, black, some like people, only with horns, or tusks, or faces on their stomachs, or, well, other bits where they shouldn't be; some of them more like giant beetles, or flies, or some kind of half-and-half thing, I remember one a bit like a toad but with a face like a hyena - and everyone screamed and turned to get away from them - and I looked at the gentleman beside me, and he suddenly wasn't there, but there was a giant centipede sort of thing, still laughing - and I screamed again and ran.

Some people jumped into the orchestra pit, some ran out through the wings, heading for the dressing rooms or the stage door. Poor old Will tripped and fell, and he was sitting there shouting bits of the bible at them - I think it was Isaiah - and when that didn't work he took a bible out of his pocket and shied it at one, catching it on the side of the head and knocking it to the ground. The demons pounced on anyone they caught up with, and started eating them, although of course people fought them off as well as they could. It was horrible. When the manager hit one with his stick the stick went through it, and the thing wasn't even dented. Someone got a sword from the prop box, but the same thing happened - it was like cutting water, the thing just flowed back together.

I stumbled down the steps and made for the stage door - and I saw Father Murphy coming in. I shouted,

68

"Run, Father, they're coming for us!"

Instead of running away, he handed me something, and then moved on towards the stage. I looked at what he'd given me - it was a long brass pump, the sort gardeners use for spraying plants with water or bug killer or whatever. Father Murphy had half-a-dozen under his arm. I stood there for a second, thinking, "What the blue blind blazes -?", and then a huge thing with three tails loomed up in front of me, and without thinking I sprayed it from the pump. It made a horrible noise, and started to burn and melt; the spray that hit the wall behind it just trickled down the paintwork.

I ran towards the stage, and joined Father Murphy and the others who were still standing, spraying the demons, who were all burning and melting. There was a lot of blood everywhere, and even more melted demon; they dwindled down to nothing at last, when they'd been hit by what was in the pumps. A thin spiky red thing was taking a bite out of Alf; I sprayed it and it made a noise like grinding metal and fell away; another, green and squishy, was coming up behind the priest - the ones that were left were converging on him. I turned the spray on the green chap and he gurgled and went down.

I looked around, and it was a great relief to see the few demons left were melting, crumpling or fading. Father Murphy was shouting something in Latin, which seemed to upset them, even before they were hit. At last there were none left - so I thought. Father Murphy was busy helping the injured, and treating wounds. One of the stage hands was beyond help - half his head was gone. They'd taken a big lump out of Alf's arm. I joined in helping, and I said to Father Murphy, "What the blazes was in there?"

"Holy water - what else?"

I suppose I should have guessed.

I helped Pauline to her feet, and then I saw that the gentleman - no longer a giant centipede - was still standing at the side of the stage. I caught up the pump again and made for him; he held up a hand and said, "Don't bother. It won't do to me what it does to these lesser creatures. We are not all so ephemeral in the hierarchies of Hell. But I will leave you now. This isn't the end - this is the beginning – an amusing little opener before the main performance, if you like. And a test – how well you did!" He laughed. "But you'll see me again."

I said, "I'll try to recognize you next time," and let him have it with the holy water anyway. He didn't burn or melt, although he did flinch as if he'd been stung; but then he simply vanished.

Father Murphy was beside me. I told him what the gentleman had said, and what he'd said earlier, about the empire.

The priest said, "It may well be only the beginning. We must be vigilant. The British have sown the wind, and it may be time to reap the whirlwind."

The Royal Navy presented a problem for both sides. Disciplined and well-armed, the bastion of Empire, it was perhaps the most organised military force that Britain had to resist the depredations of the Incursion. And yet it was, by its nature, ill-equipped for the defence of the inland cities, and crucial to the survival of coastal communities. How thinly could its gunners and marines be spread? Was it feasible to integrate its actions with civil defence groups - or with the patchwork quilt of reserve battalions and yeomanry which the Army had to spread across the land?

One surprising fact about the Royal Navy did come to light during the Incursion. Decades before, some rum-sodden Rear Admiral, or a Lord of the Admiralty who once read too deeply for his own sanity, had issued an instruction. A standing order which on most vessels had probably been lost, or opened and thrown away as a madman's jest. That long-dead madman may have given a sour laugh, vindicated, when the portals from Hell began to open...

THE MIGHTY MASTIFF

Ross Baxter

Despite his thick woollen gloves, the icy wind tore painfully at Owen's frozen hands. Out on the exposed water, the bitter westerly gales served as a constant reminder of the remoteness and latitude of the tiny Scottish island of Canna. Although the weak early morning sun shone brightly, the open rowboat had nothing to protect the two occupants from the harsh elements.

"Put your back into it, lad," grumbled Chief Petty Officer Campbell, pulling his scarf higher to cover his grey beard. "I'll bloody freeze to death by the time you've made land!"

Owen nodded and looked back over his shoulder towards the shore, judging that he had only covered about half the distance from the small grey ship behind him. He smiled; regardless of the early hour, the biting wind and the grumpy chief, he would not wish to be anywhere else. Being a Boy Sailor in the Royal Navy had been his dream ever since he could remember, and he doubted any fifteen-year old could be any happier than he was serving on board *HMS Mastiff*. Although small and out-dated, the elderly gunboat offered everything he ever wanted; excitement, comradeship, a generous tobacco ration, and three square meals a day. The fact that he also got paid the princely sum of six shillings a week was an added bonus.

"I could row twice as fast as this when I was your age," Campbell goaded good naturedly. "Although at fifteen I wasn't as small or scrawny as you are. I'll make sure you get something extra when we pick up the supplies."

"Thanks Chief," Owen replied gratefully. He liked the early morning trips to pick up fresh provisions with the Chief Cook, especially as the old sailor usually gave him some of the warm fresh bread on the way back. The bread was actually meant for the Wardroom, the officers paying for it themselves rather than rely on the navy rations - although they never missed the odd loaf purloined by Campbell on the row back.

"I can never understand why you always look so happy, boy," mused the chief, rubbing his old gnarled hands together. "Anybody would think you served aboard one of Her Majesty's capital ships, living it up cruising around the sultry tropics, rather than being stuck on rust bucket like the *Mastiff,* forever chugging around the Western Isles!"

Owen shrugged and continued to row, unquestionably proud to serve on the obsolete gunboat, wherever it sailed. He pulled harder on the heavy oars, and after a few more minutes of gruelling rowing they finally reached the first dark granite blocks of the harbour wall. Owen followed the wall in, manoeuvring the small white-painted boat skilfully towards the empty jetty. Coming alongside, Campbell grabbed a rusty wrought-iron ring next to the equally rusty ladder and bent a knot around it with the mooring line. Once secured, the old chief launched himself up the short ladder at a speed belaying his age and weight. Owen quickly followed, eager to be out of the freezing cold of the early spring morning.

Canna's small harbour appeared deserted as usual, its flotilla of three fishing boats all out in the North Atlantic plying their lonely trade. Empty herring sheds lined the short dock waiting for the boats' return, the few families of the fishermen nestled in their isolated and barren crofts scattered across the island. Only the dark squat blockhouse, set back from the harbour wall, offered any hope of warmth and shelter. The old two-storey stone building served as the harbourmaster's office, the general store and the bakehouse, as well as being home to the elderly couple who ran it.

"I hope they've got the kettle on," said Campbell through the buttoned-up collar of his jacket.

"It doesn't look like they have, chief," Owen replied, scanning the shuttered windows and smoke-less chimney.

"Nonsense," said Campbell dismissively. "Our morning visit is the highlight of their day! I told them yesterday we'd be anchored off the outer buoy till noon today."

They reached the building and moved quickly towards the heavy front door, which stood slightly ajar. Campbell rapped loudly three times on the weather-beaten door and pushed through, followed more cautiously by Owen. Inside, the small room which served as an office and small shop, was cold and dark. With the shutters still closed on the two tiny windows, the only light came from the open doorway.

"Mister McCluskie!" yelled Campbell, "Are you still in your bed?"

Only the wind against the shutters answered. Campbell looked at Owen and frowned.

"It's Harry Campbell from the *Mastiff*. We're here for our bread!"

Again, silence.

"That's odd. In all the years that I've been coming here, I've never known old man McCluskie not to have the bread packed and ready, with a mug of tea to go with it," Campbell muttered quietly to Owen.

"Hello!" shouted the Chief loudly.

Again, the only sound was the wind outside.

"Maybe they've just popped out? Owen suggested.

"There's nowhere to pop out to," Campbell answered, rubbing the grey hairs on his large chin. "The herring sheds are all empty, and we didn't see anyone. They wouldn't be out visiting at this unholy time of the morning; I think we'd better have a look around this place."

Campbell moved over to the single door behind the counter, leading to the stores and the kitchen with its small bread oven. Both rooms stood dark and empty.

"The oven's cold," he mused. "Old man McCluskie would normally stoke it up at four in the morning, to get the bread on. Something's not right."

"What about upstairs?"

Campbell nodded, walking across to stand at the bottom of the narrow flight of stairs. "Mister McCluskie! It's Chief Campbell from the *Mastiff*."

Both waited in the gloom, but the call went unanswered.

"Pass me that lamp, lad," Campbell said, beckoning to the table behind Owen. "It's pitch black up there."

Campbell fished in his pocket for a light whilst Owen raised the smoke-flecked glass cover of the oil lamp. Owen managed to use one of his own matches to light it first, always having his own tobacco pouch close at hand.

The chief took the lamp and carefully climbed the creaking un-carpeted steps to a narrow landing. Two wooden doors stood closed at either side. He paused, then moved to the door on the left and rapped loudly. Pausing again, he frowned before grasping the worn handle and opening the door. Inside the windows were un-shuttered, and the morning sun lit a sparsely furnished living room. Two spartan wooden chairs, a rickety table and an ancient set of drawers filled it, with nothing out of place.

"The other room must be the bedroom," sighed Campbell, backing out onto the landing.

He knocked again, and again received no reply. Gingerly turning the worn handle, he opened the door, holding the lamp forward into the gloom. Nothing. The flickering light revealed two empty single wooden beds, the sheets jumbled and tossed aside. Clothing lay strewn over the threadbare rug and worn wooden floorboards, and on the elderly dressing table lay the old man's pocket watch and his wife's thin silver necklace. Water from a knocked over pitcher pooled on the floor by the dresser, the broken shards of pot scattered in all directions.

Campbell shook his head, puzzled. "It looks like they left in a hurry."

"But their clothes are still here," said Owen, scanning the floor.

"Let's check the outhouses," the chief murmured, pushing past the boy sailor.

Owen followed the older man back down the stairs and out of the front room which served as the servery. Campbell paused outside, and then turned left to follow the stone wall of the building around to the back. A small plot marked out a tiny garden for growing vegetables, the soil cold and barren with the chill of early spring. Owen looked around for anything unusual, then something at the corner of his eye caught his attention. He squinted in the sunlight; something colourful appeared to be daubed on across the dull grey of the corrugated iron wall of the nearest herring shed. He turned to tell Campbell, but the chief was already walking over.

Campbell stopped about twenty feet from the wall, shaking his head as he stared at the crimson outlines of the image which covered the wall from floor to roof; a pentacle, seemingly drawn in blood.

"What is it, Chief?" asked Owen, never having seen the like before.

Campbell said nothing, and instead slowly walked forward to peer through the open doorway of the shed. Though gloomy, the shadows hid none of the gruesome details within. Old man McCluskie and his wife hung crucified from the outer herring rack, both naked and disembowelled, their entrails hanging slickly down their matchstick-thin legs. Yards of glistening intestines had been carefully placed in front of them to form an intricate pattern containing symbols and what appeared to be elaborate, incomprehensible script. Owen stood behind Campbell, unable to quite grasp the sight before him. He had seen dead bodies many times before, but nothing like this. The stench of fish and offal clawed at his throat, making his stomach heave. Then he noticed the third figure, standing watching them from the darkness at the rear of the shed.

"Jesus Christ!" stuttered the chief, unable to look away from the tortured faces of the McCluskies, which seemed to regard him despite the fact that their eyeballs had been gouged out.

"Not quite," came a voice which seemed to ooze from the back of the shed.

"What? Show yourself!" yelled Campbell, quickly coming back to his senses and seeing the dark figure.

The figure walked slowly out of the darkness towards the open door, and the two sailors both stepped unconsciously backwards. The light revealed an old man, pale, tall and gaunt, and dressed in what appeared to be sumptuous silken robes. Stopping at the corrugated iron doorway, the man regarded them in silence, with a detached indifference.

"What happened to the McCluskies?" Campbell demanded uncertainly.

The old man's look turned to one of unveiled contempt, and he answered only with a sneer.

"I'll ask you again," growled Campbell, his anger rising. "What happened here?"

"I sacrificed them," replied the old man dispassionately.

Owen stood behind Campbell, waiting for him to say something, but the chief seemed dumbstruck. Although never one to speak out of turn, this time the boy took a step forward.

"You did this?" Owen demanded, his heart racing. "Why?"

The man's eyes swivelled from Campbell to Owen, a sick and crooked smile playing across his pale, wrinkled face.

"I freed them. Their blood helps to open the gate," hissed the man with scorn. "They're better able to serve now."

Owen stared back in confusion. "To serve?"

"To serve His Highness. You will all serve His Highness."

"We don't have a king," Campbell challenged, suddenly finding his voice again. "We all serve the Queen!"

"Not for long," mocked the figure. "Her reign is over. The gates will soon be open and His armies shall march forth to crush your Queen and her pathetic Empire."

"Are you...French?" asked Owen.

This time it was the old man's turn to look confused. "French?"

"Only the French would dare to challenge for our Empire," replied Owen.

"And perhaps the Dutch," added Campbell. "And the Spanish. And maybe the Americans."

"I'm none of those" roared the figure, the volume belaying his size. "I serve His Satanic Majesty!"

"Tsar Nicolas the Second?" queried Campbell.

"No, you idiot! Lucifer, Emperor of Hell!"

Campbell and Owen exchanged worried glances.

"This barren rock is a mere gateway. I have thirty-one legions poised to sweep out and join the Armies of Darkness, to seize your pitiful nation, making your Empire our own."

"Just who exactly are you?" asked Campbell.

"I am Agares, First Duke under the Power of the East. You two should prostrate yourselves before me!"

Owen looked to the chief for a reply. Campbell looked back, seemingly considering his response.

"Well?" demanded the old man.

Campbell sucked his ample stomach in and straightened up to his full height of five feet six inches, a look of defiance on his grizzled face. "Well, I'm going to give you the beating of your life, you old fool!"

Agares laughed; a grating high-pitched parody of mirth. "That would amuse me, but I don't have the time; I need to spill the blood of three innocents to complete the opening of the gate. I'll spare you both for now. to give us some sport when my legions pour forth."

Campbell made to reply but the creature suddenly vanished, leaving only the stench of decay and corruption.

***

Lieutenant Commander Henry Lambert listened to Campbell's tale impassively. *HMS Mastiff* was his final command after nearly fifty years at sea; a chequered career during which he thought he had seen or heard everything. But the story recounted by Chief Campbell and the lad was a first. Still, as ridiculous as it sounded, Lambert believed them: he had spent long enough in the confined company of sailors to know a lie when he heard one.

"And you've told me absolutely everything?" he asked, regarding Campbell and Owen sagely across the table in his tiny day room behind the wheelhouse. Sat opposite to him, the two looked distinctly uncomfortable.

"Yes sir," said Campbell dryly. "I know it sounds like madness, but I swear every word is the truth. We're both as sober as judges."

Lambert nodded. "I do believe you."

"Really?" said Campbell.

"Yes, chief, I do," confirmed Lambert, reaching down into one of the drawers in his desk. He rummaged for a moment, before withdrawing a large manilla envelope. "As you know, each Captain in Her Majesty's Navy carries a number of secret, sealed orders, only to be opened in the event of a specific emergency. Most cover events such as striking the of colours, the capture of the vessel, the outbreak of hostilities, and so forth. However, surprising as it may seem, I should tell you that one of these sealed orders relates to what you've just told me."

Campbell and Owen exchanged an astonished glance, whilst Lambert reached for a letter opener and broke the seal on the thick envelope. He withdrew a single sheet of paper, put on a pair of reading spectacles, and carefully read the text to himself. Once his eyes reached the bottom of the page, they returned to the top and he re-read it again whilst the chief and boy sailor waited expectantly.

Finally, and with a frown, Lambert looked up. "Very interesting indeed. The letter is dated January 1871, the date of the commissioning of *HMS Mastiff*. It has rested in this drawer, unopened, for the last twenty-six years. I've seen similar sealed letters on every ship I've commanded, and always wondered as to their content. Now I know."

Owen found himself holding his breath, waiting for the captain to stop stroking his long grey whiskers and continue.

"It seems that certain parties within Her Majesty's Government believe that our Empire is at risk from attack by…" Lambert paused, searching for the right words, "satanic forces. The sealed orders do not specify what the nature of such an attack will be, but say the forces may emanate from some form of hidden gate or portal. The orders for any warship of the Royal Navy encountering such a portal are to engage the forces as close to the gate as possible, as soon as it opens, and stop them by any means possible."

Owen waited for Lambert to continue, but the captain simply folded the sheet of paper and placed it back into the envelope.

"I'm sorry, sir," started Campbell, "I'm not sure what you mean."

Lambert fixed the chief with a stern stare. "It means that we engage the enemy as soon as it shows itself, which, given what you've just told me, may not be long from now. The nearest telephony office to us is at Oban railway station, at least fifteen hours steaming from here. The nearest Royal Naval vessel is likely to be off Stornoway, which is even further. That means, gentlemen, that the initial engagement will be by the *Mastiff* alone."

"I hope there's not too many of them, sir," mused the chief.

"Well, I admit I would prefer the fire-power of a capital ship, rather than our single ten-inch gun. However, we are all that stands between the enemy and our homeland. We may be one of the smallest vessels in the Fleet, we may be one of the oldest gunboats in the Fleet, but by God we can show them what the *Mastiff* is made of!"

"Yes sir!" said Campbell, grimacing inwardly as he remembered seeing exactly what had been made of the McCluskies.

"I will address the Ships Company at once, and make ready for action. You two go and help the First Lieutenant muster the crew on the fo'c'sle," ordered Lambert.

"Aye aye, sir," said Campbell, standing with Owen as the *Mastiff*'s captain stalked out of the cramped dayroom.

***

Owen stood by Campbell at the back of the fo'c'sle whilst Lieutenant Commander Lambert briefed the Ship's Company. Despite the strangeness of the message, the assembled sailors listened quietly and none questioned what the captain had to say. Once done, Lambert handed over to his Number One for the details. Lieutenant Bowman moved forward to the guardrail at the front of the open bridge and looked down. A grizzled Welshman, he was a similar age to Lambert, but unlike the captain had risen from the lower ranks to become the *Mastiff*'s First Lieutenant. As such, he was a rarity amongst the officers, and greatly respected by the men.

"As the captain said," Bowman began, "we've got a fight on our hands. We're not sure what we're facing, but face them we will. The plan is to make steam and sail closer in, giving us more chance of having the range when the gate opens. This will also mean that if we get hit, we won't sink completely as our keel will rest on the bottom and we will be able to fight on. All hands will close-up at their stations, and rifles will be issued to the deck hands. I also need one volunteer to go ashore and act as artillery spotter, signalling the range and location of the gate, and the accuracy of our fire with semaphore flags."

"Aye sir!" shouted Owen from the back.

"No lad," hissed Campbell. "That's no job for a boy."

"Who volunteered?" Bowman scanned the rear ranks.

"Me sir!" replied Campbell loudly.

"Thank you, Chief Cook Campbell. But I don't believe you are of the age to be sprinting up hillsides to get in position before hostilities begin."

"Me sir!" Owen pushed forward. "I've been ashore before, and am as fast as quicksilver."

81

"Very good, Boy 2nd-Class Robinson," said Bowman. "Collect your flags from the Yeoman and row ashore immediately. Secure yourself a position on that hill to the left of the harbour."

"Aye aye sir!" shouted Owen, proud.

"At least let me row him ashore, sir" Campbell pushed. "I don't want him to end up like the McCluskies."

"Very well," said Bowman. "But do it at the double!"

"Aye aye sir!" Owen and Campbell chorused together as they raced off the fo'c'sle.

"Right, lads! You all know your positions." Bowman gazed down on his men from the bridge. "This is our chance to show them all that the mighty *Mastiff* has a bite. When we get back to Rosyth it'll be the capital ships saluting us, not the other way around. They'll be queuing up to buy us ale in the bars!"

The whole Ship's Company cheered as one before running off to make ready and man their stations.

***

"What are you grinning at?" Campbell grumbled, heaving on the heavy oars of the small whaler.

"The idea of *you* rowing *me* ashore," Owen chuckled.

"Don't get used to it; it'll be the first and last time."

Owen nodded and again checked his kit: after collecting the two semaphore flags, the Coxswain had given him a pair of battered binoculars and a Martini-Metford rifle with twelve rounds. Campbell had also slipped him a hunk of bread, six boiled eggs and a bottle of pale ale from the galley. He felt prepared for anything, and could not have asked for more.

Ahead the rocky shore loomed closer, and Campbell sculled skilfully towards a gap between two large boulders with a patch of white sand on which to land. Using the momentum of a wave, the chief drove the boat ashore, jumping forward at the last minute to drag the whaler up beyond the high-tide mark onto the mud and sparse grass. The landing spot was out of site of the harbour, and hopefully of the demon which had crucified and disembowelled the McCluskies.

"Just be careful, lad," muttered the chief. "I'll make sure no-one follows you up that hill."

"Thanks," replied Owen, unexpectedly feeling a lump in the back of his throat as he suddenly realised that the old chief was the closest thing to the father that he never had.

"Well, don't stand there gawking; you've an empire to save!"

Owen turned quickly back to the boat. Grabbing the flags and the heavy rifle, he dashed off at a crouch through the scabby shoreline heather, towards the tumbled rocks scattered at the base of the hill. After jumping over a low stone wall, he picked his way purposefully up the steep hillside, keeping to the lee of the hill so as not to be seen from the cluster of harbour buildings. He crested the first ridge and dropped flat to damp peaty ground. Slowly he crawled towards the angled rocky edge which overlooked both the harbour and the *Mastiff*. Dampness soaked through at his knees and elbows, but did nothing to deter his progress. He finally chose a spot in the middle of a large mound of weather-beaten heather, and inched himself carefully into position. He knew that he would likely be spotted as he gave gunnery directions via his semaphore flags, but felt he would be invisible until then.

The harbour building and the cluster of herring sheds appeared deserted. From his lofty position he could not see the open door of the stinking shed where the corpses of the McCluskies hung, but guessed Agares must be inside.

In contrast to the deserted harbour, Owen could see that the activity onboard the *Mastiff* was intense. Sailors laid out hoses on the decking and piled up the 400-pound Palliser shells behind the single 10-inch gun. Black smoke boiled from the funnel as the boilers built up steam, and the forward winch slowly hauled up the heavy sea anchor. He felt proud as the large aft-ensign came down and the smaller battle-ensign ran quickly up the main mast, knowing his ship was now ready for action.

83

Owen scanned the sparse harbour, looking for any signs of a gate opening or anything out of the ordinary. Then he spotted movement at the far end of harbour, half-hidden behind the beached hulk of an ancient trawler. He adjusted the bevelled focus wheel of the battered binoculars and squinted through to see dark shapes feverishly working at erecting some sort of wooden structure. The figures worked at speed, ripping wood from the hull of the wreck, hammering it together crudely to make what appeared to be some sort of scaffold. As he watched the activity he spied two other figures prostrate in the long grass. Unlike the half-dozen frantic dark shapes, these two were motionless, and appeared to be dressed in nightclothes. Owen realised they must be islanders, having suffered a similar fate to the McCluskies. He guessed their intestines would be soon be arranged in similar diabolical patterns as those of the unfortunate harbour master and his wife, once the demonic builders completed the scaffold, and knew the time had come to alert the *Mastiff*.

Grabbing the two yellow semaphore flags he moved the lee of the grassy knoll and started to signal the gunboat.

***

"A signal, sir!" shouted the Yeoman from the bridge wing.

Lieutenant Bowman ducked through the door onto the narrow decking and followed the yeoman's gaze to the overlooking hill, where twin flags danced geometrical patterns.

"He's requesting fire to be centred behind the beached boat off our starboard quarter, sir."

Bowman nodded, able to read the flags himself. He glanced towards the trawler, calculating the range and bearing before dashing to the front of the bridge wing.

"Gun crew!" he yelled. "Target bearing zero-four-zero, range six hundred yards, to the rear of that beached trawler. Five rounds rapid fire!"

The four sailors manning the *Mastiff*'s single gun flew into action, the two loaders ramming a heavy four hundred-pound shell into the open breach as the other two spun the polished brass elevation and rotation hand-wheels to turn and range the weapon. Despite the speed of the gunners, the gun moved laboriously slow, stopping as the aimer made final adjustments. Once satisfied, the aimer punched his hand up to signal readiness.

"Fire!" yelled Bowman.

A bright flash shot from the rifled muzzle and a deafening bang sounded as the shell flew from the gun. The aimer closely followed the trajectory, watching the round explode thirty yards to the right of the target.

"Two degrees port!" yelled Bowman, noting the frantic signals from the hill.

After ramming a fresh round into the breach, the gun crew adjusted the angle and fired again. This time the shell sailed over the wreck to explode harmlessly in a shower of sandy soil twenty yards behind it.

Bowman cursed silently as he read Owen's flags. "One degree down!" he barked.

This shell slammed into the peeling wooden hull, the explosion ripping the trawler apart and sending planks and splinters in all directions. Bowman glanced up at the flags, which signalled to keep firing. He peered through his admiralty binoculars at the target area, trying to make out what was happening in the lee of the trawler. Dark figures seemed to dart about, carrying baulks of timber to what looked like a rudimentary platform instead of taking cover.

The fourth shell smacked into the aft of the target. Bowman clearly saw the splinters and wicked shrapnel fizz in all directions, including where the dark figures laboured. At least three of the figures were scythed down by the debris, but as the smoke cleared, Bowman watch in wonder as all the figures stood back up, apparently unharmed. At the top of the hill the flags continued to signal frantically to keep firing.

"Keep firing!" Bowman yelled, his eyes scanning the figures and the platform which still stood.

Through the binoculars he watched as two of the dark figures dropped their loads of timber and sprinted around the bow of the wreck towards the shore. Both plunged forward into the waves, splashing frantically towards the *Mastiff*.

"What the devil?" Bowman muttered to himself. He watched for a few seconds more, then realised the figures were speeding towards them.

"Buffer!" Bowman yelled aft. "Prepare to repel boarders!"

On the rear quarter-deck the Petty Officer and three seamen dashed forward to the guardrail, fixing long bayonets to their Martini-Metford rifles.

"Fire at will!" Bowman roared, pointing in the direction of the two dark shapes closing on the vessel. He stared in confusion, estimating them to be swimming at an impossible twenty knots.

As the *Mastiff* sent a fifth shot towards the shore, the four sailors by the forward guardrail began to fire the heavy rifles. Bamford saw the rounds zip into the sea around the approaching figures, but their speed made them difficult targets to hit. They reminded him of his previous draft at the Royal Navy testing range at Whale Island, Portsmouth, where the new prototype torpedoes were being developed for the fleet. The dark shapes approaching seemed to have the same speed and aspect as torpedoes - although unlike the new weapon, these clearly had arms and legs to propel them.

The volleys of rifle shots seemed to have no effect, even though a few certainly seemed on-target. With only fifty yards remaining, he pulled out his heavy Browning revolver and fired all six shots at the flailing shapes, to no avail. He braced himself for the impact, but none came. Instead he heard only twin hollow thuds as the figures hit the *Mastiff*'s iron sides. Opening his eyes, he leaned over the bridge wing to peer down into the clear waters. About six feet below the surface two dark figures clawed at the hull wildly with their figures. He gasped in surprise; the figures looked like large, ugly gargoyles, something normally seen crafted from stone on the roof of a Gothic church. Gnarled

86

muscular hands hammered on the iron plates and clawed at the rivets of the ship's side.

"Buffer!" Bowman yelled, pointing over the side of the ship.

The petty officer and three seamen positioned themselves by the guardrail and started firing below the waterline at the two ghastly figures. Bowman reloaded his revolver and fired downwards from the bridge wing. Lieutenant Commander Lambert skidded to a halt by the Buffer and added fire from his own Browning. The bullets pinged into the water, leaving trails of tiny white bubbles as they drove towards their dark targets. Most hit the gargoyles, but none seemed to have any effect. Whether the bullets were slowed too much by the water, or whether the dark rough skin was too thick to penetrate, Bowman had no idea, but he continued firing nonetheless.

"They're taking out the rivets!" shouted the Buffer.

Bowman watched as the figures managed to claw out first one, then two and three rivets from the *Mastiff*'s iron plated side. As each rivet dropped into the darkness of the sea the gargoyles concentrated on the next.

"Yeoman!" shouted Bowman. "Take the damage control party to the orlop deck and check for water ingress in the galley. Do what you can to stop it!"

Bowman's thoughts span: losing a plate would be catastrophic, and no amount of damage control could save the ship.

"Leave it to me, sir!" shouted the Buffer.

Before Bowman could stop him, the petty officer dived overboard, rifle in hand. The dive took him down to the gargoyles, where he thrust the bayonet into the side of the nearest. Instead of skewering the beast, the blade broke on contact. As the Buffer struggled to bring the shattered blade back for another thrust, the gargoyle sprang off the hull and grasped the man's head in one clawed hand, his left shoulder in the other. Then in one fluid movement he tore the Buffer's head from his body. Blood billowed out in great clouds, and crimson bubbles poured upwards from the gaping hole of the trachea. The creature let go of the unfortunate petty officer and returned to prising out the iron rivets, letting the torso and head drift slowly down into the murk.

"Keep firing!" Lambert shouted to the dazed riflemen by his side.

Knowing he had one chance to save the ship, Bowman darted back into the bridge. Grasping the polished brass handles of the ship's telegraph, he rammed both levers hard forward into the 'full ahead' position. Bells sounded as the gear engaged, and the ship vibrated as the two steam engines transferred power to start the twin screws turning. The *Mastiff* jerked forward, then slowly started to pick up speed. He ducked back onto the bridge wing to look down into the water; the two gargoyles seemed momentarily confused to see the ship moving forwards.

Both trod water until they were just astern of the gunboat, and neither seemed to notice their proximity to the propellers. Bowman watched in astonishment as the port screw sucked the first creature directly into the spinning blades. He heard a series of heavy clunks, like metal impacting hard on rock, and saw limbs and body parts spin off aft. He also saw the propeller lose a heavy brass blade, and felt the ship shake from the now unbalanced screw.

The three sailors with the rifles let off a cheer, then started firing again at the lone gargoyle which swan back towards the loosening iron plate. Bowman dashed back to the bridge, stopping the port engine and correcting the heading of the *Mastiff* to point back towards the shore.

Lieutenant Commander Lambert ran panting onto the bridge, pistol in hand.

"They've buckled one of the plates; we're taking in water!" Lambert cried.

"I know," Bowman shot back, "our only chance is to run us aground. Do you concur, sir?"

"Aye," said the captain bleakly. "Do it!"

Bowman nodded, returning his attention to the wheel. Progress seemed painfully slow, the ship braked by the ruined screw and weight of the water pouring through its punctured side. The ten-inch gun continued to fire, and Bowman noted with satisfaction that the scaffold being built behind the beached trawler had been obliterated.

"Not far now," muttered Lambert, watching the rocky shoreline loom frighteningly closer.

Bowman made to reply but then the *Mastiff* jolted, throwing him heavily forwards. The sound of iron plates scraping granite filled the ship, loud and frightening.

Bowman glanced out of the port side and saw the semaphore flags marking another target, but knew he must ensure the stricken vessel was soundly grounded first. Moving back to the bridge wing he peered over the side, seeing with relief the sea bed below and, with it being nearly high tide, knowing the *Mastiff* would not sink.

"Sir!" shouted a sailor on the fo'c'sle. "More of the devils!"

Bowman looked forward, seeing three more of the torpedo-like wakes marking the approaching creatures.

"All hands, prepare to repel boarders!" Bowman shouted, dashing below to collect his sword.

***

Owen watched with horror as the *Mastiff* grounded just outside the harbour. Then he sensed a vibration, a heavy rumbling which seemed to emanate deep underground. Looking around for a source of the noise he saw something glinting in the corner his eye, and turned the binoculars northwards to a spot about half a mile inland. Agares stood on a small crest, leading three young girls who appeared to be chained together. He stared at the group for a moment, seeing the look of panic and terror clear on the girls' faces as the old man dragged them towards what looked like three hastily erected crucifixes. Signalling the *Mastiff* would be pointless; any shells directed at the old man would undoubtedly put the girls at risk. The rifle offered no better solution, the range being too great and his marksmanship not good enough to offer any chance of being able to hit him. He surmised the three girls were the innocents Agares had said he needed to complete the opening of the gate. Given what had happened to the McCluskies he guessed their fate would be bloody, and although ordered to observe and direct the gunfire, he knew he could not just simply wait and watch Agares butcher the girls.

His mind raced, desperate for a plan of action. Although gunfire from the *Mastiff* had destroyed the scaffold being built to the right of the harbour, he could still feel the rumbling in the ground beneath him. If anything, the vibration seemed to be increasing. He thought back to how the intestines of the McCluskies had been so carefully arranged; if the pattern was part of the key for opening the gate, he realised that the herring sheds should be the next target for the *Mastiff*'s ten-inch gun. He picked up the flags again and began to signal the ship to fire at the sheds. Then he saw all hands mustered on deck with weapons, including the gun crew. It looked like the *Mastiff* now had a greater priority.

If the ship could not destroy the diabolic symbols in the sheds, he knew he must do it himself. Without another thought he stood and launched himself down the hill in the direction of the herring sheds, the rifle gripped tightly in his left hand. The gradient gave him speed, although he tripped twice on the way down, rolling and picking himself quickly up both times. Darting behind the first ramshackle shed he rounded upon the final out-building; teeth gritted in anticipation of the scene within. What met him made him stop dead in his tracks - between him and the ghastly corpses of the crucified McCluskies stood something with the appearance of a huge crocodile. At least fifteen feet long, the creature stood eyeing Owen hungrily. He jumped back out of the open door and retreated another half dozen steps, warily regarding the beast which simply stood its ground. Without breaking eye contact, Owen slowly took a round from his jacket pocket and eased it into the breach of his rifle. Raising the Martin-Metford up to his shoulder, he took careful aim down the sights of the long barrel, and squeezed the trigger. The silence was shattered by a loud crack, the heavy recoil knocking him back a couple of yards.

The bullet glanced off the heavily armoured scales of the huge crocodile's neck, ricocheting noisily through the tin roof of the shed. In response, the creature remained in position, opening its huge jaws as if in mocking laughter.

Owen quickly reloaded and fired again. The effect was the same - the round deflected off the thick scales to bury itself in the brickwork. As he reloaded for a third time he felt the rumbling in the ground beneath him increase in pitch, and sensed that the gate was about to open. Knowing he was out of options he sprang through the open door of the shed and dodged right, hoping the crocodile would follow and thereby destroy the intricate patterns of the intestines as it scrambled towards him. Owen's momentum carried him to spring off the now shaking right-hand wall, and he pushed himself off it with all his strength towards the rear of the cramped herring shed. The crocodile span around and charged forward to meet him, scrabbling through the bloody symbols and smashing through the racking as it went. The makeshift crucifixes twisted and snapped, sending the bloody corpses of the McCluskies toppling down to the shaking ground. Now cornered at the back of the shed, he watched as the crocodile advanced towards him. Having dropped the rifle in the doorway he looked for another weapon, but saw nothing. All he had was the small bottle of pale ale that Campbell had slipped into his pocket, and despite the futility he grasped the neck and waved it threateningly at the creature, waiting for it to spring at him.

Seconds passed slowly, and the crocodile made no move towards him. Owen suddenly realised that the rumbling in the ground had ceased and the walls of the shed had stopped shaking. Then the figure of the old man stepped into the doorway, surveying the wrecked racking and jumbled corpses of the McCluskies. The crocodile turned to look at its master, bowing its head. Agares stared woefully at it, and it slowly turned and lumbered towards out of the ruined shed.

"My beast has ruined the symbols, and the time to open the portal has passed," Agares hissed. "But other gates are open, and I will simply take my legions there."

91

"Not before Chief Campbell has given you the beating of your life, you old bastard!" Owen shouted bravely back.

"He already tried, as I made my way here," sneered the demon. "Here, catch!"

Agares lobbed a severed head at Owen, who side-stepped so as not to be hit. The head bounced and rolled onto the floor, and the boy's eyes widened in horror as he realised it to be Campbell's.

"Then I'll give you that beating!" roared Owen, flying at Agares with the bottle of pale ale raised. The old man stood still, smiling as the boy smashed the bottle heavily against the side of his head. Despite the force and shattered glass, Owen saw the strike had no effect. Agares simply brushing away the shards and beer. Undeterred, he jumped forward and swung punch after punch at the unflinching demon. Again, the blows did nothing, and although it felt like punching solid granite Owen continued until his hands were raw and bloody, and he had to stop to catch his breath.

"I'll give you your due," grinned the demon, "mortals are usually too afraid to even dream of striking me. Whether it is your ignorance or your courage, I'm unsure."

Owen knew that most of the fingers in both of his hands were broken and further punches would be pointless, so instead he jumped forward to head-butt Agares, his forehead connecting perfectly with the demon's nose with a satisfying crack. Owen's last thought as he lost consciousness was that the sound must have been that of his own skull breaking, and not actually his opponent's nose.

***

On waking in the field hospital, Owen struggled vainly to control the pain which racked his whole body. He could not feel his hands, and his head throbbed excruciatingly. Rather than crying out he instead remained silent, trying to overcome the agony and marshal his blurred thoughts. His memories of the events on the Isle of Canna seemed too strange to be true, and he feared the doctors would commit him to an asylum.

As the minutes passed, he started to regain his full senses, cautiously feeling his bandaged head and bandaged hands. Finally, he mustered the strength to sit up in the hard bed and look around. He stared at the turmoil around him. Beds were crammed into the cramped ward; every space overflowing with dying and injured soldiers, sailors and civilians. Seeing the numbers and the state of the unknown casualties in the nearby cots, Owen realised that although he and the *Mastiff* had prevented the gate opening on the Isle of Canna, other gates must have opened elsewhere.

He stood, dizzy and in pain, but filled with grim determination. He knew his duty; to re-join his beloved ship, avenge the wicked fate of Chief Campbell, and make sure that the sun never set on the British Empire.

As for those coastal resorts which catered more for entertainment and day trips around the bay, the Incursion was not only sporadic but also close to whimsical, by the standards of the Enemy. A single Infernal being might walk the streets, or the lowest of their forces, little more than animated corpses, might raid the town like feral dogs.

What little intelligence which could be gathered on these incidents suggested that, beneath a general, over-arching plan, there were also those from Below who saw the Incursion as an opportunity to play...

THE SEA WALL

Ian Steadman

From where Millicent stands, she can see all the way along the promenade to the West Pier, its pristine buildings gleaming in the sunlight. She can just about make out the tiny figures strolling along it, although at this distance they are only half an inch high, crammed together like pilchards in a tin. They say it is Eugenius Birch's crowning achievement, this bold, manly structure thrusting its metal bones out into the sea. Millicent thinks it looks crowded and unpleasant.

"Did you see him?" Gladys asks, tugging on her arm. "Him with the moustache. Near naked he was, and proud of it too. You'd think he'd be ashamed. It's disgraceful, walking about in public like that."

Millicent almost replies that it didn't stop her companion from following his swimsuited physique along the promenade with her eyes, but she reins the sentiment in. Gladys has been kind enough to ask her along on this jaunt to the coast, so it's only right that she should keep up the pretence of civility. Instead, she mutters a non-committal "Quite," and turns her eyes to the sea.

In truth, it's the sheer numbers that surprise her more than their states of undress. When she last visited a beach – ten years ago at least, maybe fifteen – it was still the fashion for some of the men to bathe naked, a shameless display that some seemed to enjoy more than they should have. In comparison, the striped bathing outfits on display along Brighton's promenade look almost puritanical. Mind you, she is beginning to suspect that ogling young men was Gladys's main reason for coming. Her own motives are less clear, although she is finding the salt air to be surprisingly invigorating. Since the disaster of the Goodmans' séance she has needed something to clear her head. Earlier, she spotted a sign for a clairvoyant, and almost ducked through the bead curtain to seek the advice of a fellow spiritualist. When she saw the turbaned figure behind his rickety table, however, his fingers jewelled with chunky rings of paste and coloured glass, she corrected her course. She's been in the profession long enough to spot a charlatan.

An older gentleman clatters past them on a bicycle, only just swerving in time, yet somehow doffing his hat with an apologetic 'Ladies' as he passes, but Millicent's attention is elsewhere. She has laced her corset looser than usual this morning but it's still troubling her, and she finds herself panting, her breath ragged and shallow. Maybe it's the heat. She can certainly see the appeal of the gentlemen's bathing suits, and the lightweight freedom they offer. Perhaps she should treat herself to one of the striped cotton dresses that seem to be all the rage down here, instead of persisting with her heavy black gown. It and its like, however, are all that her wardrobe contains.

But no – the heavy feeling in her chest began before they felt the lick of Brighton's coastal sun. It dated back to that last séance: the Goodmans. She'd heard all kinds of rumours, of course: of the strange happenings in London, the sightings of 'Devils' in the Cotswolds. She had felt something abnormal herself on a couple of occasions when she was under, a looming darkness that sat both within and outside the spirit realm, like a crack running through it. But still, she hadn't imagined it could affect her: she was too experienced, too strong, too well-informed.

Ah, hubris.

Looking past the brightly-coloured changing huts, along the coastal resort's infamous pebble beach to the whispering waves at the shore's edge, she finds it hard to imagine that any of it was real. And yet the tightness remains, a hand gripping her lungs and squeezing, slowly forcing the air from her body. Mr and Mrs Goodman had only wanted to contact their son on the fifth anniversary of his death. True, he'd scoffed at the idea at first, accusing his wife of foolish sentimentality, and Millicent of exploiting the woman's weakness. He had come around eventually, though, and it should have been a simple summoning, one she had performed a hundred times before. Instead, she'd found herself acting as the conduit for something else, a presence she couldn't contain, simultaneously slipping through the cracks and looming massive in her mind. Apparently, the voice that had forced its way out between her teeth had been guttural and inhuman, a roaring, catlike bark that had left Mrs Goodman cowering under the table – but she remembers none of that. There was only a blackness within her, sliding like oil over her soul, and heavy, so heavy…

It's Gladys who snaps her out of it, her hand tugging at her sleeve again.

"Lord, look at him."

She turns, expecting to see another toned, sparsely-clad young specimen, so she's surprised by the older gentleman whom Gladys is eyeballing. He's more conservatively dressed than most of the holidaymakers, his barrel of a stomach suggesting that he's richer than them too, but it isn't his waistline that has attracted Gladys's attention. The man appears to be engaged in ripping the beard from his face. There are already several wet, bloody patches on his chin, and as Millicent watches he grasps a fistful of hair and tugs it out with a coarse tearing sound. There are a few gasps from the ladies nearby, but Millicent leans nearer. He is muttering something under his breath. She can't make all of it out, but it's something about a boy king, and it being wrong, all of it, all wrong.

Gladys pulls her away from him, back into the safety of the crowd, and the last she sees is a police constable attempting to pin the gentleman's arms behind his back. She's shocked, but also intrigued. She would have liked to have seen more.

"Well," Gladys says once they're moving again, their path bringing them closer to the pier, "you don't see that every day, do you? Poor blighter. Too long in the sun, I reckon. They say it can do that, and you know what these old men are like. They never pay attention to the doctors, do they? You hold onto your parasol there, won't you."

But Millicent has her own thoughts about the old gentleman, and they have nothing to do with the detrimental effects of sunbathing. There was something in his eyes, in that vacant stare, that reminded her of the oily blackness she'd felt during the séance.

She tries to convince herself that it's simply because her mind was already occupied – an echo of her own thoughts, projected onto the world. But as they near the pier it becomes clear that all is not right there either. There is a crowd gathered around two men on the floor, their hats pushed to the edge of the circle as they wrestle. The larger of the two, a heavyset gentleman with a full, bushy beard, has the upper hand, and as he pins his opponent down, his arm twisted back, there is an audible snap. The wounded party howls in pain, but instead of stepping in to stop it, a constable in the crowd wades in with his truncheon and begins to beat him about the head as if he is merely threshing weeds. One of the women in the crowd lifts her petticoats and dances around the circle, as the constable whacks the man's head back and forth, nothing more than a ball of blood and bone.

"Oh God," Gladys shouts, but her words are drowned out by the noise of the crowd, rowdy and blood-drunk. Gladys sits on the ground and covers her eyes, humming a hymn Millicent hasn't heard since she was a child.

As for Millicent, her head remains remarkably clear. Whatever was gripping her ribcage has loosened its grasp. She can't explain it, but it's as if the blackness has gone. She catches her breath, allows it to flood her lungs for the first time in weeks. Then she starts to look around. Beyond the two fighting men and the gathered crowd there's something happening on the beach as well. She can't see exactly what, but a mob has formed, ladies in their striped summer frocks, men in their suits, their skin-tight bathing costumes. There's a weird energy about the gathering, like a storm but subtler, more intense. When one of the men whoops she jumps as if it's a thunderclap.

It's when she turns her glance towards the pier that she realises just how far the madness has spread. There's an entertainment arcade there, an attraction for the bored masses. Penny ices, donkey rides, rifle ranges. Hit the target three times, win the missus a prize. Except the man standing at the range in the pea-green jacket, his hair lacquered straight and his moustache waxed into surgical points, isn't aiming at the targets. He's slowly, methodically scanning the beach, raising his rifle, picking them off one by one. A bather still in his costume; a volunteer watching the fight; a mother with her toddler still clinging to her petticoats as she falls. His rifle is indiscriminate and precise, as if he does this every weekend. When he pauses to reload, the man behind the range hands him a plaster of Paris model of the pier, barely wider than his palm. Then he begins again.

Millicent takes a moment to gather her wits, but the breeze gusts suddenly from the sea, hitting her face with a briny insistence that makes her start. She should be terrified, she knows that; but for now, at least, she isn't. Years spent channelling the dead numbs you to most eventualities.

Somebody should have noticed the rifleman by now, but as she scans the crowds her heart sinks. A few people are curled up on the ground, like Gladys, covering their eyes or their ears, weeping into their hands. But they are in the minority. Most of the holidaymakers, along the beach and as far as she can see along the pier, are fully enclosed in whichever nightmare is filling their heads. With a shriek like an owl an old woman pulls a fistful of hair from her scalp then crams it between her cracked, yellowed teeth; a young man to her left, barely more than twenty years old, has stripped off his bathing costume and appears to be mutilating himself with a knife, carving lines in his belly that draw ever lower. The din is swelling as she watches, a cacophony of screams, and yelps, and profanities that fills her ears. Only the Punch & Judy booth has fallen silent, but she doesn't have to draw near to spot the thick, red-brown puddle gradually oozing from beneath its curtain. Mr Punch lies forgotten on the ground, empty and lifeless, still grinning.

She's so numbed by the chaos about her that Millicent almost misses the woman. She's standing at the entrance to the

99

pier, her back straight, the area around her an eerie bubble of calm. Her stillness alone marks her out from the crowd, but it's the look of fear and disgust that draws Millicent towards her. Those who have been sucked into the madness are too blinkered to see anything beyond their own feverish dreams. This woman is awake, and all too conscious of the horror that's happening around her.

Millicent has to battle to reach her. Two men collide with her as she tries to make a path, their combined weight almost pulling her to the ground. They're too focused on trying to gouge out each other's eyes, however, to offer more than a passing threat, and as they spin off into the crowd she's able to regain her feet. The woman sees it happen, and it's enough to snap her out of her trance. She steps forward and reaches out a hand. Millicent grasps it as if it's a lifesaver.

"You— you see this?" asks the woman. "It's not just me, is it. I'm not imagining it. Has everyone gone mad?"

Millicent tries to ignore a small boy, no more than seven or eight, who is rolling something bloody and red down the steps beside them.

"Oh no, this is real," she says. "Do you have any idea what started it? Perhaps—" Her thought is interrupted by the *crack* of a rifle shot near their heads, and both duck. Behind them, a sturdy gentleman topples to the boards of the pier, a wet hole blooming where his eye used to be.

"We should find cover," Millicent scans the entrance to the pier for somewhere suitable. "Here, follow me."

She needn't have issued the instruction, as the lady doesn't relax her grip until they are both under the overhang of the entrance pavilion. There is a solid wall between them and the marksman, but still the lady clings on, her eyes panicked. Occasionally they hear a sharp *crack* as a projectile hits the plaster. Millicent's eyes are drawn to her feet. Beneath them she can see between the wooden boards, down to the stony beach below. They are still above dry land, just, but occasionally a wave hurries inland and she can see the foam wash into view, only to be sucked back out to sea moments later.

When the lady speaks, it breaks her reverie. "Thank you for that. I didn't know what to do. I've never... nobody's ever seen anything like this before, have they? I mean, you hear stories. But not this." Finally, she releases Millicent's hand. "I'm Rose. We might as well keep things civil, even if the world is falling to pieces."

Millicent can't keep a snorting laugh from escaping. The rules of civilised society no longer seem to apply, not in the face of this. She is afraid she may have offended her new companion, but Rose's lips stretch into a grin as well, albeit a thin one.

"I'm probably quite mad for asking," Rose says, gazing up the pier as a yell and the sound of a scuffle are carried to them on the sea breeze, "but do you have any idea what's going on here? Are we the only sane ones left? I don't know quite how to describe it, but there's a strange feeling in the air, isn't there?"

Millicent is about to plead ignorance, but then she stops. She doesn't know anything, not as such, but she does feel something. Even saying it in her head, she's aware that it sounds ridiculous, but she feels that something has come through to this world, something dark, and angry, and destructive. The presence from the spirit realm, the one she felt during the séance – it's here now, somewhere on Brighton beach. Those rumours from London no longer sound so far-fetched.

"I might know something... a little. I do, I think. You've seen the reports in the press? The Devils at Cleeve Hill, the stories from London, these rumours of demons, or whatever they are..."

Rose nods.

"Of course - you suggested as much, didn't you?" says Millicent. "We all have, I suppose. I didn't pay them much mind at first, but now... well, now I think we might have been rather naïve. I have a... let us say an acquaintance with matters of the spirits and the other world, you see. And I felt something here today, but I pushed it away to the back of my mind. It couldn't be true, could it? But now it looks as if it is, and— "

"Are you trying to tell me there's a demon, here?" Rose interrupts. "Is that what's doing this?"

Millicent nods. It's easier to hear it than to say it.

"I see." Rose's hands are shaking, and she swipes at a stray lock of hair over and over as she talks. "I've been told I am a little 'sensitive', although I doubt it's enough to make any difference. At least we have some idea of what we're dealing with, I suppose. It might go some way towards explaining this, this..." She gestures at the pandemonium around them, the deranged masses. "Do you have any idea where it is, this *thing*? You said you could feel it. Can you sense it now?"

Millicent closes her eyes, tries to block out the shouts and the terror. She recalls the presence so clearly, its emptiness, vast and slippery, and in her mind she hears the roar that she made when she barked at Mrs Goodman, not her voice but something else's, like a lion, or a cheetah. Yes, a cheetah. Unbidden, a figure rises into her thoughts, that of a huge cheetah walking upright, a crown upon its head with spikes sticking up like needles. She can see it but she can feel it too, its weight shifting from that other world to this one, bending reality around it. It has a psychic mass to it that's still sending out ripples.

Opening her eyes, she lifts a finger and points along the length of the pier, towards the far end and the open sea.

"There. It's down there. I can still feel it, whatever it is. It's on the pier."

Rose adjusts her gown, brushing her hands against her sides. "Well, I won't claim I'm not terrified, but I imagine that's where we're heading, then. Better facing the danger on your feet, as my father always used to say."

Millicent nods, her mouth dry. She's not sure she feels very courageous, but there appears to be little option. Everyone else is lost in their communal fever dream. When Rose leads the way along the pier, her feet echoing hollowly on the salt-stripped boards, Millicent follows.

They have to weave from side to side as they make their way through the crowds, dodging bodies as they hurl themselves – or are hurled – into their path. Millicent sees a woman cradling what she can only assume is a baby, the bundle wrapped unseen in a bright blue blanket, her mouth smeared with red. She turns away before she learns any more.

It's Rose who spots the change in the flow. The crowd is still in chaos, a spectacle of perversity and madness, but they all avoid a space partway along the pier, close to its end. When two wrestling men draw apart, they see what it is. The penny arcade is housed in one of the white buildings, but despite the bright signs and the promises of amusements, nobody is straying within ten feet of it. *As if it's the eye of a storm*, Millicent thinks, *or the void at the heart of a whirlpool.*

She concentrates for a moment, reaches out with her thoughts, and it's there: that dark mass, heavy and undeniable, a sinkhole from our realm through to another. The thing she felt before, the abomination.

Rose is holding her head now, and as they push forwards it becomes harder to move, as if they're walking against a current. Millicent looks at her companion and mouths, "Are you all right?"

A shake of the head. When she speaks, Rose must shout to be heard. "I hear something. A voice, telling me things, telling me… lies. Can you not hear it? The things it's saying?"

Millicent hears nothing. She had been relying on that inner feeling, but now that it's mentioned she fancies she detects a whisper, a voice coming from the arcade. She had mistaken it for the sea breeze, but it's more insistent than that. She has no idea what it's saying – if it's saying anything at all – but it writhes around her mind like a snake, working its way in, making itself at home.

She has faced possessions before, has allowed herself to be a conduit for the dead. She knows what it is like to invite another consciousness inside your head, to surrender to it – but she also knows how to keep it at bay. As Rose topples to her knees, her

103

fingers thrust into her ears, her eyes squeezed shut, Millicent draws upon all her learning and control and pushes back, forcing the voice from her thoughts. She focuses instead on the candy-striped awnings, the bathing suits, the salt tang of the briny air. These things she knows are real. They anchor her, and with a final push she is able to grasp her way back, expelling the whisper from her mind.

Gathering her black gown in her fists, Millicent runs into the arcade.

It's dark inside, the stark daylight of the seafront failing to penetrate. It's cold too, like a cave. Her eyes take a few moments to adjust. When she can see, her first thought is that it's empty. She wonders whether there could really be something here – the place seems deserted. Reaching out, though, she can still feel something. A heaviness, a vacuum—

Then, without warning, she sees movement. She can't make sense of it at first. It's little more than a flicker, or more than one, like three birds flitting through the darkness side by side. It's gone as quickly as it's seen, but she follows it, heading to the rear of the room, the deepest part of the cave. And then she sees it. The sign catches her attention first, the words 'Hall of Mirrors' written in a sickening wave, but then her eyes are drawn down and she sees it – him – standing there, watching her. She imagines he might be a painting at first, but his mouth is moving, his eyes are alive and burning.

His body is lean, muscled, but furred like a cheetah's, his arms ending in hands that still resemble paws with their short fingers and long, curved nails. His face is feline and yet there's an undeniable intelligence, albeit of the wild, untamed kind. As he moves, the light catches a crown that sits atop his head, and she remembers suddenly an image from a book, a volume on demonology that she kept on her shelf mainly to impress her customers. It takes her a moment, but his name comes back to her in a rush, as if it was waiting there all along, hoping to be found. Ose. His name is Ose, the fifty-seventh spirit, President of Hell.

She knows it without a doubt, just as she knows that she must let him in, just a little, just enough to hear.

His voice, when it comes, is deep and sonorous, fading into her consciousness like the distant reverberation of a gong.

"...what I will do for you child, what you can know. My knowledge spans worlds, it crosses aeons. I can make you wise beyond imagining, answering every question, teaching you those things that man has never known. What say you, child? What say you?"

Millicent digs her fists deeper into the fabric of her gown, her nails starting to pierce the skin of her palms. "And what do you ask in return?" she says, her voice weak and thin in comparison. "What would you have me do for you?"

Ose shifts slightly on his padded feet, and it occurs to her that he isn't there at all. His reflections warp and waver on the surface of the mirrors, but there's nothing solid, no creature here with her to cast such a reflection. *He's not made it through yet, then. Something's happened, and he's trapped.*

"There is a war happening, child. You cannot even begin to imagine how long it will be waged, and how many will die. You stand in its foothills, but the mountains of suffering and loss are vast. We are coming, all of us. We are coming. All I want is to make the victory swift, to save you that suffering. You have seen what I can do, the way the weak open their minds to me. From here I can spread the message that all is lost, I can make your soldiers stand down, make your politicians lose faith in their cause and hand your world to us. There need not be so much suffering, child. You could deliver them to the future. All I ask is that you break these mirrors and allow me to finish my work. All I ask is that you open the door."

Millicent can see it now. The mirrors have trapped him where he is, confining him in their infinite regressions. He hasn't been able to take on a physical form because they've tampered with his conjuring. And with that realisation, she sees what she must do.

105

The first mirror is hard to move, the base scraping along the floor. She isn't used to so much physical exercise, and it makes her feel a little queasy. It's as she moves the second that Ose starts to roar, a fierce, guttural bark that sets her teeth on edge and vibrates through her bones. As she pulls the frame she can feel him probing at her mind, dark flashes that obscure her sight for seconds at a time, as if someone is pouring oil down the inner surface of her eyes. There is no doubt now that it was his presence she felt before, that he was the one she touched during the séance. Each time he barks her gut clenches, and she fears she will be sick. She sticks to the job at hand, though. If Millicent knows how to do anything, she knows how to persevere.

The third mirror refuses to budge at first. She wonders if it's caught on a nail, but then she realises the truth. On a distant plain, Ose's hand is stretching out, holding his portal in place. The strength left in her arms isn't enough to move it even an inch, and she wonders briefly if she possesses the strength to do this. But when the darkness spasms in her mind again she pushes back with her thoughts, uses every ounce of her skill to repel the invader from her head, and the mirror gives suddenly in her hands. Her ears feel wet with what she imagines must be blood and yet she labours on. Half-blind, she is able to pull it into place.

When she gets down to the final mirror she can sense his roar starting to trail off, the sound no longer piercing her the way it did. It's one of the hardest mirrors to move, its strange undulations making it unbalanced and unwieldy. Twice it almost topples and twice she catches it before it falls. If it were to break he might still find a way through. The mirrors all stand in the centre of the room now, facing inwards at each other. She imagines that if she were in the middle, between them, she might see Ose duplicated thousands of times, his bestial form regressing back and back until it becomes nothing at all.

She smiles, and with a few gentle pushes eases the mirrors closer together, until the glass panes almost touch, the regression reduced to nothing.

And then there is silence.

She notices immediately that Ose's voice has disappeared, but it's a moment before she realises that silence has fallen outside too. Retracing her way through the arcade, Millicent steps out into the brilliant sunshine of an English summer. Beyond the bodies and the destruction, the trails of blood, there are pennants fluttering in the sea breeze, a subtle taste of salt on the tip of her tongue.

She steps forward to help Rose back to her feet. Her new friend is no longer clutching her head, although Millicent can make out fine trails of blood running from her ears. Still, she smiles.

"Thank you," Rose says, holding on to Millicent for a moment until the shuddering in her arms subsides. "Whatever happened in there, I have the impression that I owe you a great debt. That all of us do."

As they walk hand in hand through the wreckage on the pier, Millicent wonders what the press will make of this. Whatever story they decide to tell – an invasion from Hell, or a mass delirium caused by the summer heat – she imagines it will not mention her at all.

Away from the coast, incidents made even less sense. The city of Coventry was virtually removed from the face of the Earth by a portal which disgorged a vast, pulsating mass – yet its growth was slow enough that a lame child could out-walk the threat. Not a single life was lost.

The mass, which stopped growing when it was two and half miles wide, was ignored by other demonic appearances. It made no threatening moves, only sat and stank of brimstone. Occasional crows picked at it, but found it distasteful. Not even toxic, only distasteful. The Army's Midlands Defence Committee concluded, in consultation with the clergy, that this was either a failed experiment or a complete mistake.

Other communities reported what we assume were scouts, saboteurs and even ambassadors. The village of Burford in Oxfordshire simply surrendered at the sight of a plumed, burning figure which set fire to the local church from a distance. Noting their obeisance, the figure, over eight foot tall, walked on and was never seen again. Lone demons crouched on the edge of many towns and hamlets – and some of these Infernal visitors ventured closer...

THE SINGING STONES

Charlotte Bond

Scree felt the rush of wind, an intense pressure inside his ears, and then, for the first time in his life, he felt cold. Tentatively, he opened his eyes and looked around. The towering cliffs and burning lakes of Hell had gone. Instead, there was lush green grass around them and a black sky with pinprick stars above. Ruined stone walls stood several feet away on either side, shielding them from the world.

"I'm here," he whispered. His breath misted in the air before him and he stared at it wonderingly.

Pain shot through his head as his master cuffed him round the ear. Scree tried to shy away from Abdiel's snarling face, but he was stuck. He looked down and realised that, while they had successfully materialised in the world of the living, they'd arrived buried waist-deep in the ground, which was smoking slightly.

"You imbecile," snapped Abdiel. His scowl twisted his scar tissue, making him appear even uglier than ever. "You've got us stuck."

"Can't you use your infernal power to get us out, Master?" Scree asked. He saw the second blow coming, but trapped in the dirt, he couldn't avoid it.

"You're just a useless lump of rock, aren't you? Any half decent demon would know that my only power is to influence men's minds, not move earth and stone. *You're* the labourer, so fix this."

Obediently, Scree started to dig down into the earth that encased them. Carved from the stones of Hell, his nails gouged easily through the soft earth. A strangled cry made him look up. A man was standing beneath a crumbling archway. The human gaped at the demons before he turned and ran.

"Curse him!" Abdiel slammed a fist into the earth. "We can't be seen like this. Hurry up!" Scree redoubled his efforts,

109

managing to haul himself out before setting about digging out his master. "Why are you stone demons always so slow?" Abdiel snapped.

Eventually Abdiel was able to clamber out of the hole, and he was just brushing himself down when a voice cried, "Hold! Who are you?"

Coming through the crumbling archway was a man, tall, with muttonchops and a thick woollen coat. Behind him, hunched over and wary, was the one they'd seen before.

Abdiel stretched out his hand welcomingly. "We are messengers. From God. Who bring blessings from--" Abdiel stopped as the man pulled his coat aside to reveal his dog-collar. "Shit."

Scree shied away. No matter what Abdiel's mental powers, his master couldn't fool a holy man.

"I am John Barber, vicar of this parish. From God, you say? From the Devil more like. Michael told me that you came out of the ground, and that in itself seems to speak more of demonic than heavenly natures."

Scree glanced at his master. Abdiel had been scarred in his fall from Heaven and manipulated the minds of men to still see his angelic beauty; he hated being seen for his true self.

An unpleasant smile lit up Abdiel's twisted features. "A vicar, is it? Well, no matter. Your mind might be more resilient, but both it and your body will succumb just the same in the end, when we come for you."

"They're coming! They're coming!" screamed the hunched man. He turned and fled down the hillside.

John Barber glanced behind him, unnerved by the outburst, but he didn't give any ground as Abdiel stalked towards him.

"Who exactly are coming for us?" asked the vicar.

"We're just the scouts," said Abdiel. "Testing the waters before our main force arrives, which it will. Soon."

John visibly paled. "I had heard... rumours... but I never..." He closed his mouth, a look of resolution steeling his features. "You will not infect my home with your putrescence."

110

Abdiel glanced over the man's shoulder at the small village below. "Such a small thing. Hardly worth saving."

"I will not let you pass!" John said, fumbling at his neck for the cross that hung there. Abdiel's hand shot out, gripping the vicar's wrist and tugging hard so that the crucifix was yanked from around his neck and fell to the ground, where it was sucked down into the earth.

From beneath his cloak, Abdiel produced a knife with a long, thin blade. He pressed it to John's throat. The demon's grin was maniacal. "So comes to pass the first blood on this land."

"Yes. Yours." John gripped the demon's neck and Abdiel let out a shriek of pain, pushing the vicar away from him so hard that the man fell to the floor. In momentary agony, Abdiel dropped the knife as well. John seized it and scrambled to his feet. Scree lurched forward; protecting the higher demon was as ingrained in him as the flecks of quartz in his flesh.

Scree cannoned into John, forcing him back into the ruined wall and away from Abdiel. Scree gripped John's arms, keeping the knife turned so that the vicar could not stab him either. In the holy man's eyes, Scree saw the acceptance of the inevitability of death. Scree tightened his grip, expecting John to lunge for him. But instead, the vicar twisted the knife in his hands and stepped forward, impaling himself on the blade.

Shocked, Scree let go of John and stepped swiftly away. The man sank to his knees, his teeth gritted against the pain. He looked up at Scree and, with great difficulty muttered, "John... three, sixteen. I shall... for the... many." Then he toppled forward.

As the vicar's lifeless body hit the ground, Scree felt a tremor run through the earth, as if the man's body had sent a shockwave down through the grass into the very stone of the hill. Instinctively Scree looked to his master, but the higher demon was absorbed in his own pain.

Abdiel walked over, his hand pressed to his neck. "You killed him," he said, with grudging respect. "Well done, Scree. Maybe you have the makings of a proper demon after all."

111

I didn't kill him. He killed himself. Didn't you feel that in the ground? The words were coating Scree's tongue, but something kept his lips sealed.

Abdiel took his hand away from his neck, exposing a livid red mark. "Bastard had a crucifix ring. That'll take years to heal properly." The demon tugged his collar up, covering the mark then strode downhill towards the sleepy village below.

Away from the castle ruins in which they'd materialised, Scree marvelled at the stillness around him. He'd never been to the living world before, and everything was new. In Hell, screams echoed across the barren lands, rebounding off the forbidding cliffs. But here it was so quiet that Scree could even detect the delicate crunch of the grass beneath his feet. He realised he was shivering, his stone flesh unused to being away from the fires of Hell. He grinned; being cold was a new and welcome sensation.

"Isn't it disgusting?" Abdiel said as they entered the village, and Scree was swift to wipe the smile from his face. "Cold, wet, dismal. How long must we endure this before we can bask in the warmth of Hell again? Come along. Stop being so slow."

Scree followed Abdiel as the higher demon strode along the road and towards a dwelling with lights shining in every window. Abdiel opened the door, striding in. Scree glanced at a sign that hung to the side of the door, which read 'The Butcher's Arms.'

He had been expecting a house filled with meat, but once inside he found himself in a warm room, with a wooden counter running two thirds of the length of it. The ceiling was low, the air was hazy with smoke, and the floor was old, dead stone, scuffed by many feet. The rest of the space was occupied by tables, chairs, and people – all of whom were looking at the two newcomers. Scree wanted to back out of the door, but Abdiel walked confidently towards the counter with glasses upon it. He stopped when a group of five men stepped in front of him.

"Well, look at these two ugly louts," said one, who was no picture of beauty himself.

Abdiel stiffened. "Ugly?"

"What happened? A whole pack of dogs ate your face?" asked another. Sniggers ran through the group. Scree winced.

There was a hint of uncertainty in Abdiel's voice as he asked, "I do not appear... beautiful to you?"

One man chuckled and said, "I ain't never seen a man wot I'd call beautiful. If I did bend that way, I'd certainly not bend for you." There was uproarious laughter.

"Your powers of concealment don't appear to be working, Master," whispered Scree.

"Yes, I realised," Abdiel hissed back.

"The circus!" piped up a small squeaky voice. Everyone looked towards the doorway through to the backroom. Sitting on the step was a small, grubby girl. Her white smock was grey with dirt, her hair was tangled and her shoes were falling apart.

The landlady scowled. "Get away w'yer, Peg!" she called out, waving a stained dishcloth at the child. One of the men stepped closer and aimed a kick at the girl, but Peg darted away, nearly causing him to overbalance as his foot met nothing but air. The child stopped at the front door, casting her own scowl at the landlady before diving out into the night.

"Little Peg-head might be right," one of the men said, scratching his chin. "Are you from the circus? With elephants and all that?"

Abdiel bowed, a large smiled plastered over his face. "But of course. I am both a fire-eater and part of the freak show." Murmurs of approval ran through the crowd, no one noticing the dagger-edge to the words.

One man gestured at the mud on their clothes. "What's all this mess then? Been in some trouble?"

Abdiel's expression froze. Scree knew that normally the higher demon would have altered the men's minds so that they simply didn't see the mud.

The tension was growing as the silence stretched out. Curiosity was turning to suspicion. In desperation and against his usual timidness, Scree said, "Mucking out the elephants?" The silence stretched out a moment longer. Abdiel threw him a dark look and clenched his fist but then suddenly the men were laughing and the atmosphere was light again.

Abdiel took a few seconds to recover from his surprise and then his grin was back in place as he said, "And since I must be the ugliest man in the village, I should buy everyone drinks to distract you from my visage." The laughter turned to cheers, and the men surrounded them.

Scree shied away as hands slapped him on the shoulders or elbows nudged him. He tried to scramble out of the press of bodies, but a man caught his arm and said, "What are you then? The strongest man? Hey, lads, feel this man's arm. It's as hard as rock."

Hands were suddenly clasped around his forearm, pressing and kneading at his flesh. Scree went very still, gritted his teeth and hoped the ordeal would be over soon. Eventually, the hands released him as one man commented, "I bet you have a devilish right hook with arms like that."

The drinks were served and the men turned back to the bar, allowing Scree to slip outside. That short interlude had taught him that the handling of humans was best left to his master. Instead he wandered through the streets, looking at the houses, dead stone but so prettily arranged. The doors had numbers on them. He thought of the vicar's last words: John, three, sixteen. He peered through the window of a house with a three on its door, but it was too dark inside to make out anything.

"Are you from the circus?" asked a voice behind him and Scree turned.

In the village square, beneath a large tree, sat a small figure. It was the girl from 'The Butcher's Arms', Peg. He glanced back the way he'd come. Abdiel would likely be hours in there testing out sinful natures, trying to twist words and start fights. Scree wandered over to the tree and sat down.

Emboldened by the clean air and blissful silence, he said, "Do you like the circus?"

"I've never seen one," she said wistfully. "I want to see the graphs."

"The what?"

"The graphs. Back when my Da was a lad, a circus came to town. There were snakes and tigers and elephants and graphs."

"Oh." This didn't seem to shed much light on the matter, so he added, "If it helps, I've never seen a graph either."

"It doesn't help," she said shortly. With bitterness she added, "Da probably wouldn't pay the sixpence to let me get in anyway. He only pays Auntie Maggie one shilling a month for me because the court papers say he has to."

Scree was about to ask who her father and Auntie Maggie were, but one of his questions was answered by a shout from the edge of the green. "Peg! Get away from that monstrosity!" Michael, the man who had twice fled the ruined castle, was standing there, glaring at them.

To Scree's surprise, the small child shuffled closer. Her warm body pressed up against him, sending heat shooting through his cold, stone limbs.

"Shan't!" she called back.

Michael drew himself up. "I'm your father. You'll do as I say."

"If you're my father, how come you ain't paid Auntie Maggie these last three months?"

Michael's hands clenched into fists. He started towards them. "Don't you dare--" He stopped. Scree had stood up. Most of the time, the demon stood hunched over, but now, he straightened to his full height. His head brushed the branches of the tree and his stone chest gleamed in the cold moonlight.

In a low voice, filled with gravel, he said, "If the child wants to stay, she can stay." Michael gave a high, squeaky shriek before he turned and fled, all paternal duties forgotten. Scree sat back down.

The girl looked at him through narrowed eyes. "Why are you here?"

"Is there someone called John here?" Scree asked, deflecting the question.

"Plenty," Peg asked brightly. "Which John?"

"I don't know. He might live somewhere with a three or a sixteen on the door." Peg screwed up her face in concentration. "Well, there's John Eades who lives at Four, Peveril Road. Four's close to the three."

"No, I heard him say three very clearly."

"Heard who?"

"Scree!" The word was a low hiss, but it carried through the village, twisting its way down dark snickets and slithering across moonlight grass.

"I have to go," Scree said, scrambling up and away.

"Will you come back? And tell me about the circus?" the girl called after him.

"Scree!" The word reverberated around his head. He hurried off, grateful that he didn't have to make a promise he couldn't keep.

***

Scree ached to be back in the living world again. He thought of the song of the rocks, how calm and peaceful they were. He'd never really listened to the screaming rocks of Hell before, but now he heard it everywhere and it was agonising.

When Abdiel said they were to make another trip, Scree could barely contain his excitement. This time, he was careful to make them appear well above the ground but in the same place.

"Better," said Abdiel curtly, brushing himself down as he walked off. Scree took a moment to draw in a deep breath of air free of sulphur, before he hurried after the higher demon.

"You stone demons are always so slow," grumbled Abdiel as they walked down the hill. "Why can't you be faster?"

"Sorry, master."

Abdiel ordered Scree to wait outside the inn, and Scree was happy to oblige. The world, he liked; the humans, not so much. Across the road was a low wall. He sat on it and watched his master through the wide windows on either side of the inn's door. He noted the hostile looks of the men in there, but there was no tension in the demon's shoulders and the men's scowls slowly morphed into frowns then eventually smiles. Abdiel knew his work well.

"Our vicar's been killed," said Peg in a low voice.

Scree turned, surprised to see she'd sat down next to him soundlessly. Her words made his chilled skin feel colder. "Oh?"

"Was it you?"

Scree remembered the man's face as he impaled himself. "No."

"He was called John. Were you looking for him?"

"No."

Peg slid off the wall and stood in front of Scree, her hands on her hips. "Are you demons?"

"What do you think?"

Peg tilted her head thoughtfully. Then she leaned against the wall and nodded towards 'The Butcher's Arms'.

"They all think I'm soft in the head too, just because my Da is Mad Michael. 'Peg-head' they call me. It's not fair."

"I don't think anything is fair. You should simply accept your place in life and get on with things."

"Why?"

"Because... it's all part of the Plan."

"What Plan?"

"The Divine Plan in your case; the Infernal Plan in mine." Scree caught his breath, realising he'd made a slip. He cursed himself for letting his guard down. He waited for the child to denounce him, to start screaming.

Peg looked at him, and asked, "Have you ever seen either of those plans?"

"No."

"Then how do you know they exist? Or that they're good plans?"

How could he explain to her? The rightness imbued him as surely as a streak of quartz through limestone. It just was.

Peg sniffed. "Aunty Maggie forces me to sit and listen to her reading the Bible, but that's stupid."

117

"I've never read it."

"You're lucky. It can't even get its story straight. First it says 'an eye for an eye' and then it says 'turn the other cheek.' What's the point of a god who keeps changing his mind all the time?"

Scree was saved from commenting by Abdiel's appearance back on the street. Men were watching him through the windows, their faces scrunched up. "Come," Abdiel said curtly, "we need to report back." His gaze flicked briefly to the little girl and just as quickly dismissed her.

Scree went back up the hill again, Abdiel muttering all the way. "They just won't succumb. I don't understand it. I shouldn't have this much trouble. They say that Mad Michael or some fool told them that he saw demons, and they're all on edge because their vicar's dead. But that should dishearten them, not galvanise them against us."

Scree was aware of his master's mutterings, but he wasn't truly listening. What filled his head was the song of the living rock all around him.

***

It was virtually impossible to get hold of a Bible in Hell, but Scree managed to track down a battered copy that had been torn in half. He had to trade three centuries of extra labour for it. He waited until no one was looking, then slipped away to a small gully where he would be safe from the many prying eyes of Hell. He unwrapped the cloth around it and looked at the tattered book. It appeared so fragile. How could the Great Master be afraid of anything contained in something so delicate?

His hands shaking, he tentatively touched the cover then snatched his hand back. He inspected his fingers. They were the same as ever. It was whispered that if you touched the Bible, you'd burst into a bright white flame, hotter and more agonising than any of the fires of Hell. But Scree had touched it, and he remained unburned.

He looked through the book. It was filled with words that he didn't recognise. All labourer demons were crafted with the knowledge of writing embedded in them; it was necessary to follow the complex codes and instructions that kept Hell running. But despite that, Scree still struggled with some words, sounding out their strangeness with his rough tongue.

"Genesis... love... redemption."

He had no problems with the names, like Adam and Eve, Noah, Cain, Abel. Names were everywhere in Hell. He scanned the pages, looking for the word 'eye', but he couldn't find it anywhere. With a sigh, he turned to the first page and stopped. He saw the name John listed, and a coldness that had nothing to do with stone crept through his body. He tried to turn to the page number next to the name, but the remnant he held stopped fifty pages short.

With a curse, he flung the book away. It slammed into the side of the gully and a few pages fluttered loose. He quickly scurried over and stuffed them back in, glancing around fearfully in case anyone should have spotted him. Then he returned the book to its owner and went about his tasks with his normal slow efficiency, while his mind raced with ideas.

***

While Abdiel had a third go at corrupting the clientele of 'The Butcher's Arms', Scree waited anxiously by the wall for Peg to appear. When she did, he asked quickly, "You said your aunt has a Bible. Could you bring it?"

She frowned. "What does a demon want with a Bible?"

"I think your vicar's last words were from it. I don't think he meant John that lives at three or sixteen. I think he meant John, 3:16. Can you get it?"

Peg agreed, her eyes alight with mischief. She led Scree to a row of cottages and jemmied a window open with a piece of flint. She climbed in and, a few minutes later, climbed out.

"Isn't it your house?" Scree asked.

Peg scowled. "No. It's Auntie Maggie's place. She's very particular about that. I just *live* there. Here you go." She handed over a leather-bound book. "Auntie Maggie is very proud of this. It's brand new. Only published a few years ago."

Scree flicked through it and found the correct passage. "Hereby we have known love, because He has laid down His life for us; and we ought for our brothers to lay down our lives," he read out loud.

Peg wrinkled her nose. "What does it mean?"

Scree trawled his memory for knowledge that had been chiselled into him. "I think it's talking about self-sacrifice." An involuntary shudder ran through him. He felt acid rise in his throat and swallowed it down. "Sacrifice is old, older than me even. It has power. If we'd killed your vicar, nothing would have happened. But he killed himself, with those words on his lips. For his brothers, he laid down his life, and that sacrifice has protected this village. That's why Abdiel is having no luck with turning any of you."

"So we're safe?"

"Not forever."

"For how long?"

"I don"t know. I'm just a stone demon. I could ask my Master but..." He tailed off; Peg's expression showed she understood. He sighed. "I hope it's a long time. I like the stones here."

"Aren't there stones in Hell?"

"Yes but they're different. They're hot, black, spiky, cruel."

"How can stone be cruel?"

Scree shrugged. "How can humans be cruel? It's just part of their nature. But I like the stone here. It sings so sweetly."

"It does? Well, you'll like this then. Come on!" She grabbed his hand and tugged at him. Scree could be as immoveable as rock, but he chose to let her lead him.

"Where are we going?" he asked. Peg didn't answer but led them out of the village and up a winding path towards a massive limestone gorge. At the top of the cliffs, Scree could glimpse the ruins of the castle. Ahead of them was a cave entrance, taller and wider than a house, with a river flowing out of it. The path they were following led to a substantial stone ledge high above the river. Around him were lengths of rope, some fully formed and in coils on the floor, some stretched between wooden stakes which were either fixed in the floor or attached to a wooden board on wheels.

"This is the rope walk," Peg explained. "It's here we make all the rope for the mine. The rope-makers live over there." She gestured at some ramshackle dwellings, all of them appearing lifeless.

She lit a lamp and he followed her to the back of the cave where the ceiling sloped swiftly downwards until they were walking, stooped, along a passage. The drip of water around them was like a heartbeat. Scree wondered if this was what it was like to be a human in a womb, surrounded by flesh that matched your own and the steady rhythm of a heartbeat.

The passage eventually widened again and Scree stood straight, stretching his back. Peg giggled and pointed to a hole in the floor. "See that? We call it the Devil's Arse. Water comes gushing up it in winter, and makes this dreadful sound, like the devil himself is farting." She cocked her head, looking at him. "Maybe you could tell us if it really does sound like the Devil farting."

"I've never seen the Great Master, never mind hearing him fart. He doesn't bother with the likes of me."

"The queen came here, you know," Peg said as they set off again.

"Did she like the Devil's Arse?"

In an approximation of a genteel voice, Peg answered, "We renamed it so as not to offend her gracious majesty."

A sharp, unfamiliar sound escaped from Scree's lips. He slapped his hand over his mouth as echoes bounced around the stone walls. When they'd died away, he asked timidly, "What was that?"

Peg cocked her head. "I think that was a laugh. Come on. We haven't got to the best bit yet."

After several more twists and turns, Scree found himself in a massive chamber. The walls were stepped as if wide ledges of rock had been carved into them, but the stone was smooth and glossy with the passage of water over the centuries. The song of the rock in this deep place filled his mind, and a joy he never thought he possessed welled up from the depths of his being.

Peg used the lamp's flame to light a candle and then began scampering about the chamber, lighting other candles to help him see, although their weak light still kept the vaulted ceiling wreathed in shadows.

"What is this place?" His voice was a whisper, but it was magnified by the great space, as if a hundred Screes were talking at once. But even that couldn't drown out the sweet song in his head.

"We call it the Gallery."

"It's beautiful," Scree said. He felt wetness on his cheeks and stepped back, thinking water must have dripped onto his face, even though he hadn't felt it. He walked round slowly, running his hand across the rock. It felt cold but in a good way. He sensed that all the rock he'd ever touched had been heated beyond endurance, and that this was the temperature that rock should be, if it was to be at peace.

"What's down there?" he asked, pointing to where the walkway continued out of the cavern.

Peg shuddered. "Ghosts," she whispered, "and the river. Some say that if you follow the river that way, it'll lead you straight to Hell."

Scree shook his head. "There are no rivers like this in Hell. This one is too wet, too cold." He looked around one more time, memorising it all before he had to leave. "Thank you for this," he said to Peg, "but now I have to report back," and this time he felt tears – too wet, too cold – as they leaked out of his eyes and ran down his stone cheeks.

***

All the way back up the hill, Scree's mind was filled with the song of the stones. The further he walked from the caves, the quieter that song became. When he was back in Hell, he knew it would exist only inside his mind, and sorrow filled him at that thought. As he walked, he became aware of footsteps behind him, two sets he thought, but he was too wrapped up in his own misery to care if he was being followed.

Abdiel was waiting for him at the castle ruins, his arms crossed and his eyes blazing. "There you are, Scree. Where have you been? Slow, as always." Abdiel's eyes narrowed. "One of the men at the bar said he'd seen you and that girl Peg together. Did you learn anything?"

Impelled by his very flesh to obey, Scree told Abdiel everything he'd discovered. The higher demon's eyes went from blazing fires to furious infernos. "You let that man sacrifice himself? You idiot!" Abdiel's blow sent Scree sprawling, scraping a groove in the grass. For a moment, the castle ruins spun around him with dizziness.

"Hey!" cried an indignant voice . A small figure dashed forward and wrapped her arms around Scree's neck.

"Get out of here," he whispered urgently to Peg, but she just clung on tighter.

Abdiel was pacing, anger and relief warring on his face. "But that explains everything. No wonder we can't test this town properly. Bloody self-sacrifice." He paused and his eyes fell upon the two of them. "Still, I know how to fix this." He moved with the speed of a striking snake and seized Peg by the wrist, hauling her away from Scree and up into the air. "We'll just answer a sacrifice with one of our own.'

"Father! Help me!"

For a moment, Scree thought Peg was beseeching him. But then he followed her gaze, just in time to see the tip of a battered coat disappearing through the tumbledown archway. Now Scree knew who else had been following him. Knowing that Michael

123

was more intent on saving his own skin than his daughter's life fanned an angry fire inside him that had sparked the moment he'd stepped out of the caves.

Peg kicked and squirmed in Abdiel's grip, cursing and crying, but the demon held her fast. Scree scrambled to his feet, his mind whirling with confusion. Every essence of his flesh insisted he aid his master, but that fire within him urged him to save the girl. Inside his mind, the song of the stones rose up, full of mourning for blood on grass.

Abdiel drew his knife and leered at Peg. "You are serving a higher purpose, little vermin. It is an honour to--" The words were cut off by blood spilling from his mouth. He let go of Peg who fell to the floor and scrambled away. He stared at his empty hand, where the knife had been, then at the knife itself, buried in his chest.

Scree released the hilt and drew his hand back sharply. Abdiel looked at him, shocked.

"Was I fast enough for you this time, master?" Scree asked in a low voice.

Abdiel fell to the floor, black blood oozing out of his chest. Scree knelt down beside him and scrawled a message in the grass, using the demon's blood as ink.

This town is protected. It killed a higher level demon. Leave until last.

He watched as the blood sank into the grass, leaving scorch marks. He knew that very soon those words would be appearing on a message slate in Hell. It would be noted and filed. Abdiel would be honoured and mourned. No one would come looking for Scree. Stone demons were plentiful, and a missing one was an irrelevancy.

Abdiel gave a gurgle. He couldn't speak, but his eyes screamed: why? With his disobedient act, Scree had broken Hell's rules. The Infernal Realm's hold on him was weaker now, so he did not feel bound to answer Abdiel as he had before. But he'd taken the demon's life, and Scree felt he owed his former master an answer.

"The stone here sings," Scree said softly. "I want it to sing for as long as possible. And maybe..." He stopped. The demon's eyes had clouded over; Abdiel was no longer listening, to Scree or to anything.

Peg appeared at Scree's side. "What will we do now?"

He stood up and offered her his hand. She hesitated, then took it. "We'll go to the caves," he said, "and if you listen very carefully, I'll help you to hear the stones singing."

PART TWO

THE STRUGGLE

THE NOWL OF TUBAL-QAYIN

Phil Breach

A Ballad of the Incursion

The Incursion, scant years from the century's end,
brought such woe to Her Majesty's nation,
when the sphincters that pinched off this soil from Hell's
were splayed wide by explosive dilation.

Legion 'pon legion, the demons loped in,
each demented, cacophonous horde.
Waves of distortion lapped out from the breaches,
besmirching fair Albion's sward.

After, 'pon mounts like to great, spindly babes,
rode the ranks of the Infernal Gentry.
Behind them, each sphincter grinned wide to a maw,
dirty fangs thrusting upward in sentry.

From Land's End to Lerwick the portals peeled back,
as Victoria's realm was invaded.
Great tracts were lost to Perdition's encroach,
the very earth warped and degraded.

The constable cornered and pulled into bits,
the farmer cast wide 'pon his field.
Ruinous losses, butchers butchered on crosses,
as the bowels of all Hell came unsealed.

The sight of the lowliest fiend beggared reason,
wrought harm 'pon the unprepared mind.

127

Suicide bloomed, parents smothered their children,
with their own nails, clawed themselves blind.

Yet stories relate of some few who fought back
in those grim, early days of Incursion.
Of those who stood firm in the maddening storm
of Reality's frightful obversion.

Of Belial's imps slain and the Castle kept safe
by the brave folk of Windsor and Datchet.
Of the travelling tinker who crept 'pon an ambush,
and felled seven scamps with his hatchet.

When a rupture appeared in the gun wharf at Portsmouth,
a small Marine rifle platoon
stopped up the gap 'til the stevedores fled
with the great drift of corpses bestrewn.

And the witch, tales tell, who saved a whole village;
her name was Anjelica Brown.
She lived in a cottage on Dartmoor's south skirts,
by North Wood, where the Plym plummets down.

She came from a kindred of crooked old Craft,
learned the trade under Grey Heron May.
Her praxis was hoary, of scourge and of stang,
blood-raddled, partaking of Fae.

The South Devon valleys, as yet unbefouled
by the sulphuric taint of Inferno,
were nonetheless trembling in fear at reports
of fiends on the march down in Kernow.

Then a harbinger ranged from the Moor's hollow hills
with a burden of dole to betide.
Yet, it also held gently hope's gossamer thread;

soft as quail down, stole to her side.

Through the gloaming it came, as she scored out her
compass
in the churchyard of blesséd Saint Mary.
She leant on her sloe stang, fork-ended and stout,
and inclined her cowled head to the faery.

Its voice was belike to an antique viol,
fretted through with uncanny harmonics.
Each syllable soft-limned with sibilant silver,
weird glamours enlaced in its phonics.

"Hark well, Mistress Brown, and gather your tools
just as swiftly as ever you can;
ill dispatch has the Court of the Seelie received
from the Augur of Tir na mBan."

"Though the world shall be riven on Dewerstone Rock,
jutting forth to the north of Shaugh Prior,
one hope I yet bring from the Ever-Bright Halls,
one hope to bring halt to Hellfire."

"You must seek for the Nowl forged by old Tubal-Qayin;
First Smith, the Snake-blooded, the Hairy.
A black hound attends me, and waits at the lych-gate,
to guide you askance into Faerie."

"Hie to Brig-under-Moor, by the low path,
through the horn gate at Trowsworthy Gorge.
Look to the warden of Tubal-Qayin's Nowl
in the glimmer of Great Brigid's forge."

"I depart now to fend at the bulwarks of Fae;
Cù Sith, my good hound, he will lead you.
For Albion, Mistress Brown! Seek for the Nowl!

The people of Shaugh Prior need you."

Anjelica snatched up her stang and they ran,
to save Devon from Hell's desecration.
As they reached the horn gate, out from Dewerstone Rock
boomed the blast of a vast detonation.

The earth spasmed and twitched as they fled into Faerie,
cliffs groaning and trees all athrash.
She wept, as the forge neared, in grief for her land,
as its sinews began to unlash.

The Brig was colossal, an upthrusting dolmen
with a huge cap of whorl-studded limestone.
She stepped closer and spied, through the infra-red gloom,
a great back bent hard to the grindstone.

The figure rose up and he turned to the witch.
He was tall as a juniper tree,
and his head was belike to a heavy-tusked boar.
He approached her and dropped to one knee.

On his brow, in a kiss-curl of long, matted bristles,
the Nowl hung. She stretched up to take it.
"I am Torc, son of Brigid. Now fly, witch," he said.
"Make haste to Hell's gate and unmake it."

The Nowl; a great witch-nail, storied and keen,
ten inches of age-blackened iron,
smelted by Qayin from a tumbledown star
that slipped off from the Belt of Orion.

Ahead of its legions, Duke Forcalor strode
through the newly-stretched hole into Devon.
It was most keen to witness, ere ruin commenced,
that place many souls named as Heaven.

It looked on as the foulness that drooled through the sphincter
depraved and unknitted existence,
and smiled at Beauty's collapse all around
'neath Perdition's polluted insistence.

As it harked to the woe of the fluttering birds
in the swell of corruption encroaching,
its blood-weeping eyes were drawn down below
to the sight of two figures approaching.

It watched them fight on up the failing path,
as the feculence dragged at their pace,
and was somewhat bemused by the look of derision
the human displayed 'pon her face.

"Surely not...", panting, Anjelica sneered,
as she and Cù Sith reached the Rock.
"Surely Inferno fields finer than you?
A ninny bare fit to bemock?"

"Some high-ranking fiend, you? Some duke? Or a count?
How pathetic. D'you perch 'pon a throne?
I'd bethought me to scare up a bobby or two,
but forsooth, we shall do this alone."

I am British, you dolt, my resolve is unmatched,
and Brigid's Flame leaps in my heart.
Foolish you are to contend with a witch,
in her place; on the Moor of the Dart."

"This is the Dartmoor, you risible churl!
Coming here, you have courted disaster.
Your parvenu Devil impresses me not;
mine's a far older, far sterner master."

131

"My Lord was the Devil before you were spawned
in whatever rank crater confined you.
Now get you hence, demon, rue long your mistakes,
when back down to the Pit I've consigned you."

"Good Cù, to a worthy foe, I'd not concede
a bare inch of Her numinous ground,
so I'll not give up Devon to rubbish like this.
Prepost'rous! Now have at it, hound!"

Brave Cù hurled himself at Duke Forcalor's throat,
as the witch felt Hell rise to surround her.
With a scream of defiance she took up her stang,
and swept a swift compass around her.

Forcalor broke the hound's back and came on,
but her circle it floundered to enter.
She fell to her knees in the blistering filth
and plunged the Nowl down in its centre.

Across half the county the Closing was heard,
from the Eddystone Light to Ashburton.
Shaugh Prior's saviour, the witch of North Wood,
was gone and her fate was uncertain.

But the folk of the village, from that day to this,
though they hold she was nevermore seen,
still swear that they heard her victorious cry;
"GODDESS SAVE THE QUEEN!"

There came a time when few, if any, could deny that events were out of control, that the Government was dealing with a new and palpable threat. Not the French or the Russians; not anarchists or Fenians, nor any enemy so easily defined. And not Hell, of course, not immediately. Believing that 'murderous creatures' and 'baleful influences' were abroad did not imply anything so grand as the possibility that the Infernal Empire sought to turn the Mother of Colonies into a colony. Unthinkable - though there were social philosophers and theologians who dared to say that this might be a judgement on the British Empire and its treatment of its far-flung possessions.

The massive submarine telegraph cables were cut – no one knew how - and Europe fell silent. Some suspected the Governments of the continent to have been warned that their lands would be treated to the same Incursion as Britain if they interfered. Other believed, rightly or wrongly, that Europe waited, not entirely displeased that the Empire was under assault at its core. And it is possible that countries such as France and Germany thought Britain would inevitably triumph, but be weakened - a tempting proposition.

England bore the brunt of the onslaught. If things were worse in Scotland, it was hard to tell – communication with many Scottish centres of population was lost towards the end of the first month. We knew that fighting was stiff in Northern England – Durham and its cathedral a beacon of hope, York almost in ruins, Hull a besieged port reached and supplied when possible by sea. Armed trawlers and naval patrol boats, each with their parson or priest, kept a semblance of resistance going along the northeast coast. Hardened chapel men and women held the line inland, bolstered by what remained of the military and the police force.

133

London, and many large towns in the Midlands and South East, became battlefields. Confused arenas of war fought in burning streets, where civilians shot at anything which they could not understand, and hasty garrisons were formed from a motley of regular troops.

Religious belief itself became a battlefield. Faith and Will seemed paramount. Three devout Mohammedan students from Balliol College survived the destruction of Oxford, as the lost souls which were sent against them seemed unwilling to engage. Perhaps their piety held back Hell. A priest in Leicester stood against a spiked horde, and found that the faith he professed to his flock was a sham. He died, several times.

Christian theologians and rabbinical authorities dug deep, and found partial answers - Faith, Will, and the symbolism of earlier times. The Enochian language of Dr John Dee, whether fabricated or not, held power, as did certain aspects of the Kabbalah. The curious fact that Dee had been advisor to the greatest queen of these isles until Victoria, and that he was reputed to have coined the term 'British Empire, was lost on most. Bullets were blessed and scratched with such symbols as were known; the people turned to holy water, cold iron and silver, whatever might work.

Not that there were not older beliefs still retained in small communities across the land, half-remembered by the few. All knew that in the cities, spiritualists - those few who had a genuine gift - were being used to confuse the enemy and to provide intelligence. In rural areas, hedge-wizards and Cunning Folk had brought succour once. Did other powers still exist? What of those which predated Christianity altogether? If Church and Synagogue could awake, so might the lore of ancient days...

FORGE

Shell Bromley

Tramping home in the near dark set my thoughts to jangling.

It could just have been that I was coming home far later than my habit. Old Kit had thrown a shoe and we'd had to sort it, else she might have been run away with by the fairies. Or so Mitt said, and Mitt should know, what with him being from a strange, far-off land himself.

After that, it was already evening by the time I set off to Mam's. To the place I was meant to call home. It could be having my routine go awry that had me feeling out of sorts and worried.

Or it might be the weird, washed-out greys of the place, or the storm that had been coming on all day and still hadn't got its legs under it. The air pressed in on all sides, hunching up the thoughts in my head.

The lane lay in shadow-stripes. Walking the lanes with Brack beside me was normally a time I felt right with myself, a time I could be without having to keep watchful, but not now.

I was partway to cursing myself for daft imaginings when the lane flashed red.

Wincing at the shock of light, I tried to think what could have caused it. Brack's nose pressed against my right hand, cold on the scar across my palm. Close together like we were one and the same, Brack and me went creeping up to the corner where the lane twisted itself along the commons. From here there was no sight of the village. No sight of Pepper's farm, neither, though that and Mitt's forge were still closer than Mam's.

It was dark as we crept, but as I peered round the bulk of a blackberry bush the red flashed again, fire in the air, turning the whole lane to the colour of iron in the forge. It hit the edges of the bushes, of the drystone wall, of the dead tree that stood guard over it all. They looked strange and wrong in the forge-light, not like something that had grown right there and belonged. The red twisted and warped the lane. That wasn't all it showed.

It inked in figures, facing each other across the lane. My sense of things being real wavered as I took in a tall woman stood with her hood thrown back, hair tumbling round her head, and with her back to the storm-dead tree. That was my tree, that was, killed on the night I was born, and all the evidence most needed I'd been landed on my mam by the Fae. Whatever I was, this woman was not human.

Across the lane stood a creature that made me want to run right to Mam, to anyplace, long as it wasn't here. Least, that's what every sinew and joint in my body screamed, the hunched thoughts in my head spinning out into a mass of panic and would-be movement and fright.

My feet didn't agree. They stayed rooted, taking after my tree. Brack cowered against my leg.

That red light faded slowly, not like normal light at all. This didn't blaze and vanish. This clung. It gave me time to take in more of that beast.

I'd seen fungus growing on the corpses of trees and seen rot eat away at all manner of things. A lot of it, lately. This…this beast looked to be made from both, all bundled up and given limbs the shapes I'd seen on little crawling things, with pincers large as the scythe blades Mitt made. It crowded out the lane.

That lady stood firm. A dark smear of something spread along her cloak. She had the look about her of someone injured and trying to hide it.

All of that, I took in as the light flared and faded. Even strange and stubborn as it was, the growing night pushed it away. While it lasted, it was like stained glass in a Church, an image out of story frozen still, save for the colours were all shades of red and grey.

No. That wasn't quite right. There were other colours, mucking up the red, turning it sickly.

Dark finally washed back over the lane, and in it I could only see shapes. But now I knew what they were. When the creature moved, writhing huge against the stars, I clamped my hand over my mouth and prayed to anything that'd listen.

A third flare of red revealed the woman closer to the beast, and it looming over her. When the beast snapped a limb forward, clacking claws cutting at the air, the lady lifted a hand, like that'd do anything. She stumbled. She stumbled and fell, landing on her rear. The hanging-storm rumbled thunder as she hit the ground, but a tumble like that must have made her cry out.

Still, the storm didn't come on proper.

By my side, Brack growled, a smaller storm wrapped in fur.

Panic bit at my throat, and it was a feeling I wanted to choke up and spit out. Hiding was safer. Hiding was smart. The brand on my palm throbbed.

The lady pulled herself away from the thing, still on her back and not getting far, and the beast nigh on touching her.

Hiding was safe. Hiding was smart. Hiding should save Brack and me.

I don't think I chose to, but when the creature moved again, so did I. My feet pulled themselves up from the ground and I turned into the loud, quick thoughts in my head, and I was crouched over the lady. I was in between the lady and the thing.

The creature stank. It was almost worse than the sight of it. Almost. This close, I could see it even in the dark, a dim glow the colour of mould on bread coating it.

It writhed, shifting sideways and back, pulling itself into a hissing, humming wall that I could hear right through my feet.

"Move, child," the lady said from behind me. Ordered, I should say, and like she was used to being heeded. "Run!"

But I couldn't move and let it attack her, what with her hurt and fallen. Even without knowing her, I was sure her voice shouldn't be tight and pained like it was. And I couldn't have made myself move if I'd tried as the beast lashed out again. At me, this time.

Before I could do anything, my hound lunged at the beast, setting his teeth against the thing's pincers. He was fury like I'd never seen from him, snarling and snapping. He got a hold of the

137

creature and the thing spasmed. I didn't know if he bit it hard enough to injure it, but I saw the way his body jerked when the beast's claw caught him. And I saw the way his body thudded when he hit the ground.

Brack was still, but the beast wasn't.

It moved so fast, I barely got my hands up, and I didn't know what happened or how I survived, but there was a roar that started somewhere in my boots and a flash of light so dark it made me think the world was over, and then I was standing in the lane, Brack still on the ground, and no sign of that creature. None at all.

Gasping, I ran to my dog and crouched down, taking hold of Brack's head so I could look in his eyes. His tail wagged, one thump on the ground. Two. With my hands on him, he struggled to his feet and pushed against me. My seeking fingers found wet under the fur of his neck, and his blood on my skin was moonlight black.

Movement to the side made me startle. I had to check it was that lady. She was back on her feet, her cloak tidy and her face calm.

"He is brave, your hound," she said. "I owe him my thanks. He's given me time to muster my strength. As have you."

"He was protecting me," I said, turning back to him. "He got hurt protecting me."

"Take him home, little one," the lady said, and now she sounded farther away, even though I'd heard no footsteps. "Take yourself home and seek shelter. There is something wrong in the world for a demon to be here, where I had no warning of attack."

I twisted, still crouched, to ask the woman what in the name of all things she was going on about. Only, she wasn't there. The dead tree stood all by its lonesome, with no sign of any tall woman, hood or not.

***

I heard the voices afore I reached the yard, rising and falling in a manner that told of hot tempers and tears. The squirming storm in my belly wanted me to stay hiding, safe and snug under the dangling branches of the holly by the kitchen window. My arm hurt and my head throbbed, the pulsing pain in my hand faint echoing, but pain wasn't new and I could wait.

Brack, though, Brack was hurt bad.

Go home, the lady had said. Home. I'd lifted Brack into my arms and frowned at the path to Mam's. Pepper's farm was closer.

I left the leaves and felt the cold curve of flagstones under my feet. My toes wanted to curl about them, but they couldn't in these boots Mitt insisted I wear at the forge. Mam always said I'd to wear boots out in the world, but like Pepper she never minded if I went barefoot where folks couldn't see me.

Some man was in with Pepper, so I'd to keep the boots on. Those were the rules.

I wasn't sure how it stacked up when the man was shout-speaking, with a hard, ringing voice talking at Pepper like she was a misbehaving mule. Didn't need to hear the words clear to get the mood in there. I'd had enough practice working out when people were mad, and I would have been the kind of lady as could float in and settle tempers all graceful like, if I could. That wasn't me, though, so I clomped in with my boots saying how I felt and Brack heavy in my arms.

Pepper stood with her back to the range, drawn up and near-jangling. She had copper in her hair, did Pepper, and iron in her bones. Never could understand how so many people missed it.

She paled when she saw me.

"Hol-," Pepper said and caught herself. Holly was a name just for the two of us. "Vera. What happened?"

"Were you attacked, girl?" her visitor asked. Edward. One of those cousins of hers. It was the most concern he'd ever shown me. Pepper had explained he had odd ideas about folk without money. He made no move to come near. "I told you, Violet, it's growing dangerous. Now your farmgirl's hurt."

139

Pepper's lips pressed together and her eyes were slate as she crossed to me. The slate wasn't aimed at me, though. Pepper always looked at me soft.

"Are you hurt?" she asked, taking hold of my head and peering at me. When I shook my head, she stepped back and looked down at my hound. "Is Brack hurt?"

I nodded. My words had run away and hid and that man frowning at me wasn't making them run back.

His words wanted to fill the whole room.

"You should listen to reason, Violet. Bad enough to be a woman living alone at the best of times, but these are far from the best of times. People have disappeared, livestock has been found torn to pieces."

"People are always disappearing," Pepper said, over her shoulder. "Drag the canals."

"Don't be difficult. The canal hasn't ripped cattle apart."

He'd no call to bite the words at her. None at all.

"And this is doing nothing to help. If you want to be of use to me, cousin, fetch Mitt."

Her hands left my face and made their way to Brack, but Edward didn't move at all.

"There are dangers. Too many..." He stopped and closed his eyes for a moment. "Too many flooding into the cities, it was bound to spill over-"

"Get Mitt or get out of my home." Pepper didn't raise her voice. She didn't need to. "If you're scared to walk the lanes for fear of attack, you will have to wait until I can send Mitt with you. No? Afraid he'll turn on you? Then how about Vera? I assume you aren't afraid of her."

I wasn't going anywhere with Brack hurt, but Edward Mayhew wouldn't have let me help him out of Hell itself. Pepper had helped me see that long ago.

He stalked out like Pepper had thrown muck at him, still grumbling she'd come to harm out on her own. Pepper closed her eyes when he'd gone, just for a moment, and shuddered out a breath. When she opened her eyes again, they were heather.

"What happened, Holly?" she asked, quiet now. "I was starting to worry."

I shook my head. My words weren't ready to come back yet.

Her arm around my shoulders got me moving, and together we settled Brack by the hearth. Brack didn't move except for breathing, and that was rasping and wrong.

I'd been chilled in that lane, but this was a different sort of fear, one that dug deeper. Brack had been with me long enough that he was one of my roots, and I couldn't lose him.

"I'll bring Mitt," Pepper said, and was gone.

I stroked my hand along Brack's side in the quiet of the kitchen, the fire in the grate doing nothing to warm me, and my words came creeping back, weak and whispering.

"Brack. Brack, lad. Come on."

I didn't know if it was the touch or my voice, but he opened his eyes and struggled to lift his head, turning enough to look at me.

His eyes were clouded.

"Oh, lad," I said, and held his muzzle in my palms.

I'd seen animals with bad eyes, people too, but I'd not seen what looked like bruise yellow and bile spreading through an eye. It looked like ribbons of fur...or of fungus. Fungus right inside the eye itself.

It took me longer to find a gash, deep under the thick fur of his neck and still weeping blood, and if it had been a normal thing he'd fought, another dog or a badger or some such, I'd have called it not much to worry over. With this one, though, that same creeping fungus pushed at the edges of the wound.

My lungs felt thick in my chest and I had a flash of feeling that fungus was in me, filling up my insides.

Footsteps behind me told me Pepper was there before she crouched next to me, the hem of her skirt brushing my foot.

"What are you-" she started, and I heard the gargling shock in her throat as she caught sight of the growth. "What is that? You have to tell me, please, what on Earth did this?"

141

Square hands joined mine on Brack's coat, and I glanced up to see Mitt kneeling on the other side of my poor hound, his dark eyes puzzled and seeking. I hadn't heard him.

"Something happened on the way home," I said. I'd to stop and swallow and try again. My voice only shook a little. "It'll sound like a tale, but it's not."

"I've never known you to lie, Verushka," Mitt said. He sounded steady. Mitt always sounded steady, even when those men turned up with accusations I still didn't understand.

That day, he had been a kind of calm I hadn't recognised, and I saw it again in him now. Calm wasn't the same as relaxed, Mitt had told me after. Some kinds of calm were about survival.

Pepper took my hands and drew me away, leaving Mitt space to look at Brack proper, and she set to washing my hands clean as I told them what had happened.

"A demon?" Pepper asked, when I'd done and when she was satisfied nothing stayed on my skin to harm me, but it wasn't really a question. More a plea to be told she'd heard wrong. "That... You're saying Hell itself is out hunting?"

I nodded.

Pepper's hands went tight, pressing my fingers. "What do we do about demons?" Her voice only shook a little.

"We fight, we run, we hide," Mitt said. "Choose one."

"Else we'll die," I said, recalling Mitt's lessons on taking the right action to make sure the forging came out right. Know what the danger is, he said, and know how to avoid it.

Mitt's hands came to a halt, and the look on his face was the one he got when a job was hopeless.

"You might pick any, and still die, little one."

"Then we fight," Pepper said. "We won't be driven out of our home. Mitt, can you think of anything that might help Brack? Or anything we can use to fight with?"

I didn't like seeing Mitt go out into that dark, but I couldn't stand to let Brack stay hurting, and Mitt reckoned he needed what was back in his cottage. He didn't promise me it'd help Brack. I tried not to think on that until I had to.

142

Which left Pepper and me, sitting on the floor with Brack shuddering breaths over my legs and not a notion of how to fight off demons. Pepper and me knew each other, and I could read her face and posture and mostly work out the right conclusion. Right now, she was scared and she wasn't going to give in. She was the strongest person I knew.

Mitt had been gone a good while when Brack's ears pricked up and a whine sat low in his throat.

We all three looked to the door.

I'd all too good an idea what might be out there. Maybe if we stayed inside, all quiet and hidden, like, then the danger would take itself away. Mitt would run. He was fast. Not as fast as me, but not the slowest in the valley. I'd seen that when he'd chased after those men, shouting at them not to think of coming back.

I wasn't ready for the screaming. Took a moment, and a second set of screaming, to work out it sounded different from the roar-screech of the one I'd faced.

Brack's whine turned to a rumble, and that waiting storm rolled hammers over the sky, like it was joining him. He shifted, dragging himself upright and standing with his head low and his ears set the way they'd been that day with the bar. I caught hold of him afore he could take a step and felt the growl through his body.

"Tell me there ain't some bugger out there," I muttered.

Another scream, and Pepper got to her feet. The wild look in her eyes was new.

"Do you hear that?" she asked, sounding more desperate than frightened. "Is there someone in trouble outside?"

"If that thing's out there with them, they'll not be in it long," I said.

But those words felt sour in my mouth. From the look on her face, Pepper felt the same thing. Might be Mitt. Shouldn't be any person at all.

"Brack chased off the last one," Pepper said.

"Brack got hurt by the last one," I said. "Besides, why is anyone out there now? It's got to be near midnight."

143

The next scream came from the yard.

Brack pulled out of my grip and there was no sign of sickness in him as he ran at the door. Pepper took off after him before I could get to my feet. She had the door open and the both of them were through it by the time I got halfway across the kitchen. Cursing, I followed.

Outside, everything had swallowed itself up in darkness. The stars had no hope of giving me any light. Only a few shone, and those faintly. I paused, my whole body wanting to slide back and press against the wall, like that made even a lick of sense. I'd be no safer there, not from a creature like the one from the lane.

It took Pepper's voice to get me moving, though.

"Holly! Holly, come help us!"

I'd to get right close before I saw the man on the ground, and Pepper trying to pull him up one handed. He looked small and sort of wispish, and it took more than a second in the dark to recognise him.

Edward.

His face did something weird as I looked at him, and I'd no idea what it meant. It wasn't an expression I'd learnt. Didn't have time to fret about it, neither, because another screech ripped the air, and this time the screaming wasn't a frightened man.

"Keep it away!" Edward shouted, or might have shouted, but it came out scratchy and odd. "Get me away!"

And he grabbed at my Pepper, nearly pulling her down even as she tried to pull him up.

A few things happened at once, then.

I lunged forward to keep Pepper on her feet, and Edward's hand clamped down on my upper arm in a flail. Lightning made the whole yard bright. Seemed like the same moment the gate burst off its hinges, clattering to the cobbles as Brack barked and shot that way.

Yelling for him to come back, I jerked upright, and pulled Edward and Pepper with me. Somehow, we were all on our feet, and I wanted to be back in the house, but I wanted to get Brack back, too.

"He'll follow!" Pepper said, and shoved us all into a stumbling run with Edward half hanging between us.

We got most of the way to the table before someone lost hold. Edward landed in a heap on the floor, and the banked coals from the fire gave his skin a hellish tint that was most unwelcome.

Much as I wanted to know what he was playing at, I wanted Brack safe more, and I left him in his heap and ran back to the dark outside. Thunder met me, thunder and another fork of lightning. There was no weird light, no alien roaring. No Brack.

My whole chest clenched and flooded cold through me, and I felt the ground go unstable beneath me.

"Holly?"

Pepper's voice was a rope to catch hold of. It yanked me back enough to know I couldn't stand out in the dark when I'd no idea where the monster was. Still, it took Pepper's hand on my arm to pull me back into the kitchen, and it was her who had to shut the door.

Edward was still a heap.

"What was it?" he asked, snapping near as much as speaking. He glared up at Pepper like she was to blame. That expression, I'd seen on him many times before. "Something attacked me. Something out by your farm attacked me. What have you got up here? Something not human, that I do know."

"It was a monster," I said, and even I knew my voice was quieter than normal. "From Hell. And now it's dragged Brack there."

"You're worrying about a dog?" Edward asked, at the same time as Pepper took my hand.

"Brack is likely chasing that creature through the fields. He'll be back for his breakfast, you'll see."

But Brack never ran off and left me like that. He didn't. He wouldn't. He hadn't. And I was sure Pepper knew it, too. She knew I didn't like lies, even ones meant to wrap a sharp truth up to stop it cutting. I pulled away from her and sank to the floor before the hearth.

145

"Hell," Edward said, his lip curling. He'd made it as far as sitting up. "You said a monster from Hell." He didn't call me a liar or say I got things wrong all the time, like he usually did. "Did you summon it? You're part demon yourself, aren't you? Have you brought Hell's creatures down on us?"

"Thought you lot had me pegged as a changeling," I said. I felt numb, and it happen showed in my voice. In any case, his words didn't slice me like they might have done.

"Don't be so foolish," Pepper said. "There's been no summoning of demons here. And no-one under this roof has any sort of connection to Hell."

I had my doubts. Edward was under the roof right then. But I didn't say it.

Edward's mouth twisted. "We've humoured you, Vi, but it isn't natural, to be the way she is."

"There is nothing unnatural about Vera," Pepper said, and it always sounded odd, to hear her say my paper name, the one written down in Church records and used by people as didn't know me. "If anything has brought Hell down upon us, it's your lack of Christian kindness. Pray to God that you aren't treated the way people treat her. Or do you want me to throw you back into the dark?"

Edward's lips made twitching shapes, but he looked away and didn't say any more on the matter.

"Whatever's caused it, there's something out there attacking people," Pepper said into the silence. "We need to focus on dealing with that."

Lightning flashed with thunder right on its heels, and then again. And again. Each time, that thing screech-screamed, its cry echoing so it sounded like it was miles away or just the other side of the door and not a one of us could say which.

"Brack's out there," I said. "Mitt, too."

The next crack of thunder near shook the house. On its heels, red light filled the windows. I stared at the door.

The last time I'd stood and fought, leastways, the last time I'd done that afore tonight, I'd ended with a scar across my palm and mutterings about me not being human all through the village. I'd kept Pepper safe, though. And Mitt. Hurt though it had, there was that.

"Not alone," said Pepper.

I turned to her to find her staring right at me.

"How'd you mean?"

She came to me and knelt before me, setting a palm against each of my cheeks, and those hands trembled but she sounded certain when she spoke again.

"I know that look. You aren't going out there alone."

"No sense in us both risking a mauling," I said. My throat and my heart and my brain, too, felt clogged and cold, but something in me had decided to go out there and I felt a rightness in it. "Stay where it's safe."

Her look said what she thought of the chances of safety and of being told to seek it, and I let my eyes close as she moved in and set her forehead against mine. I felt her words as well as heard them this time.

"Not alone."

It sounded like a promise. Pepper kept those. Always. It was another of my roots.

Glass splintering pulled us out of that moment, and I swung round to see the far window shattered. Pepper clutched at my hand, a sharp breath all the other sign she gave that she saw it, too: a thing all of rot and creeping fungus, the size of a large dog, perched in the gap it'd made. It had no face to speak of, no eyes or muzzle or mouth, but the way parts of it twisted, rippled, made it look to be sniffing.

A clatter behind me only distracted me for a moment, to see Edward brandishing a fire-iron and looking halfway to throwing up.

He glanced at me, at Pepper, and grabbed up the toasting-fork. With a sharp nod, he threw it. Pepper caught it in her free hand. He didn't hesitate much at all before he threw a poker to me.

My attention jerked back to the window at a crunching noise to see the creature on the floor, treading over the broken glass, heading right for us. I stepped back, Pepper mostly behind me, and heard Edward do the same.

"Does iron work on demons?" Edward asked.

I maybe loathed him less right then, what with him setting himself to fight when he sounded so scared.

Pepper no longer sounded scared. She sounded angry.

"Strike hard and anything works."

That was Pepper, making determination do the work of experience when she had to.

A shaking roar from outside was met with rattling thunder, and in the brief silence after, the thing, the smaller demon, shrieked. It was a fox-scream dragged through poison and it had me stopping my breath.

Pepper yelled as it ran at us, darting past me and swinging that piece of iron hard enough to crack stone. The demon crumpled sideways, but it hardly slowed, its fungus flesh knitting back to a whole piece. Another shriek, and it locked on to Pepper.

I saw Edward grab her, pull her sideways, as I set myself in its path. I'd set myself in the path of those men coming after Mitt or Pepper or both, and I'd swung iron at them. I knew iron could hurt, better than most, but I'd had no iron in the lane.

The demon hissed, jaws appearing in what I'd have sworn was its neck.

I met it with bared teeth and my iron-branded palm thrust out.

The same roaring silence, pulling echoes up from my boots, the same pulse of dazzling dark, and I was gasping half-way to the floor, with Pepper's arms around me and a stinking pile of mould before me.

"How did you...?" Edward asked, but he didn't throw devil-child at me, and he made no mention of the Fae.

Pepper lowered me to the ground, and as the storm raged on outside she sat behind me with her legs either side of mine and

148

opened my palm in her hands. With her chin tucked on my shoulder, I felt her words against my jaw.

"Your scar. It's warm."

Her voice held wonder. At least one of us felt something other than shock.

I'd faced down a beast of Hell and left it in bits.

In that blankness, I thought for a moment all the noise had gone. An explosion of red light and screaming knocked me back into the now of things. Sounded like the racket filled all of outside, and the light made Pepper's kitchen wrong. The floor beneath me didn't shift, but it felt like it should have done.

"How many are there?" Edward asked. He was half-crouched, eyes darting. "How many?"

"The lady said Hell was attacking," I told Pepper. Her cousin could listen as he liked. "How big is Hell?"

Pepper didn't answer.

"The cellar," Edward said. He altered his grip on the fire-iron. "We can barricade ourselves in the cellar. Wait it out."

"No." Pepper let go of me and got to her feet, leaving some of her warmth clinging to my back. "We still need to find Mitt."

"And Brack," I said, twisting to look up at her from the floor.

She held out a hand to me and nodded. "And Brack."

I let her haul me up. My limbs still felt wrong, like someone had steamed them in a kettle until they went soft, but the heat across my palm blazed. I let Pepper tug my clothes straight and saw her take a deep breath once she'd sorted her own. She nodded, one bird-sharp movement, and we turned to the door.

"Don't be stupid!"

In the spell of quiet between those red screams, Edward's words followed us, but he didn't.

Pepper looked at me before she reached for the door. It wasn't a look I'd learnt and we didn't have time for her to explain its meaning, so I just looked back at her.

"Okay," she said, and opened the door.

149

We stood for a spell, looking out and listening, but strain as I might I couldn't make out any beasts. There were no stars and no moon. No red light right this minute. I couldn't see anything.

I went first, and we crept along the front of the house and past the first outbuilding. I trailed my hand along the wall, the gritty cold of it reassuring on a night where Hell itself was attacking and Brack was missing from my side. Thick silence clogged up the place, except for our breathing and the rasp-tap of footsteps on stone. I couldn't move as quiet in my boots as I could in bare feet and Pepper had never been as good as me at going unnoticed. Just had to hope there was nothing out there, that the rotting beast inside had been on its own. Hope made a poor shield.

We reached the corner. Mitt could be in any one of these buildings, but he'd been away to his forge, and the quickest way was through the gate at the top. Waiting for the next flash of light grated at me and at the same time I didn't want it to ever happen. Behind me, Pepper tripped and cut off a cry. We paused, then, frightened prey freezing still as there'd be no outrunning what might chase us.

Nothing attacked. I went on.

About a third of the way along that side, the next wave of red noise hit. Now I saw the whole yard. Dark clouds boiled in the sky, charcoal and crimson, and no wonder the stars were hidden. Heaven was blocked off tonight.

That beast inside hadn't come alone.

Another thing like the one in the lane screamed at the clouds. It was most of the way across the yard, nearby the gate to the lane, but it only took a second to see it was twice the size of the last one. Rearing up as it was, its limbs made dead-branch silhouettes against the burning sky.

Something got hold of my sleeve. I flinched.

"Holly." Just Pepper, her voice a whispered hiss. Pepper who normally never forgot how I felt about touches I hadn't seen coming. "Look!"

I was looking. I was looking at the hell-creature and seeing more of those smaller ones milling round it. I was looking at the space between them and us and thinking it wasn't half big enough. But Pepper leaned in close and directed my gaze to the fourth side of the yard, where the largest of the outbuildings stood.

As the red light faded, I saw what Pepper had. Mitt, crouched in a doorway halfway between the demon beasts and us.

Crashing thunder and lightning hit at the same time, the blur-white light of the storm forking through the clouds. It pushed away the last of the red and for a moment it was just a storm. Nothing devil-like about it. A storm I wouldn't normally be out in, but something of the normal world.

Another bolt arced overhead, and this time it wasn't just clouds and thunder above me. Pepper's hand tightened on my sleeve. All I could do right then was stare.

The lady from the lane towered tall, her hair made of storm clouds and her skin the night sky. My mind turned dizzy, trying to take in a person I'd met, a person who'd been human-sized, having grown into the storm.

With a scream that sounded shriller than before, the large beast reached up, and up, and up, until it stretched impossibly high. Until it reached high enough to slash at the lady. Red light stabbed at the storm, and light shouldn't be able to mix and billow and roil, like it was liquid, like it was fighting for the sky.

A hard shove sent me stumbling. I caught myself and whipped around to see Pepper had leapt the other way. One of the smaller beasts stood a few feet away, turning from Pepper to me and back again.

If it went for Pepper, she'd only have the iron held in her hands as a weapon. I couldn't see it would work any better now than it had back in the house. If she ran…

Pepper wasn't someone who ran. She didn't have the way of it. If she tried now, she'd be slow. Slower than the beast, and slower than me.

I hurled the poker right at the thing and bellowed as loud as I could. They weren't words I fired at it. Nothing so pretty and ordered as words. Didn't need to be words. Didn't know if it could hear me over the storm. Just needed to get the thing to choose me. I waved my arms and I roared and I prayed. It worked.

Pepper's wide eyes and pale face vanished behind the beast as it charged, its rotted mass blocking her from view. I hoped she would run, just this once. Run right back to the house and hide. I knew she wouldn't.

No point being quiet, now. My boots struck the cobblestone, and it would have been loud, only any sounds but thunder and screaming were drowned. I let myself be wild and shouting, and ran.

Above, the lady raised an arm and struck at the huge beast with something shining. Maybe she'd plucked down the moon itself to use as a weapon. Whatever it was, the beast fell back.

It fell in my direction, and its rotting pack came with it.

One behind me was bad enough. Now, too many to count at a glance moved about the larger thing, and the way they moved, too, was wrong. Most of them seemed to be looking up, but at least two spotted me.

Skidding, I just kept my feet under me and bolted away at another angle. Too late, I realised I was leading them to Mitt.

In all the noise and chaos I didn't know if he'd see me, didn't know if he'd have chance to get out of the way. Couldn't change course again, though. The ones chasing me had me boxed, with a high wall on one side and the rest of their pack too close on the other.

Ahead of me, Mitt craned his neck, tracking the fight above. I braced to hit him, hoped I'd land us both far enough inside we could shut the door and…and… And we wouldn't be any safer in there. There was nowhere we'd be safe.

A slice of something not yet pain slashed across my left calf. I fell. I'd fallen before, knew the jarring thump of it, the breath-stopped suddenness. Didn't have time to lie and get over it, now. With my calf growing sharp pain and a duller, throbbing hurt spreading through my knees, my chin, one of my hands, I twisted and flailed and ended up on my back.

Silence fell, short and startling. In that gap, I heard Mitt yelling my name, the one he'd called me ever since I fetched up at his forge as a kid, my thoughts caught by the glow and by the ways he could make iron take new shapes.

Mitt couldn't help me, now. Over me, bringing its stench so close that bile rose in my throat, one of the beasts opened its mouth.

I'd saved Pepper and Mitt that day at the forge, had saved Pepper and her mean cousin back in the house, and had even saved a lady made of the night-storm from having to fight on alone when she was hurt. This time, I had to save myself.

I thrust my iron-branded palm upwards and let all the quick, loud thoughts in my head narrow down to screaming silence, to echoes through all my body. To fire in my hand.

This time, I kept my wits enough to see the beast shred apart, thrashing as it became nothing but rot. I felt the burning grow, spreading wider, and the others that had chased me crumbled.

Movement either side of me had me fight to my knees.

"Holly!"

The meaning of sounds came back to me, and I knew Pepper and Mitt.

"You were supposed to run," I told her. My voice rasped.

"I did run," she said, her words a little sharper than normal. "Can you do that again?"

Gripping the wrist of my branded hand and setting her other hand against my back, Pepper peered at the forge-fire in my flesh. I dragged my attention up to the rest of the yard to find a seething mass of nightmares between us and the house. The largest creature was on its feet, its battle with the storm carried out into the lane, but there was plenty to see to in Pepper's yard.

The beasts weren't the only creatures abroad this night. Took a moment to see it, but some of the shapes weren't the

153

stinking rot creatures, and the shapes were fighting the invasion from Hell. I'd to snatch glimpses in the lighting bursts, the red light not showing them sharp enough. In some ways, they were harder to fathom than the devil's creatures. These ones moved like smoke. They formed and swept away and formed again, snapping at the demons, pulling them apart. Hounds. They were hounds made of nothing solid, and they were driving the enemy back.

Still a whole load of evil between us and the house.

"Holly," Pepper said again. "Holly, can you kill more of them?"

I flexed my hand. Smithing was about making things, but part of forging was melting the old shape down, and I had a good fire going.

"Yes," I said.

No telling how long the fire would last, and please God let the lady destroy the giant one, but I'd burn up as many of the devils as I could. When the thunder roared again, I joined it.

***

"Have they left?" Edward asked.

Dawn light was the only cause of red in the sky now. The clouds had cleared and the thunder had rumbled itself out. Piles of rot and ruin made a mess of Pepper's yard. Pepper and Mitt wore bruises and blood, and Pepper was already washing hard as she could to clear her skin of burned beast. Mitt had made a start on clearing the cobbles, even though he'd not hit on anything yet that worked. Edward finally stuck his head out of the farmhouse door over an hour after the last creature fell.

I still hadn't found Brack.

"Demons?" Edward asked, head swivelling as he looked at what was left. "What killed them?"

"The lady in the storm got the big one," I said. "Her hounds tore others to bits. I killed some of these."

154

If Edward had anything to say to that, I didn't hear it. My attention caught on movement in the lane, and I saw a tall shape over the wall. Tall for a human, but not supernaturally so. The lady reached the gate and stepped over what was left of it. Her hair was back to being hair, her skin was skin, dark and lovely but no longer the night sky. I didn't dwell on that, though. Couldn't. In her arms, she carried a shape that was too small, too still.

"No."

Pepper tried to deny it for me, but the weight of it being real struck my chest. The lady cradled him all careful like, but I knew before she reached me that she'd brought my Brack home. She'd brought his body.

We were all alive to see the morning. Brack wasn't.

***

I took Brack out to my tree.

Pepper looked set on coming, but I told her to stay with Mitt. She gave me one of her unhappy looks and tried to hand me the poker, but I carried Brack away by myself.

By myself as far as the gate, where the lady stood waiting. She said nothing while we reached my tree, keeping pace with me and not intruding.

I held Brack and thought on how it wasn't right, him being so still. He'd always been life and joy and energy, and now he was empty. I couldn't find any tears yet, but Mam had explained not to dig for them, back when Dad had died. They'd come when they were ready, she'd said. No need to force them for show.

Brack had never needed me to put on a show. Didn't matter what name I went by or what I had on my feet. I was his and he was mine, and neither of us needed to make it tangled like people tended to do.

I laid him down amongst the roots of the tree, where they twisted up out of the earth. In a bit, I'd find stones to build him a cairn. For now, I settled on the ground and stroked my branded hand along his fur. If I could have forged him anew, I would have done it, but all I seemed able to do with my fire was unmake.

The lady sat cross-legged next to me, and it was hard to believe she'd been the storm sky a few hours before.

"Your hound was brave, little sprite," the lady said

"You got rid of them." I said, still looking at the roots that now cradled Brack, still feeling his fur under my fingers. "All of them demons. How?"

"You are brave, to question me," she said. Her voice had something of the storm in it. "I don't hunt alone. You saw my hounds, I think. And I have been hunting for a very long time indeed."

I thought I should be scared or awed, and I was. A little. There was something wild in her, wild and deep and sweeping, and it was like standing on the edge of a cliff, wondering what it would feel like to fall.

"You hunt demons?" I asked.

I looked at her then, and she met my gaze. There might have been something like sorrow on her face as she tilted her head, watching me.

"No. This was…not planned."

She sat with me then, not speaking or troubling me, just sitting and breathing and being, and I felt the tears in the base of my throat. They pushed up into my jaw and into my cheeks and into my eyes, crumpling my face and escaping, my grief trying to leave me like Brack had.

"I am sorry," she said, after she'd listened to me cry for a time. "He was brave and he was loyal and he joined my hounds to fight back the danger to his home. This was not part of the natural order of things."

My head throbbed now. My words were sodden.

"They say I'm not natural."

"Who is 'they'?"

I shrugged and scrubbed a hand across my face. "People round here. I'm odd, they say. Wrong. Don't belong. Must be a changeling."

The curls around her face shifted as she tilted her head. They put me in mind of twists of yarn, soft and thick and lovely, but I was in no mood to admire them. "Who are they to judge what is natural?"

I nodded at the tree.

"They say this happened as I was born. Say I caused it. And there's this." I held out my hand, flattening my palm to show her the scar. The brand. "Hot iron. There was… Some men came after Pepper or after Mitt. Wasn't clear. There was this bar."

I stopped, more tears threatening. That day was seared in my mind as much as in my skin, and aside from only noticing when it was done that I'd used burning iron to beat them away, I recalled Brack sitting with me after.

"Well, then, you're no changeling, child. A changeling could not touch iron, hot or otherwise."

As she spoke, she reached out and tapped my hand. The burn tingled. Didn't hurt, mind. Just…a ripple of something ran along it, lit it up inside, sank into me, and vanished.

"I held hot iron," I told her, holding my hand out again as though she might have missed what the scar meant. "That ain't normal."

"Perhaps not," she said, "but it isn't Fae. And you carry a mark from it. You're human, and you burn like a human."

I felt she didn't just mean my skin against that past-iron, but she went on before I could ask.

"Whatever you are," the woman said, and there was kindness in her voice and the whole night in her eyes, "you are a brave soul, and what you saw here, what you helped with, makes you a friend to my Hunt. We will not call you strange, but we will call you friend. And we will remember, for all the long years to come. As will your hound."

I felt another thing then, in with the wet, weighing tears. Anger.

"He's dead," I said. "Gone. Can't remember anything when he's dead, can he?"

157

"I can't bring him back to you," she said, as though I'd asked her to. "But I can take him with me."

"What?"

Maybe I wasn't the only one who had to learn expressions and remember to use them, instead of it being built in: there was nothing human on her face now, nothing at all human in her eyes. What there was, was nothing, slate blue and strong, and the feeling of standing on the edge of the cliff, with the great, sucking sea below.

"For the sake of a hound who will protect his mistress with his life, who will fight Hell itself to keep her safe, and for the debt I owe him, it may be I can find him a place in my Hunt. He is brave enough to let the storm carry him."

"Would-?" I had to stop and swallow around the clog in my throat. It didn't occur to me to doubt what she said. Not after the night we'd had. "Would he be happy? Would you love him?"

She lifted a hand and placed it on Brack's shoulder. "I promise. He will be my hound and he will be loved and he will remember his first mistress always."

I wanted to ask if I'd see him again, if he'd become one of her hounds now, where I could see, but I couldn't face being told no. Instead, I asked something different.

"How did I kill those things? If I'm not a changeling child, then how'd I have any power like that?"

She took my hand again and I let her, watching as she turned it over to show my scar to the sky. I trembled, just a little, as she traced her finger along that ridged skin, and the same ripple as before followed along.

"You have the power you called to yourself," she said. "Not all magic is locked in words. You've given yourself a weapon, little sprite, with your own actions. There is a power in making the choice to protect. To belong. Mind you use it well."

And as that ridge warmed and ripened, turning the same forge-red as the iron that formed it, I met the eyes of a lady who might be all manner of things, who had promised to take my

Brack and make him part of the storm that hunted, who for certain wasn't human, and I promised.

We do not know why London was such a target, nor why all manner of monstrosities were sent into and against it. Symbolic, we supposed, or was it simply that huge concentration of people, all neatly packed within its boundaries? The Government, ever keen on its own preservation, dispersed into areas of relative calm; the aged Queen Victoria and her immediate family were pressed, against her initial wishes, to relocate to the South West, which was holding better than most regions. Venerable Pendennis Castle, used to guard Cornwall against invasion for centuries, became the centre of a new resistance.

The sole royal dissenter was, to almost everyone's surprise, the Prince of Wales. Prince Albert Edward, 'Bertie', forsook his baccarat tables and his socialising to enter the field, commanding the Army of the North, as it was popularly known. None had expected that he would show the military acumen that he did, or that he would shed his fine tailored suits to crouch in the mud with weary soldiers and stiffen their resolve.

Meanwhile, the capital was assailed by plagues of brimstone-scented sickness; great pallid worms which oozed acidic pus; seeming legions of misshapen demons and the damned. The damned were worse, because they wore a shell of humanity, and bore lost faces...

AD MAJOREM SATANAE GLORIAM

Damascus Mincemeyer

The flames were all he knew.

Long had the fires of perdition incinerated everything that could be called man; his past, his life, even his own name, were lost to the fiery abyss. The reasons for his damnation were gone, too, eaten away by every carnivorous lick that had reduced his soul to ash.

Yet there had been a dawning, a rising through the embers, and he found himself among a writhing horde of gnashing teeth and flailing limbs, all of them moving upward through the pit to a destination unknown. And above it all the Voice spoke to each of the million screaming souls, clear above the chaos:

The time has come to war with the Creator, to turn His world to blood and dust, it said. *You are the hordes of Damnation, and shall fight to the last, from the clay of the earth to the gates of Heaven.*

Then the flames were gone. No, not gone. Different. Fire still surrounded him, but now there were streets and carriages and buildings ablaze, the wailing agony of men and beasts symphonic in the night.

He stood there, the Nameless damned soul, the taste of sulphur in his mouth, bewildered by the anarchy around him.

Forward, the Voice urged.

And the Nameless One obeyed.

***

Calvin Woolery stood in the open doorway of the narrow terraced house, watching the night sky above London dance with flames.

"The line at Hampstead was breached last evening," Martin

161

told him, thumbing through *The Times* at the parlour room table, so fresh an edition the ink was still practically wet, his usually jovial tone sober as he read. "They say the VRC have fallen back to a position in Regent's Park and have all but abandoned St. John's Wood and Paddington, and there's another line retreating back through Bethnel Green and Spitalfields to bolster up the police contingent along Brick Lane." He rapped the paper with a knuckle. "This article claims the Sappers will burn all the bridges to prevent the enemy from crossing the Thames if necessary. I tell you, lad, if those Russian bastards reach the Isle of Dogs, they'll have us by the inexpressibles then, no question."

Calvin said nothing, though his uncle's assessments held truth - the Isle of Dogs was the main hub of London docks, a short march from where they were in All Saints Poplar, and a shining strategic target for the enemy force besieging the city. It was also a powerful indicator of the desperation in the struggle if the Royal Engineers were indeed considering demolishing spans across the river.

Martin set the paper aside, ripping a chunk of bread from the mouldy loaf on the table and emptying the last wine from a bottle into his glass. "Come and eat, Calvin. We might as well enjoy what little we've got left."

"I'm worried about Anne." Calvin said. Martin laughed.

"The one thing I'm decidedly *not* concerned about in all this is that daughter of yours. She's the most head-strong woman I've ever met, besides your aunt, that is. You made the right choice sending Stuart and James to Brighton with her."

Calvin's fingers brushed against the Webley service revolver tucked in his waistband. At one time he'd been robust, but a decade in the regiments and that old spear wound from Rorke's Drift had transformed him from youthful soldier to middle-aged dockworker before he knew it, and that was before his wife Louisa had been eaten alive by consumption, leaving him with three young mouths to feed and little money to do it with. When the current calamity began, his primary instinct was to protect his children, but sending them south had been a difficult

162

choice, despite what the papers said about the protective zone the military had established there.

From outside, another round of screams punctured the night, followed by the distant rumble of artillery. Martin went to the window, watching a herd of panicked people rush down the street. He withdrew a pipe from his vest, tamping it before lighting up. "I tell you, lad, I always knew the Russians would make a move on us one day. Tsar Alexander just couldn't resist Queen Vicki's plum pudding, so to speak."

Calvin looked at his uncle. "I don't think the Russians are capable of launching an attack on this scale. On the continent, against France or the Germans, yes. But not here."

Martin frowned. "Don't tell me you're one of those who think the enemy's some phantom army of the Devil. I thought you level-headed enough not to believe in such superstitious nonsense. From my worthless drunk of a brother I'd have expected it. But not you."

Calvin bristled at Martin's casual condemnation of his father, even if the description was apt. "I don't know what to think, uncle. But it doesn't seem God's hand is in this."

Though the newspapers loudly championed the military response to the invasion, there were conflicting reports as to the nationality of those launching the assault upon Britain's shores. Many assumed, like Martin, that it was the Russian Empire making a violent power play, or even a surprise French attack. But there were other, darker, rumours whispered by those who had actually seen the enemy first-hand. Tales abounded about sinister soldiers with charred flesh and burning eyes, monstrous creatures so perverse they could have only come from a Bosch painting, about beings that belched brimstone and could turn river-water to boiling blood and men to bone with a mere touch. And despite the press's refusal to acknowledge the tales, Parliament had hastily formed a new cabinet ministry consisting of a cabal of England's most notorious occultists, psychical researchers and ritual magicians, an act giving weight to theories of the enemy's otherworldly origin. Despite that, Martin still only laughed.

"Heard a fellow when I was out today swear up and down a cadre of vicars and priests had set out to bless the Thames. Mad as hops, he was. I mean, it would take a blessing from the bloody Archbishop of Canterbury himself to just combat the stench from that miserable river," Martin looked to his nephew, his laughter fading. "Chin up, lad. Anne and the boys will be fine. You'll see." He put his pipe out. "Maybe we should try to get some sleep."

Martin waited a few minutes, but Calvin didn't budge from the doorway, and eventually he sighed, going upstairs alone.

***

Something stirred within the Nameless One as he marched with the legions of the Damned; around him whirled a cataclysm of burning shops and collapsing houses, the bodies of the slain mingled among the wreckages of carts and cycles, carriages and omnibuses, yet there were things in his surroundings that triggered memories from a time before the flames claimed his soul, words and places that seemed somehow familiar: Shoreditch. Liverpool Street Station. Bishopsgate. Gracechurch Street.

Amid such destruction there remained, astoundingly, pockets of defiance; a detachment of riflemen had staunchly erected a stubborn defensive perimeter along Cannon Street, complete with securely nested Maxim Gun. As the Damned approached, the riflemen opened fire with well-practised aim, but though they howled as bullets struck them and their charred flesh bled sparks of fire, the Damned did not die. They proceeded forward despite the onslaught, obsidian-tipped blades and halberds in hand.

More insidious were those commanding the hordes, things the Damned themselves would have difficulty recognizing as having ever been remotely human: the demons. All of them were different, yet similar in their hideousness--some were tall and thin with ten heads and twenty hands, while others were squat creatures with rows of sharp teeth and bones protruding from mottled, raspberry-like flesh; there were those that shrieked and collected the skins of their victims as trophies, even as their compatriots whipped the Damned forward with tendrils of fire.

Unlike the Damned, the demons had names, whispered in the heads of the infernal infantry: *Beleth. Amdusias. Leraje. Eligos.* Those, and dozens more, were the Earls and Dukes of the Abyss, the generals of the dark crusade upon the earth. The Nameless One saw his own commander appear in the midst of battle astride a viper the size of a horse, directing the offensive: Haborym, who appeared as a handsome man in body, but possessed three heads--one of a serpent, a man, and a cat. In its hands the demon carried a lit firebrand with which it sprayed flames so intense upon a group of retreating riflemen they disintegrated into white ash. The sight was a horror even to the Nameless, but Haborym's heads bellowed with unholy laughter.

Once the line had been breached and the rout began, the Damned poured down Cannon Street, driven by the Voice and Haborym's ruthless prodding, and at first the Nameless did not know to what end the assault was for until he saw the baroque dome of St. Paul's Cathedral rising from beyond the thick billowing smoke.

***

A pounding on the front door woke Calvin with a start and he lurched from the chair he'd nodded off in, hand automatically pulling the Webley from his waist before he was fully on his feet. The grandfather clock in the parlour room's corner read half past three, which told Calvin he'd slept barely twenty minutes, yet despite the lateness of the hour the room was lit with a soft amber glow from the flaming sky; under other circumstances the way the furniture and decorations were illuminated would have been picaresque, but as it were it seemed an ill omen.

There was another furious hammering at the door, followed by muffled cries for help that had become all-too-common since the attack upon London began. But not every entreaty was necessarily genuine: Calvin had witnessed his fair share of looters and ruffians taking advantage of the chaos. Calvin walked to the closed door, grip tight on the revolver.

"Go away!" He shouted. "We've no food or water here!"

There was a pause, then another plea, one that took Calvin by surprise: "Father? Father, let us in. Please."

"Anne?" Calvin asked, turning the knob almost involuntarily. Part of him remained cautious, but his daughter's voice was unmistakable; when the door was open Calvin saw Anne standing on the step with a group of strangers, all of them looking ragged and filthy and exhausted. When Anne had departed two days earlier, she'd been in her finest dress, hair coifed neatly beneath a bonnet; now her clothes were torn and mud-spattered, her teenaged face bruised and scratched.

Calvin pulled his daughter close, but the embrace was short. One of those behind Anne, a bloodied, grey-headed vicar, tried to shove through the door. Calvin blocked him, raising the revolver.

"My daughter may stay. There is no harbour for the rest."

Anne glanced at the vicar, then to Calvin. "Please, Father, let them in. You don't understand what we've been through."

Calvin scrutinized the refugees. There were five all told: besides Anne and the vicar were a heavyset fellow in an expensive matched derby suit and a bowler hat, and a woman who looked like a typical East End factory girl, clutching a small boy. Two others he expected in the group, however, were nowhere to be seen.

"Where are your brothers?" He asked Anne, the hesitation before she spoke telling Calvin everything, and his heart sank.

"They're...They're dead, Father," she finally said, tears streaking down her face. "We made it no farther than Brentwood. Somehow those...those *demons* circled around and cut off the rail lines and roads out of Havering... I tried to hold onto Stuart and James, but there was too much commotion, too many people. Stuart stumbled and was trampled, but James... Oh, Father! It's too terrible to speak of!"

166

Anne buried herself, sobbing, in Calvin's chest, and slowly he lowered the Webley, motioning for the refugees to enter. Once they crossed the threshold, the man in the derby suit immediately went to the bottle of wine on the parlour table, frowning when it proved empty. He tore a piece of bread from the half-eaten loaf, ate it, and was about to rip another when Calvin told him, "For the child first, sir."

He bristled, but begrudgingly did as he was told. The factory girl came over to Calvin, soot marring her otherwise attractive features, saying, "Don't pay no mind to Mr. Cornthwaite, sir. He told us he's from Hampstead and his whole house done burned down." She patted her scruffy boy on the head as he devoured the bread, and Calvin felt a pang. "My name's Margaret, by the by. Thank you for the shelter."

Martin's voice called out then, "What's all this ruckus, lad? And who are these people in my house?"

Calvin's uncle came down the stairs in his nightclothes, staring at the newcomers; when he spotted Anne his face drooped. "Anne? I thought you and your brothers would be well away from this madness by now." He glanced around the parlour. "Where *are* your sons, Calvin?"

"The devils took them," the vicar said, sitting down. "Just as they'll take us all."

"Devils?" Martin sneered. "Did they have horns and pitchforks? Perhaps the Russians will employ leprechauns and wood nymphs as hussars next."

The vicar furiously launched from the chair. "Do not mock me, sir! My entire congregation in Ipswich was massacred right before me not more than a week ago, from spinster to infant all! So do not presume to tell me our adversary is anything but from Satan's own dominion!"

"And do not presume to come into my house, an uninvited stranger, voicing such rubbish!" Martin roared back. The vicar shouted again, but Calvin heard the argument as if it was from far away. His only thoughts were of his sons, neither yet ten and already gone from the world, and he glanced at the hand holding

167

the revolver; it trembled uncontrollably.

"Quiet! Both of you!" He yelled, and the two men silenced. "This is no time for division. Anne says these invaders are inhuman as well, uncle, and I believe my daughter."

"Is there no way out of the city then?" Martin sounded fearful for the first time. Calvin looked at Anne.

"By what way did you return?"

"Through Dagenham and Canning Town, but the whole of Barking and Newham are clogged with people, and the police have been unable to stop rioters and arsonists from burning half the buildings."

"I've seen much of that here, too." Calvin said.

There was a frantic cry from the street. Calvin went to the window; outside, an overstuffed wagonload of people clattered by, one of the passengers yelling, "Tower Bridge is on fire! Tower Bridge is on fire!"

The vicar tossed his hands up. "It's all over for us now!" He collapsed back into the chair, rocking back and forth, repeating, "It's over. It's all over."

"Get a hold of yourself, man," Martin chided, then whispered to Calvin, "I want this madman out of my house!"

Before Calvin could reply, a dull rumbling, deeper than any artillery barrage, shook the ground; the windows in the house rattled, plaster from the ceiling broke loose, and the grandfather clock tipped on its side in front of Margaret and her child. As the quaking ceased Mr. Cornthwaite pointed out the cracked windowpane.

"By God! Look!"

In the distance a pillar of flame soared into the night, reaching higher than anything Calvin had ever seen.

A heartbeat later it began raining fire.

***

There were many jewels coveted by the demons in their black campaign, none more so than those places dedicated to the reverence and worship of their great enemy, The Creator. Ever since the Incursion began it was the triumph of triumphs for the infernal commanders to capture, and spoil, and desecrate the churches and temples and mosques they came across. From quiet country chapels to vast Gothic abbeys, all offered delight, and the greater demons competed with one another for the chance at violation each presented. If worshippers and holy men were discovered within, the pleasure only increased.

So it was in London there was no greater prize than St. Paul's. The cathedral was so awe-inspiring, so resplendent in its features that it became a lusted-for object, and Haborym was determined its legions would possess it after dislodging the defenders from Cannon Street.

The Damned surged up St. Paul's Churchyard and Newgate Street and stormed Ludgate Hill, finding thousands of the Creator's devoted cowering inside, those frightened or foolish enough to seek refuge from the invasion in His house and offer supplications that turned to screams as the Damned began their massacre.

Despite the boldness of the Inferno's war upon the world, there remained firm rules even the demons had to obey. Unlike the souls it marshalled, Haborym, being born of the nether-realms, could not set unholy foot upon the sacred ground to celebrate its victory; instead, the fiend commanded the Damned to use the blood of the slaughtered in the creation of a seal upon the cathedral's central nave to deconsecrate the area, allowing Haborym access. Once inside, the demon revelled in its small conquest, repeatedly striking the main altar with its firebrand, and soon the ground began to quiver, then split and fall away as a fiery chasm opened, spewing smoke and churning magma.

As the floor gave way, the walls shook, columns crumbled, and the dome itself cracked; the two towers of the west facade were failing as the fissure widened, sliding into the pit, and soon the whole of the cathedral disappeared like a ship sinking into an ocean of fire. There followed a series of ever-more violent spasms from the crevice where St. Paul's had stood, the quaking

169

intensifying until a spire of flame erupted heavenward, bursting and showering incendiaries upon the portions of London thus far unscathed by the legions. From the well-to-do estates of Greenwich and Blackheath to the immigrant enclaves and silk weaver's sweatshops of the East End, the city began to burn.

Dawn came, but the sky remained black, the sun blotted by the volcanic smoke from the wound in the earth Haborym had opened, and the Damned regrouped.

East, the Voice commanded, *So that The Dragon may soon come.*

***

The terraced houses and shops and pubs all along Poplar High Street were ablaze. Everywhere, people desperate to escape the quick-moving flames swarmed into the road; fire brigades were overwhelmed, and soon lawlessness reigned throughout All Saints.

Calvin Woolery gripped his daughter's hand tightly as they rushed from his uncle's burning house, dodging a mass of carts and cabs and cycles. All around, the din of hysteria assailed the senses, and to Calvin the noise of the flames as they claimed building after building was like a thousand chariots beating together over stones. Close behind, Martin, Mr. Cornthwaite and the vicar staggered to the sidewalk; Martin, robe hastily thrown on over his nightclothes and carrying an armful of possessions, angrily protested the evacuation.

"My house! Damn the Tsar to hell!" He shouted, waving a defiant fist in the air; a second later a man on a bicycle collided with him, both of them tumbling to the ground, the assortment of coins and silverware Martin held scattering across the pavement. The man who'd struck him was dressed in a railway porter's outfit, and he scuttled to his feet, seething.

"Bloody Christ, you old bastard! Get out of my way!" He grabbed his bicycle, still swearing as he rode off. Calvin hoisted Martin up; next to them the vicar raised arms to the still-black sky, then dropped to his knees, wailing, "This is the Revelation! The Day and the Hour has come! Mercy! Mercy on us all!"

Calvin reached for the vicar, but Mr. Cornthwaite intercepted his hand.

"Leave him, sir," he said, "The man's mind is gone. Just leave him."

Calvin hesitated but eventually turned away, quickly loosing sight of the vicar amid the crowd. Behind him there was a creaking from Martin's house as the roof caved in upon the upper floor, showering the street with cinders. Calvin dodged a chunk of falling masonry, but Margaret and her child were not so lucky; in the panic they had not fled quickly enough and the buckling front of the building crashed down upon them, the pair disappearing under the flaming rubble.

Martin unleashed a slew of obscenities, thrashing as Mr. Cornthwaite pulled him away from the blazing remains of the house and back towards Calvin.

"This is intolerable!" Martin yelled, angry tears rolling down his cheeks. "Where are we supposed to go? *Where?"*

Calvin had no answer to the question; his only immediate thought, like everyone else's, was escaping the maelstrom, but he possessed little in the way of an actual plan until Mr. Cornthwaite said, "The ferry from the Isle of Dogs to Greenwich might still be running. The roads south were passable yesterday afternoon."

"It may work," Calvin agreed, but before he could take a step something landed on the street beside him; the way it wriggled and flopped he didn't recognize what it was, but then another hit the ground a yard away, flapping wildly and on fire, and Calvin realized what they were. *"Pigeons,"* he said, watching the flock of birds, their wings ignited by the inferno, fall from the sky. "The pigeons are on fire..."

A hot, rank breeze started up; the air in the East End always smelled foul from the noxious odours of factories and tanneries and the docks, but there was something else tainting the wind that now rankled Calvin's senses: the overpowering stench of sulphur.

"Make way!" Someone in the crowd shouted. "They're

171

coming! The devils are coming!"

In the distance there was a shrieking made by neither man nor beast, a cacophonous, tortured howl, and from far down the burning street a figure appeared through the smoke, charging headlong into a throng of people, brandishing a long, sinister blade. It was quickly followed by a second attacker, and a third, before an entire host of them swarmed Poplar High Street like locusts, hacking and slashing at all in their path, their screeching worse than any Zulu war cry Calvin had heard. At first glance they looked like men, but their skin was blackened and blistered, eyes ember-red, and around their necks were collars of flame, linked between each like a chain. To Calvin the lurid tales of demonic invasion seemed abruptly real.

Mr. Cornthwaite stumbled past Calvin and ran, but made it no more than a dozen paces when the closest of the skirmishers caught up with him, plunging its blade into his back. He gasped, blood spewing from his mouth, and Calvin instinctively fired the Webley at his attacker. The demon - what other word was there for it? - reeled from the closeness and force of the shot, a sputter of quick flame spurting from the wound, but the thing did not fall, only merely staggered a step before rebounding, withdrawing its weapon from Mr. Cornthwaite's fallen corpse and slashing at Anne. She screamed, and Calvin pushed her away, firing point blank at the creature; there was second burst of fire from its flesh, but the thing's momentum was too great and it tackled Calvin to the ground, the Webley slipping from his grasp.

Despite its ghastly appearance the attacker was no stronger than Calvin, but its skin was hot to the touch, its breath reeked of brimstone, and as they wrestled Calvin grabbed for the weapon it held. His own flesh seared when it brushed against the blade, and he swore from the pain.

The creature brought its weight to bear upon Calvin, its face coming so close to his that he could clearly make out features - the heavy brow, that off-centre nose, the cleft chin - that seemed familiar to him despite the inhumanity of its guise. Yet only when Calvin's gaze locked with those burning eyes did he truly realize what he was struggling with; Martin noticed it at the same time, and Calvin heard his uncle feverishly cry, "Good Lord, it can't be! *Stephen?* It *can't* be!"

Until then the creature had been intent on driving its blade into Calvin's chest, but abruptly it relented in its assault. Lowering the weapon, the attacker looked down at Calvin even as it straddled him, and their eyes met again; this time Calvin saw not fury, but despair deeper than any bottomless pit.

The lull lasted only a moment. Shoving the brute back, Calvin snatched the Webley from where it had fallen, lashing the creature's skull before scrambling upright and practically dragging Anne with him down the street, Martin trailing close behind.

They went along blindly, turning down byways and alleys, wherever the fire wasn't, but as they neared Bow Lane and All Saints' Church, Anne stopped, slumping against a gas street-lamp.

"I can go no further," she rasped, face suddenly pale.

"Nonsense," Calvin pulled her up, shocked when his hand come back smeared with crimson; Anne quickly collapsed to the pavement the spreading spider-web of blood splotching her soiled dress from the wound in her left side visible to Calvin. The demon's blade had found its mark after all.

Calvin tried to scream, but his mind was too numb, too full of the horrors that had been so swiftly thrust upon him, and he fell to his knees, cradling Anne. Weak, she touched his face.

"Take me to the church, Father," she whispered, "I need to be cleansed of my sins..."

"You have committed no sin, Anne," Calvin said, burning tears welling up in his eyes. "If there's any sin here it belongs to me, for my failure to protect you and your brothers."

"Oh, but Father, I've done terrible things," Anne coughed, bloody spittle dotting her chin. "I did not tell the whole truth at the house. Stuart was indeed crushed by the crowd in Havering, but James... I knew there was no way out of London, knew we were all going to die horribly, and I thought surely you were

173

already dead, Father. I just didn't want poor James to suffer, so we walked to the Thames...and I drowned him. Sweet boy he was, trusted me right up to when I held his head under the water..." Her voice grew faint. "I *murdered* him, Father. I wanted to protect him from those demons, and God above, now I'm going to *become* one..."

Anne coughed again, gurgled and choked, her body writhing in Calvin's arms before the life slipped out of her and she slackened, eyes open and staring yet seeing nothing. Calvin knelt there, the numbness spreading throughout him before he summoned enough strength to lift her body.

"Where are you going, lad?" Martin asked.

"She wanted to be in the church," Calvin replied. "That's where she's going."

Martin shook his head. "It's bloody pointless, lad. That milksop vicar was right. We're finished. *All* of us. Londoners. Britain. Everything. There's no salvation for anything now..." he pulled at his thinning hair. "I never thought The Devil and Hell more than pabulum to frighten the flock, but now I know how wrong I was," Martin grabbed Calvin's jacket. "That...that *demon* who attacked you and Anne--did you *see* its face, lad?"

Calvin nodded. "Yes. But it's not possible. It *couldn't* be *him*. You said so yourself."

"But it *was,* lad. I'd recognize my own brother anywhere, even after fifteen years in the grave," Martin's grip tightened. "That was *Stephen*. That was your *father.*"

***

Hell had been cunning.

For untold millennia the Kings of the Abyss designed their campaign against Creation, and it had been decided early on that drafting the endless multitude of condemned souls as foot soldiers to spearhead the attack was essential. Much time was spent organizing the legions in such ways that the Damned would be intimate with their surroundings, so they would better know the terrain, the cities and villages, and the people with whom they were to war.

So it was when the Nameless One marched eastward after the destruction of St. Paul's that the memories of his past life became more vivid with each step. With no need for rest, or food, or any other worldly succour, the Damned pressed relentlessly on past Tower Hill and proceeded down the Ratcliffe Highway through St. George's Street East, and flashes of existence, like shards of glass, pierced his mind. First the visions came randomly, but as the column of dead souls moved unencumbered through High Street, Cock Hill and Broad Street to Limehouse and then to Poplar High Street, they became more intense and increasingly unpleasant, filled with the mean-spirited spitefulness of a life lost to drink and senseless violence, the reasons for his recruitment into Hell's invading force slowly making themselves clear.

It was as the legions entered All Saints Poplar that the Nameless realized he was where everything began and ended for him: *this* had been home. Was that not The White Hart, the pub that had claimed so many of his nights, now burning to the ground? And there - was that half-collapsed rubble the brothel he had repeatedly abandoned his wife to visit, and where his life had finished with a knife to the gullet?

There was no time for reflection despite the revelations; the sepulchral intonations from the Voice drowned all else with its constant urge - *forward, forward, forward* - and he could not help but obey, finding himself in the vanguard of the attack as the Damned stampeded into a crowd of alarmed civilians.

A house collapsed nearby, a handful of people narrowly eluding the falling ruins; one of them was an elderly man, white-headed; another portly and dressed in an expensive suit, yet a third man among them stood clasping a revolver, shielding a young woman from the debris; despite his shabby dock-worker's clothes, the Nameless could tell this one was no stranger to battle.

The large man, however, was not so steadfast; as the Damned gained ground he ran, and the Nameless set after him,

175

wolf to hind, thrusting obsidian blade through his spine. Before the corpse could even fall the dockworker opened fire, the bullet's sting enraging the Nameless, and he lashed out at the woman the dockworker protected, catching the girl by surprise and driving his blade under her left arm, between the ribs. The dockworker fired again, but the pain only further fuelled the Nameless's ire, and he hurtled towards the man, both of them going to ground with crushing force, the revolver clattering out of the dockworker's hand. Together they were a mass of thrashing limbs, and the Nameless swung his blade down, but the man grabbed his wrist, the pair wrestling for control of the weapon.

As the dockworker strained under the weight of the struggle, the Nameless caught a glimpse of the man's eyes. Those eyes - *those eyes!* - where had he seen them before? From someone in his earthly life to be sure, but who? A friend? An enemy? No--*NO!* They were closer than that - a part of himself, were they not? Indeed, there they were - the eyes of a son, grown to manhood and looking back at him.

From the pavement, the Nameless heard the elderly man cry out, "Good Lord, it can't be! *Stephen?* It *can't* be!" And that, too, sounded familiar.

Martin. His brother. But he hadn't been old before, had he? And that name, Stephen - why did it feel so wont?

Something roused in the Nameless that he had not felt since his unholy resurrection, and only rarely before that, and for the briefest of moments he remembered the boy who was now a man: Calvin. In his mind the Voice goaded him to kill, but the memories supplanted compulsions to perform another atrocity atop the ones he'd already committed, and he let the weapon fall to his side, simply staring into his son's eyes, wondering - was there recognition, a spark bridging the gap between living and dead? If there was it did not show, and Calvin retrieved the fallen revolver, striking the butt end against the Nameless' temple before escaping down the street, pulling the woman and Martin with him.

Watching them flee, The Nameless stood, looking then at

the obsidian blade, thoughts of the innocent blood it had shed suddenly disgusting to him, and he threw the weapon down even as his fellow Damned rushed past, still eager for mayhem.

A gravity overcame him, like the very ground was trying to swallow him whole; somewhere deep within he knew what was coming and why, and all the horrors he had inflicted, both in life and afterwards, were washed away in one final kaleidoscopic wave and the last fragment from his existence fell into place, even as the Voice berated him.

You have failed us, soldier of darkness. Mercy has no place in Hell, and by showing such you shall burn until nothing that can be called man remains.

The tone was furious, yet even as the flames of immolation kissed him, the dead, damned soul tried to speak while his unholy vessel was dragged back through the embers into the furthest recesses of the Abyss. When the unquenchable fires began to engulf him once more, the words were lost, but Stephen Woolery was at last no longer nameless.

***

The churchyard surrounding All Saints' was a large garden enclosed by railings, its perimeter lined with trees, from the centre of which the church itself rose impressively, unscathed by the ruination surrounding it, the ionic columns of the portico supporting a steeple that towered over the terraced houses on adjoining streets.

A mass of people had assembled seeking safe haven, filling both interior and exterior beyond capacity with frightened fugitives praying to a suddenly distant God. Together, Calvin and Martin manoeuvred through the crowded churchyard, the weight of Anne's body draining to Calvin's arms, though he barely felt the pain; his only goal was getting her inside - a futile gesture, but one that to Calvin signified the final act he as a father could perform for his daughter.

A man in a filthy coachman's uniform clawed at Anne's

177

dress when Calvin and Martin passed, his eyes crazed as he tore at the fabric. "The body of Mary, all for me?" He said, repeating, "Pretty, pretty, pretty."

Martin shoved him back, but the coachman only laughed manically. Calvin didn't even look twice; the wounds to his spirit were too vicious for him to care. He just kept walking, up the steps and into the church itself.

Inside All Saints' were grand galleries on all sides and a raised, ornate cast-iron altar positioned in front of a cracked stained-glass window. As in the garden, people packed the building, stuffing each pew and kneeling on the floor in every available space, weeping endless lamentations. Despite the desperation, there was a strange, calm atmosphere inside the church, palpable to Calvin as he made his way toward the front altar, where he laid Anne's body on the floor. He knelt there, looking at her pretty, blood-speckled features, knowing that she, and Stuart and James too, would never enjoy life as he had, never grow to adulthood, marry or have children of their own, and the thought sickened him.

"My *father* killed her," Calvin said to Martin as he stood, the words unbelievable even as he spoke them, though he knew they were true.

"Your father was a brute. You and I both know that," Martin replied. "It doesn't surprise me a jot his soul ended up where it did."

Calvin could not argue with his uncle's statement; his father *had* been a brute, the man's meanness the keystone of Calvin's youthful memories. Before his mother's death from typhoid she had borne the brunt of his father's rages, and afterwards Calvin sought escape from the cruelty in the regiments, a place where, ironically, the harshness of his father's abuse had bequeathed a survival instinct that served him well.

"Will Anne be one of those demons like him, I wonder?" Calvin asked.

"Your daughter wasn't like Stephen."

"No, but you heard her. My father was many things, but

178

murderer wasn't one of them, and if *he* is one of hell's soldiers, what will become of *her?*"

Martin sombrely shook his head. "I... I don't know, lad. I truly don't."

Outside there was another rumble, perhaps from artillery, perhaps from something more wicked, and a chorus of uneasy screams rose from the assembly. Calvin was no theologian, and religion had never been a major facet in his working-man's life, but he had no doubt that Hell - whatever it proved to be - was responsible for the battle ravaging London, though whether the city, or Britain, or the world would survive whatever apocalypse had been unleashed was not for him to speculate. His war was over, and he had lost on all fronts. What happened from now on out, to himself and to England, was inconsequential. His daughter had confessed to murder, yet out of mercy, not malice; Calvin had killed, too - willingly, if not eagerly - countless times in Africa. Did that mean *he* was damned? He glanced at the Webley. How many times had he fired that weapon in anger on the battlefield? How much blood had it shed?

"Do you believe in the Devil now, uncle?" Calvin asked. Martin slowly nodded.

"I've no choice, not after what we've seen."

That hollow numbness spread throughout Calvin once more, and he closed his eyes; opening them again, he could barely see Anne's body through the bitter, burning tears.

"If the Devil truly is real, I pray he guides my soul steadier than God ever did," Calvin said, "For if my daughter is to be damned, then so shall I."

Quickly Calvin raised revolver to temple; from far away he heard his uncle scream, but before Martin could stop him, Calvin pulled the trigger, a white heat searing his final thought in the ether.

***

Day, night, day, night; sky black as pitch, hour slipping into hour, few were able to distinguish between the two.

Despite the damage done to London, there remained flickers of hope in the resistance to the incursion; the Royal Engineers following volunteer forces retreating south of the Thames demolished each span across the river, from Tower Bridge to Blackfriars to Albert Bridge, in a bid to buy time for reinforcements moving up from Woking.

Soon after, the Damned, having advanced through All Saints Poplar and Blackwall, made their way to the Isle of Dogs, the legions wading into the waters only to find their infernal flesh blistering and melting as if the Thames flowed with acid, the sulphuric stench of their dissolving bodies thick on the wind, and Haborym recognized the ploy with equal parts rage and bemusement: the river had been blessed, and the entirety of the Thames now ran with holy water--a crude spiritual blockade, but one that was nonetheless effective, however temporarily.

Yet even as commanders on both sides reorganized and counted casualties, the fires of perdition opened and more souls from the abyss blossomed, black roses upon the earth, all of them moving upward through the pit to their ultimate destination.

And the Voice spoke to them, clear above the chaos:

The time has come to war with the Creator, to turn His world to blood and dust, it said, *You are the hordes of Damnation, and shall fight to the last, from the clay of the earth to the gates of Heaven.*

Then the flames were gone. No, not gone. Different. Fire still surrounded them, but now there were streets and carriages and buildings aflame.

Among them a soul stood, confused, the taste of brimstone in his mouth, bewildered by the anarchy around him.

"Forward," the Voice urged.

And Calvin obeyed.

With London badly wounded, and so few experienced soldiers or sailors available, militia action was essential to survival. Communities organised their own patrols, often fragmented and disorganised. In some areas, there was a semblance of order. Watch-posts, rotas and the equivalent of Army platoons, bolstered by what regulars there were...

INFERNAL PATROL

A. F. Stewart

"Bloody Hellspawn! The brimstone's turned the milk again!" Henry Ellis stared into the can of spoiled dairy and then scowled at the delivery boy. He waved his empty jug at the youth. "I can't fill my pitcher with this sludge!"

The lad snivelled and whined, "Can't help it. That filth's everywhere since the Battle of the Thames last week. It's bound to get in some." The boy gave a sneer as he fastened the cover back on the can. "And it ain't in every one. Rest of the street was clean enough."

Henry snorted. "Well, isn't that just a dandy bit for them. But that don't help me none. What am I supposed to do, then?"

"Keep your knickers on. I got extra. You'll get your milk." The boy stowed the polluted can and rummaged in the back of his cart. He pulled out another tin, and on inspection found the milk untainted. "This one's good. Hold out your jug."

Henry held the container and watched the fresh milk fill it to the brim. Mollified, he managed a brief smile as the delivery boy continued on his way. He paused for a moment to glare at the red sky, and the still burning silhouette of the HMS Purgatory on the river. Then he scurried back inside his lodging house.

"Here's the milk, Mrs. Pinch." He shouted down the corridor and followed the echo into the kitchen. He placed the jug on the table.

"Good." A scrawny grey-haired woman with one red eye glanced at the jug and then gave it a sniff. "Don't smell. That's a change. Breakfast'll be ready in a bit. Fried herring and eggs." She grinned. "The hen laid decent size eggs last night. Shells are grey too, not black like they 'ave been. Herring didn't turn,

182

neither. Or talk back like yesterday. I bloody hate having to kill my breakfast after it's already been done by the fishmongers."

Henry gave a snort. "I think they come out of the water dead, Mrs. Pinch, the fishmongers have naught to do with it." At her glowing red-eyed glare, he hastily added, "But I know what you mean. All the brimstone and hellfire's played havoc with the livestock." He gave a sigh. "Glad to hear the hen's on the mend, though. Them eggs the past few days tasted a bit like match-heads they did."

"I know. Nothing to be done, though, and the taste won't kill yer. Not like some taints." She rubbed the corner of her red eye and Henry remembered the month of her sickness, the brimstone infection that nearly killed her and left her scarred. Then she snorted, and snapped at him, "Now go rouse that lackadaisical friend of yourn and get back here to eat. Can't be late for the Whitechapel line, and the two of you need something in your bellies, walking patrol duty all day."

Henry shuffled off to obey, wandering down the dilapidated hallway to the room of his friend Jim Dunn. He knocked on the slightly ajar door, with a "breakfast's ready" and a quick peek inside. His friend sat on the bed in his Whitechapel Corps uniform, head lowered, his eyes staring at a spot on the floor. Jim grunted a greeting and got to his feet. Henry scuttled back as the door opened.

"Fine morning, ain't it, Jim? Sulphur smell's hardly noticeable today."

"One day's same as the other." Jim moved past Henry, shuffling his feet against the worn rug in the hallway.

"Bad night, then?" Henry nearly reached out a hand but thought better of the gesture.

"Had worse, but yeah. Dreamed again. Back to before I came here, when I was..." His words trailed off, but Henry knew what Jim meant.

"Those days is gone. Them papist priests took care of you. Got rid of the thing. You're right as rain now."

183

"Am I? Still got the memories. Unspeakable things. No priest is ever taking that away."

Henry let out a small sigh at the sight of his friend's dejected face. "Can't change the past, can't do anything but keep living." This time he did reach out and patted Jim's shoulder. "Things'll get better. 'Sides, we got herring for breakfast. They'll put you to rights. Nothing like fried herring to cheer a man."

Jim finally grinned at Henry. "True enough. Simple pleasures, and all that. Come then, let's eat."

The pair ambled to breakfast, laughing and chatting with Mrs. Pinch between bites of food and taking care not to spill on their uniforms. Then they said goodbye and headed off to catch the company troop carriage for the Whitechapel Defense Station. Henry snitched two slightly shrivelled apples on his way out to feed to the carriage horses, Roscoe and Bucephalus.

They rode the carriage in silence, perched on a spot on the roof and trying not to cough from the smell of sulphur in the air. Conversation from the other volunteer soldiers inside wafted upwards and the chatter mixed with the clatter of the wheels on the cobblestone streets. Henry smiled at the overheard complaints about food, wives and tedium of patrol duty.

Atop the carriage, they jostled against other men as they bumped along, grunting and bracing against the vehicle until they rolled to a stop. Then the carriage emptied of men and moved off. Henry and Jim walked down the street towards the headquarters building.

"Well, if it ain't the great heroic Jim Dunn, Defender of the Tower! And his cohort, Henry Ellis. How you two fine gentlemen, today?" A nasal voice hailed them. The pair stopped and turned to see a fellow soldier, Nigel Plaskett.

Henry scowled as he watched Jim's face turn bleak, "Lay off, Nigel, you know he don't like mention of what happened at the Tower. 'Sides, we're no gentlemen. Just volunteers, same as you."

"Yeah, yeah, sorry." Nigel scuffed his toe along a thin patch of grass. "Shouldn't sneer. Jim did good, killing those demons, defending the Tower."

"Did my duty." Jim's quiet voice startled the other two. "That's all. And added to my collection of bad memories."

Nigel's face turned pale and abashed. "Oh." He chewed on his lip and added, "We all got those, I guess."

Jim nodded. "Yeah, we do." He smiled a bit. "No hard feelings."

"Thanks." Nigel scuffed his toe again, this time in the dust, and added, "A new royal dispatch's been posted. Things are looking better up north."

"Really? Come on, Jim let's go see."

Henry strode off with a wave to Nigel, Jim trailing, and made a beeline to the Whitechapel Volunteer Corps headquarters. He stopped to read the news bill tacked to the front of the building.

"Well, I'll be the devil! The Prince's Rifle Regiment defended York against an attack! And pushed a division of Fifth Circle Hellspawn back towards Hull! Bless Prince Bertie, the man's a born soldier, he is!"

Henry then grinned at Jim who asked, "What else does it say, any news of the Prime Minister?"

"Let me see...yeah, here it is. Looks like he's on the mend. The priests did an exorcism. Seems to have rid him of the demon possession." Henry chuckled. "That's good news. Leastwise the Queen won't have to get herself a new Prime Minister. She's got enough on her plate. I wonder if there's truth to that rumour she'll be leading the charge to retake Oxford."

Jim shook his head. "Doubt it. They wouldn't risk it. But she might come down and review the troops. Boost the morale. Those Oxford boys could use it."

"Maybe the sixth time will be the charm." Henry shrugged. "Last time they did get the holy water into the river. Wiped out a whole troop of the marching horde and got the lower town cleared."

185

"But they've never managed to come close to the university." Jim gave a small sigh. "Those damnable ghosts siding with Hell. That's what's the problem."

"True words, Jim." Henry nodded at his friend. "Bloody academics. Can't trust them, alive or dead." He checked the dispatch again. "Don't seem to be much else. The Kent boys are holding the line and the Cornwall defence took down a pack of Hell Hounds again." He chuckled again. "Wouldn't want to tangle with that bunch. And that's it, so I guess we best report in for duty."

They entered the building, an old tavern requisitioned as a military headquarters, and reported to the sergeant checking names for the daily roster. He looked at them with a sour glare and raised a pen.

"Names?"

"Volunteer Private Henry Ellis and Squad Commander Jim Dunn, sir."

The sergeant scanned his lists and checked off their names. Then he studied another list. "Dunn, you're in charge of 5th Squad today, with street patrol. Ellis, you're in 5th Squad today as well. The rest of your men are waiting in Black Lion Yard." The sergeant put down his pen with a sigh. "We had a report last night. Some jeweller shops in that area were fire-bombed with brimstone. Buildings got scorched and damaged, but no injuries. Looks like we've got demon infiltrators there stirring up trouble." The sergeant cast a final glare. "Get to it then!

Henry and Jim saluted and hurried off to join the waiting squad. Six men milled together in the street, smoking, chatting, or kicking pebbles in front of brimstone scarred businesses, some with boarded-up windows. They snapped to attention as Jim and Henry walked up and formed a line. Henry joined them as Jim faced the men and addressed his troops.

"As you can see, there was an incident last night, and that means demons are loose here in our part of the city. It's up to us to make sure they don't get up to more mayhem. So be sharp on patrol today, boys, and don't let any of those possessed bastards get past us."

A chorus of "Yes, sir!" answered Jim and he led the way down the street, the men moving into patrol formation.

***

Midday found Henry perched on an abandoned crate sniffing a purchased meat pie for taint whilst Jim leaned against an alley wall. He took a bite, then wolfed down the apparently edible pie. As Henry licked the crumbs and grease from his fingers, a small noise attracted his attention. He looked up the street and noticed one of his fellows confronting a civilian.

Henry nudged Jim, who also glanced at their comrade-in-arms. "What's Little Tom on about over there?"

Little Tom had stopped a gentleman dressed in a scruffy coat and a bowler hat, and was waggling his gun at the man and glaring.

Jim returned Henry's nudge, with an order. "Find out what he's doing."

Henry scrambled to his feet and grumbled under his breath, "Bloody youngsters, thinking they can harass folk."

Henry took a step into the street to intervene when Tom yelled, "State your business!" Henry heard a loud growl and then Tom abruptly jumped backward, screaming, "Infiltrator! We got an infiltrator!"

The entire company snapped to alert, watching in horror as the intruder sloughed off his skin in smoking chunks of flesh and fire. Little Tom screamed again—this time in pain—as flaming debris hit him and he went down.

Henry shouted, "Hellbeast!" as Jim gave the order to the squad to open fire. The air erupted with the thunderous discharge of their rifles and the acrid smell of gunpowder as dozens of consecrated bullets engraved with holy symbols slammed into the infernal creature. The echo of sizzling and thuds cracked the air along with the pong of sulphur.

The creature roared and fell to all fours leaking black fluid and embers. It tried to crawl past a writhing Tom, its claws scraping gouges across the cobblestones.

"Fire again!" Jim shouted another command. "Kill the bloody thing!"

Another volley of bullets pierced the Hellbeast, silencing its growls for good. At Jim's nod, Henry walked over and nudged the scaly corpse with his gun bayonet, staying clear of the head and claws. It didn't move and he breathed a sigh of relief.

Henry shouted back to his fellows. "The thing's been sent back! Naught but the human shell left." Then he shifted to check on a moaning Little Tom as the rest of the squad moved forward. "Tom's burned up some, but he'll live."

"That's good." Jim knelt down beside Henry and Tom. "We'll get a medic down here, son." Jim turned his head. "Rollins, go fetch a medic and report this in. We'll need clean up and the higher-ups will want confirmation of infiltration."

With a relieved look and a "Yes, sir", Rollins took off running. As he left, the remaining men milled round Tom, guns raised, and avoided looking at the demon corpse. Anxiety coursed high and Tom's nerve-wracking moans only made the mood worse.

Henry heard Jim whisper, "I hope Rollins gets back soon." He eyed the twitchy men and silently hoped the same thing.

***

Rollins' return brought Tom medical attention and his groans subsided as opium was administered to relieve his pain. Henry heard sighs of relief pass among the men. At least until a new voice spoke up.

"Blast it! That's the fourth one this week! Bloody fiends are planning something!"

All eyes turned to the speaker. A captain, standing with his aide, staring at the demon body being wrapped in canvas for disposal.

The aide slipped a small notepad and pencil from his pocket and replied. "Indeed, sir. Mammon's spies have increased activities of late." He jotted something on his pad while being ignored by his captain, who continued ranting.

"God, I hate this war. Look at the poor bugger. Nothing left but char. Damn Hellbeast class demons. Never leave their hosts alive."

"No, sir." The aide responded. "Rum bastards the lot of them. At least with the upper-class echelon of demons, you have the possibility of exorcism. Far more sporting."

Several men around them squirmed, but neither man seemed to notice until Jim cleared his throat.

The captain frowned. "I suppose we should finish up here. Anyone get a look at the host before you opened fire?" He shot a quizzical look at the assembled.

"The injured man, sir. Tom Perkins." Jim nodded at Little Tom, being trundled off on a stretcher.

"He'll live?"

Another nod from Jim.

"Good." The captain turned to his aide. "Make a note to visit this Perkins later. We may have some luck and he can describe this scorched bastard well enough to identify him off the list of the missing civilians."

"Yes, sir." The aide nodded, scribbling on his notepad.

"Well, that's it then." The captain sniffed. "You men! Back on patrol!"

Jim saluted and ushered his men back down the street, glad to be rid of the captain.

***

Come the evening, Henry and Jim sat in his room discussing the day's events. Neither ate much supper, and Jim was in a particularly melancholy mood. He slumped in his chair staring at a glass of cheap gin. Henry looked at him, wondering how to cheer his friend.

189

Jim sighed. "Today brought it all back. That could have been me, had my luck been worse." A low cry escaped his lips. "I can't stop seeing it all in my head. What happened at the Tower... and after. The memories keep playing like a perverted zoetrope." He pushed off the bed and started pacing. "The Hell Hounds attacking, the fight, the victory. Me standing over one of the beast's corpses as the other thing walked out of the shadows." Jim shuddered. "It was all glowing crimson eyes and smoulder inside a human being." Jim stopped and whirled, looking Henry in the eyes. "I didn't even hesitate, didn't think of the poor bugger the demon was using. Just plunged my bayonet in his guts. I took *pride* in it. Until it was my turn. Until I was the one possessed."

Jim curled his fingers into tight fists. "I don't know why the fiendish thing decided on me. Maybe revenge for the other spawn I killed, maybe it just tried to survive. Maybe it sensed something in me, something evil." Jim walked over to his armchair and flopped down. "I killed four of my men before someone doused me with holy water. I can't describe the pain of that moment, but I welcomed it. I don't remember nothing after that, until I woke up in the church, the priest standing over me, trying to exorcise the beast."

Henry stared at his friend. "I'm sorry, Jim. Truly."

"I know Henry, and that helps, it does. Having someone to talk to about what happened. Everyone thinks I'm some hero, Defender of the Tower. You know the truth. That's why I need you to know something else as well." Jim leaned forward. "I don't ever want to feel that helpless again, watching my body do things I had no control over. And seeing its thoughts, the bits of Hell it showed me..." Jim shuddered again. "I can never get that out of my head." He looked up at Henry, anger and horror reflected in his eyes. "That's why I joined back up. After the exorcism. They would've let me go, but I wasn't having it. I want to find it, Henry, and kill it. I had demon killing bullets done up just to end it." He patted his sidearm, tucked in its holster, slung on the back of his chair. "I had them special made, silver-laced, blessed with holy water and salt, inscribed with some unnatural runes. Keep my revolver loaded with them. I know it's out there somewhere in London. I can feel it."

Henry frowned. "I'm all for revenge, but how would you know it, out of all of them? Especially that type of demon. It could be possessing anyone. Seems hopeless."

"It brands its hosts. Scored its mark right into the flesh of my arm. A crescent moon under three claw marks." He rolled up the left sleeve of his shirt and displayed a faint scar. "See. It was brighter, all red and glowing, when I was possessed, but the mark's still there. I find that on someone else, I find it."

Henry stared at the scar, and swallowed hard, his guts churning at the thought of what branded Jim. "Right. I'll keep my eye out too. If we see it, we'll kill the thing."

"You're a good friend, Henry. The only good thing I found in this war." Jim saluted with his glass and took a swig of liquor. "When you say it, I almost think it'll happen someday."

***

Two days later, Henry and Jim were back on patrol in Whitechapel. Several more demonic incidents had occurred and the fear and tension rolled through the streets like the morning fog off the river. Rumours of a full-scale invasion had both citizens and soldier on edge.

"Stay alert, men. We—" The remainder of Jim's words went forever unsaid as a warning bell clanged, splitting the air in an unholy clamour. Jim and his men scrambled to the side of the street as several Volunteer Corps wagons raced by, horses galloping as if their tails were on fire.

As the vehicles sped by, they all heard shouts:

"It's an invasion!"
"The Tower has fallen!"
"Marching hordes swarming in from the river!"
"Demons all the way to Whitechapel Road!"

191

"To arms, men! Follow those wagons!" Jim's command galvanized the men and Henry's guts tightened in fear and anticipation as the squad dashed down the street towards Whitechapel Road. His fingers tightened their grip on his rifle as they burst into a scene of chaos.

The howl of Hell Hounds sounded above the screams of men and the snapping sizzle of other hell-born beasts. The crack of rifle shots and revolvers mixed with the screeching demons wearing the shredded skins of possessed men and women. The stench of sulphur filled Henry's nose and burned his lungs. His boots slipped on bloody cobblestones as he waded into the fray, shooting at the enemy, his heart beating a wild drumbeat.

He emptied his rifle into the advancing hordes until the gun clicked on an empty chamber. He fumbled to reload, fingers scrabbling in his ammunition pouch, barely missing being chomped on by a hell-beast. He rammed the bayonet through the skull of the three-horned, six-eyed creature and pulled it out in a waft of sulphur and smoke. The thing fell dead at his feet and Henry thrust more bullets in his rifle's magazine.

He looked around, his squad nowhere in sight, his position now wedged behind other soldiers retreating from a demon onslaught. The strategic withdrawal pushed him back in a wave of scurrying men until the company reassembled rank and file for a new defence. With no other choice, Henry joined the line and opened fire on the invading demons and their beasts.

The reverberating boom of gunfire echoed in his ears, not quite masking the inhuman shrieks as the horde advanced against the hail of bullets. The stink of sulphur made him cough and a haze of smoke encircled his head as he fired at his enemy. They fell, creature upon creature, the beasts climbing over corpses, pressing forward until the click of an empty chamber sounded again in his rifle. With shaking fingers he reloaded, watching others engage in hand-to-hand combat, only to be shredded by the claws of things that crawled from the foul pits of Hell. He shoved his last bullet in the rifle's magazine, raising both the gun and his head. He stared into red, blazing eyes and a grin that used to be human.

Henry pulled the trigger without thinking, a bullet smashing into the flesh of the possessed man. He fired again, and again, two more bullets slamming into the chest of his enemy. He took aim to fire another, but the man went down in smouldering embers, whatever demonic spirit possessing him burned away or fled.

Only then did Henry realize he heard hoarse cheers, and the wave of advancing demons were gone. Bodies littered Whitechapel Road, but the marching hordes of Hell were retreating. Somehow they won. Somehow he survived. Henry took gulps of acrid air, coughing, hands shaking, still gripping his rifle.

He listened to murmurs and snatches of conversation around him, and muttered prayers of thanks. To his left, a small fire burned in the street: the remains of an incinerated corpse. Other bodies surrounded it, and he watched survivors crawling away over spent bullet casings and moving past the carcasses of demons. Suddenly he knew: he needed to get away. To leave the sight of the carnage. His feet moved and he started walking.

As he staggered through the aftermath, Henry ducked the smouldering embers floating in the air and rubbed his nose against the choking smell. Bodies spread out across the ground, both human and demon, and some halfway in-between. He saw the corpses of men he had joked with only hours before. Around him, he heard moans and screams, saw his wounded comrades. Henry tried to look away, but it was impossible. Everywhere he saw the injured: some missing limbs or with hellfire burns, others bitten and bleeding or wearing claw marks gashed into their guts.

"God save us." The whisper slipped out, even as he wondered if God had abandoned them to the forces of Hell. He knew the priests and the ministers would say different, but standing here, in this street of slaughter, Henry felt like God had turned his back. A hand touched his shoulder and he whirled.

"Hey, it's me, Nigel." The man took a step back, hands raised. Henry relaxed.

"Good to see you made it. You seen Jim? I got separated from my squad. I should find him and any that's left."

Nigel shook his head. "I got pinned down, lost my squad too. They're herding survivors over towards Aldgate. That's where I was headed."

"Sounds good."

Henry and Nigel picked their way through the bodies, walking down Whitechapel Road as the medics and corpsman carrying stretchers for the dead passed them. Henry sighed.

"Did we win, Nigel? I don't even know."

"I expect we did. Leastwise, the demons retreated. Though why they attacked..." Nigel let the words trailed off, and Henry nodded.

"Yeah. None of it makes sense."

Nigel suddenly stopped, his face turning pale and a sickly expression settling across his features. "Henry," The name came out of his mouth slowly, hesitantly. "That body over there...the uniform... I think... doesn't it look familiar?" Nigel pointed, his hand shaking, to a bloody corpse of a man with brown hair and a face Henry recognized.

"Jim." The whisper was soft and empty, flying away with the last bit of Henry's hope. He moved closer to make certain and stared down at his friend's lifeless countenance. Looking at the corpse, Henry fought back tears. Jim was dead.

Henry stared at his face, so serene and peaceful.

"Why you smiling, Jim? Why?"

Henry didn't understand until he glanced at the body next to his friend. A dead man, clearly from the enemy ranks, with half a dozen bullet holes in his chest...

And the brand of a crescent moon under three claw marks, clear on his wrist.

Wales was its own mistress, less troubled in the early days. Chapel was strong, and after centuries of English meddling, communities were suspicious of outsiders. More than one scouting demon found itself cornered by Welsh women with sharp sickles. But the fighting spread, and the sickness, and soon the Welsh border was either aflame or burdened under the weight of strange growths and even stranger creatures. Cardiff's water was thick with sulphur, and pitched battles began in the larger Welsh towns.

Back on the border, each aspect of the Incursion had to be dealt with as it came, and once again old ways had to be remembered...

YAHN TAN TETHERA

J. A. Ironside

Cadi Owens didn't give the war a thought as she leant into the sharp autumn wind. The fighting had been confined to the coasts and cities, and even though her brother had joined the South Wales Borderers eight months ago, the war seemed distant. Information had been sparse, and what did arrive in the Border, had stretched local credulity. Inhuman invaders? Supernatural creatures? *Demons?* Border folk were stoic and unexcitable in general. They spoke English when required to go to the sheep market in Hereford, or Welsh at the one in Abergavenny y Fenni. At home they spoke the inscrutable Border dialect – a mixture of the two and some much older language. For the most part Border folk kept themselves to themselves, and were Her Majesty Queen Victoria's loyal subjects only insofar as they paid their levies and caused no trouble if they were not interfered with. They would wait and see as far as the truth of war reports went.

Cadi was glad Pa wasn't with her today. The cold and damp always made his leg pain him, and then her normally even-tempered father gained all the contrary moodiness of a wounded bullock. She skipped back and forth between countries as if she were still a child, rather than a grown woman of nineteen. Shadow frisked around her feet, leaping side to side with her, tongue lolling in a doggy grin that said this was fine sport. Blue, a much older dog, trotted just ahead, every so often pausing and casting a glance of disdain back over her haunches.

"Come on, Blue, you're not so old as all that." Cadi made another neat leap as Shadow crashed heedless through a puddle and drenched her skirts. For answer, Blue curled her lip a little and lifted her leg at a tree stump, apparently considering Cadi to be wasting time when they ought to be moving the sheep. Cadi chuckled, adopting a more appropriate gait as they reached the village.

Wych Hill had only one street, cottages staggered at intervals either side of a narrow, unpaved road that was fast turning to silty mud in the drizzle. She heard children's voices raised in a singsong chant before she saw them.

"You're in Cymru, I'm in Lloegyr,
I know you for a saucy rogue!
Yahn. Tan. Tethera.
Methera. Mumph.
Hithier. Lithier!
Your house is straw, mine is gold,
In the winter, you'll be cold!
Anver. Danver. Dic!"

Two teams spread out along either side of the street. Every time the caller – currently a skinny girl called Beca Carrag, whose pinafore skirts were mud-splashed to the knee – gave a count, all the children jumped to the opposite side of the street. If you fell in the mud, you were out. If the caller forgot the count, then she was out and another took over. The winning team was the one who made it to the end with the most players still 'in'. Cadi counted the children silently, almost without being aware of it, and frowned. Over half were missing.

"Where's your Billy?" she called to Beca.

The girl jumped, just missing the mud. "He's sickly. So's th'others."

The light didn't change, Cadi was sure of that, but it felt like a shadow passed over the scene and a cold foreboding gripped her. And something – something she only half remembered? – dangled for a moment on the edge of her awareness like sheep's wool caught on hawthorn. She shook the feeling off. "Give him my best." Children sickened and grew well again. Why should it bother her? Behind her the chant began again.

Cadi had once asked her Granny Owens why the song, which was so old no one remembered where it had come from,

197

used the old shepherd's language. Granny had given Cadi one of her wizened, bright-eyed, gap toothed smiles.

"Where is our farm, girl?" Cadi, a wee slip of seven or eight, had been confused. Granny had cackled. "The Shepherd's Tongue is used for counting the things that matter, Catrin. Sheep, grandchildren…and the number of steps from one country to another."

She'd repeated Granny's words to Pa later that evening. He'd told her to fetch the family bible. Most people who had such a book used the blank flyleaves to record the progression of the family – deaths, marriages, births – from one generation to the next. There *was* an Owens family tree but there was also a beautifully drawn map, inked in by one of Pa's great uncles.

Pa had pointed to a wavy line. "This is the Usk and here is the Wye."

"Is that our farm?" Cadi had jabbed a small finger at point between the two rivers.

"That's right." Pa's smile had folded deep creases around his eyes in his weather beaten face. "Now, in which country do we rear our flocks?"

"Wales? High Meadow is in Powys… Oh, but the low pasture is in England?"

Pa had traced another line with a blunt tipped finger. "The Border runs right down the centre of Wych Hill. Houses on the left are in Wales. On the right, they're in England. Don't make no earthly sense when it's just a line on a bit o' paper. Wych Hill was here long before the Border between two grousing countries was decided. Be here long after the Border's forgot, most like. Owens Farm sits smack in the middle of the Border."

The game was all mummery for the skirmishes the Border folk had seen between England and Wales in the old days. Cadi had laughed, pleased she finally understood. But the idea of the border, the thin, invisible line of division, had sunk into her mind that day. And sometimes, when she was drifting off to sleep, it seemed to her that the Border was not a barrier, but a crack. A narrow aperture through which the dark creatures of Granny's tales issued forth to cause mischief amongst the living.

Granny's voice sounded in her memory. *The devil is real, Catrin. Those who live elsewhere are always watching with envious eyes...*

Blue gave a wheezing yip, recalling Cadi to the present.

"Alright y'old bossy boots, I'm coming." Cadi said, then realised Shadow was pressed against her skirts, shivering in fright. Blue's slate coloured fur rose in ridges along her stocky body. "Why are you all affrighted, Blue?" The lane seemed suddenly dark, the hawthorn and hazel hedge oppressive. The air was colder than frost, almost slimy. Unbidden, other memories rose in Cadi's mind. Tales Granny had told her as a small child. *Galleytrots* and *Ddafud ddu*. An icy-dank gust stroked Cadi's neck and a stench of decay rose, bringing another story sharply to mind. One she couldn't fully remember but which filled her with nameless terror. She thought she might be sick as the stench ripened into full blown sweet putrefaction. Blue gave a sudden low growl raising the hairs on Cadi's arms. It was here. There was something really here. Something that meant her harm...

She tried to speak but the words died in her throat as if all air now belonged to whatever was making that rotten-egg-spoiled-meat-sulphur stench. She brandished her crook in both hands like a staff, sucked in a breath and gagged. "Who's there?" Shadow whimpered, almost retreating under her skirts. All the performers of Cadi's childhood nightmares rose and fell behind her eyes. *Cú Anwnn*, white as death with jaws like a steel trap. *Diod Gwaed* – the blood drinkers who haunted byways waiting for lone travellers to prey on. *Cysgwyr ar y stryd* – the restless sleepers. And *sluagh*...

When it felt as if she might faint from lack of air, or from oppressive, unnameable fear, the feeling faded leaving nothing except a vague sense of foreboding. Blue trotted back to Cadi, looking up with a little whine, then trotted forward again. She glanced back at her mistress.

199

"I don't know why you won't just give in and talk, Blue," Cadi muttered shakily, following the dog with Shadow still pressed to her calves. "Plain as pie-crust you want me to look at summat. T'would save time if you just said so."

Blue stopped abruptly, shoving her nose forward like a pointer with a whuffly snort of disgust. Cadi saw a scrap of brilliant red. She crouched down beside the dog, resting a hand in the coarse grey fur of Blue's ruff.

It was some sort of weed. Redder than holly berries, thin strands creeping out from fleshy leaves. The stem shone with slime. The spread fronds weren't even as wide as Cadi's hand but she felt an instinctive shudder of disgust. She'd never seen the plant before, which should be impossible. There wasn't a root, bud or leaf Cadi hadn't known since earliest childhood. Not that grew wild anyhow. She leaned a little closer, trying to examine the plant like Miss Morgan had taught her. Cadi wondered if even the indefatigable schoolmistress had ever seen anything like it.

If it wasn't for the colour, it would belong in the salt marshes at the other end of the Usk. Miss Morgan had taken Cadi's class there once and shown them a pallid, repulsive plant called 'Corpse Candle', which didn't need sun or rain, but fed on the bodies of animals rotting in the salt marsh. Dilys Morgan called herself a 'naturalist' and the inhabitants of Wych Hill regarded her as an eccentric, though on the whole, one they were proud to own. She was always examining bits of bones or plants found in the marsh. Her small library of books was controversial. And then there was all that business with the foundling sixteen years ago.

Cadi liked Miss Morgan, who'd had been very disappointed when Cadi had said she'd be staying to mind Owens Farm, rather than going away to attend one of the new ladies colleges. It had rather put a crimp in their friendship but Miss Morgan was clearly the person to consult in this instance.

"I'll take her a sample." Cadi reached out to break off a stem but Blue growled, snapping at her fingers. "Blue! Get on you daft dog!" She nursed her nipped hand, frowning, but she

200

didn't reach for the plant again. "Come on. The sheep'll be moving themselves at this rate." Blue seemed happy enough to leave the red weed behind and as they moved up into the meadow, Shadow became his old rambunctious self.

But the red weed played on Cadi's mind and she took a circuitous route uphill to check the new pasture. As soon as they were through the gate, the dogs let her know what she would find – Shadow once more cowering and Blue near snarling. There were splashes of scarlet amidst the verdant green like some knight of legend had slain the Questing Beast there, liberally splashing the ground with its blood. It grew oddly. Not scattered in greater and lesser clumps like gorse or bramble, but in tufts of varying sizes along some invisible line. As if a giant knife had wounded the hill side.

Cadi's disquiet grew. "I can't take the sheep in there. They'll have to go to Cooper's Barrow." She spun away from the tainted field, running headfirst into something warm and solid. The girl had come up unseen and unheard behind her, apparently either undetected by the dogs or untroubling them. Cadi bit back a rude word, trying not to glare at the girl. She knew her, of course. Everyone knew everyone in Wych Hill. Probably everyone this side of Hereford would recognise Aneira because she didn't look at all like one of the Border folk. She was taller than some of the men, and very pale, her skin never picking up the slightest tint from the sun. Cadi felt the usual choked mixture of guilt and awkwardness looking at her. They'd played together as small children, always together, close as sisters – at least until Granny put a stop to it.

Aneira gazed at Cadi uncertainly, twisting a long hank of silver-pale hair between her fingers. Cadi took an involuntary step back and slipped. Aneira's hands flashed out like white swifts, too fast to see almost, steadying her. Cadi swallowed and shrugged the pale hands off. "What do you want?"

Aneira's large, violet eyes registered hurt at her ungracious tone.

Cadi felt a pinch behind her breast bone. "Sorry. You gave me a fright."

Aneira shrugged and her pale hair rippled. It was the oddest hair, silky fine and almost white. Aneira never plaited it and it never tangled in revenge. Cadi privately swore she'd seen it subtly lift and resettle itself like a pelt. As far as Cadi knew, Aneira had never spoken. Not once in the last sixteen years. She had very expressive eyes, though, and a way of communicating what she wanted you to know without making a sound. Heat crept along Cadi's jaw as the girl continued to hold her gaze. Aneira bent and scratched Blue's head, as if she'd seen Cadi's discomfort and was giving her a moment to compose herself. Blue received the attention with the delight of a lively puppy, not a dignified working dog of advanced years. Animals inexplicably took to Aneira. People, perhaps not so inexplicably, did not. Miss Morgan had found her alone and abandoned, barely more than baby, on one of her trips to the salt marsh, and in a move that had scandalised the villagers, adopted the girl. Aneira had never really been accepted though, merely tolerated. Only fear of the schoolmistress had stopped the crueller children throwing stones at the interloper. Granny Owens had warned Cadi to stay away from Aneira, although she would never say why.

Aneira gave Blue a last pat and straightened.

"Did you come to help me move the flock?" To Cadi's irritation, Blue and Shadow danced at the girl's skirts, happy to abandon her and go wherever the silent girl led. "I'm taking them to Cooper's Barrow."

Aneira canted her head to one side. *Why?*

"There's all this slimy red weed and I don't want the flock eating it."

Aneira's mouth tightened.

"Do you want to come?" Cadi said.

A rare smile curved Aneira's lips. Cadi whistled the dogs back to her heels, wondering if she'd been trying to make the other girl smile, and what it meant if she had.

It was the fastest Cadi had ever moved the flocks from one pasture to another in all her years of sheep farming. She could have done without the dogs entirely thanks to Aneira, but it was one of the strangest things she'd ever seen. Aneira walked into the field and stood there for a few moments, motioning Cadi to wait. Cadi watched with growing amazement as the sheep gathered around tall, pale girl. When Aneira had the attention of the full flock, she turned back to Cadi and nodded. The dogs came forward without any whistled commands, running the perimeter of the gathered flock. Not that there were any stragglers for the dogs to round up. Mouth rather dry, Cadi led the way and in no time at all, they were at Cooper's Barrow. Even the counting didn't take long, almost as if each sheep politely waited its turn to go into the field.

"*Yahn. Tan. Tethera...*"

Whenever Cadi reached *jigif* – one score – Aneira had scratched a line in the mud with the point of a stick, and they began at *Yahn* again. The last ewe hung back. Cadi whistled Blue up from her crouch but Aneira laid her hand on Cadi's arm and shook her head.   "Why mustn't that ewe go with the others?"

Aneira bit her lip, the corners of her eyes tightening in concentration. She laid a hand over forehead, then repeated the gesture over her heart, then pointed at the ewe with a grim expression, shaking her head once more.

"You think she has some sickness?"

Aneira frowned. *Yes.*

"I can keep her in the little fold out here? Until I know if she's sickening?"

Aneira nodded.

Puzzled but certain she was doing the right thing, Cadi shut the lone ewe up in the little pen. Blue sneezed in canine approval and she realised that for all the dog had obeyed her command, Blue hadn't wanted to approach the ewe. Aneira caught Cadi's arm, gesturing back towards Wych Hill.

"Alright. Let's head back."

***

Miss Morgan brandished a newspaper at Cadi as soon as Aneira led her through the schoolmistress' cottage door. "Have you seen this, Catrin?" she demanded. "Aneira, put the kettle on the hook, there's a good girl."

"No, Miss Morgan," Cadi said, uncomfortably aware that she'd never seen the schoolmistress het up before. Even stranger to see Aneira bustling about, doing mundane tasks when she looked so ethereal. Like watching a unicorn pull a plough. Cadi bit her lip, glad Miss Morgan was too distracted to notice her discomfort.

"Read this."

Cadi took the newspaper. It was several weeks out of date and her eyes grew wide as fragments of sentences swam up out of the close set type. "London has been attacked? And Plymouth? Where did you get this?"

"I went all the way to Hereford and haggled. It seems many printing presses have met with accidents." Miss Moran's heavy black brows drew together. "Most of the major port towns and cities have suffered heavy casualties." Miss Morgan paused again, nostrils flaring alarmingly over the grim pressed white line of her lips. "We are not winning the war. This truly isn't an enemy we've seen before."

Cadi sank into a chair, thinking of her brother. Of that last strange letter Garth had sent her weeks ago.

'Cadi, but this is an enemy like no other. There's no reason to think they'll come so far inland but you must be vigilant. Watch and stay safe...'

"Do you think they really are...demons?" Cadi said.

Miss Morgan gave her a very grave look. "I don't put much trust in talk of magic but why shouldn't there be an undiscovered genus or two? An entire race...several races...coming from their own land. Did you know the farmers of Edge lost almost their entire flocks last night?"

"Last night? But how?"

204

"The shepherd who brought the news was near hysterical. I have suspicions, farfetched as they will seem. But you spend almost all of your time out of doors. Have you noticed anything strange?"

Cadi didn't miss the way Miss Morgan avoided her question. "There's this red weed. Never seen anything like it. Growing all strange in a line. I was going to bring you a bit but Blue snapped at me."

Miss Morgan's dark eyes narrowed. "Show it to me."

***

The children weren't playing in the street when the three women emerged from the schoolmistress' cottage, with the dogs trotting at their heels. Cadi supposed the children had gone home to be scolded for getting so mucky, before being given their supper.

"Miss Morgan!" Cadi recognised Beca's mother. "Oh, Miss Morgan! Please will you come?"

"Mrs Carrag? Whatever is the matter?" Miss Morgan said.

Cadi felt a small warm hand clutch her arm and looked up to find Aneira as wide-eyed with suppressed fear as the dogs now shivering at her ankles. "What is it?"

Aneira didn't reply and Miss Morgan's voice rose, making both girls look at her sharply. "What do you mean 'Billy's been sleeping since yesterday'?" she demanded.

Cadi winced thinking that this wasn't a tactful way to speak to an anxious mother but Mrs Carrag was too worried to be offended. "He went up to bed early last night and didn't want any supper. Now I can't wake him. No fever and he looked alright. But now he's so still..." Mrs Carrag wiped her eyes. "Mrs Williams said two of hers are the same. And Cery Bragg's oldest."

"Have you sent for Dr Grey?" Miss Morgan's face was grim.

"My husband's gone to fetch him now. Can't you have a look at Billy, Miss Morgan? Put my mind at rest?"

Miss Morgan laid a comforting hand on Mrs Carrag's shoulder. "Dr Grey is the best person to look after Billy, and I have something I must do–"

"Oh please! It'll be hours before he gets here."

Miss Morgan gave a reluctant nod. "I can't promise I'll be able to help."

Cadi motioned for Shadow and Blue to lie down outside the cottage, glancing at Aneira. The tall girl shook her head, clearly intending to wait with the dogs. As Cadi followed Miss Morgan into the Carrag's cottage, she wondered what exactly Aneira knew that she did not.

Billy might be asleep but he was definitely not at rest. His thin little face was pinched and though he lay deathly still, there was a tension about him. His lips were peeled back from his teeth turning the cheerful row of half-grown incisors and erupting canines into a demonic sneer.

Mrs Carrag watched Miss Morgan examine him. "It's bad, isn't it?"

Miss Morgan swallowed. "I don't know yet."

Cadi remembered how Aneira had refused to come in. How her dogs had been jumpy and fractious all day, the ewe that wouldn't go into the field. Standing there, in the Carrag boys' room, Cadi felt as if she was surrounded by dank, icy shadow. As if all the light had been extinguished and with light, hope. The air reeked sulphurously and a thin, dark line in her mine glowed red as berries and cracked slowly, inevitably wider...

"Come on, Cadi. The sooner we go, the sooner we have answers," Miss Morgan's crisp voice cut through the waking dream. Cadi followed her downstairs, resisting the urge to wipe her mouth with the cuff of her dress.

She sucked in great lungfuls of cool, fresh autumn air when they were back outside, unable to forget the still, tense way Billy had lain. The way he had bared his teeth. She thought about how many other children had fallen to this strange sleeping sickness and Granny Owen's voice mocked her from the recesses of her memory.

"The devil is real, Catrin..."

Cadi slammed the door hard on the thought and whistled for the dogs.

***

"It can't be the same weed," Cadi said. "It was nowhere near so grown earlier."

The hand span of red fronds now stretched from one side of the lane to the other like a stair runner. Or like...like *hands*.

"This is no natural plant," Miss Morgan began but Cadi had finally seen the shape of the danger and her stomach roiled.

"It's the Border," she said. "I don't know why but this red stuff is growing right along the Border."

"What are you saying, Catrin?"

Dimly, Cadi was aware of Aneira's hand slipping into hers, a silent offering of comfort. "The war's come to us. We're under attack."

"Explain your reasoning," Miss Morgan said in a schoolmarm tone that made Cadi automatically stand up straighter.

"It's the Border, isn't it? Neither one thing nor the other." Seeing that Miss Morgan didn't understand the connection she went on. "In Granny's stories, all the...*things* come through from the Between place. The Dead follow their own roads and other creatures... The Border is one big Between place. A crack in our world that they can come through. Maybe the crack's been too narrow before but they're pushing it open. S'what that red weed is for."

Aneira touched Miss Morgan's arm, nodding fiercely.

Miss Morgan's lips flattened into an unhappy line. "Yes, I think you're right."

"But why would they attack here? We've no army. Nothing except sheep and land and people who mind their own business."

207

Miss Morgan raised an eyebrow. "Why would they not attack here? Or any other farming community? If you want to take a country, isn't it easier if their army is ill fed and worn down? Or if they can't trust the communities they must trade with? Take the farms and the food, and you've half won the war."

Cadi's tongue felt thick and gluey in her mouth. "The...the *things*..."

"Demons, Catrin. Always call a thing by its proper name–"

A hissing, sucking noise from behind them made all three women turn. Blue leapt away from the red weed snarling and Shadow practically climbed Cadi's thighs, whimpering. They watched in horrified silence as a slime coated stolon pulled itself laboriously out of the wet mud and sent a questing tendril across the lane.

"It's alive..." Cadi breathed, well aware that this was a stupid observation.

"I think we should continue this conversation elsewhere." Miss Morgan's face was white in the gathering gloom. The small group headed back to the schoolmistress' cottage, where they huddled over hot cups of tea. Cadi had brought the dogs inside. Blue now lay, tense and wakeful, in front of the fire, tolerating Shadow's clingy nuzzling with greater forbearance than usual.

"It's a weapon as well," Miss Morgan said into the silence. Cadi exchanged glances with Aneira. "There was red staining on Billy's hands. I'd have to see the other sleepers but I'm willing to bet all of them had direct contact with the weed."

"You think the demons are trying to make us sick?" Cadi said. "But that doesn't sound very..."

"Demonic?" Miss Morgan suggested. "Think about it, Catrin. Invading armies have a long history of physically weakening the population they mean to oppress, whether that is in poisoning wells, destroying crops, or introducing sickness. Why should an army of demons be any different?"

"But my Granny Owens says–"

"Folk tales will not save us!" Miss Morgan snapped. "We need logic and strategy."

Cadi sat back in surprise. Of course the schoolmistress had been known to bridle at the old wisdom, just as Granny had been heard to mutter darkly over 'newfangled thinking'. Aneira had been smoothing rough patches on the crook. She set her knife down with a loud clack, giving her guardian a reproachful look.

Miss Morgan rubbed her eyes. "I'm sorry, Cadi. Your granny knows a lot but these aren't creatures out of old tales. Spitting on their shadows and turning to face the sun will not vanquish them. Those old stories got a lot wrong. Besides this is an organised force. Everything they are doing serves a greater plan."

"So what do you suggest we do?" Cadi said. "Wait for the demons to arrive and let them roll over us?"

"How do you fight a demon?" Miss Morgan meant it as a rhetorical question but Aneira stood abruptly making her chair screech on the stone floor. She looked for a moment like a doe at bay, then snatched up Cadi's crook, gesticulating fiercely.

This! You will use this! You!

She thrust the crook into Cadi's hands and made several more gestures, too fast and angry to follow. Cadi looked sidelong at Miss Morgan. Her fingers found new grooves on the rod, smooth and regular as if the girl had carved some sort of design.

"You want Cadi to see the demons off with her crook?" Miss Morgan sounded as if she felt she was saying something silly.

"I don't understand," Cadi whispered apologetically.

Aneira slumped back into her seat, eyes full of frustration. Cadi and Miss Morgan fell into a low rumination on what exactly the weed and the sickness might mean. Neither of them came up with a satisfactory hypothesis, and all the while Cadi felt Aneira's reproachful gaze upon her and felt sure she had missed something.

"I need to go home," Cadi said finally. "Pa'll be worried if I'm not back soon."

***

209

Aneira walked part of the way back to Owen's Farm. In the twilight Cadi thought she saw new splashes of red peeking out of the mud on Wych Hill's one street. The infection was spreading. And then they were out of the village and alone together on a lonely track winding uphill to the farm and Cadi's growing unease took another direction. Reforming itself to encompass the guilt she felt always around Aneira. How did you apologise for something you did ten years ago? Wasn't it too late then? And anyway it hadn't been Cadi, it had been Granny Owens.

As if sensing her discomfort and knowing the cause, Aneira pulled Cadi off the path, leading her to a disused barn. It was on Owens' land but it was too far from the pastures to be used regularly and had fallen into disrepair. She and Aneira had played here often as children. They'd been playing here the day Granny had turned Aneira away with furious words.

Pharisee's child.

The words were so clear in Cadi's mind. *Faery's get. Changeling.* She remembered how Aneira had stood, small and pale and trembling, eyes brimming with pleas she could not utter. And she remembered how she'd been too afraid to tell Granny she was wrong. Aneira had run away. They'd never played together again. Aneira had avoided Cadi as much as she avoided the other children after that. Shame rose hot and acidic in Cadi's throat. Perhaps she'd only been a child but she'd known it was wrong and she hadn't spoken out. Hadn't even asked Granny, letting months and years, and declining health and confusion muddle the answer until it Granny could no longer give it.

Then last summer, Aneira had happened upon Cadi trying to get a ewe out of a ditch and had stopped to help. Cadi had shared her lunch with her. After that Aneira had made several infrequent visits when Cadi was with the flocks. Sometimes she just watched from a distance but gradually, Cadi's grudging greetings had grown warmer. She'd stayed – a few minutes at first, then half an hour and then an hour. The girls had sat together companionably in the warm sun, looking down over the valley.

Cadi wanted to say that she'd never wanted to stop being friends. To say she was sorry for being weak. She drew a breath but Aneira had moved over to examine part of the ancient stone work and waved her over. Perhaps she had never expected an apology? It was an odd moment – Cadi dwelling on a past slight she had dealt, while Aneira had had a completely different purpose in taking her to the barn. She beckoned again, eager, excited even. Cadi rested her hand against the stone. Her fingertips traced the slashes, whorls and grooves cut into the stone and a wave of nostalgia lifted her. She and Aneira had discovered them when they played here. Markings in an ancient language, now long forgotten. Pa had once said it was writing used by the people who lived here before it was the Border, who spoke the language that came before the shepherd's tongue. For a moment the marks flared in Cadi's mind with the same eerie significance as the imaginary line of the Border had, but brilliant gold instead of ruby red.

Aneira laid a hand on her arm. *Remember?*

Cadi met Aneira's gaze and for a moment she couldn't breathe. She gently shrugged the hand off. "I still don't understand."

Aneira pursed her lips and led the way out of the barn, leaving Cadi once again with the feeling that she had missed something important.

"I need to go now."

The pale girl just looked at her, gaze almost hostile. Cadi kept herself to a brisk walk but all the way home she felt as if that hostile stare stabbed between her shoulder blades, making the cool night even colder.

"You've got a face on you like a Poll and Down ewe," Pa said caustically when Cadi shut the door behind her. "What ails you? Young man playing fast and loose, is he?" He eyed her damp, messy hair and the panting dogs.

Cadi frowned. "No, Pa. And let's not argue tonight. There's this red weed." She poured out the tale as she helped Granny to the table. It wasn't one of Granny's good days, she was more

211

confused than usual. More and more of late the sharp tongued, sharp minded old woman who'd raised Cadi when her mother died, seemed to fade back behind a vague and muddled stranger.

Pa was silent a moment when Cadi finished explaining. "She's a clever woman, that Dilys Morgan."

Nothing further seemed forthcoming. "Well? What do you think?"

Pa set his spoon down. "Doesn't matter what I think, Catrin."

"But–"

"Miss Morgan is likely right. But wars are also fought in making the enemy doubt and distrust each other, so their attention is turned inward instead of looking out for the next attack."

"Is that what you think is happening?"

Pa tamped the tobacco down in his pipe. "Hard to say. Best to watch and not make judgements. They'll be enough folk running scared if it's true. Or even if it's not."

"Never follow the Judas sheep," Cadi said a touch bitterly.

"Exactly." Pa smiled but it didn't touch his eyes. "Use them brains of yours and don't let no one decide aught for you."

"*Sluagh*," Granny said suddenly.

"What did you say, Granny?" Cadi said.

"Don't pay no mind. She's wandering again."

Granny Owens' eyes were bright and sharp. "The sheep, Cadi. Don't forget to count the sheep."

Cadi wasn't sure that Granny was wandering at all.

***

She couldn't sleep. Memories of the day rose whenever she shut her eyes. It felt as if a fire had started in the warm, damp thatch of a cottage. She knew the danger was there but not where exactly and by the time the smoke appeared it would be too late. The flames would leap from roof to roof and burn the village to the ground.

Count the sheep...

The ewe. The one Aneira had stopped her turning loose into the field. She should have gone back to check on her. Cadi threw off the blankets and got dressed. The dogs stayed close to her heels as she headed towards Cooper's Barrow. The utter silence was disquieting, as if the darkness was listening to her. The night wrapped around her, clinging like wet wool. There was no reason for the fear, Cadi had been out in the dark before after all. Sometimes all night by herself in lambing season. And yet as she arrived at the sheep fold, she knew with a prey animal's instinct that she wasn't alone. There were *things* in the dark. Unnatural things very carefully not making a sound.

The devil is real, Catrin...

She believed it. In that moment she believed it completely. Intelligent, alien beings that bore no love for human kind. Perhaps they sought souls, and their science was magic. Creatures of nightmare were invading her country. They had arrived here, in the Border, like fiends stepping out of the Between place in a bedtime story. Cadi felt them in the dark, watching her. Felt their hunger.

A harsh, skittering noise came out of the darkness. Blue growled. Shadowed skipped back, yipping. And something that might once have been a sheep crashed through the gate of the little fold. After all the thinking and fretting, all the attempts to puzzle out what shape the danger would take, Cadi wasn't prepared at all. She heard a faint bleat of distress from the flock high up on the barrow...and then a snarling mass of matted fleece, snapping teeth and sharp hooves tore through the wooden gate and lunged at her. Sheer instinct made her dive to one side. She caught a glimpse of burning red eyes, then Blue lunged for the demon sheep, snapping and growling. Shadow gave a howl of fear and joined the fray. The sheep lowered its head, snapping with fangs no grass eater should have, and Cadi watched stupidly, trying to force her mind into action.

There was a yelp of pain and Blue jerked, side-limping from a vicious bite to her hip. Shadow's yipping gained a hysterical quality as the sheep butted him aside and turned its attention on

Cadi. And still she couldn't make her frozen limbs move. Hell bright eyes. Curved fangs bared in a gaping maw of hunger. And the weight of its presence. Terror that pressed on her mind.

I'm going to be the first shepherd killed by a sheep...

A white hand reached out of the darkness and pulled her to her feet.

Aneira looked as incongruous as a stray shaft of moonlight at the bottom of a well. She had her gaze fixed furiously on the charging demonic sheep. At the last moment, she side-steeped and brought something down with violent crack on the beast's skull. There was a flash like lightning and a hideous cry from the ewe before it staggered a last few steps and fell to its knees. Cadi thought she saw something black and amorphous sliding away across the grass away from the sheep's belly but she couldn't be sure. She took a tentative step towards the now docile sheep but Aneira caught her arm and pulled her back. She thrust Cadi's crook into her hands, pointing towards Wych Hill.

"I left this at Miss Morgans," Cadi said. "How did you know...?" How did Aneira know she needed help, here, now?

Aneira tugged on her arm again.

"I have to check Blue over. And the ewe."

Aneira slashed both hands out sideways. *No Time.* She pointed again, then stiffened, clutching Cadi's arm. Something was happening in the village. Aneira gestured frantically. *Now! We must go now!*

Cadi whistled for the dogs, praying Blue would be able to keep up. They ran, feet almost numb with cold, cracking through the thin film of ice on puddles before squishing into the thick, cold mud beneath. She heard a crash and a whooping that grew louder. The night thickened like mist around Cadi until she felt as if she ran underwater and her mind finally began to work.

The red weed had widened the gap so the demons could come through but it had also made the children sick, and the sheep. Cadi was sure the flocks in Edge had eaten the weed and some had turned like her ewe and torn apart the others. Yet somehow Aneira smacking it with Cadi's crook had stopped it.

She remembered how her fingers had hooked in the ancient carved writing in the barn. Over that lay a memory of her fingers feeling the new grooves Aneira had carved into her crook. Impossibly through all of that, came the image of Beca Carrag counting...

The village was in chaos. Lamps swung wildly painting hell shadows on cottage walls. There was a group of villagers clumped across the street. Several families had their longbows out, arrows nocked. She saw guns too. What was going on?

"Cadi!" Several voices cried out at once. "Aneira." Miss Morgan stood with Pa, who carried his old fowling piece. No one was shooting though.

Aneira pulled her to a halt and Cadi's mind resolved the other half of the equation. There was a ragged group of half-grown shapes spread out across the street between her and the villagers. Cadi saw now why no one was shooting at the demons.

"Billy?" she gasped.

The boy whirled, reddened eyes flashing, teeth bared. He didn't look like a child. He looked like a fiend. His hands opened and closed convulsively as if he couldn't control his desire for violence.

"Mother of God," Cadi cried.

Aneira nodded and Cadi realised that she'd already worked it out. How do you make an invasion successful? Stealth. Poison the food. Sicken the inhabitants. Stamp out the will to resist before you even meet your enemy on a battlefield. And then, if you are especially cruelly brilliant, send in troops that your enemy will hesitate to strike down. Send in their children bound to your will. Why risk your own troops? It all came together in a blinding flash of terrible sense. *Sluagh*. Shadow creatures who took the weak and sick, riding them like demons in an old tale. No one wanted to fight their own children but the children wouldn't hesitate to tear their parents apart, just like the flocks of Edge. How did you stop creatures like that?

215

Cadi glanced at Aneira in despair but the pale girl had a determined look in her eyes. She made a series of gestures that Cadi had no difficulty understanding. *Count them.*

She stared at Aneira, feeling she almost had it. Her fingers found the groves cut into her crook just as she realised that all the children she'd seen playing yesterday were huddled behind the adults. All the children she had counted in her head, like sheep.

The Shepherd's Tongue is used for counting the things that matter.

A language so old it pre-dated the Border. A language spoken by those who had carved the stones with strange letters and told tales about demons but called them *sluagh*. A language that had the power to keep things safe.

Aneira let out a soft gasp and Cadi looked up to see that the fiend-ridden children had thrown themselves into a charge. Not against the adults, but towards her and Aneira. Blue snarled and Shadow howled. But Cadi stepped forward and jabbed out with her crook, catching Billy by the arm. "Yahn!" she cried. *One! This one is mine! It belongs to my village so it belongs to me! Billy is ours!*

There was a flash of light and the symbols Aneira had carved into the crook lit with an eldritch glow. Billy went limp and an oily shadow slid away from him. Cadi hooked another child. "Tan!" And a third. "Tethera!" She caught child after child, and at *Jigif* she reached Pa and he drew the tally in the mud so she could start again. Children held by numbers. Numbers held by marks. Marks enclosed in the Shepherd's Tongue.

But Cadi wasn't alone now. More crooks flashed and more voices cried out the numbers. Cadi paused, breathing hard. They had counted all those who had fallen to the sleeping sickness, and everyone else for safety. "We need to close the Border."

Miss Morgan was throwing salt water on the red weed where it hissed like acid. "How?"

Cadi turned to Beca and the other children. "Let's play a game."

***

Later, when the folk of Wych Hill sent out word to the other Border Folk, no one could quite remember the words they had chanted when they'd played a game of crossing the Border with deadly intention. It didn't seem to matter so long as everyone kept the count and cleared the mud. It wasn't just the children, everyone in Wych Hill had played the game one time or another, and everyone had counted. Cadi saw it in her mind – the glowing red seam of the Border stitched closed with the words and intentions of the folk who lived there. The sleepers had all recovered. The flocks were safe. Considering it was the first battle fought in the Border for centuries the fact that there was only one casualty – the demonic ewe – was miraculous.

Everyone now had the symbols Aneira had carved into Cadi's crook on their own crooks, arrows and bows, staffs and even etched onto guns. Aneira had shown many people what symbols to use. The foundling had never been so accepted or so popular. When Cadi went to see her friend a few days after the Battle of the Sleepers, as it was called, Miss Morgan's parlour was strewn with posies of autumn flowers and berries. Cadi raised an eyebrow at Aneira, who blushed for perhaps the first time she could remember. Even Granny had warmed to the pale girl, muttering 'pharisee's child' without real rancour.

If anyone else had noticed what Cadi had seen that night, they chose not to reveal it. But Cadi remembered how she had been turning from one child to another and for a moment she'd seen Aneira, darting about with preternatural speed like a white deer, catching the oily shadow creatures. And crushing them into thick black dust between her slim pale hands. Something that perhaps no one who was entirely human would be able to do. She didn't say anything to Aneira. Nor did she mention it to Miss Morgan, who was leading an exhaustive hunt for and destruction of the red weed. Just like Granny, the schoolmistress had learned some acceptance. One for the new and one for the old. It seemed fitting, the Border was a place of contradictions after all.

217

Cadi turned to Aneira, determined this time not to let what she thought slide by unsaid. "Thank you, for saving my life. And I'm sorry. I never... I mean, I was always your friend, even when I didn't act it." She felt her face warm.

Aneira gazed at her a moment, then smiled and kissed her swiftly on the cheek. Cadi linked hands with the pale girl, reflecting that sometimes you had to choose a side. The war wasn't over. There would be further battles. But the folk of the Border would no longer keep to themselves.

There had always been a feel about the South West – Cornwall and Devon had their own identity, far from London, more akin to the North than to the rich South East. Bleak moors and mining; remote fishing villages and people steadfast in their ways. Between stubbornness and a sense of history, after centuries of providing the fleet with some of its finest sailors, the South West held.

Naval units gathered in Falmouth and Exeter, whilst people whose families went as far back as the Monmouth Rebellion took up arms. Not against the monarch this time, but for her.

Victoria rode openly to review her troops, and won the hearts of those who, a year before, would have seen her rot. They might have still doubted the crown, but not the wearer. The men and women around and beyond the Tamar recognised courage. And answered with their own...

REINFORCEMENTS

Frank Coffman

A Tale from the Great War with Hell
(being Excerpts from the Diary of
Corporal [Brevet Lieutenant] Gareth Williams, Royal
Welsh Fusiliers)

16 June-

This has been the worst season yet in our struggles against the demon hoard and the various other spawn of Hell. Our regiment has been more than decimated—just over the past two weeks. And we were at half our original strength before that.

Word has it that the Scots lost half their numbers in the fighting near Glasgow and most of the Highland Regiments have retreated back whence they hail from to attempt to guard kith and kin. The cities of the North are mostly laid waste as we understand it. But news travels slowly—and poorly these days. But here near the Cornish coast—not far from Tintagel—we've regrouped ourselves.

Some local men have joined our ranks—civilians, some actually with farm implements for weapons! "Swords from plowshares" I guess, so to speak. But we've had some trouble finding actual weapons for them—not that even true swords would do much good.

All for now. I'm tired as ~~Hell~~ SCRATCH that bloody word! Tired as a man alive and awake can be.

St John's Eve – 23 June-

There's news reported today that a new force (don't know about strength of numbers: brigade?, regiment?, company?) has actually attained a victory or two! At least holding actions are reported.

One report—most likely myth or wishful thinking—says that one sizable "Helliment" (as we call them) of demons was actually defeated up near Glastonbury. Wonderful news—if true. I'm more than weary of the other sort of news. Mum, when and if you see this journal, I hope you and young Dylan are all right. I've heard nothing more about Da's company.

St John's Day – 24 June- (Midsummer's Day to the pagans)

It was a glorious day today. At least as "glorious" as days in these impossible times will permit. Reinforcements have arrived! A sizeable regiment of men, well organized and marching into our encampment in well-formed, well-disciplined ranks. I'm guessing made up of mostly Cornish chaps, based upon their accents.

Their general is a most imposing fellow. He rode in at the head of the columns on a handsome white stallion—reminded me of our trusty old Gwyn back on the farm. God! It seems like ages, yet it's only been a few months! I've heard nothing of Da's unit. I haven't seen him since we lost Anglesey, and that's been three months ago.

This group seems to indeed be the regiment that has achieved some defenses and even victories in recent weeks. But there are some really strange things about them. What ISN'T strange these days, for that matter? For one thing, though obviously well-trained and hardened troops, they are totally irregular in dress, looking more like a collection of farmers or folk from small villages just finished with chores and saying,

"Ho-hum. Might as well go off and join in that war against the Devil thing."

No uniforms. But they're carrying banners. Another queer thing, the banners are not regular guidons or flags, but, rather things that hang in front of the suspending carry-poles, square in shape and held by a horizontal rod. In the old illustrations of Roman legions in books I've read they're called "vexilla." Nothing on them by way of a design—only the capital letters "RQRF"—and that ain't the "SPQR" that I learned in Latin class. Really odd bunch.

But that general is certainly a striking fellow. About average height, dark hair—but greying, looks like in his 50s, but a wiry, solidly built man. His big tent is pitched just across from our tents, with those of his men behind and around. In fact, his tent is just opposite mine.

I'm going to try to find out more about this bunch. Dog-tired now. We were on alert all day, and the sounds of battle echoed through the hills around our camp. But it was a bright, clear day, without much wind, and sounds <u>will</u> carry. All for now.

25 June-

Have met some of the blokes from the "Odd Regiment"—as my guys have begun calling them. They don't speak much. They'll greet you if spoken too, but they're very tight-lipped. They are definitely not regular army—and we'd already guessed that. But they're unbelievably disciplined for a group just gathered together. That speaks to the quality of their general and his immediate staff of officers I'm sure. Many of them MUST have been regulars before this damned war. Only way to explain it. I tried to pin this one fellow down with a couple questions. He did offer that they call themselves the "Logres Legion"—whatever that means. At the same campfire, I overheard one of them speaking to another in a very low voice saying "...we must save Albion, Gavin. It's our sworn duty." They are definitely a queer bunch—but I'm very happy they're on OUR side.

222

26 June-

An interesting night. I can't remember the last time I sang! But sing I did tonight. And so did all my company—indeed our whole force in chorus. The "Oddies" have an officer named Tally (obviously a fellow Welshman) who led us in song: Cwm Rhondda, and Hen Wlad Fy Nhadau, and Sospan Fach! The fellow even plays the lyre! And his voice is the finest high tenor through deep baritone I've ever heard! What a range! He strummed some tunes we didn't know, but the melodies were marvelous. All the while, their general sat in his big folding camp chair and sang and clapped along. He even got up and danced about to one tune! What an amazing group it is that has joined us.

27 June-

We've been called to the battle. The front is only ten miles away. If this is my last entry, May God have Mercy upon my Soul…Amen—and my eternal love to You Mum, and to Dylan bach, and Da, Please God that he still be alive!
Your Loving Son, Gareth...

29 June-

We have a victory! And, obviously, I lived! What a wonderful thing to say: "I'm Alive!" If we can win this war—and I'm beginning to think now that it might be possible—I'll go home to rebuild my LIFE! Our LIVES! And never take this wonderful world for granted again.

It's due for the largest part to the Odd Regiment's actions, deploying immediately as our vanguard as we approached the howling forces of Hell. Those demons and walking monstrosities that they use as shock troops always lay down that stinking

223

miasma of thick greenish fog, so that their front ranks are only seen as silhouettes and dim shadows.

But the Odd Bunch plunged directly into the fray. I was amazed by the effect that their "special" grenades achieved! One of their officers, knowing that we are technically named "Fusiliers" (even though the grenade is a very little part of our arsenal or our training) showed us the "difference" in their grenades. This fellow, an officer, Lieutenant Percy Knight, showed us that they remove the firing mechanism from the Bickfords and remix the powder inside with powdered silver! That or any silver coins or silver chain or parts of watches or any bits of silver-containing powder they can find: silver nitrate (from the photographer's bunch of chemicals) and other salts.

He claimed the resulting weapon was devastating—and that proved true! Upon explosion, the fiery sparks of the powder and the flying silver bits quite literally destroyed—or at least made disappear whole droves of our demon foes. They disappeared in large swaths—almost like mowing down the corn back on the farm!

The strangest thing about that battle though was the sight of their general, riding directly into the fray on that great white horse at the head of his phalanx of soldiers. His sword was drawn and he was shouting out commands that I could not hear (certainly could not understand in the roar of battle), but his regiment followed with a furious rush. At first, they fired pistols and rifles at the walking monstrous wraiths—those somehow reanimated corpses. But then as we all entered the fog, I could see them brandishing swords and spears—and even axes! It was like looking back into a history book. Some fellows of their regiment were firing arrows from longbows! It was like being at Agincourt in a dream!

I really can't explain the things I saw today. I can't remember half the things I did. Battle will do that. You get so ~~damned~~ mad! "That demon ~~son-of-a-bitch~~ is trying to kill me! We can't have that!" [sorry, Mum, for the language]. I'm only truly glad that my company had made up several of those "silver grenades." They worked well when we hurled them too.

Then it was over! No bugle sounding the usual retreat. The diminishing sounds of Hell retreating were something new. We had won! Thank God! God!, Queen!, and Country Forever!

This is the kind of thing legends used to be written about. Today was worth an epic poem that will, likely, never be written. But I was there—and I know! Move over Ulysses. Move over Jason. Move over Roland, etc. The Armies of God and the Queen have scored a victory—not won the war yet, but my hope is renewed.

30 June-

Here's something new! I've been summoned to THEIR general's tent. More when I find out what this is about.—

What an unbelievable thing! Their general, a man named Pendrake—I guess I haven't written that down before? With that name, he's almost certainly Cornish—as most of us had guessed about their regiment. "By Tre-, Pol-, and Pen-..."—and all that. But that's not the unbelievable thing. He called me by my name and praised my courage in yesterday's battle. God knows I didn't do anything more than the fellows beside me. But he singled me out. Well, me and four other chaps from my regiment were all escorted into his tent.

And one by one, we each received a field promotion! When it came my turn, he said to his adjutant, "Lance, bring corporal Williams forward." When I was positioned directly in front of him (and I don't mind saying my knees were a bit weak standing there) he said, "Corporal Gareth Dafydd Williams of the Royal Welsh Fusiliers, Company D, for conspicuous gallantry in the face of our infernal and damned enemy in action on 29th June, instant, and under my authority, you are hereby promoted to the field rank of Lieutenant in your company, and are being further

225

commended for the Victoria Cross with Legion of God Ornament"

I was flummoxed. You could have "knocked me over with a feather"—as the saying goes. What an amazing turn of events! Thinking on it know, I know it means even more worry! Men under my command! Men I will have to send to death—or worse!

But that's not the strangest thing. Certainly, that is strange enough, but the general then said to me, "Kneel, Gareth Dafydd Williams." I must say, I was so taken aback by that order that I delayed somewhat—enough that the adjutant had so repeat: "Kneel." To that, I complied.

Then the officer I knew as Percy Knight—the fellow who showed us the way to make the altered grenades—brought out what I thought was a red plush pillow! "'Odd' doesn't do these chaps justice!" I was thinking to myself.

Just then, Percy Knight bowed and, lowering the "pillow," I saw that its upper surface was depressed by the weight of the most beautiful sword I have ever seen!!! It's not a military sword, Mum. There's no u-guard to protect the hand and it's not a sabre, but a double-edged straight weapon with a point. The hilt is simply an ornate golden "T." But the thing must be worth a "king's ransom!"—as they say. I've never seen a blade shine so brightly!

At any rate, General Pendrake took up that sword and—just like in the storybooks, Mum!—he dropped the flat of it, first on one of my shoulders and then the next, finishing with a touch of the flat to the top of my head!

Then he said, "Arise Gareth Dafydd Williams, Liegefellow of Logres."

I'm certain nothing stranger or more wonderful will ever happen in my life—But I've said that before. All for now. Wheeew! That's enough, ain't it!

2 July-

More amazing news! I thought our recent victory and my field promotion and "Liegefellowship" (if I can make a new word?) topped all. <u>But the Queen herself is coming to our encampment!</u> That's the word—Victoria herself! But again, so many rumors and myths and untruths. Some correspondent back in the Crimean War days said something like, "The first casualty of War is Truth!" Ain't THAT the truth—at least usually. Still, the "Oddies" are talking about the Queen's visit, and they seem to be a pretty trustworthy and knowing lot—aside from other words to call them like amazing, unbelievable, mysterious, strange, even weird. Well, time will tell. It better be a short time too. I hear we're preparing to move out. An actual advance! Taking an offensive!

3 July-

The rumors were true. Her Majesty, Victoria, by the Grace of God of Great Britain and Ireland and of her other Realms Queen, Empress of India, Defender of the Faith reviewed our assembled soldiery today. What a proud occasion!

The Queen is of shorter stature than I had imagined. Wearing her customary black with a white hat and veil draped down the back she is, nonetheless, a most imposing presence.

But, yet again, I was mistaken in my belief that—if she should indeed come to our camp—that would be the high moment in and of itself! But such proved—yet again—not to be the case. Another day of wonder upon wonder! Each one keeps topping the one before for strangeness and even greatness in a way.

She addressed our assembled units in a fine, bold voice, urging us to fight on as "The True Army of God" and "Defenders of the Realm, nay Defenders of the Earth." She awarded medals to several among us—including my Victoria Cross! What an honour for the Queen herself to place the ribbon 'round my neck! Ivor Jones—you remember Ivor from over across the valley? took photos of it—I hope we can actually develop them some day! God willing! The medal has the words "For Valour" on it, but I

227

still don't see how my "valour" was any greater than the lads around me—and certainly not equal to the bravery of the "Oddies." Ah well, a great honour just the same. And now I have to lead my boys in the coming battles! I hope I'm worthy.

The Queen was then finishing the presentation of medals and was now proceeding toward the large tent of General Pendrake, her retinue trailing behind—including our Colonel Roberts and OUR entire group of senior officers. Our lads were all in as good a form as possible, wearing our caps with the white hackles. "Y Cymry Brenhinol!" we shouted all together and saluted as the Queen passed by. We were flying the Gryphon Flag. Even our regimental goat, Old Billy (he's actually got the rank of Lance Corporal, ya know) was in fine form—he's been safely kept away from any fighting in our encampments, well cared for by Goat Major Owens.

But here's the stranger thing—believe me or not— <u>WHOEVER might read this journal as it might be in days to come</u>. As she and her retinue proceeded toward the General's tent, I realized that Lieutenant Percy Knight of the "Odd Regiment" was standing beside me.

"You're a Liegefellow now," he said. "You need to know more about what that means."

"Yes, please," I answered in a whisper.

"General Pendrake has taken a liking to you—you and those few of your fellow Welshmen he decorated the other day."

"I'm deeply honoured. But what exactly does 'being a Liegefellow' entail?"

"You will be formally initiated into the Order this evening at sunset, my boy. But you must have some idea of the import of the other day?"

"I'm afraid I have to say that I'm struggling to make sense of it all—indeed, sense of any of it," I answered.

"Well, we know you fellows call us the 'Odd Regiment.'"

I'm sure I blushed a bit—them knowing the not necessarily complimentary appellation we'd given to them.

"It's perfectly fine, my lad. We ARE, as most would say, unusual. 'Odd,' as you say, in many ways. But I will give you the answer to the First Mystery of our Order. You have noted, I believe the lettering on our vexillas?"

"Yes, and I've asked about, but none of your bunch would tell me what 'RQRF' stands for. They would only answer something like, 'Time might tell' or 'Not really your business, lad—at least not for now.'"

"Yes, but now you're ready. Now IS that time. The words of our motto and our oath are Latin: 'Rex Quondam, Rex que Futurus.' "

And it was then that the truth hit me. It was a harder hit than an artillery shell—at least to my mind! Talk about wonders. Mum, Dylan, Da—I hope you can read this someday—or better still, that I might tell you the story straight. I know it will be hard to believe, but then, who would have believed an attack from Hell itself and the armies of the Devil?

I turned in amazement to see General Arthur Pendrake nod his head slightly to Victoria. Then—to the amazement of the "normal" soldiers in our ranks—the Queen curtseyed before the man who had come to save Britain in its hour of need—just as prophecies had foretold!

"Yet somme men say in many partyes of Englond that kyng Arthur is not deed /
But had by the wylle of our lord Ihesu in to another place / and men say that he shal come ageyn...
I wyl not say that it shal be so / but rather I wyl say here in thys world he chaunged his lyf / but many men say that there is wryton vpon his tombe this vers
¶ Hic iacet Arthurus Rex quondam Rex que futurus. "
—from *Le Morte d'Arthur* by Sir Thomas Malory
Wm. Caxton, Printer, A. D. 1485

PART THREE

DAYS OF DOUBT

THE CHARGE OF THE WIGHT BRIGADE

Phil Breach

Half a league, half a league,
Half a league onward,
Out of the valley of Death
Lurched the cold hundred.
"Forward, the Wight Brigade!
Lunge for the guns!" it said.
Out of the valley of Death
Lurched the cold hundred.

"Forward, the Wight Brigade!"
All to a man decayed.
Rot-black and livid blue
Half-rent and sunder'd.
No tongue to make reply,
No mind to reason why,
To do but no more to die.
Out of the valley of Death
Lurched the cold hundred.

Living to the left of them,
Living to the right of them,
Living in front of them,
Stumbled and blunder'd.
Unstopped by shot or shell
O'erweening, their putrid smell.

232

Out from the maw of Death,
Out from the gape of Hell,
Lurched the cold hundred.

Gore-smeared their cleavers bare,
Clotted with brain and hair,
Charging an army, while
Abigor thunder'd.
All wreathed in sulphur-smoke,
Right through the line they broke;
Soldier and sailor
Reeled from the cleaver stroke
Skulls split and plunder'd.
Victorious, black with rot,
The putrid cold hundred.

Living to the left of them,
Living to the right of them,
Living in front of them,
Stumbled and blunder'd.
Unstopped by shot or shell
Quick, before Dead they fell,
Choked on the foetor'd smell.
Back thro' the maw of Death,
Back thro' the gape of Hell,
All rot had left of them,
the putrid cold hundred.

When can their fell glory fade?
O such a lurch they made!
All the fiends cheered and thunder'd.
Honour the woe they made,

Honour the Wight Brigade,
The putrid cold hundred.

Despite many small victories and successful holding actions, the kingdom was no longer united. The Midlands and the South East had been gutted. Communications were poor or non-existent; a number of seasoned troops and naval personnel had been lost in the initial engagements – trained and resolute, they stood, brave enough, and fell just as bravely. And it was hard to fault the thin lines of reserves and volunteers as they crumbled at the sight of horned, screeching horrors, or under the onslaught of the almost silent damned.

Had this been a co-ordinated invasion, the heart of Empire would have been destroyed within weeks. But it was not. As devastating as any one incident or battle might be, there was no clear link between them. Strange, luminescent beasts stalked Lincolnshire, but made no attempt to join the fiery legion which had encamped around Hull, a mile across the Humber. Ten towns within a county might become the hunting grounds of night-things and demonic creatures too foul on which to gaze, whilst an eleventh would be completely spared for no discernible reason.

No consistency in nature or actions; no evident strategy beyond the blockading of the ports and the frequent, frenzied assaults upon London. Scholars and Ministers debated that this might represent the nature of Hell itself – that the Infernal Prince, if he existed, presided over Dukes and Barons of Chaos who could not be coerced into mutual support. Where humans fought for survival or for the Queen, their opponents fought for any portion of British flesh and soil they could grasp. Perhaps this was not one great Incursion, but many, each with its own agenda.

Not that this would matter in the end. Each local victory parade was matched by utter defeat elsewhere. Faith and resolve strengthened in some, but weakened in many others, who saw no end to this fight except death or servitude. Clergy faltered and died; supply lines failed. Surviving towns and cities struggled with refugees, becoming unwilling enclaves of resistance rather than mighty fortresses against the brimstone.

In private, Government officials and senior military figures began to wonder. Was it possible that they they were witnessing not a campaign between two powers, each with its strengths, but the slow and certain subjugation of their own people?

"Of the United Kingdom of Great Britain and Ireland, Queen". The Irish were, as ever, conflicted about the occurrences across the water. For many, their arguments with the British Government were tempered by reports of the devastation wrought amongst the British people. A Gloucester seamstress who died in agony under a demon's claws was no different from a Cork woman who might face the same fate.

Others saw the Incursion as one more reason to accelerate their political efforts towards a Free Ireland. And they told themselves that Ireland had been spared thus far because their cause was just. A few, especially the religious, wondered if such horrors could be contained so neatly. A number of Catholic priests took passage to South Wales and Cornwall in order to bolster the resistance there – Liverpool and much of the North West having been lost. Most arrived safely, their small craft missed or ignored.

As for the staunchest Fenians, they made individual choices – to wait and watch in their home towns, just in case, or to continue their plans for disruption of British rule...

PROFANED BY FEELINGS DARK

J S Deel

October 7th, 189-

Ganey had travelled up from Waterford with Patrick Higgins, and they had met a third man in Limerick – a fellow named Hanlon, a friend of Higgins from some socialist society. He was a man in his early thirties, tall and thin, with a pinched, hawk-like face that Ganey didn't like the look of.

Ganey tried to avoid conversation by reading the newspaper. In the centre of the front page was an illustration of a shadowy monster, shaped like a man with bat's wings, which had been sighted in Liverpool. Had a similar picture appeared in the same paper just two years before, the monster would have had Parnell's head, with 'Land' written on one wing and 'League' on the other, and it would have been swooping on a fainting woman representing Ireland. What a shame that the Incursion had robbed the caricaturists of their favourite clichés.

Hanlon waved to catch Ganey's attention. Ganey ignored him for as long as was feasible, and then reluctantly looked him in the eye.

"I don't know if you've been told, *a chara*," he said, "but our friends want you to know that they value your hard work, and they appreciate your willingness to share your findings."

Ganey looked back to the paper, pretending to read. He spoke through gritted teeth. "They're no friends of mine. Ten years is a long time to be left out in the cold."

"For Christ's sake, man," Higgins said, "you've been vindicated. All those years in America with the spiritualists and table-tappers and medicine-men – your efforts are about to be rewarded."

237

"We'll see."

Ganey folded the newspaper and turned to look out the window. Everything in this country seemed wet and chilled and miserable.

Why on Earth did I come back? I could have just vanished, taken a new name and forgotten it all; I could have escaped.

If I had, though, it would have all been for nothing. And with that, the daydream of flat, empty prairies faded. He was, once again, sixty years old, shivering on the Limerick-to-Killaloe train, and very, very tired.

Higgins was in his late twenties, and slightly too old to still be so optimistic and cheerful about everything. Ganey was not the only one to remark that Higgins had the wrong temperament for a revolutionary – he was a romantic with utopian dreams, but he detested violence. He made for a passable research assistant, though, and he had made himself useful during the Dublin survey.

"What's the story with our transportation once we get to Killaloe?" Ganey asked him.

"Nobody wants to go all the way to *Clais Cama*," Higgins said. "There's some bad business going on up there. Scores of paupers being turned out of their homes."

"Really? How come there was no mention of it in any of the papers?"

"The Incursion," Hanlon said. "That's the only thing the papers want to print these days. Anyway, this James Carmody fellow behind it all is a gombeen man with enough pull to keep the eviction story quiet."

There was no figure in rural Ireland quite so hated as the *fear gaimbín* – the gombeen man, the scavenger who profited from the misfortune of his neighbours. Such men were like crosses between usurers and class traitors, and loathed as much as both combined.

"Aren't they all," Ganey grunted. "So, how will we get there?"

"There are four stables in Killaloe," said Higgins.

238

"Is it wise to ride around in the open when people are shooting at each other?"

"Shooting?" Higgins shook his head. "Nobody's shooting up there – the poor bastards can barely afford to feed themselves, let alone buy guns."

***

By the time they reached Killaloe, evening was setting in. Just outside the station, a substantial crowd had gathered to listen to a Redemptorist roaring about the Day of Judgement. There were paupers and smartly-dressed professionals alike in the crowd; the shoeless and bedraggled stood alongside the well-fed, all of them soaking in the drizzle, all rendered equal by terror.

Hanlon sneered at the red-faced priest as they walked past. "I don't know whether those lads believe in God at all. They only ever talk about hellfire and damnation. I bet they're secretly delighted."

"I never understood the attraction to fire-and-brimstone sermons," Ganey said.

"The people will come to their senses," Higgins said. "When they see that the clergy is acting against their interests, they'll return to the cause."

Ganey shook his head. "The Incursion changed everything. The Empire and the Church will be stronger than ever now."

They left the station and walked down the road known as Royal Parade. Higgins, Ganey learned, had chosen their hotel very carefully. There were two hotels in Killaloe, but the Shannon View was owned by a local businessman with a line in every trade and scores of employees; Higgins reckoned there was too great a risk of gossip spreading through the town if they stayed there. Thus, they would be booking into the Royal Hotel instead.

After they had checked into their respective rooms, the two younger men came to Ganey's room to compare notes. Higgins open the discussion by asking, "D'you think we're going to find anything?"

"The remains of an infamous sorcerer lie somewhere in that lough outside," Ganey said. "Biddy Early used to live up in the hills behind us. And in this area, there have always been sightings of strange and terrible creatures. To have so many spell-casters in such a small geographic area, 'the talent' must run in families. This stretch of country probably has more spellcasters in it than anywhere else in Europe."

"But do you not think that they might have gone to ground?"

"Oh, probably. But the more of them we find, the more likely we are to meet one who can be reasoned with."

"And how many 'reasonable witches' have the two of you found so far?" Hanlon asked, an edge of annoyance to his voice.

Ganey responded with an exasperated sigh and said nothing further.

"You surprise me, Phelim," Higgins said. "I thought you were a believer."

"The fact of the Incursion does not make every other myth true by default," Hanlon replied.

Ganey snorted. "Think of our history, bearing that *fact* in mind. The French Expedition of 1798, scuppered by 'freak storms' before they could help our Rebellion; the uprising in '67, prevented by a sudden snowstorm; think of all the accidents, mistakes and quirks of fate that have undermined every plan we make. Is it all just coincidence? Are we simply unlucky?"

Hanlon raised an eyebrow. "You mean to say that the British have been using magic to maintain their rule?"

"I've never been surer of anything in my life," Ganey said. "I'm not looking for a secret weapon, Mr. Hanlon; my priority is to ensure our side is evenly matched."

"What about the Famine?" Hanlon asked. "Was that the work of British wizards as well?"

"It's hard to say." Ganey cleared his throat. "Anyway, what have ye found?"

Acting on Ganey's advice regarding the different kinds of evidence of diabolism, Higgins had made discreet inquiries into

240

the Petty Sessions records around East Clare and North Tipperary, making note of every case involving interference with a grave; he paid particular attention to cases where only part of a body had been taken, such as a hand, the internal organs, or subcutaneous fat. He discovered to his revulsion that this kind of selective thievery was more common that he imagined.

Hanlon's research had borne its own fruit. Most of East Clare happened to fall within the Poor Law Union of Scariff. The Medical Officer and Registrar for that Union, and a great many of the Dispensary Districts contained within it, was a butcher's son from Killaloe who had gone on to study at both the Royal College of Surgeons of Ireland and the Royal College of Physicians of Edinburgh. That man thus had inside knowledge of the Scariff Workhouse, as well as proud parents who would talk about him at length with a little encouragement. Sure enough, having visited the family's shop on the pretence of buying a pound of sausages, one of Hanlon's associates managed with very little effort to get them talking about their son's achievements, and then steered the conversation towards the odd things he must have seen in that Workhouse.

In the overlap between their inquiries, one place-name popped up – *Crom-an-Broc*. It was, by all accounts, little more than a crossroads on a bare hillside, but it loomed large in the frightened testimonies of superstitious farmers and the ravings of lunatics in the 'Idiot Ward' of the Workhouse.

There was a cottage there, the stories said, and living in that cottage was a woman who was not to be trifled with.

"What does the name mean?" Higgins asked.

"'The Badger's Crescent,'" Hanlon said. "And *Clais Cama* means 'Twisted Ditch.' I admit, if you were going to find a witch anywhere, those sound like promising places to look."

"Will you join us in the morning, then?"

"Absolutely not. I'm here to gather intelligence on the eviction and those involved – magistrates, process clerks, RIC officers and other hired thugs. I will leave the witch-hunting to your good selves." He stood up and turned to leave the room.

"Are we to be party to an assassination, then?" Ganey asked.

Hanlon smirked. "Only if you know about it. Good-night!"

"Your friend seems remarkably at ease with the thought of murder," Ganey said.

Higgins squirmed a little. "He copes with awful necessities by treating them flippantly. Once you get to know him, you'll see he's a sound, moral man."

"I'm sure."

***

The following morning, Ganey and Higgins set about organising transport to the tiny townland of Clais Cama.

Of the four stables in Killaloe, two were owned by the hotels, and a third was owned by a man from a well-established local family with a variety of businesses. To limit the chances of word spreading, Higgins and Ganey went to the fourth. After much arguing, posing as journalists wishing to observe the evictions, they were able to hire a man to drive a coach up into the hills.

Long before they came anywhere near Clais Cama, they heard church bells ringing across the landscape. The coach pulled off the main road into a small laneway and halted. Higgins opened the door and leaned out to talk to the driver.

"Why have we stopped?"

"Best to leave it a while, sir," the driver said. "They're ringin' the bells to warn everyone the peelers are comin'. There'll be war up there soon."

Ganey rolled his eyes. "We're not paying to hide in a ditch all day," he said, not quite loud enough for the driver to hear him.

"Is there any other way to get to Crom-an-Broc?" Higgins asked.

A strange look came into the driver's face. "Why do ye want to go there?"

"That's our business. Just tell us, can we get there without going past the evictions?"

The driver shivered. "Yes, sir. I can bring ye, but if it's all the one to you, I'll not linger outside that cottage."

"Why not?" Higgins asked. "Who lives there?"

The driver shook his head. "I'll not draw her on me. When she was a child, her shadow had a life of its own; that's why she only ever sets foot outside her cottage at night, never during the day."

Higgins chuckled. "Do you believe that?"

The driver scowled. "You've heard there are demons walkin' the earth, haven't you? Why would I risk it?"

Higgins sighed. "Grand. Take us as close as you will dare, then."

***

Higgins did not know what to expect from a witch's cottage, but he felt somewhat disappointed by the sight of it: it was a plain cottage, with stone walls and a thatched roof. Smoke curled up from the chimney, and a couple of speckled hens scratched at the ground outside. Higgins noticed that the windows were covered with boards, but that was not unusual – country folk who were behind on their rent often blocked up their windows and doors to impede bailiffs.

"Have we come to the right place?"

"Let's ask," Ganey said. He walked up to the door and knocked.

The door of the cottage opened slightly, and an eye looked at them out of the dimness.

"We're looking for the lady of the house," Ganey said. "Have we come to the right place?"

The person on the other side of the door stayed silent.

"We're not with the police, or the newspapers, or the bank," Ganey explained.

The door closed again, and then opened wide enough for them to step through.

"Come in," said a woman's voice, "and close the door after you."

They stepped inside. In the light that briefly came through before Higgins shut the door, he saw that the inside was just as unremarkable as the outside – it was an ordinary one-room cottage, with some basic, hard-wearing furniture, and there was an open fireplace in the back wall, complete with an iron spit, a pot and a kettle. There were no strange symbols on the walls, no grimoires or strange idols. Once the door was closed, however, the interior was suddenly very dark, save for the ruddy glow of the fire.

The woman who stepped forward to greet them was on the far side of middle age, but her hair was still long, thick and blood-red. "What do ye want?"

"I am Tom Ganey, and this is my associate Patrick Higgins," Ganey said. "Forgive me, Madam, but nobody in the locality would tell me your name."

"No matter," the witch said. "I wouldn't have given it to you anyway." She scrutinised them both. "What do ye want, I said?"

"Do you speak to the spirit folk?" Ganey asked.

"Sometimes," the witch said.

"Can you command them?"

The witch cocked her head to one side. "Why d'you ask?"

"If you could," Higgins said, "such a gift might be put to good use in the service of Ireland."

The witch chuckled. "Why would I want to do that?"

Higgins gestured in the general direction of Clais Cama. "Barely a quarter of a mile from here, dozens of families are being evicted from their homes. Who is to say that it won't be your home next?"

The witch said nothing, but smiled knowingly.

"Ah," Ganey said, "you believe you're safe because the locals fear you. What will you do when that changes, and the Church sends an army of the faithful to tear down this cottage?"

"That'll happen whether I help ye or not. Helpin' ye might even hasten my destruction."

"We can protect you," Ganey said. "You can hide in Philadelphia, until the Incursion ends and the people come to their senses."

The witch considered this for a moment. "I can't 'command' them to do anythin', Mr. Ganey. They repay favours. Since this 'Incursion' started, it's easier to hear their voices, but you should think carefully about what you want from whatever takes the offerin'."

"What kind of 'offering' is required?" Ganey asked.

"A blood sacrifice," the witch said.

"We are all willing to lay down our lives in service to our country, Madam," Higgins said, puffing his chest out. "No higher purpose exists, than to—"

"I mean it just as I say it," the witch said. "The only sure way is to offer human blood. Someone will have to be killed."

"Oh." Higgins briefly looked disturbed at the thought, but he nodded and set his face in an expression of grim determination. "Carmody, then. God knows he deserves it."

"Carmody's already dead," the witch said.

"What? Since when?"

"Not important. Someone else will have to be found." The witch grinned. "I can make the choosin' easier for ye."

"What do you mean?" Ganey asked.

"Your comrade-in-arms—the one who refused to come here—is a spy."

Higgins gritted his teeth and advanced on the witch. "You're lying! You—"

The embers in the fireplace suddenly roared into sheets of flame that bathed the single room in red light. Skittery, spider-legged shadows danced all over the walls.

"Don't even think about liftin' a hand to me in my own house, Mr. Higgins," she snarled. "I've done ye a favour, tellin' ye what I know."

Higgins jumped back, as from a rearing snake. "I apologise, Madam. I meant no disrespect."

The witch's point being made, the flames died down to glowing coals again. "Come back to me when ye've made yer decision."

Ganey cleared his throat and gave her a little bow. "Thank you for your time, Madam." He opened the door, gently pushed Higgins out, and closed it again; then, the two of them set off back for the coach at a brisk walking pace that quickly turned into a sprint.

***

The coach driver took them back by the main road past Clais Cama. The brawl was over, but the scene was still chaotic. There were pools of blood all over the ground. Young men and old, looking dazed and frustrated, shuffled up the road towards their homes; there were sticks and clubs and scythes over their shoulders, and sticky red rivers flowing from open wounds on their scalps. A screaming crowd was kept at bay by mounted constables, while a bald, middle-aged priest called for calm. Twenty men had been arrested, and were handcuffed to each other on the side of the road; their braces had been removed, forcing them to use their free hands to hold their trousers up.

The coach carried on down the road, past the village proper, but the roadsides were still full of wounded locals and uniformed policemen.

"Jesus, there must be two hundred of the bastards," Ganey continued, his voice quiet.

"She was lying," Higgins said. "She must have been. Hanlon would never betray us." He paused, breathing heavily. He went silent and stared out the coach window, his face pale and his forehead glistening.

246

Ganey sighed. "I know what you're feeling, Pat. The Fenians were always riddled with informers and spies. It was always a terrible shock to discover them."

Higgins took a deep breath. "We have to confirm it. There's a stationer's office in Killaloe. I'll go there and send a telegram to our friends in Dublin. If he really is working for the British, then they'll have been following our movements."

They passed the remainder of the journey in total silence.

***

Higgins was not in his room the following morning, so Ganey went down to the hotel dining room to eat breakfast alone. The news carried word of suspected Incursion-related events in Belfast and Wexford, and of the death of Charles Stewart Parnell. Ganey wanted to read Parnell's obituary, but he found it impossible to concentrate amid the hubbub of conversation from the other guests. Most of the chatter concerned the death of James Carmody, who had been shot in the face while travelling back to his fortress-like home outside Ennis. The Constabulary were now scouring the hillsides, raiding almost every farm and cottage in search of the assassin.

Ganey looked up and saw Higgins enter. There was a harried look on the younger man's face. Ganey waited until he had gone up the stairs before following him. On the first floor, he found Higgins knocking on his door.

"Oh, there you are. I've heard back from our friends in Dublin."

Ganey gestured for him to be quiet, opened the door and ushered him inside. "Alright. Tell me."

Higgins took a crumpled telegram out of his pocket. "I went down to the stationery office as soon as I awoke. This was waiting for me."

Ganey took it and felt his face grow hot as he read it. The Irish Republican Brotherhood had their own codes and ciphers to which disgraced old Fenians like himself were not privy, so the message had been disguised with easily-parsed innuendo:

DEAREST PATRICK **[STOP]**
NEW FRIENDS INVITED TO SPEND COUPLE NIGHTS AT LT'S HOUSE **[STOP]** LT HOPES YOU WILL JOIN THEM SOON **[STOP]**

The amateur occultists that they had spoken to in Dublin had been arrested; the "Lieutenant's House" could be nothing other than Dublin Castle. As the reality of it sank in, Ganey cursed himself for being so stupid. The British government were keeping an eye on would-be warlocks and sorcerers – of *course* they were.

"Bloody hell," Ganey said. "They've been on to us from the start!"

Higgins nodded. His expression was one of barely-contained fury. "Yes. And the only way they could know—"

"Is Hanlon."

"What do we do now, then?"

Ganey felt a degree of sympathy for Higgins; Hanlon was a dear friend, after all. He had experienced the same thing, too many times.

"I've been thinking about it," he said. "We'll have to convince him to come with us, back to the witch's cottage. If we reveal that we know he betrayed us, we'll be forced to keep him prisoner here until nightfall, and then somehow get him all the way out to Crom-an-Broc without raising any suspicions. It'll have to be during the day, too."

Higgins gawped at him. "You want to go through with it?"

"If we turn back now, it's all for nought. Would you prefer that we gave him a traitor's execution? If he must die one way or the other, let's make use of it. If it liberates Ireland, his sacrifice may even redeem him."

Higgins nodded. "You're right," he whispered. "Of course you're right."

248

***

Higgins never lied more convincingly than he did to the coach driver at the livery. The cottage at Crom-an-Broc was not a witch's abode, he explained, but a safe-house for Irish patriots wanted by the RIC. He repeated all the gory details of the previous day's eviction and the cruel landlord's assassination, and told him that the gallant fighter who had ended Carmody's reign of terror was hiding in the very place that everyone was afraid to approach. Their business was to help that hero to reach safe harbour, and the coachman was only too willing to be a part of it.

Ganey had taken responsibility for lying to Hanlon, but he had the harder job of convincing a sceptic to come and meet a witch with actual magic powers.

"I've seen more than my share of frauds, Phelim. Believe me, this woman is a miracle-worker, and she wants to help us."

Hanlon scoffed. "Why are Fenians so bloody gullible?"

"It's not gullibility," Ganey snapped. "It's open-mindedness. That was always the strength of the Fenian Brotherhood – we never dismissed any idea out of hand."

"And look what you have to show for it – the invasion of Canada, that ridiculous submarine, the Manchester fiasco—"

"Our successes were just as dramatic as our failures; you just choose not to acknowledge them. What are you afraid of? That you might have to change your mind?"

Hanlon gave him an exaggerated weary sigh. "Alright. I will go with you to see this wise-woman, but you must give me your word that you won't complain when I mock you at every opportunity afterward."

"I'm sure there's no fear of that," Ganey said.

***

The coach driver still would not approach the witch's cottage; Higgins quietly thanked him for his service to the cause

249

and asked him to come back in an hour. Hanlon took advantage of the walk to lecture the other two on the principles of historical materialism.

"Magic and romanticism are insubstantial foundations," he said. "Lads, ye need to stop going after magic solutions to the situation. Everything has a *material* cause."

"What about the Incursion?" Ganey asked.

"That has a material cause, too. It has to; there is no such thing as the supernatural, only sciences that we haven't yet discovered." He gestured disparagingly at the cottage ahead. "You can't build a nation on the likes of *that*. We need to seize the canals, the railways, the ports, the factories—"

Higgins, who had been walking two steps behind, suddenly lunged and cracked Hanlon over the head with a rock. Hanlon fell straight to the ground like a sack of potatoes. Ganey hunkered down and examined him.

"Still alive. Good Jesus, what were you thinking?"

"I couldn't listen to him anymore," Higgins muttered.

Ganey scanned the hillside for anyone who might have been watching. "Right. Hurry, take his feet."

***

The witch was not pleased when they carried Hanlon's limp form in through her door.

"He has to be conscious," she said. "Otherwise it won't work."

Ganey and Higgins busied themselves tying Hanlon to a chair, using strips of cloth taken from his own coat. When the job was done, Higgins stood up and smacked Hanlon across the face repeatedly, until Hanlon came to and looked around the room, confused and groggy.

"Why're you hittin' me?" he slurred. His voice sounded plaintive.

The witch stepped forward with a little flask in her hand; she opened the lid and wafted it under his nose, causing him to gasp and rear up in his seat, suddenly wide awake. The witch replaced the flask of smelling salts on one of her shelves.

"What's going on?" Hanlon asked. "Pat, what are you doing?"

"We know you betrayed us," Higgins said. "Don't bother trying to lie; just have *some* honour and tell us why you did it."

Hanlon fumed in silence for a moment, and then sighed. "It had to be done. For the welfare of the common man."

"That's what we're fighting for," Higgins said.

Hanlon shook his head. "The workers of this country—of the world—need a revolution of peace, not of 'heroic' bloodshed."

Higgins's jaw dropped; his eyes bulged, and his face went deathly pale. "Good God … you're a *Fabian!*"

Hanlon nodded in Ganey's direction. "You said it yourself, Tom. There's no gainsaying the Empire now, not when demons walk the Earth. There's only one viable plan now – let the Empire spread over the entire globe, and then implement socialist reforms at the centre of it."

"What was the price of your cooperation?" Ganey asked.

"Free rein to give James Carmody what he deserved."

"That was some bloody business for a man who claims to disdain conflict," Higgins said, struggling to stop himself from shouting.

"Excising a parasite hardly counts as 'bloodshed,'" Hanlon retorted.

The witch cleared her throat. "Shall we begin, gentlemen?"

Ganey nodded and stepped back, pulling Higgins after him with a hand on his shoulder.

"Ye'll need to move further back than that," the witch told them as she took her position behind Hanlon, a long knife in her hand. "The blood shoots out a fair distance."

Ganey and Higgins stepped back further, as advised; they were now standing by the door.

"This is nonsense!" Hanlon screamed. "Empty superstition, nothing more! This'll accomplish nothing!"

251

The witch raised her knife. "That's good. Keep roarin'; it'll make the blood nice an' hot."

"Murderers! Murderers all of—"

Hanlon's final cry was cut short with a gurgling howl of pain, as the witch drew her knife across his throat. The blade bit deep and opened almost every vein and artery in his neck. She had not exaggerated: jets and sprays of blood flew in every direction, spattering the walls and the furniture. Higgins flinched when he felt some hit his face, and he crumpled to his knees in open-mouthed horror, making a hollow moaning sound. The witch ignored him as she muttered rhythmic phrases in some strange, harsh language that Ganey could not identify.

Ganey considered all the times in his life when he thought a line had been crossed. *If I give up now, all of that will have been for nothing. That heartbreak, that abandonment, that humiliation, that loneliness, those deaths – they will count for nothing if I stop now.*

Only at this moment did he truly believe it; that imagined sense of commitment had now taken on a horrible, razor-sharp clarity.

There was a gunshot outside, somewhere down the road. It was an alarm, a policeman firing into the air to attract his comrades' attention. The coach driver had sold them out. Ganey pressed his ear against the door, trying to determine how far away they were. The shot did not sound very close, but the frantic shouts which followed were not distant enough away for his liking. He gripped the door handle and began to pull it open.

"Leave it shut, you stupid pig-fucker!" The voice had come out of the witch's mouth, but it did not sound like her. When Ganey looked at her face, he saw that her eyes were sunken, and her lips were tinged with a dark substance that looked almost like tar. Hanlon was still not dead.

Higgins had curled himself into a ball on the floor, moaning and sobbing. Through the door, Ganey could hear the RIC men more clearly as they advanced on the cottage. And then, very suddenly, all was quiet and still. Ganey's vision blurred and swam, and he felt nauseous. With tremendous effort, he turned to face the thing that had appeared in the room.

"What do you want, little man?"

"The RIC men," Ganey blurted. "The ones outside, and the ones who took part in the eviction yesterday – kill them all."

***

In the barracks at Ennis and in Ballina, and on the cold hillside at Crom-an-Broc, men of the Royal Irish Constabulary fell screaming to the ground as their flesh was sundered and peeled away. Every death was a new offering, bringing another outsider through, and when the boon had been fulfilled, the unleashed horde ran wild across the countryside in broad daylight, unrestrained. They fell upon every man, woman and child in their path, killing and devouring the rich and the poor alike. Killaloe and Ballina were reduced to blood-soaked ash, and word travelled fast as the demons rampaged through Limerick and Tipperary: the Incursion had finally reached the banks of the Shannon.

Ganey stood on the hillside, looking out across the landscape at the thick plumes of smoke rising in the distance. He closed his eyes and tried to retreat into some dream-world, as though he could will himself to follow Higgins into a catatonic state. He tried to conjure up memories of American prairies, lonely railroads and painted horses, but they would not come to him.

"Nothing," he whispered. "It's all for nothing."

The witch had already walked halfway to the ruins of Killaloe, laughing, her shadow dancing on the road behind her.

We do not know how many isolated townships suffered – in some there were no survivors, in others no one would speak of what they had endured. When Scarborough was relieved by Prince Bertie's famous charge against the damned, a bishop on either side of him and a Parsee elder chanting from horseback as they broke the enemy line, there were no cheers. The victorious troops were met with the faces of people who no longer understood the nature of their world. Fisher-women looked up at the bloodied Prince of Wales in silence and then trudged home to see if they could feed their children.

The aftermath of many a victory could be worse than the combat. With an enemy abroad in such varied and appalling manifestations, madness was to be feared as much as physical harm. Minds bent; some broke. Demonic whispers turned family members into spies or open foes – other folk saw little but their own personal plight and had no charity for their neighbours. Were these the weaker souls, or had some Infernal influence always dwelled with them? How deep were the roots of the horror only now showing itself?

And so the Incursion brought doubt and deception, more potent than a demon's claw...

WE'VE ALWAYS LIVED IN A COLONY

S. L. Edwards

The screaming night had given way to a calm, foggy morning. Dortsmouth was covered in acrid, smoky mist carrying the scent of wet decay and sour, bursting rot. The miasma was worse than death, a reeking corruption of something that rested beneath the flesh and sat heavy in the stomachs of all who breathed it in.

In Dortsmouth the people talked with each other, speculating as to the nature of the fog over bitter teas and coffees. It was evidence of deliverance, some said, proof that their lads were beating the enemy at sea. It was evidence of damnation, others said, the proof that the stain of infernal infiltration was a scar.

Bridget Braddock only thought it fog. Pungent and infernal fog, but nothing more.

Bridget had not liked England, had not cared much for the English either. In London she had been biding her time, travelling along the edges of several circles of discontent to discover what could hurt Britannia the most. She watched the pretty socialist boys give their grand orations in empty factory cellars, and she walked beneath the billowing coal smog to watch the impassioned anarchists beat their chests and raise their fists as they decried the evil of empire and championed liberation of all men from its yoke.

All men.

For all her life, Bridget believed there were only two types of men: those who were too selfish to love and those who were too stupid to live. The pretty socialists were the first sort, beautiful things with bright eyes and delicate faces who would confess all the love necessary to compel some stupid little girl to make a bomb and die for them. Bridget's brothers had been the other sort, reckless young boys who threw themselves before an English firing squad because they couldn't imagine living another day under the yoke of a tyranny they had barely come to understand.

She believed she had learned everything she could from those two types of men.

But after arriving in Dortsmouth, she learned there was another sort man; a type who could temper their selfishness and eagerness to live long and fruitful lives, the kind who thought in terms of decades rather than minutes. There was a kind of man who did not rush headlong into death, but who prolonged their life so that they could squeeze every hateful drop from it.

Her horse's hoofs fell softly as they could against the drawbridge, the beast whinnying as it snorted the stream rising from the holy water bog. She didn't turn back to look at the wall of wooden spikes that impaled winged forms in black armour, the severed red heads with glowing eyes that still occasionally followed her has she went out on patrol. The fog was heavy, but she had learned not to be afraid of what she could not see. Every animal had a sense of self preservation, and she trusted her horse to run if it sensed danger.

She inhaled, taking in the cold air as she unslung her rifle from her shoulders. The winter grass was wet and brown, poking out from sheets of melting ice pock-marked with black ash. In all directions the fog seemed to go on forever over the flatlands, an endless white and yellow horizon for a droll, ceaseless existence.

It was in the mornings that she felt most like her brothers, stupid though they were. Through the phantom clouds of her of her frosty breath she recalled the smiling, idiot boys who tussled her hair and dared her to be strong. Brave, stupid boys that they were. Considering the world as it was, she supposed there were worse things to die as than brave and stupid.

Her horse stopped.

Bridget kicked its sides, trying to motivate it forward. The horse didn't cry out, nor did it bray up in fright. She carefully dismounted, raising her rifle's butt to her shoulder and lining up the sights. She tried tensing her muscles, sending small shocks to every nerve in her body. She thought of her own death, of how it would feel to be scraped apart by long, hooked teeth or torn by claws. But to no avail.

Try as she might, she couldn't find her fear of death.

The grass bent beneath her feet, a frigid wind blowing frost and ash against her face.

She pointed her rifle at the dirt and brought a sleeve to her forehead.

The wind rose and pushed the fog away, and as it cleared she saw an enormous yellow eye peering out at her.

She brought the gun back up and shot. The bullet dug into a sucking mass, tar black ichor billowing out from the wound on the bursting eye.

She moved forward again. The eye was as large as her torso, slanted and broken as it was. Around it ran red flesh as coarse as leather.

The gusts of wind blew to a fury.

Her rifle fell to the ground.

***

At midday the tower stood clearly against a mottled sky.

It was tall enough to loom over Dortsmouth as Big Ben rose above London. It was covered with eyes and mouths. The eyes were yellow and black, some wide as doors and others as small as grapes. They blinked sporadically, undulating with the rippling red wall of flesh that connected them. At intermittent intervals mouths leered out, full of broken yellow teeth and piercing white fangs. Black worm lips pursed together and smacked wetly as the gigantic tongues behind them sat still.

"I've never seen anything like it."

Vicar Johnson was a kindly man. Shorter than her by a head, his squat shoulders were growing more bent every day, his eyes shadow-marked with the lack of sleep which came with ceaselessly pouring over books for answers which weren't there. Beneath his winter cap he had grown bald, more a monk after the Incursion than he had ever been before it.

"Neither have I," Bridget answered distantly.

In London the creep had been slow - horned shadows walking the darkness of alleys, as members of parliament suddenly sprouted wings and hooves. By the time the Horde made itself known, it was too late. As Bridget fled across Britain she had seen man-like gelatinous forms which seeped in the spaces of abandoned houses, looming horrors in spiked armour that adorned themselves with the severed heads of men and women. She had fought and killed her way until she arrived in Dortsmouth.

But she had never seen anything like the tower.

The eyes did not seem particularly interested in either Bridget or the vicar as they circled around it, nor did the mouths have anything to say. Hot breath poured out in waves, sour as curdling milk. Aside from long, white, spine-like hairs the tower was merely a stack of flesh, eyes and mouths which rose into the thick grey clouds above.

"Any ideas as to what it is for, Vicar?"

He smiled weakly and shook his head.

"The same thing all of this has been for...to test our love and dedication to the Lord."

"Then tell me, Vicar," a bitter and scraping voice came from behind them, "How many more tests does your God have for you and the rest of his sorry sheep?"

Bridget heard the vicar shudder and sigh. She turned, resting her eyes on the man who had dismounted his white horse. He was tall, but age had stooped his spine and stripped away the flesh from his bones. His skin had gotten tighter across his jagged skeleton, deep cavernous eyes almost as black as his coat, peering out from the darkness of his face.

He put his cane down hard, walking as deliberately as he could towards both the tower and the vicar.

"General Carthill," the vicar began.

Carthill brushed him aside and continued towards the tower. He stopped before the wounded eye and dipped a crooked finger into the thick black ichor. He lifted it to his nose and laughed with a sharp, jaundiced smile.

"You shot it then, did you, Ms. Braddock?"

"Yes sir."

Bridget regarded General Carthill as she always did, coldly and carefully. His height had folded in on him with the weight of his years, but his stature had not. Long grey hair poked from beneath his hat, and with his frost covered beard he seemed almost and lupine.

"Good show. Though I dare say you haven't killed it," he smiled.

Bridget did not respond. It was part of how she handled him, denying him the ability to provoke and chide her. A strategy which he seemed aware of, and seemed to enjoy. His smile widened as his lips closed over his teeth. He turned away from them and back to the tower.

"Vicar, I'll need you to go over your books. Go over them again and again until you can give me an idea as to what this is."

"Sir," the vicar began, "Genevieve Dodd's young boy remains unbaptized, and I had hoped to get to him today."

"Your job," Carthill's voice hissed with boiling steel, "Is not to bless babies. It is to bless moats, bullets, and to figure out what the bloody hell it is I'm looking at. And if you forget that, Vicar, I can just as well put a bullet in you. There are plenty of good lads in the village who can stand over water and sing songs from some dodgy old book. Do I make myself clear?"

The vicar bit his lips, his face playing out a battle of righteous anger and creeping fear as it reddened and shifted.

"Yes, General…"

"Good." The smile did not return to Carthill's face. He looked up at the tower, putting a hand over his eye to block the sun as he searched for the peak.

"Big bloody thing."

***

Dortsmouth and the people in it had been Bridget's salvation. They had taken her in, fed her; given her a place to bathe, gave her clothes spun by soft-faced women who doted on the new stranger as if they were attempting to gain God's favour through kindness. After running for so long, she was thankful for the kindness.

Her rescuers told her stories about how they had fought the horde, how they beat them back with spears and guns, with songs and prayers. How Vicar Johnson blessed the moat they made around the fortress town, and how no infernal thing had ever been able to enter Dortsmouth since.

Bridget imagined it, a little community of housewives and old men fighting a full-fledged insurgency against the Horde. And she had imagined that these people, attempting to court God's mercy, were responsible for their own salvation.

But in the days after her arrival, she learned that a demon had lived in Dortsmouth long before the incursion.

"What do you make of it?"

General Carthill's home was a large estate, the gift of a military family that had served the Crown since the early 1700s. It was big enough and empty enough that Bridget only needed to see the General when they took their meals together.

He spoke to her from the end of the dining table, knife pointed towards his lips as pink lamb's blood dribbled into his beard.

"Of the tower?"

"Yes."

Whether his offer that she stay with him had been out of loneliness, curiosity, or cruelty, Bridget could not be sure. When

260

he had first invited her into his home, Bridget refused. She was young and pretty and knew enough of the world to know the dangers of old, sabre-eyed men. Then one day he had found it, the right sour promise to lure her into his home.

"I'll tell you what I did with those bloody Fenians. You're a Mick. Little anarchist, bet your father taught you to make bombs. Bloody savages, sending children to fight their wars. Would you like to know, lass, what we did over there?"

That had been enough to draw her in.

"I think," Bridget paused to consider her words. "It's a stake."

"Oh?" Carthill dipped his fork into mashed potatoes, not looking up at her but straining shoulders to lean towards her voice.

"If they're like us," she continued, "They'll leave signs for each other. Markers. That's what it is, a sign."

"Good theory," he wiped his beard with a cloth napkin and coughed. "You know what I think?"

She had an idea.

"No."

"I don't think they're 'like us.' I think they are us."

She had heard this before, so she toyed with her potatoes and let him speak.

"None of this makes a difference, mind you." He continued, unaware or indifferent to her lack of interest, "They've always been here. I've seen them before, on the faces of sepoys and Irishmen. I've seen their eyes looking up with the sort of hatred that only a man can muster. I've wielded that hatred too. Oh, I've never hated a man for being different than me. If there's one lesson to be learned from all of this, it's that we're all the same. But I despise weakness, the inability of people to keep what's theirs. That makes it ripe for the taking, doesn't it?"

She cut into her lamb chop and bit down. It was chewy, sliding right down her throat with all her bile and anger.

"That's all this is," he said. "It's us trying to keep what's ours. If we can't keep it, then it isn't ours, is it? Weakness," he began chuckling, aware of some secret knowledge he couldn't help but share, "*That's* the great sin! *That's* what earned us this! Not bloody unbaptized babies."

He continued chuckling to himself as Bridget ate in silence.

***

Bridget slept on the second floor of the home, in a corner room which had belonged to Carthill's son, who left England when he was a boy. The room remained decorated with naval propaganda and toy boats, painted pictures of luxuries and aspirations which she had never had in Ireland. Her two large windows were closed, creeping white frost shining in the orange gaslight as just outside the darkness went from deep blue to black.

The general's wife had left some articles of clothing, Bridget's night gown among them. Wearing it, she could not help but smile at the wry irony that wove itself into every part of Carthill Hall. For all his insistence on the virtue and primacy of strength, the general could not keep his family. His wife had left him for some Texas rancher, and no one in Dortsmouth had heard from her in over twenty-five years. His boy, who used to dream of the great ships and smile brightly, was now a man across the ocean.

A man who Carthill would never be strong enough to meet.

She moved across the room to a writing desk, opening it up and removing a bottle of whiskey and a clean glass. The nights were always full of screaming. Vicar Johnson had told her they had once sent a party out, to make sure that it was not some poor soul in need of help. But the search party never returned, and they found a horse torn in two just beyond the blessed moat the next morning. Since then, the people of Dortsmouth had learned to live with the screams as part of the environment, as natural as the setting sun.

But the screaming wasn't the only reason she reached for the whiskey.

Since arriving in Dortsmouth, there was an emptiness in her. Once it had been anger, driving her onward to make bombs that would kill some bastard outside Buckingham Palace. After that, it had been the drive for survival, running from one burning town to the other just to live as long as she could.

But in the routine stillness that came with security, Bridget could not sleep.

The whiskey was thin and smoky, a cheaper stock she was making herself finish before breaking into the general's cellar and looting his Scotch.

After all, he wouldn't be able to stop her. Carthill may have split throats and hung boys from trees, but he had been a younger man then. Now it was just Carthill, Bridget, and the cook alone in the house.. And the cook wouldn't mind, the way Carthill had been kicking the poor bastard since the day he walked through the front doors. No, the cook would probably give Bridget the knife to slice the general if she asked.

She let the whiskey hum against her lips, and sat down in a velvet-cushioned chair.

She didn't hate Carthill. 'Hate' wasn't the right word. But night after night of listening to him describe what he had done in Ireland was tiring. All his horrible stories had become as old as the general himself, and his keen military mind did not have many more lessons to divulge. His cruelty would shift from a blessing to a burden for Dortsmouth, and when that moment came there would be no weighty decision. She would either go into his room at night and slit his throat, or she would shoot him in broad daylight, without announcement or declaration.

A single moment and it would be done.

Bridget put down her whiskey with a start. A chill ran down her spine and she stood quickly, jumping up to peer out the dark window.

There were no screams. The night was silent. She had never had such thoughts before. But in the quiet, still night, they came to her in her own voice.

With a fear she had not felt since she first fled London, she poured the rest of the whiskey in her mouth, and fell asleep to the sound of her own roaring laughter.

**

The morning was unkind to her. Her stomach lurched and churned with drunken emptiness; the back of her throat remained dry despite all the water she drank. The taste of whiskey mixed with the sharpness of the frost as her boots crunched against the thin layer of snow. Around her the meagre stone buildings of Dortsmouth were sealed, the inhabitants having boarded up most of their windows long ago. A few faces peered out from what windows remained, some of them guilty and others confused.

Not one of them had moved to help the vicar.

Word reached the Carthill Hall quickly, as all words did in Dortsmouth. The frantic knocking on the door woke her, crashing against the throbbing pain in her head. The poor frantic man at the door had expected the general, and stammered fearfully at Bridget in her gown as he averted his eyes to the ground. She then moved quickly through the quiet streets, turning to the vicar's residence and not waiting to knock.

The house was a mess of ripped pages, split furniture and broken glass. The darkness seemed to stretch from every shadow, pouring dimness onto every surface. Bridget moved quietly, knife drawn and ready.

But the vicar was alone when Bridget found him.

His kindly face was gone; only a red smear at the end of a ragged torso remained. By his bed, the figure that was the vicar slumped, his undergarments drenched in brain, bone and blood. In a puddle of gore the murder weapon, a limestone rock the size of a large grapefruit was flecked pink and grey.

"He told me everything."

Ellen Johnson's voice was small and far away. Her red-silver hair was wild, caked in sweat and grime. The vicar's wife peered at Bridget from the corner of the room, hugging her knees like a scared child.

Her guilt was written in the stains of her husband's blood.

"Mrs. Johnson-"

Ellen Johnson made a hissing intake of breath and held her dripping fingers to her face.

"I never saw him move…in the dark. But he told me everything. About all those girls. Those…those…"

She seemed on the verge of frantic tears.

"Harlots," she spat.

Her eyes fell on Bridget. The weight of the stare fell on Bridget's shoulders, forcing her still as the vicar's wife rose like a limber spider from her crouch.

"He told me about you-"

"Mrs. Johnson-"

"He told me all of this was his fault, his sacrilege. He told me that all of it would go away. But…"

She stopped, only a foot away from Bridget.

"But it's still here, isn't it?"

"In here, or out there?"

They hadn't heard Carthill enter. His coat was redder than Ellen Johnson, bright and crimson against the winter that swirled around outside. His face showed no emotion, bored and disinterested as he stood above the vicar's corpse.

"In here, or out there, Ellen Johnson?" He repeated.

The sound of his voice dredged up the vicar's wife from whatever madness had claimed her. She shivered, looking first from her fingernails to the form of her late husband, shuddering violently as she stammered out.

"I…I…"

The general raised the sabre of out his lion-headed cane ever-so-slightly.

"Do you prefer to die in your own home or do you prefer to have your bloody carcass paraded through the street? Either way madam, it will only be a short labour on my part."

265

***

The winds were picking up, frigid knives slashing Bridget's exposed face. Through her tears she could see Ellen Johnson, and guided her trembling body with a soft hand on her shoulder. The self-made widow was crying, the howling air only barely concealing her panicked wailing. Dortsmouth was quiet as they crossed the moat her husband had blessed and stepped beyond into the horde-lands.

No one other than the General, Bridget, and whichever boy poor they selected to take the vicar's place would be brave enough to approach the tower. Through the blinding white its grey shadow stood firmly and silently, mouths and eyes sealed tight against the biting storm.

"If it is any comfort to you," Bridget shouted over the wind, "I don't know what the vicar told you, but it was a lie. I never touched your husband, Ellen Johnson."

Ellen Johnson moved slower and cried louder.

They finally stopped before the tower.

"Would you like to pray?" There was no concern in Carthill's voice, no evidence that he felt anything other than a procedural interest in the matter.

Ellen Johnson stopped crying for a moment, as if in consideration.

Then she raised her face, peering out through snow with wounded, hateful eyes.

"He says you're lying!" She roared.

Bridget's eyes had drifted away from the weeping widow and towards the tower of mouths and eyes. A pair of dark blue lips moved slowly and silently behind Ellen Johnson. A yellow eye opened wide and fell upon her, locking her feet and knees as she watched the mouth word noiseless syllables, little tufts of steam billowing out like the factory smoke over grey London. The world drifted away into sweeping winds which overtook Ellen Johnson's lumbering shadow and Carthill's dangerous, angry shouting.

Ellen Johnson's fingers were at Bridget's throat, the woman's weight knocking her down to the ground. The grey sky became dark violet as Bridget's head hit the hard earth beneath the snow, as from somewhere in the storm her own gentle whisper confirmed what she had always known.

There was no reason to be afraid.

The world become dark and comforting, her own voice telling her all would be well.

Warm drops on her face brought her back. Ellen Johnson's throat gaped open above her, pouring out into her nose and mouth. Bridget heaved herself up, pushing the dying woman off her as bitter tears welled up from just behind her eyes. Bridget spat the blood out of her mouth, wiped it from her forehead. Ellen Johnson shook gently, and then, with a final twitch of her wrists, the poor woman was dead.

The general knelt beside her, wiping his long knife against the snow.

He stopped, transfixed by Ellen Johnson's slit neck. He bent forward, putting his fingers in the wound and parting it as if to peer in. Bridget's breath shook in her chest, and to stop herself from screaming she shouted at the general:

"What the hell are you doing!?"

The general seemed surprised and, for the first time, ashamed.

"I...It..." He stopped, wiping his bloody fingers against his pants as the metal returned to his glare. "It's nothing. You've got to be more careful, you daft girl! Bloody woman could've killed you!"

"I thought I saw something-"

"What? What did you see?"

He was desperate and scared. His eyes shook, desperate for a confirmation.

It was a way she had never seen him before.

"Nothing...It was nothing."

The general stared at her a moment, searching for any further elaboration. When she offered none he shrugged, sheathed his knife and headed towards the hall. Bridget followed close behind, keeping her eyes firmly on the general's back.

***

After Bridget cleaned herself she sat in front of the fireplace, watching orange flames dart up into the dark air for fleeting moments before snapping into dancing embers. She held her teacup with two hands, lifting its warmth to her mouth to quiet the voices in her mind.

She had never enjoyed killing. She remembered how hard she had cried as her father made her slaughter her first lamb; how her brothers had consoled her, the oldest lifting her up and cradling her to his chest as he explained that there was a certain hardness she would need for the world. That the hardness wasn't natural.

She had believed that, until she met the General.

She brought the warm, bitter tea to her lips.

Killing came too easy to Carthill. His coldness had brought Dortsmouth together, but after the new vicar was trained, there was no telling what would happen. The general was old now, already only a few steps away from death. And he had never hidden his spitefulness, his incapability or scorn of the small mercies of human decency.

And she thought of the way he peered into Ellen Johnson's wound, as if he were dissecting her. Either he was losing his mind, or he was finally revealing the deepest layer of who he had always been. Neither would keep Dortsmouth safe for long.

Her stomach lurched with the tea, empty and upset. She stood, draping a blanket over her shoulders before walking slowly towards the kitchen. The house was soundless save for the creaks of its walls as it stood against the whirls of snow and ash. Moving so slowly, Bridget became aware of how exhausted she truly was. How her knees ached, how her ankles pulled and her back pulsed. But the growling in her stomach compelled her forward. She needed something before she could entertain the thought of whiskey.

She found the kitchen and opened the door.

Carthill knelt above the chef, the little man covered in savage wounds that the General had torn apart with his hands. Carthill turned to her, his grey eyes alive with electricity and ecstasy.

"I was right."

The excitement tremored in his voice. Bridget breathed slowly through her nose, doing her best to hide the fear boiling beneath her ribs.

"I was right!" He said again, lifting a bloody hand towards Bridget and motioning for her to approach. He turned back to the chef, dipping his hands into a long cut.

Bridget grabbed a butcher's cleaver, terrified that it made too much noise as it scraped out of its block. But Carthill seemed too enraptured in whatever he was reading into the chef's wounds to notice.

"I saw them in Ellen Johnson and I knew it, they've always been here!"

She was close now, only a foot away. The body of the chef had been ruined, and Carthill had stained his uniform so bloody and it squelched when he shifted so she could get a better look. Her wrists hurt, right palm closed tight around the handle of the cleaver.

"They were us, all along! Just as I said, there was no difference!"

She lifted the cleaver above her head and brought it down with two hands.

But Carthill moved quickly. He moved his head as the blade bore into his shoulder, almost splitting it from his torso. From the torn flesh of that ragged shoulder a black tendril spurted out. Bridget tried to scream, but the panic overwhelmed her. The tendril was as thin as a pen, thrashing wildly as it reached into the open air. The general turned and looked at it, laughing wildly as a child watching some performing seal.

269

"It's what we are!" The general was roaring now, moving so savagely that Bridget only saw the glint of the knife as he ran towards her.

Her mind fled as her muscles took over, the cleaver coming up and into his chest with the wet snapping of ribs. He fell backward, dying, as the tendril from his shoulder continued to probe and search its surroundings. The cleaver came down again and again, tears clotting her sight as the general's body became a dripping mass of tendrils sprouting from seeping gashes.

It was the burning on the back of her wrist that seared through her horror and brought her thoughts back to her.

Carthill had managed to get a cut in, something that tore through her gown and into the flesh beneath.

Frantically she tore at her sleeve, her heaving breathing making her queasy and ill.

From the small wound a yellow eye looked up at her. Bridget fell backwards as thin black tendrils no thicker than horse hairs searching gingerly and blindly from the cut. She ceased breathing, petrified as the things grew longer, gingerly caressing her face and feeling outwards around her. They enfolded her lovingly, petting her as if to quiet the crying that died just beneath her throat.

Outside, gentle whispers rode the dark, winter wind.

We knew, through such messengers as dared ride by day and night, that as with the South West, parts of Wales remained defiant. Around Cardiff, Jews who had fled the Russian pogroms of a decade before were reluctant to flee again, and there were tales of rabbis and chapel ministers side by side, blessing farm implements and holding fast against the forces of the Incursion. The rabbis, it must be said, did not find sense in the Incursion of a Christian Hell, but that they faced 'demonic' creatures from some Elsewhere could hardly be doubted. Faith and Will were still needed.

The area around Abergevenny was not so fortunate. Between the Black Mountains and Offa's Dyke, great slaughter was done – flesh burned and weapons failed. They say that a self-styled Duke of Hell was there, whipping and tearing at any Infernal beasts which hesitated when the Enochian bullets hit. Those companies of human troops and volunteers left in any order after the battle retreated towards Cardiff – lone survivors fled into the hills and surrounding countryside, glad simply to have lived...

THE ONES THAT WERE LEFT BEHIND

Martin J. Gilbert

The countryside was shrouded in smoke and dust, and it had been for days. A column of the infernal beasts had come through the valley, tramping through the fields and trampling the crops. While they passed, the sounds of thundering footsteps and beating wings, of screaming prisoners and snarling voices, had filled the air. The smell of smoke, of blood, of burning villages and villagers.

And then they were gone, leaving behind the smoke and the dust and the smell. And just one girl, in a small cottage set a little back from the road, hidden in a tiny copse that had somehow managed to avoid the attention of the horde.

The memory of them, of the noise and the flames, still lingered in the cracks and the corners and behind the trees when she emerged a few days later, alone, walking slowly through the devastation.

"Hello?" she called out. "Is there anyone left?"

She sniffed the acrid air, listened out for voices, but heard only silence. She turned her head and shouted again: "Hello?"

But there was no answer.

The nearest village was a husk, empty of life but filled with smouldering embers and the stench of burning. The demons had been thorough, she thought. They had left nothing alive behind them.

She smiled wryly to herself. Well, except me. They left me.

There was food in an old storehouse at the edge of the village. From it, she took bread and honey, as well as some meat that smelled palatable, and she carried them all back to the house. The food, along with water from the stream that flowed down

272

from the hills behind the cottage, and passed through the copse, were enough to satisfy her hunger, for now.

As the days passed – as the smoke faded and the dust settled on the ground – it grew apparent that she was the only creature alive in the valley. There was no sound of birdsong or rustling of small beasts in the undergrowth. No rabbits were caught in the traps that had been laid out in the thick grass in the days before the horde had passed through.

No living soul was left in the place, she thought one evening, sitting on a heavy wooden stool outside the cottage. Not a soul of man or beast or child.

Only me.

***

Another week passed before, at last, someone came to the valley.

It was in the hours between the rising of the sun and its light penetrating through the mists of early morning. A man – a soldier dressed in red with dark trousers, a white belt and brass buttons – limping and coughing and barely able to walk in a straight line, stumbled out of the mist. He might have wandered straight past the house hidden in the tiny wood, if she hadn't seen him and called out.

"Hello!" she said, her heart thumping with excitement that someone had come at last. "There is shelter here."

He stopped and squinted at her, looked around the empty valley as though checking to see if she were a delusion. His mouth opened and closed, and his brow furrowed, but he said only one word.

"Sh-shelter?"

She smiled and nodded. "Yes," she said. "I have shelter here, if you want it."

It took a minute for her words to seep into his brain, but when they did, his shoulders sagged and his face lit up with joy.

"They aren't here?"

"The horde passed through nearly two weeks ago," she said, "but they are done with the valley."

He half-stumbled, half-ran towards her and then, just as he got within a few yards, he tripped on a hidden root and fell at her feet. Laughing, she lifted him up.

"Come on," she said. "I'll take you to the house."

His uniform was muddied and torn, so she put it into a wooden trunk in the large bedroom. There were spare clothes in a closet and she set them out for him while he bathed himself.

She paused for a moment outside the room and listened at the door. He hummed a soldier's song, pausing only to hiss and gasp in pain when the water touched upon an open wound. She had never seen a naked man before, and curiosity impelled her to try to sneak a peek through the half-open door, but she resisted. She hadn't invited him into the house to leer at him.

When he came out, dressed in clothes that were a little too big for him, she smiled and handed him a plate of sliced bread and cold meat. He hesitated for a moment, then fell upon it ravenously. She watched him in silence as he ate.

He was young, and short for a soldier. His hair was pale, almost colourless, and his chin was covered in wisps of dark hair. His face was gaunt, covered in cuts and bruises, and his green eyes were sunk deep into their sockets. He was tired and bedraggled and had the look of a man who had left behind hope, passed through despair and had come out the other side with nothing of any use.

When he had finished the first plate of food and had slowed down a little midway through his second, she spoke to him.

"Where have you come from?" she said.

"Just now, or...?" he said, blinking uncertainly. Then he smiled. "Of course, that's what you mean. The battle of Abergavenny. Though I suppose it was closer to here than to Abergavenny, wherever here is." He picked up another piece of meat. "Maybe they'll call it that, in the end," he said. "The Battle of Here, wherever it is."

He kept eating and didn't look at her. It was clear he had no intention of asking where 'here' was.

"And how did it go?"

He barked a laugh and looked up at last.

"Look at me, girl," he said. "The victors of a battle don't look half so bedraggled as this, nor are they wandering through the valleys on their own two days later.

"No," he said, gritting his teeth. "We lost, and we lost badly. Besides me, I doubt there's many of us left. They don't like leaving the living behind."

He shook his head, then glanced out the window. "Though I don't suppose you need me to tell you that?"

She smiled sadly. "Seems we're both of us the ones that were left behind."

He smiled back, looking her in the eye for the first time.

She was barely fifteen, or so she appeared to him. Dark of hair and pale of skin, she was so skinny that she could have passed for ten, but her eyes were older. A deep blue like the ocean, with worry lines surrounding them. The eyes said she could be twenty or more, but her body said ten, so he settled on thinking she was probably no more than fifteen.

She held his gaze for a long while, and he was the one who first looked away.

"I appreciate the food," he said. "And the bath and the fresh clothes. But I should be on my way."

The girl's face fell.

"No!" she said. "Please – no. Not yet. I've been alone for too long."

Her eyes opened wide, and he felt a void opening up in his gut. Her family had clearly abandoned her, or had been taken by the demons. How could he leave her here, alone?

"Please," she said again, "stay here for one day – one night at least."

His decision to leave suddenly seemed both selfish and foolish – where would he go, after all? He relented.

"Only if you'll allow me to make myself useful."

Her eyes sparkled, and he smiled at her.

He spent the afternoon chopping logs in the small clearing in front of the cottage; fetching water from the stream; slicing vegetables in the kitchen. While he busied himself, the girl wandered down to what was left of the village to gather whatever unspoiled food was there.

When she came in, as darkness began to crawl down the hillside towards them, she found him sprawled on the bed in the large bedroom, snoring. She pulled his shoes off gently and covered him with a sheet.

As she did, her hand brushed his thigh and she felt a strange tingle of excitement run along her back and down her spine. It was a strange feeling – something new and formless. A kind of nagging hunger not easily satisfied.

She shivered, shook her head, and went back into the kitchen.

***

It was the smell of cooking that woke him. The last of the meat from the village, a few vegetables and some potatoes, all being stewed in a pot on the range. The girl stood over it, stirring distractedly.

She didn't know he was there, so the soldier watched her for a few minutes, thinking that this was a glimpse of what it might be like to have a wife. Someone to take care of him; to cook for him; to bear his children; to share his life. To share his bed.

She would make someone a good wife, he decided. Probably sooner rather than later. At fifteen, she was certainly old enough, if she could cook like this.

"Smells good," he said, at last.

She turned to him with a start and an absent look in her eyes. She blinked a couple of times, then wiped her hands on her once-white apron and gestured towards the table.

"Sit," she said. "I found something for you to drink."

276

There were two dusty brown bottles of beer on the table, and his eyes opened wide when he saw them. Soon, the first one was half empty, and he was sitting back in his chair laughing.

"You know," he said, "I've had many drinks that tasted finer than that in my life, but I've never had one that made me half so happy."

The girl ladled the stew into a bowl and put it in front of him.

"Are you not having any?" he asked.

"No," she said. "I couldn't wait for you, so I've already eaten."

"I'm sorry," he replied. "I didn't think I was…"

"Don't be," she interrupted. "You seemed very much at peace."

He swallowed a mouthful of stew and nodded.

"I was," he said, "for the first time in months. These… things have made life unbearable. And we can't seem to stop them."

"They are winning, then?"

"From what I've seen, yes." He finished one bottle of beer and opened the second. "What can we do to stop them? Their skin is like stone, the ones with wings can fly far above our artillery. Half of them are the size of elephants and five times as hard to damage." He shook his head.

"And when they get close, they have the viciousness of beasts, but with the intelligence of a man." He sighed. "They gave us a rifle to replace the old Emily, and it does seem to hurt them, but the bullets are so heavy, it's just impossible…"

He shook his head and drank a long draught of the beer. It was warm, a little bitter, but it was good.

"I'm sure you don't care about military matters, miss," he said, waving his hand and focussing on what was left of his dinner.

"I don't mind," she said, standing up and walking across to a cupboard. She opened the door and took out another two bottles of beer. "It's just nice to hear someone talk. I've been alone too long."

"They came through here two weeks ago, was it?"

"Twelve days," she said, sitting down. "And that already feels like a lifetime." She looked away and sighed. "Why do *you* think they've come?"

She emphasised the 'you', as though she had her own theory, but he didn't seem to pay any attention.

"The demons?" He barked a laugh and opened another beer. "I'll be damned if I know." Realising what he just said, he chuckled. "Though I guess we're all damned now anyway, aren't we?"

She smiled at him and her eyes seemed to dance.

"I don't know," he said, looking away. "All the officers had different ideas. One said it's the end times – Book of Revelation and all that. 'The world is doomed, and we should just get used to it,' he used to say.

"Another one, a posh lad who fancied himself a vicar or somesuch – came down from Oxford with a degree in something or other – said it was more than that. 'Retribution,' he said. 'The Empire is the new Tower of Babel,' he would say, all pompous and full of himself, 'and just as God destroyed that in punishment for man's desire to reach heaven, God is destroying the British for our desire to be gods to lesser men.'"

He smiled at the memory. "Arrogant toad," he said.

"And then the real men of God – the vicars and priests and rabbis and the whole lot – they said that was all nonsense. 'It's a test,' they told us. 'A test of faith. Only true faith will win the day,' they said, and they gave us holy water and crosses and little amulets and stars to wear. The day of the battle, I could've done with a few more of the big bullets instead of those on my belt."

"Do you still have your gun?" the girl asked.

"No," he said. "Lost it shortly after running out of bullets. But I have my sword." He laughed again and shook his head. "My fucking sword! If you'll excuse me, miss. But a fat lot of good that would've done me, even if I'd had the chance to use it."

278

She leaned forward. "May I see it?" she said.

He blinked, surprised at the request. "It's a bit odd for a woman to be interested in that sort of thing," he said. "Are you sure?"

She nodded. "I've never seen a sword before," she said. The eagerness burned in her eyes, and he was reminded again that she was young. And living in a place like this wouldn't have afforded her the opportunity of seeing much of the world.

In a way, her enthusiasm was endearing.

He nodded and went to fetch it. On the way into the bedroom, he felt his feet wobble a little, and he had to hold on to the door frame to stay steady. "Too much beer," he mumbled to himself.

The sword wasn't in the chest with his uniform, but he found it at last, thrown away in a corner of the room. He must've left it there in a daze after coming into the house. He bit his lip – his commanding officer would have had him taken outside and lashed for that sort of carelessness back in the barracks.

'Uniforms pressed and buttons shiny,' they were always told. 'Sword sharp and rifle ready.'

But when the demons had come, they hadn't been intimidated by rows and rows of well-pressed uniforms nor blinded by shiny buttons. Bullets and swords hadn't fazed them either, though a few of the lads swore that the demons' skin burned when they were hit by bullets that one of the vicars had blessed. Or one of the priests, or a rabbi. One of the holy men anyway – to him, now, they were all a blur of useless sanctimony.

He picked up the sword and looked at it. It was filthy; he'd fallen down in the mud not long after the bullets had run out and the demons had swarmed the battlefield. Like a fool, he'd charged them, sword swinging wild circles, shouting for them to go back to hell or he'd send them there himself.

He shook his head and smiled. Such reckless bravado – the intoxication that a man feels when the heat of battle is on him and death is staring him in the face. The desire to kill – to release all the pent-up rage and nervous energy; to feel that all the training,

279

all the preparation, had been for a reason. The desire to do something foolhardy and idiotic rather than do nothing. And what had it got him – or any of them?

Death or glory, they sang on the morning of the battle. Well, there'd been no glory, and plenty of death. But here he was now, with neither. All he had was a mud-coated sword and a crumpled uniform with dirty buttons.

He'd tripped and fallen before he got near any of them, and he hit his head on a stone. By the time he'd woken up, they were all gone. A few dead soldiers were left, but the horde had taken the others – for meat, or a sacrifice, or some revolting reason he didn't want to imagine – and he was the only one left alive.

And now he was here, with her. A girl who'd been left behind by the horde, much like he had.

He found a piece of cloth in a drawer and wiped his sword. She should see it clean, at least. Even if it was neither bright nor shiny.

He returned to the kitchen when he was done. But in the time he'd been gone, she'd fallen asleep on the table, her head resting on her arms. He walked around her carefully, quietly, to make sure she didn't wake. As he passed behind her, he paused. The way she was resting on the table had made the apron pull her dress tight around her hips, and he lingered to look at the shape of her.

He moved his jaw from side to side, bit his tongue. She had a more womanly figure than had appeared from the shapeless drape of her dress earlier. Her body was older than ten, he was sure of that at least. He could feel his temperature rising, could feel the blood flow and gather in his cheeks, could feel his… It had been a long time; they'd been too busy preparing for the horde's arrival, for the battle, to spend time with the women who loitered in the bars outside the barracks.

Improper thoughts filled his head. He gripped the hilt of his sword and a low moan escaped his lips.

She jerked upright and turned around, a tired smile on her face.

"Oh," she said. "I wasn't sure if you were coming back out. Do you have it?"

"I do," he said, his voice hoarse. His face was flushed; he lifted the sword in one hand and slowly clenched and unclenched the fist of the other.

"May I?" she said.

Only half conscious of what he was doing, he turned the sword around and offered her the hilt.

"Be careful," he said.

She took it from him and looked at it. "It's heavy," she said. She took a step towards the door, tried to brandish the sword, almost dropped it.

"Be careful!" he said again, though his eyes weren't on the sword.

"Or what?" she said playfully, turning to face him. A girlish grin played on her lips. She pointed the blade at him. "I'm the one with the weapon now," she said. "What can you do to me?"

The soldier stood still for a moment. He felt breathless; his mind was filled with thoughts of the battle, of charging at the demons. Thoughts of her. Her body, her hips.

Once again, he felt it – the need to do something.

His sword.

Quicker than he intended, more forcefully than he had expected, he slapped the blade to one slide.

"Ouch!" the girl said, rubbing her wrist. She dropped the sword and it clattered to the floor. "That hurt!"

He ignored her and picked up the weapon. He struggled to get his breath back. He couldn't look at her until he could breathe normally again. Until his senses returned.

"You didn't have to do that," she said. Her voice was pained, in shock and fright.

"It's the way I was trained, miss," he said at last, speaking in little more than a whisper. "It's what we do."

There was silence; he still couldn't look at her.

"If you wanted it, you only had to ask."

"I'm a soldier, miss," he said, turning back to her. "When it comes to our weapons, we don't ask. When we're at war, we're taught to take what we need when we need it, even if it means using force." He picked up the sword and pointed it at her. "That's what this is for. If you have the weapon, then you can take what you want. It's called the spoils of war. Those are the rules of war."

She looked at him without speaking, her eyes wide. She had taken a couple of steps backwards, but he had followed her – the point of the blade was still only a few inches from her face. She shook her head.

"You only had to ask."

***

That night, she lay awake in her small bedroom near the pantry. She could hear the soldier pacing in the other room, muttering and mumbling to himself. When his footsteps came to a halt by the doorway, or close to the wall that separated them, she imagined she could hear his breath, heavy and loud and threatening.

She just wanted him to go to bed now, to fall asleep because of an excess of beer, like men are supposed to.

But he didn't; he kept pacing, muttering, mumbling; pausing and breathing.

Until he stopped, and she realised she'd been holding her own breath the entire time.

And then the door opened.

It was pitch black; she couldn't see him, but she knew he was there. Heavy footsteps came over to her bed; his breath was over her. He stopped, and then she felt the point of the sword against her throat.

"Stay still," he hissed.

She felt the weight of him on the bed, one of his hands on her shoulders. The sheets moved; her clothes pulled up. The edge of the blade now on her throat.

"There's a good girl."

He was on top of her. She tried to move away, but the sword, his arm, his weight pinned her down. It hurt; he was hurting her, outside and inside.

"The spoils of war," he whispered.

***

The next day, she got up with the sunrise, straightened her dress.

He was at the dinner table, dressed in his crumpled uniform, eating a slice of bread with the last of the honey she had found in the village. He didn't say anything to her when she came into the kitchen.

She cleared her throat.

"Is there any bread left?"

He jerked his head towards the cupboard. "Some," he said.

She fetched the bread and sat across from him. Her heart beat rapidly; a part of her wanted to eat, but another part of her was repulsed by the thought of it. She looked at him; her stomach lurched, and she made up her mind.

She took a deep breath.

"I'd like some of that honey," she said.

He glanced across at her, then looked at the empty jar of honey.

"It's all gone," he said, turning his attention back to breakfast.

She stood up and stepped around the table.

"I said I'd like some honey," she said again. Her voice was determined, defiant, demanding.

Different.

"And I said it's all gone," he insisted. He looked up.

His eyes opened wide and he tried to stand. But his feet had gone numb; the chair skittered across the floor and he fell.

"No!" he said, but his voice was little more than a hoarse whisper.

The girl was standing in front of him, but something else was occupying the same space. Something massive with red flesh and black talons. It was her, but she wasn't a girl any more. She was a thing of flame and fury.

Her mouth opened wide – a great gaping maw that could swallow the world.

"And yet," the demon said, her voice sounding as if it was coming from a great pit deep within the bowels of the earth, "I want it."

The soldier opened and closed his own mouth, like a thing pulled suddenly into the air from the darkness of a great lake. He couldn't speak.

She moved to stand over him and leaned down. He could feel her fiery breath warming his face, could feel his skin begin to blister and crack. Her mouth opened wide, wider still, until it was wide enough to envelop him.

And then her teeth were on him, biting everywhere at once, cracking the bones and splitting the flesh. Hurting him, inside and outside.

As he passed into oblivion, he could hear her repeat the same words, over and over:

"The spoils of war."

With the losses at Abergevenny, and the costly failure of an expeditionary force to retake Birmingham, the fractured British Government was in disarray. The Palace-in-exile at Pendennis had forces pressing east, but too slowly; Prince Bertie's Army of the North had reached a position of stalemate. Where men had fallen, women took up arms and crucifixes, marching on Leeds and Manchester. Thousands of female mill-hands, shop-workers and flower girls confounded expectations by driving back demons unprepared for an army which fought with knife and cunning, which never stood in line of battle, but conducted its own war of attrition.

These women won back their homes, but homes which lay within the charred remains of once great cities. Food was scarce, and sanitation poor. Worse, in those places where Infernal forces settled rather than grinding their way through, they seemed to grow stronger with the passing weeks, as if acclimatizing to their new realm. It was as if not only the creatures of Hell, but the Inferno itself was entering the mortal world.

At last the cry went out, to scholars, scientists and spiritualists, to prioresses and priests, anyone who had even briefly contemplated that which lies Beyond. To witch-women and engineers, to artificers and antiquarians, to every name which could be named, it went - by telegraph where the lines were intact, and by volunteer riders where they were not. It was smuggled along the coast in fishing smacks, and semaphored from hill-tops.

This time it was no orderly request for advice, nor summons to council, but a cry of desperation. It came, without royal sanction, issued jointly by the Lords of the Admiralty and Marquess Lansdowne, the new Secretary of State for War.

"We are losing. In God's name, help us."

And none could doubt his Lordship's sincerity – the charred head of his predecessor was nailed to the great door of the ruined House of Commons, an inverted cross branded upon its forehead...

A SWIG IN HELL

Charles R. Rutledge

'E'll be squattin' on the coals,
Givin' drink to poor damned souls,
And I'll get a swig in Hell from Gunga Din!

Rudyard Kipling

Somehow the demons had managed to flank him. Captain Thomas Gordon, of the Royal Fusiliers Regiment, used the last of the ammunition in his Enfield to drop two of the screaming creatures as they rushed out of the mouth of Bow Street and into Long Acre, effectively cutting off his retreat. How had the things gotten so deep into the city? Were the wards finally failing?

Only moments before, Gordon had been on patrol with a dozen of his men. He hadn't really expected to run into the enemy, but there had been reported sightings of demonic creatures near Drury Lane. His superiors had considered that unlikely, as the city had been well protected by Enochian wards since the battle of Hampstead Heath, but they had sent out a patrol anyway.

Without any warning, a score or more of what the padres called the 'Marching Host', horrors of low intelligence but savage ferocity, had converged on the patrol, scattering Gordon's men in all directions. Standard procedure called for all soldiers to try and get back to base if separated from the unit.

Gordon backed up until he slammed into the wall of an abandoned boot shop. He pulled his Webley revolver free of its holster, but didn't relinquish his grip on the Enfield. He was six shots away from needing the rifle as a bludgeon.

The things came scurrying toward him. They were a misshapen lot, no two of the creatures the same, just shambling collections of flesh, teeth, and claws. One with a long, snake-like neck, but the head of a goat, got ahead of its comrades and Gordon sent a bullet crashing through its brain. Gordon said a silent prayer of thanks to the unknown metal smith who had etched the proper symbols on that bullet.

Other creatures were crowding in around him. Gordon pushed at the shop door with his shoulder and it fell inward. He moved quickly inside. At least this was a more defensible position. The things could only come at him one at a time.

That was what he thought anyway, until something that looked like a seven-foot tall pig that walked on two legs smashed into the doorway and a mass of other gibbering things crowded in behind it. Gordon had seen plenty of the denizens of hell, but he knew he would never get used to it. The smell of corruption and brimstone was overwhelming, and the very air around the creatures felt wrong somehow.

Gordon kept firing as he backed further into the room, being careful not to trip over the ruined shelves and other furniture. The Webley clicked on empty and he pulled the trigger three more times before he gave up and jammed the pistol into its holster.

A slug-like thing flowed into the room and started toward him. It opened a gaping maw and howled like a wounded child. Gordon felt his stomach clench and he raised the rifle like a cricket bat, both pleased and amazed to see that his hands weren't shaking. The thing came forward and a stink of rotted meat rolled off of it.

A second later, what passed for the slug's head burst and Gordon heard the sound of rifle fire. He looked past the dying monster and saw Sergeant Randolph Baine standing in the doorway with his Enfield levelled. Baine picked another target and fired. As he did so, a huge, but totally human form swept past him into the room. Sergeant Gavin Doyle roared as he cut into the creatures with a long single-edged sword with a basket hilt. The blade gave off a pale, azure glow, showing that it had been etched with Enochian letters.

Gordon marvelled at the sheer ferocity of the big Scotsman. Doyle was always the first into the fight and seemed happier using sword and dirk than firearms. He was the only man known to have ever killed a demon with his bare hands, and he had three ugly scars on his face to prove it.

Baine was Doyle's exact opposite. Small and wiry, he was cat quick and probably the best shot in the regiment, though Gordon flattered himself that he could give the man a run for his money.

The two sergeants continued their grim work until the room was cleared of hell spawn. When they reached Gordon's side, Baine said, "Sorry it took us so long to work our way back to you, Captain."

Gordon said, "I'm hardly likely to complain, Baine."

"We should go," Doyle said. "There are more of these things in the streets."

"And you hate the thought of someone else killing them but you, Doyle, me son," said Baine.

The big sergeant didn't say anything but he smiled.

Gordon said, "Sergeant Doyle is right. We should get back to Covent Garden and let the major know what we found. The beasts have gotten into the city."

The Royal Fusiliers had been stationed in makeshift barracks in Covent Garden for the past several weeks. As the communities and towns around London proper became increasingly overrun with the demon hordes, it made a centrally located base from which to sally forth from the city in whatever direction was required.

The trio made it back to the market without further incident. As usual, the place was a hive of activity, with career soldiers working side by side with civilian volunteers. Flags of various regiments fluttered from tents, including freshly minted and hastily contrived banners for new, combined regiments formed from the survivors of those that had been all but destroyed by the conflict.

A private came running up to Captain Gordon as he and the two sergeants trudged into the camp. His red uniform was soiled but otherwise neat. Standards had understandably fallen as the situation had worsened, but they tried to hang on to order and discipline. Sometimes Gordon thought it was the only thing keeping them in the fight.

The private saluted. "Major Murphy sent me to find you, sir. He said you were to report to him as soon as you returned and to bring Sergeants Baine and Doyle with you."

"I had planned to seek him out anyway, though what he wants with these two I can't imagine."

"I'm sure I don't know, sir."

"Well, we'll find out soon enough. Come along you lot."

Major Campion Murphy was quartered in an abandoned lace shop on one corner of the market. He was seated behind a small writing desk that had been left in the place, looking at a stack of reports.

Gordon and his men waited until Murphy looked up. Murphy said, "Don't bother telling me, Gordon. The few men who made it back from the patrol gave me the bad news. Our defences are failing. The blighters are getting through. These dispatches tell the same story. All over the country, the wards and blessings are losing whatever power they had. Our situation becomes more desperate every day."

Gordon said, "Is there nothing to be done, sir?"

"That is a question, Captain. And coincidentally, it has something to do with the reason I told you to come here and to bring these two men with you. An escort is waiting to take us to Whitehall."

***

Professor Bernard Wake tried to remember at what exact point he had stopped believing in God. He couldn't recall, and oddly enough, it had made no difference in his career as a theologian of Christchurch College, Oxford. He had gone right on, teaching classes and writing papers just as if he believed, and even when the demons had come, he had still not regained his faith.

Demons? He didn't even like to use the term. They were creatures. Animals from some other plane of existence. Demon was just a word. And yet, the language of Enoch, 'discovered' by Doctor John Dee and reportedly used by 'angels' gave the monsters pause.

Of course later it had turned out that ceremonies and relics from other faiths also worked against the demons. From Shinto, Hebrew, Islam, and Hindu. That had certainly sent many of Wake's peers into fits. Many weapons and defences from many religions. Faith, it seemed was the key, not a particular system of belief. And in the end, perhaps that was why all of them had begun to fail. Because men had begun to lose faith.

Wake looked at the small wooden box that sat on his borrowed desk in his borrowed office. The object inside it had enormous power to the faithful. It was perhaps the last and only thing that could do what the world needed it to do. And he was the only one who knew how to use it. The ultimate symbol of faith, wielded by a man who had long since ceased to believe in anything.

***

Stand at attention you louts," Major Murphy said. "This is the Secretary of the State of War, the most honourable Marquess of Lansdowne."

Gordon was already standing as straight as he could. Baine made a show of clicking his boot heels together. Doyle just glowered. It was his perpetual expression. The three men had indeed been ushered quickly to the fortified government buildings at Whitehall and taken to an office deep with one of those

291

structures. Aside from the major, there were only two men in the room, both seated behind a heavy oak table.

"Thank you for coming, gentlemen," Lord Lansdowne said. He was a thin man with a high forehead and a heavy moustache. He gestured toward the man seated beside him. "This is Professor Wake of Christchurch. The professor is a theologian and he has been one of our greatest assets in the battle against the demon hordes.

"As you men doubtless know, the demons are winning. We've fought a long hard fight, but they are wearing us down with numbers and sheer savagery. Professor Wake has offered a possible solution. A way to stop them. I need you and many more of our brave soldiers to help him."

"Just tell us what we need to do, my lord," Gordon said.

"That, I fear, will take some explaining, Captain. It comes down to the portals. The gates. They must be shut for once and all."

Sergeant Baine said, "Isn't that what the padres and wizards have been trying to do, your lordship?"

The major shot Baine a look. The wiry man smiled.

Lord Lansdowne said, "Indeed, sergeant. But we may at last have a way. I'll let the professor explain."

Wake stood up. He was slender, with dark hair which had gone grey at the temples. "You men know how the portals work. They open and the creatures flow through them, and they close. From studying them over time, we've learned that it takes tremendous eldritch energy to keep them open. There are limits it seems, even to the powers of Hell.

"But there is one portal that never closes. As near as we can determine, it was the first one to open and it has stood open ever since."

Gordon said, "And why is that sir?"

"Because it has to. It is the link between our plane of existence and the one occupied by the demons. It took them centuries to open it, and it has to stay open in order for the other,

292

more short lived, portals to function. Close that one and you close them all."

"How did we learn all of this?" Gordon said. "I can't imagine the demons just told us their plans."

Lansdowne said, "Not all of our own mystical weapons are offensive, Captain. The spiritualists and seers. The clairvoyants. All of them have turned their talents to probing the minds of those entities intelligent enough to form thoughts as we know them. And many of those seers have paid a terrible price for their efforts."

Gordon nodded. He was a fighting man and hadn't really considered how magic could be used as anything but a weapon. Magic? Ah, how he would have scoffed at that idea just a few short years ago.

"Excuse me for pointing this out," Baine said. "But if you throw me out of the pub and close the door, I can come back in later when you're not looking."

Wake smiled. "You could, Sergeant, unless I put something there to kill you if you tried."

Baine said, "That would change things a bit."

Gordon said, "Do we have such a thing?"

"I believe so," said Wake. "A way to close the portal and keep them from reopening it. To undo their centuries of toil."

"Can you tell us what it is?" said Gordon.

Wake shook his head. "The very air has ears, I'm afraid. Not all demons are as visible as the ones you fought today. You'll just have to trust me."

"It's not as if we have many options," Lord Lansdowne said. "Professor Wake believes he can close the gates. Major, I need you and your men to give him the chance. The portal is guarded by many demons. We're going to send all our available regiments to attack."

"Won't that spread us thin across the rest of our defences, my Lord?" Murphy said.

Lansdowne said, "It will. But we've reached a point where we have to make bold moves or we are surely lost. Pulling our remaining troops from their current positions is a risk, but one I don't think we can avoid.

"Major, I want your regiment to fight through to the portal and get Wake to it. Captain Gordon and his two sergeants will be the professor's personal guards and stay with him the entire time."

Wake said, "Tell them the rest please."

The secretary took a long breath. "Yes, the rest. One thing you men should know. The portal can only be shut from the inside. You'll have to follow the professor into Hell and there's little chance you'll be able to come back."

"How little?" said Baine.

"Virtually none, I fear."

Gordon said, "We'll get him there."

"Er... do we actually get to volunteer?" said Baine.

"You volunteered when you put on that uniform, Sergeant," Gordon said.

Baine shrugged. "I don't recall this part being mentioned at the time, but as you say, sir."

"I've no doubt of your bravery," Lansdowne said. "The operation begins tomorrow. The permanent portal is close to Canterbury. You'll meet up with the other regiments tonight and be ready to fight at dawn. The demons don't like the daylight, and they seem to abhor sunrise most of all. We'll take any advantage we can get."

"Transportation, my lord?" said Gordon.

"The rail lines are clear as far as Chartham and the portal is just beyond that. A train will be ready for your regiment at 4:00 this afternoon. Now, if you gentlemen will excuse us, I have some matters to discuss with Professor Wake."

"Back to the barracks, men," said Major Murphy. "Best rest while you can."

Wake said, "I'll be taking the train with you men. I'll see you this afternoon."

***

294

The train wasn't ready on time of course. It was close to dusk when the whistle finally sounded and the train began to roll. It was a former passenger train refitted for the use of the army. Every seat was taken, and soldiers sat in the aisles in some of the cars.

Except Gordon, his two men, and Wake, who had a compartment to themselves. Wake seemed lost in thought and even Baine was uncharacteristically quiet. Gordon gazed out the window and watched the city roll past. He saw more fires than on previous night patrols, and a haze of dark smoke hung low over the rooftops. In the crimson light of the setting sun, London had already begun to look like hell on Earth.

Gordon closed his eyes. As usual, in quiet moments his thoughts turned to his late wife Nancy. She'd been killed early in the incursion, and now he found that it was becoming more difficult to imagine a clear picture of her face. He did his best, though. He needed to remember. The bible said that vengeance was the Lord's, but it was going to be Gordon's too. After all, what was the worst that could happen to him? Going to hell? This train was taking him to that very place.

Full dark came soon enough as the train rolled eastward. They made no stops. As they passed one platform, Gordon saw that several soldiers had been impaled on stakes driven into the ground. Not far beyond that, weird and terrible shapes danced around a fire bordered by a ring of human skulls.

"This is what we have to stop," Professor Wake said.

Gordon hadn't been aware that Wake was staring out the window as well. He said, "Do you really think you can?"

Wake said, "Nothing is certain, but yes, if I've read my myths and legends right, I think we have a chance."

"Myths? Then you're not a Christian?"

"Not for a very long time."

"Isn't that unusual for a theologian?" said Gordon.

"More common that you'd think. The study of comparative religions often leads someone to conclude that all are equally invalid."

"But you plan to use a holy relic to stop the demons?"

"Such things have been shown to work."

"So you'll use it, even though you don't understand it."

"I don't fully understand how an electric light bulb works, Captain, but I can read by its light just the same."

The train began to slow. Gordon checked his pocket watch and then looked out the window. He said, "Something's wrong. We shouldn't have reached Chartham yet."

The train lurched to a halt, spilling everyone from their seats. Gordon got to his feet and threw open the compartment's door. When he saw Doyle and Baine about to follow he said, "Stay with Professor Wake. I'll see what's wrong."

Gordon stepped into the corridor and made his way to the closest exit. Outside, various members of the regiment were lighting lanterns. There was a lot of noise and activity near the front of the train. Peering into the darkness, Gordon could see... something in front of the train, a large, amorphous shape that seemed to quiver in a sickening gelatinous fashion.

As the soldiers with lanterns got closer to the thing, Gordon saw that it was a worm of gigantic proportions. Part of its mass was on the track. Gordon knew that the demons, whatever they were, sometimes came in the form of giant creatures. He had once seen a thing, over twenty feet tall, that walked on two legs but had a face like that of a lamprey. They had brought it down with cannon fire. There were no cannons available here, the artillery regiment having gone to Chartham earlier.

Without warning, the worm made a loud gurgling sound, and a stream of yellow ichor spewed from some orifice in its face. Anyone the liquid touched began screaming and trying to get away. In the light of fallen lanterns, Gordon saw the men's flesh was melting from their bones.

Gordon was filled with horror and with sympathy for his comrades, but he also knew they had to get the creature away from the tracks if they were going to get Wake to the front.

He began gathering men and telling them to fire their rifles at the beast, but to stay well clear of it. Many of the soldiers were still in shock, but duty and discipline won out over fear, and they followed Gordon's orders.

The men fired at the 'head' of the worm where hopefully whatever passed for its brain resided. Gordon could see fluid leaking from a dozen wounds and the ground burned where the worm's blood fell.

"Keep firing and backing away, men," Gordon shouted. "You lot! Take their positions while they reload."

Slowly, the worm began to lurch after the retreating riflemen. It gurgled and hissed, and shot forth another burst of acid, but the soldiers were far enough away to escape harm. Soon the behemoth was clear of the tracks.

Major Murphy came running up to Gordon and said, "Quick thinking, Captain, but you shouldn't have left Professor Wake."

"Doyle and Baine are with him, sir. Anything that can get past those two would make short work of me."

Murphy grinned, a rarity for the major. "True enough. Now get back on the train. The drivers are already getting her back in motion."

With a quick salute, Gordon rushed back to the train.

***

As dawn threatened the horizon, the men of the Fusiliers and the other regiments trudged away from Chartham toward the field where the permanent portal rested. They had two cavalry regiments, two other infantry regiments and one artillery. None were at anywhere near full strength, not after so long a struggle.

The train had arrived at Chartham station close to midnight, and the regiment had caught what little rest they could. The plan was to make a slow, quiet approach to the portal, and then to attack as soon as the enemy became visible. The demons had never shown much skill for scouting, so likely they would be caught off guard. Gordon couldn't imagine that they would ever expect the humans would attack such a well-guarded area, filled with so many demonic troops.

Baine, Doyle, and Gordon walked along with Wake, keeping him in their midst. Doyle was in the lead, of course. He wore his kilt that morning, the traditional uniform of the Highland Regiment of which he was now probably the only survivor. Several of the Fusiliers had come from other regiments that had been decimated in the war.

Baine brought up the rear, rifle at the ready, scanning their surrounding with quick, bird-like tilts of his head. Gordon and Wake walked side by side. Just before they had left the train station, Wake had shown his bodyguards the small, flat box he carried. He still hadn't told them what was inside.

"We don't have to get far into the portal," Wake had said. "In fact I want to leave this just over the threshold to close the door and hold it closed."

"Do you think we might be able to nip back over to our side if we're quick?" Baine had asked.

Wake had only smiled grimly.

Runners came hurrying back through the ranks, warning everyone to shutter their lanterns and keep the talking to a minimum. They were getting close. One also hailed Gordon.

"Major Murphy wants you four at the front of the group, Captain."

"Wonder what that's about," Baine said. "I thought we were supposed to follow the cavalry in."

"We'll find out when we get there," Doyle said.

"Ah, you're as cheery as ever, Doyle, me son," said Baine.

The four men stepped up their pace and hurried forward to where Murphy and some other officers were gathered. As they arrived, Murphy said, "This way, lads."

They followed the major away from the main body of troops until they reached a small wooded hill. Murphy kept going until he was almost at top of the hill.

"We'll have to crawl from here, men. You can see the enemy encampment from the top of this rise, which means someone might see us. I brought you here so you could see the path you'll be taking and get some idea of what we're up against."

They belly crawled to the edge of the rise and peered cautiously over the top. Gordon had been aware of a weird radiance emanating upwards as they approached and now he could see that the baleful light came from the portal. The gateway looked like a big, ugly scar hanging in the air.

The light that poured from the portal flickered crimson and yellow, as if a raging inferno blazed within. But then, what would one expect from a window into Hell? And he was just going to waltz right in there, draw a line in the dirt, and dare Old Scratch to cross it.

A host of demons was gathered in front of the hellmouth. They swarmed like ants, about whatever business demons had. Gordon had never seen such a profusion or variety of the enemy. Many of them were what he'd come to think of as the standard model. Roughly like men with the faces of animals. Some had wings. All had claws. Among them he saw specimens of the less human marching host, like the ones he'd fought in London.

Here and there were things that defied description and he didn't dare look at them for too long, lest his mind be blasted. The men slid back down the slope until it was safe to stand up. Gordon was glad to be out of sight of the things.

"How many of them down there, you think?" said Baine.

"Too many," said Gordon. "At least a thousand."

"We'll get through them," Doyle said. "We have to."

The major said, "Sergeant Doyle is right. Like it or not, that is our path."

"I assume we have a plan, Major," said Wake.

"As best we can. The first infantry regiment will open a field of fire as the sun comes up. After that we'll hit the things with a burst of artillery. See if we can shake them up a bit. Then the cavalry will make a charge with lances and swords. We'll move the other two infantry regiments up in columns and fire from whatever positions we can find.

"I want you four men between the second and third regiments. The Fusiliers will come last, so your comrades of long standing will be behind you."

The major looked as if was about to say something else when he suddenly looked down. Three sharp pointed objects emerged from within his shirt, tearing through the front of his body. Blood ran from the wounds and trickled from his mouth. Behind him, Gordon saw a dark shape looming from the trees behind the major.

"Dear God", Gordon said.

The thing rose to its full height of about nine feet, lifting Major Murphy off the ground as it stood. The demon was tall and thin, almost emaciated looking. Its eyes were black, without iris; its mouth was a wide grin full of shark-like teeth. It cast the major aside and stalked forward. Baine reached for his Webley, but Gordon caught his hand.

"No shooting," Gordon said. "Can't give away our position. This one may have just stumbled across us."

"Right," Doyle said, unsheathing his sword.

The demon came forward, swinging its long arms, with claws extended to rake and cut. Doyle didn't try to dodge, but instead drove a powerful cut into the nearest arm, severing the demon's hand at the wrist. Gordon could hear the grunt of effort as the big man chopped into the creature.

The demon caught Doyle with a backswing of its bloody stump. The blow sent the Scotsman stumbling back. Gordon had drawn his sabre and he dodged in and stabbed the demon in the torso, then moved away before it could grab him. While the thing's attention was on Gordon, Baine ducked behind the monstrosity and cut at the back of one of its legs.

300

The demon stumbled and dropped to one knee. Doyle rushed in and cut the head from the creature's shoulders. The demon toppled into the grass as its head rolled away.

Gordon hurried to the major and knelt beside him. He hadn't held much hope the man might still be alive, and now he could see there had never been any chance. Major Murphy had been torn open as he was thrown free of the claws.

Wake said, "He was probably dead before he struck the ground, Captain."

"I know. I had to be sure. I liked the man."

Wake said, "You certainly avenged him. You three made short work of that creature."

"We've been close quarters with the enemy before," said Gordon.

Baine said, "No more seem to be coming to attack us. This one must have found us by accident, as you said, Captain."

Gordon said, "We were lucky. All of us, except the major."

Wake said, "We should get back to the troops. It's almost dawn."

Gordon nodded. "We'll have to leave the major for now. If any of us survive, we'll come back and give him a proper burial."

They hurried back to the group and Gordon sought out Major Billing of the South Staffordshire Regiment. He explained what had happened to Murphy.

Billing, a stout man with a red face, said, "A good man lost. Like so many. Have your men take their positions, Captain. We're almost ready to move forward."

Gordon and his comrades went in search of the Fusiliers. They found a Second-Lieutenant named Miller organizing the groups of riflemen. He hailed them as they approached.

"We want you lads dead centre," Miller said. "We're going to form a wall around you as we push in after the other regiments. Where's Major Murphy? I have some reports for him."

Gordon said, "We lost the major, sir." He explained about the demon on the hill.

Miller said, "I'm so weary of losing friends to these things, Captain. We must succeed today."

"I'm sure we'll all do our best, sir."

A bugle sounded one sharp note. Miller said, "That's it, then. We're attacking."

The sun was just clearing the horizon as Gordon heard the sounds of gunfire. That would be Billing's Regiment, opening a field of fire, just as the major had said.

The Royal Horse Artillery had worked through the night getting their 6-pounder and 9-pounder cannons into position, and now they began firing. Padres and rabbis blessed and sanctified each shell, assuring maximum damage to the hordes of hell. Not only would the explosion and shrapnel kill the creatures, but the entire blast area would become deadly for them to cross.

The air was rent with the sound of man-made thunder, and blue-white light flashed where the shells struck. Gordon could hear the demons howling in pain and rage. It was a sound he had never gotten used to. A sound not meant to be heard on Earth.

Gordon saw the 1st Royal Dragoons Cavalry start forward in a trot. They would pick up speed as they approached the enemy and go in at a full charge.

The Yorkshire Regiment took its position in the lead of the column behind the cavalry. They began to move forward. Gordon, Wake, and the two sergeants walked behind them and the Fusiliers brought up the rear.

Gordon had seen terrible things during the war against Hell. This moment seemed unreal somehow, like a waking dream. The column plodded forward, and occasionally groups broke off to form lines and fire at the approaching enemy. Gordon could hear the howls and growls of the demons and the screams of the men as they moved deeper into the field. The demons were all around, a flood of shrieking evil, slowly closing around the column.

Baine and Doyle were using their rifles like the rest of the men, firing outward into the crush. Gordon had his revolver drawn, but he was keeping a close eye on the professor.

As Wake had said, the demons didn't care for dawn. He could see them squinting their eyes and hunching their shoulders. Well, Gordon didn't care for the more unhealthy light that was pouring toward them as they got closer to the portal. Fair trade, he supposed.

The Fusiliers had to step over or around more and more bodies as they went. Gordon saw what was left of a horse to his right. The Dragoons had paid a high price for their charge.

Gordon heard a clamour off to one side and then a wave of demons were suddenly in view, breaking through the wall of infantry.

"Here they come," Baine said, firing into the mass of attackers.

The Enochian bullets at least seemed to still be doing the trick. Demons fell left and right. But there were far too many of them and the gaps in their ranks were quickly filled. The soldiers fired until their weapons ran dry, then pulled their blades and fought hand to hand. Gordon saw one man get his head bitten from his shoulders. Others were torn apart, their blood raining across the faces of their comrades.

A thing with great, bat-like, wings came hurtling out of the sky, directly toward Doyle. The big man exhausted the ten rounds in his Enfield, then tossed the weapon aside. He drew sword and dirk. As the flying demon swooped in, Doyle leaped inside the reach of its wings and split its skull. The impact bowled Doyle over, but he scrambled quickly to his feet.

"Ah, but you're a rare prize, Doyle, me son," said Baine.

Gordon said, "Good work, Sergeant."

"I'm afraid we're still too far from the portal and loosing ground," Wake said.

Gordon raised his head and looked to where the remnants of the cavalry and the Yorkshire Regiment were in fierce combat with the demons. The men were dong better than Gordon would ever had suspected, but he could see now that it wasn't likely to be enough.

Gordon said, "Are you up for a sprint, professor."

303

"We're going to run?"

"We're not retreating, if that's what you're worried about. There's still a little room right in the centre of the column. Looks like one of the artillery shells exploded their and the demons don't like it. I say we make a run for the portal. The demons don't know we're guarding the bigger threat. We may be able to slip through in the confusion."

"I'll run as if the very hounds of hell were on my trail."

Gordon dropped his rifle and drew his sabre. He said, "There won't be time for aiming rifles, lads. It's Sergeant Doyle's kind of fight now. We'll cut our way to the portal. Doyle, you take the lead. Baine, you're on that side of Professor Wake and I'm on this one. Let's move out."

Doyle charged, hewing with sword and dirk as he went. The others ran close behind. Something with tentacles instead of arms reached out for Gordon, but he left the tips of the extremities twitching on the ground.

A massive creature with the head of a stag and the body of a bull came charging their way. Doyle ripped upward through its abdomen, spilling dark and steaming entrails. The big Scotsman slit the thing's throat for good measure. Gordon shook his head in admiration. Whatever warrior gods the man's ancestors had worshipped were surely with him that day.

Baine vaulted a dead horse and skewered a more man-like demon. It snapped at him as it fell, but he dodged away. Gordon cut and slashed at anything that came within reach. All around the running quartet, the surviving members of the various regiments fought on. Though none of them knew exactly why the man from Oxford had to get to the portal, all were ready to fall and die so that he might.

The portal all but filled Gordon's vision now, and a weird, unpleasant, buzzing sound filled his ears. It made his already tired legs feel even heavier.

"I was afraid of this," Wake called. "Just being this close to a gate to another plane of reality is having ill effects on us."

"Keep pushing through," Gordon said. "We're almost there."

Gordon caught a blur of motion out of the corner of his eye and a thing that was almost a snake, but which was equipped with arms and covered with spines, sprang in front of the group. It opened its mouth wide and snapped forward, clamping onto Baine's right shoulder with two inch fangs.

Baine grunted in pain and fell, with the writhing horror on top of him. It held him fast with its arms and bit him twice more before the others could get to him. Doyle hacked at the thing, almost severing its head. The creature's coiled body thrashed about as it perished. Baine didn't move.

Gordon swore under his breath. He'd fought shoulder to shoulder with the wiry man, and though Gordon had technically been Baine's superior officer, he'd never thought of the man as anything but an equal and a friend.

Gordon saw Doyle hesitate for just a moment, but then the big man snapped off a quick salute to his fallen friend and ran forward, hacking with renewed fury at the things that sought to bar his way.

Gordon and Wake ran close behind Doyle. The buzzing seemed to grow louder so close to the gate. Gordon could feel it in his head, sapping his will. The portal itself was a glowing oven of malevolence. He could see nothing inside of the hellmouth, just that malignant glow.

Gordon was also aware that this close to the gate there were no other soldiers to help them. Keeping Wake between himself and Doyle, Gordon chopped and hacked at the things that ran at them. Gordon risked a glance forward. The portal was only a few yards away, but there were perhaps a dozen demons in their path.

Doyle said, "Swing wide of them, Captain. I'll cut them off."

"There are too many!"

"I'll make them all come at me, sir. Now go!"

Doyle went to the right, drawing the mob of demons. Gordon grabbed Wake by the shoulder and led him in an arc away from Doyle and the creatures.

Gordon could see Doyle slamming into the midst of the horrors, his two blades rising and falling. His helmet was gone and his red tunic all in tatters. For a moment he was unstoppable, like some Celtic deity of old. And then the demons swarmed over him. That was the last thing Gordon saw before he shoved Wake through the portal and threw himself in behind the professor.

Time seemed to slow. The glow became a roaring waterfall of despair. Gordon could hear his heart hammering in his chest. The buzzing was gone, replaced by wailing and screeching, like all the lost souls beyond were warning him away.

Then time and gravity snapped back into place with a vengeance and Gordon was lying on his back on hot, black sand. He rolled over and pushed himself to his feet, feeling a sharp pain as shards of glass in the sand cut his hands. The light on this side of the portal was diffused and crimson. All around were chunks of what looked like black, volcanic rock. The air was moist and warm and it reeked of sulphur.

Wake was seated on the ground a few feet away. The tall professor also managed to stand. Both men turned to look at the portal. Gordon could see the battlefield beyond but the combatants looked frozen in place, like angry insects trapped in amber. Time apparently worked differently in Hell.

"I'm sorry about your men," Wake said as he fumbled in a leather satchel. He removed the flat wooden box that held the mysterious relic.

"Men die in war," Gordon said. "The ones you liked and the ones you didn't."

Wake nodded. "Best get this done. I doubt we have much time."

"Nothing seems to have followed us through."

"They don't need to. We're in Hell, Captain. Once the things that dwell here take notice, I imagine the past few days will seem like a stroll through Regent's Park."

Even as Wake spoke, Gordon became aware of sibilant sounds coming from around them. Things were moving in the crimson twilight beyond the rocks. Gordon hefted his sabre and wished he had saved some rounds for the Webley.

Wake placed the box on the ground and used a small key to unlock it. The rustling sounds grew louder and Gordon looked back over his shoulder. A dozen insect-like creatures were crawling their way. They were something like scorpions with shiny, dark red shells. They had claws and stingers, but their faces were disturbingly human, with large eyes and gaping mouths. Those were just the beginning. Behind the scorpion things, large shadowy forms were gathering in the haze.

"Best hurry, Wake," Gordon said.

"There's a ceremony I have to perform. Try and keep them away from me."

"I'll do my best," said Gordon.

The scorpion things were close. Gordon could see trails of dark drool falling from their fanged mouths. A thing like a legless bat lurched behind them on membranous arms.

Wake lifted the still unopened box. He held it out toward the portal and then he spoke in a loud clear voice. "I forbid you these lands. I forbid you these people. In the name of the Alpha and the Omega, I forbid you this world!"

The demons, as if sensing something was very wrong, began to surge forward, perhaps with some idea of stopping whatever was happening. Wake turned back toward the onrushing horrors. He opened the box and a bright, white light blazed forth from inside.

The air was filled with hissing and wailing as the demons shrank back. Wake reached into the box. It hurt Gordon's eyes to look at the shining object, but it appeared to be a shard of wood.

"What is it?" Gordon said.

"A genuine fragment of the True Cross. Secreted away for centuries. It took a long time to track it down, out of so many purported such relics."

307

Wake knelt and dug into the black sand with his hand. Small bits of glass cut and scratched him. When he had a hole a few inches deep, he dropped the glowing bit of wood into the opening and quickly covered it.

"This is the hard part," Wake said. "And I've no one to ask to take this cup from me."

Gordon said, "I'm not sure I understand, sir."

Wake said, "I'm not sure I do either, but a sacrifice is required. It's an old story, Captain, and like most old stories, it begins and ends with blood. This blackened ground is my pool of Urd from which Yggdrasil shall spring."

Gordon didn't understand the reference, but he saw that something was happening to the dark sand. The ground erupted as something white thrust up from below. Seconds later, he realized it was a tree, branches spiralling out from the central trunk. The tree shimmered with a hazy white light as it grew upward toward the scarlet sky.

"Etz haChayim," Wake said as he stepped closer to the tree. He spread his arms as if waiting for something. "The Tree of Life. The map of reality."

Gordon wondered what came next. Was the tree meant to close the portal somehow? He couldn't see any change in the gateway. Wake seemed lost in his own world. Gordon was about to speak when a questing limb shot from the tree and stabbed through Wake's chest.

"Wake!" Gordon said.

Wake shook his head. "Stay back. It only requires one sacrifice. Just like the last time."

"You knew this was going to happen."

A crimson stain spread out from the wound, soaking Wake's chest. He coughed and said, "I knew. Had to be done, Captain. For the sake of the world. Couldn't ask anyone else. Couldn't..."

Wake slumped forward and then his feet left the ground as the tree continued to grow and his body was lifted upwards.

308

Limbs and branches lanced out, spearing any of the demons in reach. The air was filled with screeching and roaring.

Gordon looked toward the portal. It was closing from the outer edges, its ovular shape growing smaller by the second. He saw something else. The soldiers beyond the portal were moving again. Time was equalizing as the portal closed. Maybe he could get back through. Maybe, if he was fast enough, he could escape.

He spared one last glance for Wake. The professor hung high in the branches of the tree. Gordon saluted, then he ran for the opening. The demonic creatures around him were scurrying about in blind panic. He dodged past one and vaulted over another. The portal was perhaps three feet wide now. Gordon reached it and went through head first, like a man diving into a pond.

There was no sensation of slowed time. One moment he was in the hot, red world, and the next he was rolling on the grass. He felt his ears pop. He rolled over on his back and looked toward the portal. It was gone.

Gordon got painfully to his feet. He looked around for a weapon. The portal was closed but there was doubtless mopping up to do yet. Or perhaps not. He saw fallen weapons, but he also saw fallen demons. Not a one of them was moving. Had closing the portal somehow also closed off some link necessary to keep the things alive?

He stared again at the place where the portal had been. He could see nothing, but he knew that on the other side, a tree grew in Hell, and a man who didn't believe hung in its branches, guarding a world.

"Captain Gordon," a familiar voice said.

Gordon turned to see Sergeant Gavin Doyle limping toward him. The man was nearly naked, and covered with deep gashes and bite marks. But he was alive. By some miracle he was alive.

"Good Lord, Doyle," Gordon said. "You actually managed to outfight all of those demons?"

Doyle shrugged his wide shoulders. "Most of them, sir. I was holding the rest off when they all of a sudden fell dead."

"That was Wake's doing."

"I owe him a drink then."

"I'm afraid he didn't make it back, Doyle. He gave his life to save us all."

Doyle said, "Then I'll have a drink to honour him when I drink to Baine and all the others we've lost."

Gordon nodded. "Agreed. We'll both have a swig for the professor. At the first pub we can find."

AFTERWORD

These are only some of the stories of the Incursion. The true fate of many parts of Scotland, or how widely the destruction visited Ireland, were not yet known – nor was the impact on the British Empire as a whole. Was Britain strengthened in the end by its resistance to the forces of the Infernal Prince, finding a new purpose and unity? Or was it fatally weakened, made vulnerable to the ambitions of other nations?

And if it could happen here, it could happen elsewhere. This point was surely not missed by the survivors. One great portal to Hell – or to a malevolent plane of existence which took Hell's guise – had opened without warning, and allowed fractures to appear across the land. When and where would the next one appear? People would ask if the Inferno's ambition and ingenuity been broken forever – and they would also ask, were we truly free now?

What had Hell left behind, buried inside of us?

WITNESSES TO THE INCURSION

After thirty years at sea, **Ross Baxter** now concentrates on writing sci-fi and horror fiction. His varied work has been published in print by several publishing houses in the US and the UK. He won the Horror Novel Reviews Creation Short Story Award in December 2014, and has a short story on the 2017 HWA Bram Stoker recommended reading list. Married to a Norwegian and with two Anglo-Viking kids, he now lives in Derby, England.

Charlotte Bond is an author, ghostwriter, freelance editor, proofreader, reviewer and podcaster. Under her own name she has written within the genres of horror and dark fantasy. As a ghostwriter, she's tackled everything from romance to cozy mystery stories and YA novels. She is a reviewer for the Ginger Nuts of Horror website, as well as the British Fantasy Society and the Jane and Bex Book Blog. Her articles have appeared in such places as Tor.com, War History Online, The Vintage News, and Writing Magazine. She is a co-host of the podcast, Breaking the Glass Slipper, which in 2018 was shortlisted for a BFS award for best audio and was longlisted for a Hugo.

Phil Breach is a storyteller and poet, and an archaeologist during work hours. Mother Nature is his foremost inspiration in life, and She informs most of what he writes, one way or another. He is also fascinated with the mythology, ancient traditions, and folklore of Albion's isles, with particular interest in Celtic myth, the Fae, and the Arthuriad. The Compleat Arte Mephitic, his current work in progress, is a commingling of these elements with the dark cosmic horror of the Lovecraftian Mythos. He lives near a boats' graveyard on the South coast of England. To find out more visit philbreach.com

Shell Bromley is a writer of speculative fiction. She is a founding member and co-editor of the Random Writers, and has short stories in several anthologies. After many years teaching Literature in England, she recently moved to a Scottish island where her neighbours include sheep, eagles and the occasional flying wheelie bin.

Frank Coffman is a retired professor of college English, creative writing, and journalism. He has published speculative poetry and fiction in a variety of magazines and anthologies. His books include the newly released collection of poetry, The Coven's Hornbook & Other Poems; a chapbook of weird and horrific poems, This Ae Nighte, Every Nighte and Alle; and his edition of Robert E. Howard: Selected Poems. He is a member of the Horror Writers Association and the Science Fiction and Fantasy Poetry Association. He is currently finishing work on a new verse translation of Kháyyám's Rubaiyát.

Jack Deel is the pen-name of editor, writer and researcher Jack Fennell. In addition to having translated a number of short stories for The Short Fiction of Flann O'Brien (2013), he has published essays on a variety of subjects, from comic books to haunted spaces, and he is the author of the academic study Irish Science Fiction (2014). More recently, he compiled the well-received anthology A Brilliant Void: A Selection of Classic Irish Science Fiction (2018). He lives in his native County Limerick, Ireland, but has been known to venture further afield in search of an interesting monster.

S. L. Edwards is a Texan currently living in California. He enjoys dark fiction, poetry and darker beer. With Yves Tourigny he is the co-creator of the webcomic 'Bockchito: Occult Doggo Detective.' His debut fiction collection, 'Whiskey and Other

Unusual Ghosts' is forthcoming from Gehenna and Hinnom Books later this year.

Martin J. Gilbert is based in north county Dublin in Ireland, where he lives with his family and their dogs. He always had a passion for writing, but only began to dedicate significant time to it after his children were born, when he realised he couldn't ask them to pursue their dreams if he was unwilling to do so himself. He has had novels longlisted twice for the Bath Novel Award (2015 & 2017) and once for the Caledonia Novel Award (2015), in addition to publishing several short stories. His stories are generally fantasy tinged with reality, or real-world stories with a touch of fantasy.

John Linwood Grant is a professional writer/editor from Yorkshire, who lives with a pack of lurchers and a beard. Widely published, he writes contemporary weird fiction, and dark period stories of murder, madness and the supernatural – such as the 'Tales of the Last Edwardian' series, including the 1920s hoodoo-woman Mamma Lucy. His latest novel is 'The Assassin's Coin', with Mr Edwin Dry, the Deptford Assassin, who also features in his new, expanded collection 'A Persistence of Geraniums'. He is editor of Occult Detective Quarterly, plus a range of anthologies. He can be found on Facebook, and at greydogtales.com, which explores weird fiction and weird art. And lurchers.

J. A. Ironside (AKA Jules) is a SFF and historical fiction writer, who masquerades by day as member of the Gloucestershire County Council library service, which funnily enough has rather less to do with books than you would think. Otherwise you will find her writing, reading or doing martial arts. She grew up in rural Dorset, in a house full of books – which set her up as a lifelong bibliophile. She writes both adult and YA fiction, often with fantastical elements. Jules has had several short stories published in magazines and anthologies, as well as recorded for literature podcasts. All seven books in her SFF Unveiled Series are now available, along with associated novellas and short stories. She also co-authored the sweeping historical Oath and Crown Duology, available now from Penmore Press. Jules co-hosts the popular speculative fiction podcast, Dissecting Dragons, where she talks about all aspects of writing as well as fantasy and science fiction. She lives near the Cotswold Way with her boyfriend-creature and a small black and white cat. You can find out more at her website - www.jaironside.com

Exposed to the weird worlds of horror, science fiction and comics as a boy, **Damascus Mincemeyer** has been ruined ever since. He's now a writer and artist of various strangeness and has had stories published (or soon-to-be published) in the anthologies Fire: Demons, Dragons and Djinn (Tyche Books), Bikers Vs The Undead, Psycho Holiday, Monsters Vs Nazis (Deadman's Tome Publishing, books for which he also provided cover art), Crash Code (Blood Bound Books), the Sirens Call ezine, and the magazines Gallows Hill and StoryHack. He lives near St. Louis, Missouri, USA, and can usually be found lurking about on Twitter @DamascusUndead.

Marion Pitman writes all sorts of fiction, most of it short, much of it supernatural. Her first collection, Music in the Bone, is available from Alchemy Press. She also writes poetry. She grew up reading M R James, Dorothy L Sayers and Algernon Blackwood among others, which explains a lot.

Charles R. Rutledge is the author of three books in the Griffin and Price supernatural suspense series series, written with James A. Moore. His work has appeared in numerous anthologies, including Clickers Forever, Widow Makers, SNAFU Black Ops, and The Mighty Warriors. Recently he has brought Dracula and the Frankenstein Monster into modern times in the novella Dracula's Revenge. Charles lives in the metro Atlanta area with a cat named Bruce and a vast collection of books and comic books.

He once wrote Chinese comic books for a living without being able to speak a word of Chinese. It's complicated.

Ian Steadman is a writer from the south of England. His stories have most recently been published in Black Static, Unsung Stories, The Lonely Crowd, STORGY and Coffin Bell, as well as in the anthologies Shallow Creek, Humanagerie, Night-Light and The Year's Best Body Horror. You can find him at www.iansteadman.com, or he occasionally manifests on Twitter as @steadmanfiction.

A steadfast and proud sci-fi and fantasy geek, **A. F. Stewart** was born and raised in Nova Scotia, Canada and still calls it home. The youngest in a family of seven children, she always had an overly creative mind and an active imagination. She favours the dark and deadly when writing—her genres of choice being dark fantasy and horror—but she has been known to venture into the light on occasion. As an indie author she's published novels, novellas and story collections, with a few side trips into poetry.

Matthew Willis is a writer and historian with an interest with things that go bump in the night and things that go boom on the sea. Matthew's first published novel was the historical fantasy Daedalus and the Deep, based on a historical sea serpent sighting in the 19th century. His short stories have been published in The New Accelerator and Flash Flood, and he was shortlisted for the Bridport Prize in 2015. In August 2016, he spent three days conducting archaeological fieldwork on the naval defences on Portland harbour breakwater - an experience that inspired the setting for The Battle of Alma.

41470368R00179

Printed in Poland
by Amazon Fulfillment
Poland Sp. z o.o., Wrocław